More Praise for
Hollywood Buckaroo

"*Hollywood Buckaroo*'s witty and engaging love-hate relationship with the industry it so vividly portrays is as entertaining as a trip to the movies itself."

— Ed Solomon, Screenwriter, *Men In Black*

"*Hollywood Buckaroo* is not just funny and entertaining, it's smart. Readers will not be disappointed. DeBrincat is an author with an original voice, who can be funny and challenging all at once. Don't be fooled by this novel's quirky, witty pace. The writing is superb— here is a writer whose writing talent shines far beyond her wit and intelligence. No plotless wonder, DeBrincat will make you laugh and admire her ability to tell an infinitely readable story and wish it didn't have to end so soon. I realized partway through that I was holding my breath as I was reading it. Sander's incredible experiences in Buckaroo may be strange, but they are never boring."

— Leslie Schwartz, author of *Angels Crest* and *Jumping the Green*

D1518281

For monsieur Peel

"Guess now who holds Thee?"
"Death," I said.
The Silver answer rang,
"Not Death, but Love."

— *Some tombstone somewhere*

1

MONDAY MORNING

There's a Death Clock on the Internet that determines your expiration date. I enter my birthday (March 19), sex (M), height (5'9" in shoes), weight (178 on the right day), and consider the pre-determined personality "mode" options. Let's say I'm feeling pessimistic. In that case, I'll officially kick the bucket Friday, July 16, 2016, with 249,869,065 seconds left to live and counting. If I pretend my mode is optimistic, my last day on planet Earth reconfigures to Saturday, June 7, 2059, with some 1,619,220,588 seconds before I croak. That's a whole 43 additional years. Over a trillion seconds. With just one little lie, I could live longer than I've lived already, and then some. If I click the normal mode, I'll die April 14, 2034. All these dates are bogus, of course, as my current mode is neither pessimistic, optimistic nor normal. What I am is—I determine with the help of another website—numb, stunned, stupefied, paralyzed. I sit here checking boxes, calculating and recalculating my death, waiting for the taxi that will take me to my father's funeral, which began fifteen minutes (a measly 900 seconds) ago.

Forest Lawn's entrance gates are tall, black and ornate. The jacaranda trees flanking them explode with violet fall blooms. Two large white trucks and a Star Waggons trailer are parked nearby; a handful of guys lay cable and set up lights and scrims. Great. I'm going to be even later to Dad's memorial because they're shooting a damn movie. A traffic cop in jodhpurs and knee-high boots motions for my Checker Cab to stop, then directs a hearse, limo and a procession of cars to exit the park. There is ample time to find poetry in this; Angelenos die the same way they live: in traffic. Ample time to consider that no site, however sacred, is off limits to moviemaking. Ample time to wonder whether Mom gave in to my younger sister Ellie's constant ragging about upscaling and designering Dad's funeral, or whether Mom stuck to her guns and honored Dad's wishes for a plain memorial. Ample time to re-read the cemetery's promotional brochure, which describes Forest Lawn as the Eternal Resting Place Born of a Dream of Dr. Hubert Eaton, Who Believed, Above All, in a Christ Who Smiled. Ample time to ponder this bewildering description before the cop finally signals it's our turn to move.

As my taxi enters the gates, we pass a sleek Chrysler Towne Car waiting to exit. The back window slips down with uncanny timing, and Ellie sticks her head out for some air, something she's done for as long as anyone can remember, often causing Dad to remark she must be part dog. I duck down in the back seat, but too late. The last thing I see before gliding through the suburban lawn landscape of Forest Lawn is Ellie slitting her finger across her throat, and glaring at me. Fucking shit. No Christ smiling here.

The marble halls of the Sanctuary of Memory are shadowy and cool. Brackish marigolds and cheap carnations decorate cabinets behind which burned flesh and bone are locked and filed away. At the end of the east wing of the Columbarium of the Sanctuaries (*Columbarium Enema*, Ghost-Dad whispers in my ear), Robert Edward Sanderson lies in a simple pine casket—no brass, no carving—on a cloth-covered riser. Good on Mom. Two Filipina workers in gray uniforms collapse folding chairs that have been arranged in front of the casket on a square of red carpet. Smoke rises from two tapers, recently extinguished, in tall candlesticks. The women see me approach and back away, beckoning, "Come, come," ostentatiously bowing themselves against a far wall. The younger of them silently speed-walks to Dad's casket and holds a lighter to the tapers, then rejoins her colleague. They both stare at the ground.

"I didn't mean to miss the funeral." My voice cracks as I stand there in my outdated, ill-fitting all-purpose suit, unable to move any closer to the casket. "My car broke down. I couldn't find my jumper cables." The red carpet swirls at my feet. I am loath to step onto it. Somehow, the red carpet means what has happened is true. Dad is dead. Life is not, as I have often fantasized, reversible.

"Psssht, psssht." One of the ladies frowns, waving impatiently. A family of four down the hall gathers in front of another drawer. The mother weeps into a kerchief; the children are wide-eyed, holding hands. The father is somber, consoling wife and kids with constant touches and encouragement. He murmurs something, I imagine a prayer, and the others join in, their invocation echoing in the chamber. On the strength of their spiritual white noise, I move toward the casket. Dad hated the idea of spending dough on a fancy viewing box when he was ultimately going to be cremated, and would have been happy to have been rolled up in newspaper if it were legal. Instead, he'll be launched into the afterlife in a receptacle resembling an entertainment console from Ikea. (How would it be listed in the catalog, I wonder. Mørtivit? Embålmbed?)

When I finally look inside, my gut curls in on itself. Dad's stocky chest sinks in the middle, like a shelf that's been piled with too many books. His complexion, ruddy from years of outdoor work, is old deli meat, jaundiced around the eyes. His lips are stitched vinyl. Some animal instinct inside me hankers for a sniff. I dare myself to breathe. If he still smells like Dad, like Old Spice and Pine-Sol and the scented hair pomade he wore to diffuse his workaday aromas, then maybe I'll believe this is him. I hold my breath, and stumble to a chair. Close my eyes. Concentrate on the words from the family down the corridor, whatever, whoever they are.

The Saturday Dad died was one of those rare Los Angeles days when the sun sparkled in a pollution-free sky, puffy white clouds hopped around like bunnies, and the breeze made everyone's hair look like they just got laid. A gorgeous fucking day. The afternoon sounds of birds, weed whackers and turbo-charged vacuums ricocheted through a bucolic canyon in the Hollywood Hills. Bougainvillea vines cloaked the lush garden walls around a faux Tuscan villa while Dad and I labored to liberate its occupants' crap from a clogged sewer line. The only reason I was there was because of the flowers. Dad's other employee, Fabrizio, had an allergy attack that prevented him from working outside. This was the first outcall I'd made since I'd been banished from client contact six weeks ago. Six weeks since I'd worn the blue El-San Pipe & Drain coveralls, identical to Dad's except for "Sander" stitched above my breast pocket and "Bobby" in red above his. I noticed Dad rubbing his chest a couple times, taking shallow breaths and yawning, but each time he caught me watching, he'd turn away.

The problem at hand: a clay sewer line, riddled with roots from a nearby ficus hedge. Dad and I'd worked all morning digging a five-foot trench on either side of the short stretch of old clay line that needed to be replaced with PVC. His catcher's-mitt hands had always been remarkable in their grace, but his usual efficient moves were clumsy today. When I was ready to make the cut, I pulled on my protective mask and motioned for Dad to do the same. He ignored me. Typical. He rubbed his chest again. "You all right Dad?"

He nodded his big, balding head once, sharply, so I waved for him to stand clear; a standard safety precaution. He ignored me—also standard procedure—and nodded again.

I snapped on my ear mufflers, pulled the chain on the saw, and set blade to pipe. After easily shearing through the clay, I turned off the saw and noticed Dad's hands were clutched at his chest. Was he having trouble with heartburn? Wiping his dirty hands on his shirt? As I tried to make sense of what I was seeing, a familiar sound traveled through the cast-iron sewer pipe from the direction of the house. Before my brain recognized the sound of an untimely flush from inside, my body snapped into action. I dropped the saw and flipped myself up and out of the trench like a gymnast, escaping being sprayed with sewage by a mere tenth of a second. Dad didn't react quite so fast. A geyser of waste burst from the pipe, exploding at his chest with amazing force. Adrenaline pumping, I lunged at Dad, wiping shit from his face, putting my lips to his, thinking *Not yet not yet not yet.* Trying to remember the steps I hadn't thought about since Duck and Cover days in grade school. Pinch. Breathe. Press.

When the lady of the house ran out on the deck to apologize for forgetting not to flush, she saw what was going on and quickly called 911. For being up in the hills, the paramedics got there in really good time. Ultimately, it made no difference. Dad's heart had already quit.

Across from the Sanctuary of Memory, artificial flowers and metallic balloons decorate headstones and statuary in rows on a grassy slope. When did people start putting party decorations on headstones? Yellow hillsides accentuate the artificial golf-green of the cemetery lawn. Beyond those, downtown's skyscrapers huddle behind a dirty blanket of October haze. There's no sidewalk here, as befits its hometown; this cemetery is made for driving. I slip my flask from my pocket and take a swig of whatever's in there since the last time I filled it. Stale, smoky whiskey singes my throat as I stroll down the middle of the road.

Below me, at the entrance gates, a director stands in the back of a truck next to a mounted camera, yapping static into a walkie-talkie. For the first time since Dad died, I am reminded of the brand-new laptop and titanium VMX3000 camcorder that recently maxed out my VISA, and my half-cooked plan of quitting El-San to write a screenplay and film it. That stupid screenplay. Bane of my life.

"Mr. Sanderson? Sandy?" The polished voice is at once reassuring, familiar and kind of fake.

That's freaky. No one calls me that except Dad, and not since I was a munchkin. I turn to look into a bespoke lapel, its perfect, tiny stitches marching along a contoured seam. Above that, a chiseled, tan jaw below startling hazel eyes. "Paul Street." I forget about the man's use of my annoying nickname as he offers his legendary hand, a hand that has caressed a legion of starlet asses, pointed countless silver-gray prop guns, placed and pulled cigarette after cigarette on his snarled leading-man lips. "I was a tremendous fan of your father."

This guy was on *Celebrity Profiles* a few weeks ago. He's one of those actors who's appeared in over a hundred B-movies. Science fiction, Westerns, action adventures, dramas. Noirs, comedies, war epics. Back in the forties, if there were ten movies in production in one week, Paul Street was in at least three of them. Some were okay; most were mediocre. A few of them were bad—rip-roaring, cult-worthy bad. He's since retired from acting to become a celebrity spokesperson for beauty and exercise products, but his silver screen aura right here in Forest Lawn cemetery is undeniable and larger than life. He's got to be close to seventy, about a decade older than my old man, but he looks years younger, his skin healthy and unlined. A *Profiles* tidbit I'll never forget: at thirteen, the pony he was riding bolted straight into freshly-laundered sheets breezing on a clothesline. His mother looked on as the line caught Paul around the neck and sliced his throat open from earlobe to earlobe. After his recovery, Paul transformed himself from gawky teen to high-school heartthrob, and dedicated his life to his acting career.

I find myself surreptitiously studying the underside of the man's jaw, searching for the scar that changed his life, but find nothing. He must have had an excellent surgeon.

"He loved his work, his life and his family." Street delivers the line like a priest.

He can't be talking about *my* father. "You're talking about Bobby Sanderson?"

"Oh, yes," Paul Street says, eyes closing, going private. When he opens his eyes, they're *brimming with tears.* "Bobby was my good-luck plumber."

God, he's good. I offer my flask.

He sips daintily and makes a face. "I'm more of a champagne man." He mops his eyes with a silk pocket square.

"How did you meet Dad?" I still can't believe this guy is our client. I know all the names on our roster and each of their plumbing quirks. There is no file for Paul Street.

He takes another sip. "A movie I was in was up for an award. Academy thing."

"*No One Ever Dies,*" I say, struggling to keep a straight face in light of the circumstances and our location. "It was a great film." It was drivel. "I'll never forget it." It *was* unforgettable in its way. As a teenager, I watched it from the top of a pickup on the other side of the fence behind the old Olympic Drive-In, where I got my first handful of Marti Jo Johnson's right boob.

Paul's used to compliments and waves mine away. "I was a beefcake. Lucky, yes. Hard-working, absolutely. But only and ever a beefcake." He nods. "Anyway, this nomination was the closest I'd ever get to an Oscar, unless I accidentally shoved one up my ass. Pardon the French."

"Ouch. Not good for the plumbing."

He smiles, a momentary strobe of bright denturnalia. "I was throwing a big to-do at the ranch. Night before the party, the entire septic system ups and regurgitates years of contents from all orifi. I was a wreck. Your father worked through the night, cleaned it all up. Saved the day."

"That was *your* party my parents went to!" I was eleven years old, Ellie was six, and we were left in the care of our dope-smoking babysitter Trish, who worshipped Jimi Hendrix and whose cookies we worshipped. Mom and Dad stood looking at themselves in the hall mirror, splendid and surprising in their finery. I remember waking up from a chocolate-chip coma on the sofa much later, when they came home tipsy and quarreling. "Dad would have been just about my age now. Thirty-three."

Street flicks his eyes across my face, then takes another sip before returning my flask. "From then on, if my septic was acting up, your father was my man. If they gave Academy Awards for plumbers, Bobby would have received a Lifetime Achievement."

"Fantastic," I say, contemplating an oversize replica of Michelangelo's David—"the largest in the world!" proclaims a plaque on its pedestal. David's foot is the size of my torso.

Paul Street throws open his arms, like he's about to burst into song. "So who are you, Sandy?"

"Sander."

"Of course," he smiles. "What turns you on? What makes you glad you're alive every day?"

Is he joking? Acting? Trying to make me feel bad?

Snippets of annoying advice, in my ex-girlfriend Ashe's voice, echo through my head. *The next person you talk to might change your career. Have a snappy personal bio at the tip of your tongue. You never know where your next gig will come from. Always make 'em think you're on your way up.* I never listened to her when we were together; why start now? "Not married. No kids. Had a steady girl, but she dumped me. Been working with Dad at El-San. Who names a plumbing company after their kids anyway?" It feels good to talk, if that's what you call my little rant, to a stranger. The cab driver honks. My fifteen minutes are up. "My family's waiting. Will you stop by the house?"

"Your mother's house?" Paul Street's hazel eyes darken ever so slightly. "I'm sorry, I can't." He grasps both my hands in his—they are smooth, warm and hairless—and maintains the grip for what seems like a full minute, though it's probably only a mature second or two. "But I'd love to talk some more. Why don't we get together?"

I hesitate. *Is he coming on to me?* I wonder, then hope I'm not so transparent that the thought was evident.

"I'm throwing a little soiree," he clarifies, eyes twinkling. "With lots of other people. You'll be safe."

Yes, I'm completely see-through. I laugh. Not the good laugh, but the donkey-sounding one. "Okay. Sure. I guess so. Why not? Absolutely." Have I left out any other possible response?

Smelling of high-end herbal shampoo, Paul Street leans in and palms me his card. "Next Saturday then. Eight-ish." He turns on his heel and jogs up the gray concrete stairs of the Sanctuary of Memory.

The cabby's radio plays some kind of Middle Eastern music with repetitive percussion, a wailing sitar and a guttural male vocal that sounds part human and part animal in distress. "What is that music?" I say quietly, so the driver will have to turn down the cacophony to hear me.

The driver, Middle Eastern himself, catches my eye in the rearview mirror and smiles. "You like?" He turns it up louder. His white turban bobs to the beat. The Checker surges forward, darting out of the carpool lane to cut in front of a truck in the fast lane.

"I hate it." I smile, knowing he can't hear me, betting he can't understand me. "My father just died."

The cabby nods yes, yes, smiling now, showing off big yellow teeth, still bobbing to the hellish caterwaul over a bass line of tree frogs on steroids.

"We weren't speaking because of a stupid argument we had six weeks ago. I was out on a routine plugger in Beverlywood."

"Beverlywood," he nods. "Nice."

"Unplugging a plugger is like hooking a catfish and then opening up its guts to discover the garbage inside it. And the garbage in this lady's pipes clogged the unclogger! I had to pull it out with my hands! You ever stick your hand in a pipe full of shit?"

"Very nice," he agrees.

"No," I shake my head emphatically. "Very not nice." Perched on the edge of the seat now, I press my face against the circular speaker, hands on the glass. He notices, and I notice him noticing, turning down the music. Doesn't want to stir up the crazy ones. Sometimes all it takes is the wrong song. But too late. I am already shaken and stirred.

"And what did I find? A lady's glove. Pink. Like a little hand buried in excrement. Now, plumber's moral code is, you don't talk feces with the client, you just eliminate it. So after I sump it into my shit bin, the client asks me if I found anything unusual in there. That's crazy, right? Normal people say, 'Does my toilet work now? Fine. What's the damage?' Am I right?"

"Right?" The cabby repeats, unsure of the shifting rules of conversation. He removes the cassette and inserts another, hoping to calm me with something familiar and Western. He smiles with delight and cranks up the Bee Gees' "Stayin' Alive."

The overly familiar, not-so-very-Western disco song does not deter me from the telling of my tale. "'Sorry,' I say. 'The glove is gone. Kaput.' 'It's extremely valuable,' she screams." I do my best to imitate her watered-down British accent. "'It was my great-grandmother's. She was an actress.' As soon as the lady says 'actress,' I can't help thinking of Ashe, who had dumped me the night before. 'Aren't you freakin' all!' I shout and instantly regret it. I apologize, but that's not enough. She wants it back." I realize I'm screeching and must sound like an idiot.

I shut up, letting the throbbing soundtrack have its way with us.

The cabby smiles, appreciating me appreciating the Gibbs. "Good, yes?"

"No," I tell him. "Terrible."

"Aliiiiiiiiiiiive!" Amazingly, the cabby hits the high note as we sail back into the carpool lane.

"So I dug through the muck and put that lady's glove right in her lily-white hand." I throw myself against the back seat, flinging my arms wide. The buildings fly past us now. U-Haul, U-Rent, U-Make-It, U-Sell-It, Signs 4 U. The client lodged a complaint. Her actual words were: "I'm telling your father." Like I never heard *that*.

We got a complaint today, Dad said when I clocked out at the end of my shift. *Lost a repeat customer.*

She got what she wanted, I said, but I remember thinking: *just like I never do.*

Customer's always right, Sandy, he said, hanging his coveralls on a hook by the bathroom door. *How do you plan on fixing it?*

Send her a gift certificate to Bitches R Us?

I came in late the next morning, and we both acted as though it hadn't happened. Typical. But Dad reassigned me to scheduling calls and ordering parts and supplies from the office. "Fine," I said. "It'll give me more time to work on my screenplay." Working title: *Blank Document.*

"Go to it," he said, then hired Fabrizio, a guy he found down at the Home Depot parking lot. Contrary to doctor's orders after a mild heart seizure last spring, Dad started going back out on calls himself, bringing Fabby with him. I knew Dad wasn't supposed to be so active and that Fabby was a stand-in for Dad's ungrateful, misbehaving son, and I felt guilty of course, which kept me from making any progress on *Blank Document* at all. That was probably part of Dad's evil plan.

One hour, fifteen minutes and far too many songs into the *Saturday Night Fever* soundtrack later, the cab lays serious scratch as it rounds the corner onto my old block, where leafy trees shelter SUVs parked bumper to bumper. I give the driver all my cash and apologize for the lousy tip.

"Fuck you!" He grouses. That, I understand.

2

MONDAY AFTERNOON

The house I grew up in is one of those *Sunset* magazine-style homes: single-story ranch, river-rock siding, wide windows and a split-personality garden with both desert cactus and tropical foliage. The front door is open, and a gaggle of relatives whose names I forget cluster in the foyer, clutching each others' elbows and craning their necks at the small thatch of celebrities inside. Big deal. Dad had movie star clients. He kept their toilets flushing regularly, their pipes gurgling like spring water in a mountain brook. He built a special water tower for one famous actress—to remain anonymous—so she could fill her toilet tank with Evian. As though her shit were too good for L.A. tap. Before I can slip around back, my mother materializes. "There you are." She grabs my hand and pulls me into the crowded living room, where the sofas that used to be blue are now white. Redecorating is like crack to Mom—she's always somewhere in a perpetual cycle of refinishing, redraping and reupholstering. I imagine she's been simmering with rage, waiting to lay into me.

"I can explain," I begin, suddenly feeling shaky and wondering if it's because I haven't eaten all day.

She narrows her eyes. "Not now." Mom's normally clear voice sounds strained, hoarse. In her simple black sheath, she looks wired, tired, and smaller than her already petite self. "Are you hungry?"

She often reads my mind like that. When I was little, she told me that when I was growing inside her, a piece of her brain swam through the umbilical cord and became the seed that grew into my brain. Therefore, whatever I was thinking, she was actually thinking, too. This was a great mind control device for a while, but I finally looked it up in her big Doctor Spock book when I was twelve and realized it wasn't true, which was a great relief as I had resisted masturbating because of it.

Mom gestures around the room filled with people. "Look at this turnout. So many clients! Everyone loved your father."

Right. Dad was paid to wade into and clean up shit, which he did with no time off for thirty years until his heart failed that day on the hill. If that's love, count me out.

"Oh, Sander." A cloud of Opium perfume precedes my ex as she approaches from across the crowded room. Ashe Standish is done up like a nineteen-forties grieving vamp in a sexy black dress, pumps and gloves. Her silver-blonde hair (touch-ups by Rudy every three weeks) falls in shining waves to her shoulders. Porcelain skin radiates a knowing innocence; red slashes her lips and dances at the tips of her short fingernails. Her eyes glisten and my stupid heart pounds when she says, "I miss..."

"I miss you too," I blurt, leaning into the familiar jut of her breasts. Never mind I've sworn off relationships in the six weeks since she plunged her traitorous knife into my heart; desire surges through me. I pull her close.

"Whoa." Ashe steps back. "I miss *your dad*, Sander." She locates a hankie and dabs her eyes without smudging her mascara.

Crying on cue is one of Ashe's talents, but I can tell she's not acting right now. "How are you holding up?"

I shrug. "I'm gonna carve his name on my chest right below yours."

"Aw, San," she says in that little cartoon-character voice she has, the one that got her the gig on the cat food commercial, and puts her hand on the nape of my neck like she used to. For a moment, it's comforting. For a moment, we are not here at all. We're alone together and we're new, and it is a morning after we've had hang-from-the-chandelier sex, and she has her foot on the sink painting her toenails a vixenish burgundy while I am yodeling in the shower and there is the possibility that together we can make good things happen. Good love, good art, good careers, maybe a good kid or two. I never expected stratospheric, blockbuster success, but when I was with her, the vision of a good life was something I actually toyed with. "It wasn't your fault." Ashe's hand casually falls away, leaving my nape naked and vulnerable.

"Why would you say that?" We are *so* back in my family's living room and my voice might be getting a little bit loud, but all I can think of is how when she left me, she took my future, my dream. "You think it's my fault?"

"I didn't mean..." she starts, and that crease that makes her look her age appears between her eyebrows.

But I'm connecting the dots. Ashe sends me the break-up email. The next day, I lash out at the lady with the glove. Dad and I stop talking. Dad goes back out on service calls. "If you hadn't broken up with me, my Dad would still be alive today." This proclamation turns a few heads our way. "You sent me an *email*, Ashe! We were *living* together!"

"Shut up!" Ashe hisses, her nostrils flaring not so charmingly.

I know I'm an idiot and what I've said makes no sense, but there's no going back once Oggie Bright joins us, casually hooking Ashe's elbow. There they are: beauty and the beast. One thing about Ashe, the girl's not shallow. I mean, I'm no Adonis and I certainly don't consider myself handsome, but it sucks to be dumped for a toad. And as if his protruding eyes, gray teeth, fuzzy hair and flooded cords aren't bad enough, the guy's a sensation. In the ten or so years since he and I were in film school together, Oggie managed to write a small, quirky comedy that won a screenplay competition. Then he wrote a couple of commercial thrillers, which earned him enough cash to direct and produce his own-low budget drama, a breakout hit. Word in the recent trades is Ashe is being primed for his next project, a big-budget studio period gangster piece—which could spell either disaster or Oscar. But what gets me most: he's my age. I wonder how long the Death Clock gives him till he's pushing up daisies. Fucking overachiever will probably live forever. "I am truly sorry for your loss." Oggie offers his hand.

"Thank you," I mutter, clasping my hands together firmly in front of me, while inside my head I'm yelling, *All right, Svengali, she's yours!* I get it. Dumping me for Oggie Bright was a good business decision on Ashe's part. She and I hardly even went out to dinner the last few months we were together. Before Fabby entered the picture, I was always busy with Dad, cruising around in the El-San van, entering the inner sancta of hill homes to Roto-Root the rich and famous. When I wasn't working, I was trying to write my Great American Screenplay, which for the most part left me banging my head against my laptop and surfing the Internet for inspiration on sites like Check Your Death Clock and Name Your Penis. Had I been in Ashe's shoes, I would have dumped me too.

"Quiet, everyone." Mom taps a glass and tucks a fallen strand of hair behind her ear to make her blond bob even and neat. Conversations fade and the guests cluster into the living room. "As I was saying to my son, Sander," she extends a hand toward me and all heads swivel my way; I turtle down into my suit, "it's so lovely to see all Bobby's friends and clients here." Her voice is clear now, no trace of strain or fatigue. "He considered all of you his family." She's turning it on for the crowd. How can she say that when his only son, his actual family, barely feels like family?

"*Ay, Dios.* Mister Bobby is a saint," a voice from behind me addresses the group. A hand grips my shoulder and pulls me into a muscular embrace. When I come up for air, I barely recognize Fabby, in his street clothes instead of standard-issue El-San coveralls. I've tried blaming his allergies for Dad's death, too. If Fabby had been out on that Saturday call instead of me, Dad might have been saved. Of course, Dad still might have died, but it wouldn't have been on *my* watch and for that I would pay a million bucks, if I had it. "I miss him so much," Fabby says in his halting English, and tightens his arm around my neck before launching into the story of how Dad took him in when he needed work and was planning to help him become a citizen, how my Dad became more like a brother than a boss. Fabby, who is shorter than I am, has me hunched over and jammed up into his armpit in a headlock the entire time, while his son Sam looks reverentially at the floor and clasps my other shoulder in some kind of bereaved father/son brotherhood. Matching gold crosses dangle from their necks. Sam grabs his in his hand, kisses it, and rolls his eyes to heaven before saying a prayer in Spanish. When everyone else joins in for an "amen," I twist myself out of his grip.

Mom shoots me an eye dagger, then resumes her gracious mask. "Gracias, Fabrizio, Sam." Mom does a little *namaste* prayer thing with her hands. First time I've ever seen her do that. In some way that is unfathomable to me and totally instinctive to her, she is handling this. "Would anyone else like to share a word or two about Bobby?" Mom purposely ignores me and gloms onto my sister across the room. "Ellie?"

Of the two of us, Ellie's the one who resembles Dad, or used to, before she dieted herself into a rail. When we were kids, Ellie was the athlete, obsessed with, at various stages, volleyball, surfing, roller skating, tennis, golf, downhill skiing and badminton, and was constantly trying to get me to join in. I shunned her as often as possible; I preferred watching movies, alone. My sister actually is gorgeous, even though she has Dad's facial features and ruddy complexion. His brown, sun-streaked hair; pond-green eyes. The broad brow makes her beauty tolerable to those not as beautiful as she, and she knows it, though if I ever need to get a rise out of her for no good reason, all I have to do is call her "Neanderthal Girl" and she cracks. Yet even in grief, Ellie perfectly complements her dark, Armani-clad prince of a husband. Right now, Jerome has one arm around his wife and is filling an ice bucket at the bar with the other. Ellie cutely sets his hand at his side and clears her throat. "What can I say about Dad except I'll always be his little girl?" she begins, her chin quivering. "He was the best. I remember him telling me, always follow your dream." She looks up at Jerome. "And I did. And the reason I love Jerome is because he's just like Dad." She buries her face into Jerome's chest. He kisses the top of her head. Their matching black-and-gold, diamond-studded Rolexes sparkle in the afternoon light. *Barf city.*

There's a big "awww" from the room and another guy steps forward. I recognize him as a screenwriter for whom my father had installed an aboveground septic tank housed in a marble-lined gazebo. "Bobby was a phenomenal plumber, an upstanding citizen, an outstanding specimen..."

This could take all day. From the corner of my eye, Oggie jots notes on a 3x5 card. Sooner or later, it's going to be my turn to share in this round-robin grief-o-rama. My back stiffens as I suddenly realize: I don't know what I'm going to say. That me and the old man weren't getting along when he died? That I failed to resuscitate him? That he never told me he loved me, or encouraged me to follow my dreams? Maybe I'll tell the story of the afternoon I told my parents I wanted to go to film school and direct my own screenplays.

The living room walls were pine-paneled and the upholstery was avocado green in those days. Dad had his feet up on the Danish modern coffee table in front of the console television, a mere silhouette against the blue light flickering from the screen; a silhouette with a voice. "Margaret,"—he always called Mom "Margaret" when he was talking to her about me—"tell your son that film school is for arty-farty kids and fags whose parents have too much money."

A wooden spoon came hurtling across the room from the kitchen, with Mom yelling, "Robert!" She never called him Robert.

Dad rubbed the back of his head, but just went on. "You and I both know it's not talent that matters; it's connections. Better he should get a real job to support himself and his family, if he wants one. The film world is a jungle. Only a few people are successful. The others? The ones who can't make it? Their lives are ruined! Ruined."

I was standing right next to him, snotty and righteous as all get-out. "Mom, tell your husband that *maybe* I do have talent and the best way for me to make connections is through film school. I've saved my money. It's not that expensive. And since when is a *plumber*"—I spit the word like it was a turd—"an expert on the film industry?"

Mom came in from the kitchen strangling a sponge, like maybe she hoped it was one of our necks. "Cool it, both of you!" She rarely yelled, but she did then, and a vein appeared in her forehead from the strain of it. "Bobby, Sander isn't the same as you. He might want different things from life. And Sander, your father just wants you to be able to support yourself. There's nothing glamorous about being a starving artist."

Dad stood up, swooped the wooden spoon from the floor, and punched the TV dial. Even though we were about the same height, he always seemed to tower over me. I've seen his broad shoulders hoist toilets and septic tanks. But he walked over to Mom and put the spoon in her hand, then said very calmly, "Plumbing is good, honest work that pays well. He can work at El-San while he goes to school, but he needs to be prepared to inherit the company when I die. I'm not going to live forever you know."

Famous last words.

Back in the now, Ashe Standish is stepping forward to say a word about Dad, Oggie Bright's paw large and supportive on the small of her back. "Even though I only had the opportunity to know him the year I was dating his son, I got the clear impression Bobby Sanderson was the kind of guy everyone liked to be around." *Oh God, no!* I put my hand in my pocket and give my flask a little shake. It makes no sound. Muttering, "Pardon me," I back out of the crowd and the room.

My old bedroom looks nothing like my room anymore. My creaky, kid-sized bed is still here, but my desk and dresser, posters and ancient stereo equipment have been replaced. One wall of shelves display a freakish collection of porcelain dolls Mom started buying on the Home Shopping Network after Ellie left for college. On the opposite wall, a behemoth TV screen is mounted on the wall across from an equally large BarcaLounger. In the back corner of the closet, I shove aside Mom's sewing kits, photo albums and bags of doll clothes, and punch the floorboard lightly to see if it's still loose. It pops up and eureka! A half-full bottle of Jack Daniel's. Nicely aged too; it's been there since I was sixteen, when my best friend Nate's uncle died and we took the opportunity to express our grief by raiding his dad's liquor cabinet, drinking half the thing, then puking our guts out in a neighbor's backyard. Neither one of us ever craved that particular brand of whiskey again, but we hid it away safely in case we ever changed our minds.

Ellie appears at the doorway. "Nice going, jackass." She kicks off her heels and flops on the bed. "Where were you?"

"Betty died, okay? The cabby got lost on his way to my place. I didn't plan it." I automatically hand the bottle to Ellie. Some of our best drinking was done when I was in college and she was in high school. I expect today to be no different.

"So Betty is finally Rubble?" Ellie cracks. She tips back the bottle, then returns it to me. She knows I named my Jeep after Jean-

Jacques Beineix's *Betty Blue*, but somehow, Betty Rubble is the name the stuck.

"Almost." I slump into the cool chocolate leather of the BarcaLounger while the whiskey burns around the hole in my chest. "Do you think Betty Rubble is a swinger?" I always enjoyed the shape of Mrs. Rubble's saber-tooth dress and wondered if Fred felt the same.

A funny look comes over Ellie's face and she spits her mouthful into a fake potted something or other. "Yuck," she says. "It's old."

"Aged, they call it, my dear, and you will be too some day. Have you been in here lately? What's Mom's new theme anyway? Nightmares of the Living Dead? Valley of the QVC Dolls?" I'm referring to the life-size babies on the shelves. With oversized eyes and rouged cheeks, they wear elaborate getups and hairdos, like miniature JonBenét Ramseys. Some sprout angel wings, some have church lady hats. One just looks plain homicidal.

Without getting up, Ellie reads off their names. "Autumn Crisp, Winter Waltz, Spring A'Daisy, Summer Swing. That's just the bottom shelf."

"And these are new, aren't they?" I slap the lounger's arms and nod toward the giant TV.

"Jeez, Sander, when was the last time you were here? Dad set this up as his screening room after the first heart attack. Mom wouldn't let him do it anywhere else. Said oversized furniture was vulgar."

"Bobby's in-home theatre." Dad's shape is molded into the seat cushion and I can feel the places—shoulder, hip, knee—where our bodies don't mesh. I take another drink from the bottle. "You think Mom's still mad at me?"

"Yeah, that's all she's worried about right now. Like *you're* the center of her universe." Ellie squints her eyes, looking just like Dad, and stares up at the ceiling, tracing her hands around her flat belly in figure eights.

"That would make me the sun. Get it?"

"That would make you a dick. Just wait until things settle down, and Mom remembers her only son missed his only dad's funeral." She reaches over and slugs my arm.

"Go ahead. Hit me harder. I deserve it."

She looks at me with tear-brimming eyes and pats the place where she just slugged me. "It must have been weird to be there when it happened."

This is my cue, but I can't bring myself to talk about that Saturday. Dad splattered with shit; me drenched in helplessness, stupidity and guilt. This may sound harsh, but Dad hasn't been gone long enough for me to miss him. Not yet. Not like I *really missed* my jumper cables this morning. In the movie *Missing*, Sissy Spacek and Jack Lemmon go to some Central American country to look for their lost husband/son. How long would I have to be away for Dad to have missed me?

When I say nothing, Ellie tilts her head back and continues. "He was a good dad, wasn't he?"

"You asking me or the ceiling?"

She won't look me in the face. "You should have been there." She says it quietly, and I wish she'd yell, because quiet is worse. "No matter what."

"I know." Does he, can he, possibly know I intended to be there? If I think it hard enough will he know it now? I remember that

Saturday on the hill, thinking, *Not yet not yet not yet*, and hoping he could read my mind as well as Mom could. Or am I just *saying* I feel that way because I feel guilty that I don't?

Ellie starts weeping the way she used to when she was little and she'd fallen down and wasn't yet sure how badly she was hurt. I sit next to her on the bed and rub her back in little circles. Her skeleton is practically discernible through her dress, her spine like a keyboard. Even her feet look too thin and too rich. Through the blinds, I can see people emerging from the living room, spilling out onto the patio. "The sharing is over," I say, nodding in their direction.

Ellie wipes her nose on my sleeve and peers outside at Jerome, who has his arm around Mom, helping her into a chaise. "He'll be a good dad someday, won't he?"

I hate that Jerome Green-Sanderson has hyphenated our family name with his. Probably so he and Ellie can create their own enlightened dynasty. Jerome always wears shades, both indoors and out, and has a habit of standing around like a security guard with his hands in his pockets. He has an annoyingly meaningful and successful career as a freelance hospice nurse, and contracts privately to help wealthy clients live out their days in comfort, but I suspect his trust fund allowance is what Ellie loves most about him. Between client deaths, the two of them travel to islands that belong to Jerome's friends or to Switzerland to attend weddings in castles or to Paris for cotillions for the children of Jerome's parents' friends, and Ellie has the life she's always dreamed of. I imagine he'll be a perfect dad, and if the two of them ever get down to it, their kids will be perfect too. But today, Jerome's normally trim black hair bushes out at the sides, with sideburns and chops threatening to fill in soon.

"What's with his hair? And is that a paunch?" He's no Hitchcock, but Jerome's definitely sporting a baby beer gut.

A true L.A. girl, Ellie hates physical imperfection, especially in the form of weight gain. I've heard her discuss her ideal weight in ounces. But her eyes are soft when she considers Jerome. "He's been working a lot. He's stressed out."

"Stress, sure, that explains it. I thought maybe he was going through some kind of childhood phase."

"No." She crinkles her nose and slugs me. "That would be you." I push her. She laughs, rolling melodramatically onto the floor. "Help me up. I have to pee."

When I see her next, it's through the venetians. Ellie points to me at the window. Jerome and Mom shade their eyes (or shades, in Jerome's case) to look. I close the blinds and raise the bottle to Autumn, Winter and Spring A'Daisy.

The flowers on the buffet are all white. The only ones I can name are roses and hydrangeas; they were favorites of all the moms on the block. I've heard white is the Asian version of black for funerals. But my family is whiter than white, and Mom's spread proves it. Tiny triangle sandwiches of roast beef with horseradish or ham with mustard; bowls of extra Miracle Whip; Dutch Krunch rolls; platters of Italian salami and pepperoncini, antipasto and marinated mushrooms, miniature hot dogs wrapped in bacon, a cheese platter mounded with slabs of American, Swiss and cheddar, bowls of onion and clam dip with Ruffles, guacamole and salsa with tortilla chips. Nothing appeals to me, so I plunder the kitchen, dig up a can of Easy Cheese and a box of Ritz crackers, and make ready to disappear.

As I'm cutting through the dining room toward the back yard, Jerome materializes at my side. The shades, the well-cut Armani, the Florence Nightingale vocation, the trust fund he never talks about but we're all extremely aware of for not having one of our own: his very existence exhausts me. "How could you miss your own father's funeral?" He spoons a blob of guacamole onto his paper plate, which buckles under its weight.

I tap my flask, which I've refilled with Jack, in my pocket. Good Jack. "It was unfortunate, unavoidable and none of your fucking business," I retort and then, unable to resist, "Guacamole is a condiment, not an entrée."

"You smell like liquor," he says, only Jerome says it *likkah*. Ellie always tries to explain that his accent comes from being exposed to lots of languages in boarding school, but I say it's just pretentious. He piles his plate with lunchmeats, cheeses, chips. "Is that how you want everyone here paying tribute to your father to remember you?" He surveys me with evident repulsion and digs into the guacamole.

For the second time today, I have nothing to say. I squirt cheese on a cracker in the shape of a skull and crossbones and shove it into my mouth, followed by the remainder of my well-aged bottle, wondering how many millions of seconds are left on my Death Clock before I die. I make it as far as the living room before the first wave wracks my gut. Ellie sees me bend at the waist, and hits the carpet running. "Not on the sofa, Sander, NOT ON THE SOFA!" She yanks my arm so the stream of amber puke flies in a circle around us. The words "graceful lariat of vomit" loop through my brain, as though I'm not even remotely involved in its creation.

3

TUESDAY MORNING

Despite the fact that my legs splay off both sides of a too-small mattress, my back aches from its lumpy springs, minky fuzz coats my throat and my head throbs, I've an impressive case of morning wood. It must have something to do with sleeping in my boyhood bed, home to years of wet dreams and furtive wanks. Mom's freakish dolls judge me ruthlessly: Loser. Ingrate. Rotten son. I point my finger at each one and pull the trigger. *Bang!* Autumn Crisp takes a hit! *Pow!* Eskimo Pie gets iced! *Kerchunk!* Spring A'Daisy gets sprung, Mochaccino Baby gets creamed! All twelve of them, in slow motion. To the whistling, hupping score from *The Good, the Bad and the Ugly.* I roll over to face the opposite wall and get a grip on myself for some customary relief, but am met by my own reflection in Dad's giant TV screen. The BarcaLounger's cushion buttons stare me down, two pair of relentless eyes. My room is no longer my room, and hasn't been for a long time. It's as though after Ellie and I left the house, my parents founded a new civilization upon the ruins and detritus of our childhoods. So long, morning wood.

In the master bedroom on the other side of the wall, closet doors slide open, plastic hangers crash onto a bed. Mom's voice is low, her words unclear. *Is she talking about me?* Then Ellie. "Remember we were supposed to spend a weekend in Ojai for our anniversary last month, but Jerome cancelled? He said he was tired, then went shopping and came home with a new Harley-Davidson. He rides around in full body leather now, like some Hells Angel."

My laugh sounds like a barking seal. I can't help it.

Ellie bangs on the wall. "That is *so* rude!"

I put on yesterday's funeral suit because that's all I have and join them. Mom's still in bed, looking even smaller than usual in one of Dad's old T-shirts from the eighties. "Plumbers do it with pipe." Classy. Propped among the flowered throw pillows and surrounded by piles of Dad's clothes, she leafs through a stack of sympathy cards. Ellie surveys the walk-in closet. She's wearing a fashionable track suit, like she's going to do lunch before laps.

"You're getting rid of Dad's stuff already?" I blurt.

Mom sets the cards on her lap, removes her pearly, cat-eye bifocals and folds them carefully before slipping them into their white leather case. She sears double-barreled holes through my chest with her eyes, then looks out the window.

"Shut up, ass," Ellie hisses as she shakes out one of Dad's many velour sweat suits, folds the pants lengthwise, and stacks them on the bed. "Nice puking last night."

Ah, yes. My memory returns with a stab to the temporal lobe. "Thankyouverymuch," I say, all deep like Elvis, dipping my hand into a chaotic pile of ties. Dad didn't wear them much, but we all knew he had a thing for ties, which is why he got at least one every Father's Day since I can remember. When he and Mom would dress up for dinner parties, Dad would slide his hand down the length of his tie and tap the tip against Mom's nose before tucking it into his suit jacket. My favorite is hand-painted, a fifties job with an abstract design that's a cross between a nuclear explosion and a dental office oil painting. It's cut wide, soft and cool to the touch. Without thinking, I fashion it into a noose and drop it over my head. "Dang," I twang. There's something about being in my childhood home that makes me act like an idiot child. I don't much like it, but right now I'm incapable of stopping.

"Where in heaven's name were you yesterday?" Mom snaps.

Finally. I toss the tie into the pile. "Betty's battery died. I couldn't find my jumper cables. The cabby was late. There was traffic at the cemetery." This sounds lame even to me. I slide Dad's suits down the rod, wondering if Mom's constant redecorating contributed to my insecurity and low self-esteem.

Mom hooks her finger through the loop of a teacup on a saucer on the nightstand. She's used that china every morning for as long as I can remember: blue flowers on a yellow background that she rescued from a yard sale down the street for a quarter. We all thought it was hideous, but she always said that by loving something ugly, it was possible for it to become beautiful. "Your excuses don't cut it anymore, Sander." She quietly sips her tea.

"They're not excuses! They're facts. Observable events with cause and effect." That sounds better.

"Ooooh," she says. "Facts. As in things we all know to be true." Sip.

"Now you're getting it, Mom." This should all blow over quickly now.

"As in, we all know for a *fact*, if Ashe hadn't broken up with you, you wouldn't have acted up at work and Dad wouldn't have had to go back out on calls. I'm sure there's some reason it's my fault, too." She returns the teacup on the saucer with a jangle.

Ouch, that stings. "Did Ashe tell you I said that?"

Mom's hands plop into her lap. "There comes a time, Sander, when you have to take responsibility for your actions and do what you say you're going to do. Stop blaming everything and everybody else for your own mistakes."

"I wanted to be there! I tried. Hey, I've never seen this one before." I pull out a suit on a wooden hanger and hang it on a hook on the door. The tweed is soft with greens and golds. The jacket has a forties cut: single-breasted with patch pockets, set-in waistband, back vent. The trousers are high-waisted and pleated, with a trustworthy cuff.

"Ha! Try these." Ellie lobs a pair of blue coveralls at me. The legs catch me around the neck and the arms dangle at my legs—an ominous 69-position of my future—with El-San Pipe & Drain embroidered on the back and "Bobby" above the breast pocket.

I give my sister the finger, both hands, then turn back to the suit. The jacket's silk lining is black, olive and ochre paisley. It's wolf-whistle gorgeous. "Where'd he get this?"

Mom barely glances at it. "I don't know. Your father got gifts from clients all the time. Take it."

"Thanks." I toss the coveralls onto the bed and slip the suit hanger over my shoulder, wondering when I'll have enough cash to make alterations.

Mom turns back to me, eyes blazing, chin wobbly. "He shouldn't have been going out on house calls in his condition. That was your job."

Just because a part of me blames myself for Dad croaking doesn't mean I thought she would. "I didn't *make* him. He didn't *have* to pull me off calls. And what if I didn't go? What if Fabrizio was there? Would you have blamed him for killing Dad?"

Our argument follows a careening logic all its own—that is, none. "All he ever did was make things easy for you, Sander. And how do you repay him? By practically kicking him into the grave and then missing his own goddamn funeral." Mom begins to cry, and in reaching for a tissue, whacks the teacup to the floor with the back of her hand, where it shatters with a hard crash, splashing tepid Earl Grey everywhere. She reins in her tears and coolly, calmly turns to me. The brazen morning sun spotlights the lines on her face and makes yesterday's perfect hair look thin and greasy. "Get out. I can't see you right now." She snaps the venetian blinds shut and pulls the comforter up over her face.

I thought it would be a relief to get past the tempest, but I'm wrong. I'm paralyzed. My feet won't move and a lead ball hangs in my chest.

Ellie pulls me out of the room. I don't realize my teeth are chattering until she places her hand under my chin. "Breathe, now. In. Out."

I gulp a few times until my lungs work again, my head stops pounding, and images of Ashe, Oggie, Dad and Fabby stop swirling through my head and I'm normal again. Sort of. "Give me a ride home?"

Car-lessness in L.A. is a condition akin to castration. Walking the ten miles from the West Side to the East Side is out of the question; the bus is for losers, my bike tires are flat, taxis are too expensive for anything but special occasions, and the girlfriend as occasionally willing chauffeur is no more. I point Ellie down Sunset Boulevard, three lanes thick with battered pickups and vans, past small storefronts boasting *Carnes* and *Mariscos*. I can't help feeling that Dad dying is a punishment for something I've done, including, but not limited to, bad CPR, the glove incident, lack of talent, going to film school, getting nowhere as a result. You name it.

"When was the last time you had an attack?" Ellie asks.

"I don't know." But I do. It was when Dad died. Before that, it was when I read Ashe's email: a hot, prickly wave swept from the top of my neck, up the back of my skull and into my eyes. El-San swam around me and my head crashed to my desk, resulting in a purple knot that looked like I'd been in a fight with a horseshoe. At the next corner, I point for Ellie to take a right.

She takes the hard turn too fast. "Shit!" she cries, slamming the brakes to keep from running over a yellow dog in the road. The animal's sole response to his brush with death is to raise his sleepy head from the asphalt, give us a withering glance, then fall back into his road-dog dream. I wonder what last thoughts Dad had when he died. Was there a montage of his life? The MTV version of the best parts, or the Lifetime network version of the worst parts? Did he float above his dying body on the hillside, think about coming back down, but upon seeing me there, change his mind?

"Why do you live here?" Ellie grumps.

"I like it." Living where I do makes me feel like I'm a member of a big family to whom I have no obligations and am not remotely related. Exotic street food abounds. There's always music, whether it's kids thrashing on drums and guitars in a garage, mariachis waiting for gigs on street corners, or car stereos blasting reggae to their brothers in the hinterlands. Children play in the street while their parents and grandparents hang out on the porch. Animals roam intently or nap without care. It's warmer over here, and the beauty is less calculated than the West Side's, with its wedding cake houses, postcard sunsets and scrubbed thoroughfares. This side of town can be rough and broken down, but at least it's colorful, sincere. There's something tenacious and heartbreaking about scraggly palms pushing up through concrete. Plus, it's cheap.

My single is at the top of Echo Park Boulevard. The front is overgrown with vines; my back windows have a view, if you can call it that, of the black ribbon of Interstate 5, the concrete L.A. river, and the dust-brown Angeles Mountains, when they're visible through the smoky haze. When I'm there, it feels as though I can't see where I've been, and the places I can see, I have no desire to visit. It's comfortable and anonymous, makes no statements or demands.

"You can just drop me here." I'm all about clean exits.

"I haven't seen your new place yet," Ellie demands. "And I have to pee."

Since the taxi picked me up yesterday, a baby-shit green love seat has appeared on the street. I push the sofa onto the sidewalk and watch Ellie bounce her Rover a million times against my stalled Jeep—which now has a ticket—before she positions the SUV a foot and a half from the curb and then quits.

"Can you give Betty a jump?"

"Sure," Ellie says, slinging herself out of the driver seat. "But first I gotta go." She follows me down the steep, uneven stairs, and paddles through the circling flies to my door.

"Which way?" she calls out as she beelines past me, and

then, "God! It's hot in here!" Followed by, "Ow! Jesus, Sander!" as she crashes into my towers of cardboard boxes.

I crank open all the windows so the brown hot air outside can freshen up the stale hot air inside, then carelessly restack the boxes while she's doing her business. The freeway roar floats up like a continuous ocean wave.

"It's hard to believe you and Ashe aren't together anymore," Ellie says from behind the bathroom door.

"No, what's hard to believe is that we lived together and she broke up with me in an email."

"No, what's hard to believe is that you let her go." Ellie emerges from the bathroom and surveys my impressive lack of furniture and decor. "And that this is all you got. You guys had such a cute place. And you haven't even unpacked."

"Not true." I point to the built-in bookshelves flanking the nonworking fireplace, where my DVDs and tapes have been filed alphabetically by genre, then director, then title. I may have even dusted them yesterday. "Ashe kept all the cute stuff." It was hers anyway. "And I've been busy." Being depressed. "So Jerome got himself a bike, huh?"

"And a *tattoo* of the frickin' Harley logo," she spits out. "It's Celtic and kind of cool actually. Orange and black to match his bike."

Suddenly, I remember my star encounter with Paul Street. Ellie will die when she hears. "Guess who I bumped into outside the sanctuary at the cemetery?"

But Ellie's off on her own tangent. That happens sometimes when you're the youngest child, the golden daughter who thinks everyone dotes on your every word and, for most of your life, everyone has. "I mean, I understand why he'd want it. Every guy wants a Harley, right?"

"Every douchebag."

I wait for her to defend her beloved, but she's on a roll. "And it's not that he just canceled our trip to Ojai, which I thought we were really looking forward to. But he went and bought the bike and got the tattoo and didn't even *tell* me about it. If he loved me, how could he not tell me about it? I mean I could have helped him pick it out. Or something." Her voice trails off, as though she suddenly knows more than she wants to. She laughs loudly, which makes no sense at all, and which is how I know she's worried. "But I interrupted. What were you saying?"

That's when I decide Paul Street belongs to me and I'm not sharing. Ellie'll just tell me I should use him to make some kind of work connection anyway. "I forget. You thirsty?" I wash a glass and dribble what's left of some flat Calistoga into it.

"The reading of the will is next Monday. Can you believe it, after all these years, you're finally gonna get the business? Might as well go with the flow." She honks at her own lame joke and drains the water in one long gulp.

"I am *not* the future of El-San Pipe & Drain." I carry her empty glass into the kitchen.

"You got something else going on? A secret career plan I don't know about?"

"There's kind of a plan." I haven't told her about buying the computer and the camera to write and film my movie. That way if it doesn't pan out, the only person who'll know what a loser I am will be me.

Ellie continues. "Ashe looked gorgeous, didn't she? She was

telling me she's in a commercial Oggie's directing with Destinée in it. I can't imagine what Destinée's doing out of rehab already, but anyway, it sounded like a great break for Ashe. How about you? Seeing anyone special these days?"

"Jesus, it's only been six weeks! Maybe I should be looking to meet that special someone who can jumpstart my career, too. Maybe Ashe can give me some tips!" I wedge the glass into the sink with the rest of my dirty dishes until it shatters.

"You'll find someone, big brother. You'll see."

I pick up the bigger shards of glass, look for the nonexistent trash, and then toss them back into the sink. "You don't think it's my fault Dad died, do you?"

She touches my shoulder. "Mom will come around." And then she's back to her old self. "You'll be back in the fold, working at El-San, in no time."

"That's it." I push her in the direction of the door. "Time for you to go home."

Ellie's arms fly around her head. "I didn't mean..."

"You never do. Thanks for the ride."

She climbs the brick stairs to the street and bumps the Rover out of its spot in only five tries. After she's gone, I remember she was going to give my car a jump.

Oh well. Finally. Alone. I strip down to my briefs, flop on the futon, and power up my laptop, where *Blank Document* waits. I still haven't even thought up a concept or characters. Write what you know, I was taught. But damn Ellie and all her questions. The only thing in my head now is Ashe. It's hard to lose someone you think is perfect for you. But if she were perfect for me, wouldn't she still be with me?

Truffaut's *Jules et Jim* was the matinee feature at a ratty art house theatre where more than half the seats were broken, which didn't matter because the place was never more than half-full. At the snack bar, I stood behind a girl with silver-blonde hair who bought the same items I always bought: coffee and a Violet Crumble. I followed her inside with my identical snack and sat where I always sat: right side, three rows from the back, on the aisle. Right behind her, one row in front of me, one place to the right. That girl put my body on autopilot. Without my usual second thoughts or crippling analyses, I moved up a row and took the seat next to her. We unwrapped our Crumbles together, and when the lights went down, we sank down into our seats and put our arms on the armrest at the same time. I felt her smiling when I refused to relinquish the armrest, and the only reason I knew this was because I was smiling, too. We experienced each other through our elbows, inhaling and exhaling, then snorted in laughter, self-consciously at first, but then we realized, we had no choice...*this was Truffaut.* At the end, when Jeanne Moreau got in that car and drove toward that bridge, Ashe leaned over and kissed me full on the lips. "At least we're alive," she said. I was a goner.

But how to write that without writing our own story? And what happens next? The guy gets dumped, his dad dies, the end? When I click the "sadistic mode" on my Death Clock, a window pops up with the date Tuesday, December 17, 1990, and this: "Sorry, but your time has already expired! Have a nice day."

Dad's suit hangs from the otherwise empty curtain rod. I put on the jacket, knowing it won't fit, but somehow, oddly, it does.

How old was Dad when he was the same size as me? The garment smells of my parents' closet, a commingling of shoes, Old Spice and the vanilla trace of Mom's Shalimar powder. Above the inside breast pocket, the monogram PS is embroidered in immaculate gold loops. Could it be? I thumb through the pages of an old college text and locate a photo of Preston Sturges wearing the *exact same suit.*

In honor of my favorite director, I pop *Sullivan's Travels* into the VCR. It's one of the greats, in which a successful director of shallow, pie-in-the-face Hollywood comedies goes undercover to experience the life of the common man in order to make an "important" film, and learns that what the common man really wants is shallow, pie-in-the-face Hollywood comedy. On my tiny TV screen, a freight train roars through nighttime snow. As I settle into the black-and-white film, my family and my life disappear. I tuck my legs under me to get comfortable on the lumpy futon, and my ankle knocks into something cold and hard. Goddamn jumper cables.

4

SUNDAY NIGHT

This is me, naked, in the mirror. Neither tall nor short, heavy nor thin. There's a bit of Mom's softness around my chin and jaw, but I have never been able to pinpoint Dad's features in me. Not the way he's there in Ellie's Neanderthal forehead, or the way she squints her eyes right before she delivers a zinger. No, I am the proverbial milkman's child, astounding in my standardosity. Strikingly average. Splendidly pedestrian. Magnificently mediocre.

With the El-San office closed all week, I haven't had much to do since the funeral except not work on my screenplay, and dread Paul's "little soiree." Fabby came by in the El-San van to give my Jeep a jump, but even that failed to resurrect Betty, who now probably *will* become rubble. My ride's true flaw has yet to be determined, but my gut says repairs will cost beaucoup bucks. My computer and camera have gone untouched; their mere presence mocks me. And here's how I picture tonight's party scenario: Disco or some other trendily ironic music will blast over concert-quality speakers. Development boys and girls will competitively namedrop, trading cards and numbers. A handful of exotic human specimens will be scattered about artfully uncomfortable furniture. Almost actors and actresses will pass around decadent libations and flashy, unpronounceable appetizers. There will be at least one asphyxiating cigar room. I will say hello to Paul, attempt to mingle, talk to one person who after five minutes will find someone else more beneficial to talk to, find my host to tell him what a wonderful time I've had and then flee into the sunset, never to see the likes of Paul Street again.

I try on that suit from Dad's closet. The Sturges more than fits—it *suits* me. The gold in the tweed turns my dishwater-brown hair blond; the olive turns my eyes green. The coat's cut triangulates my torso. I am cool, confident and collected. Cool, confident... The cabby's beep interrupts my pre-party pep talk. Amazing. He's right on time.

Forty minutes later, we're motoring on Mulholland above smoggy valley vistas. We turn up a drive flanked by cypress spires, and the cabby stops at the end of a line of cars waiting for the valet. I pay up and watch the cab make a tight U-turn in the narrow drive. I have become accustomed to being the sole pedestrian on empty walkways, the only white guy at crowded bus stops, and now the only guest hoofing it up to the flamingo-pink, Spanish-style villa.

Paul Street is waiting at the arched, dark wood front door. "Bienvenidos a mi casa," he says, arms open wide. He fingers my lapel. "Nice suit."

"Gracias," I say. "It was Dad's. Check it out. Preston Sturges." I flap open the jacket, then quickly close it. How nerdy can you get?

"Nice," Street smiles. "You like movies?" he asks, putting his hand to my back and guiding me inside the grand foyer. To my nod, he asks, "You in the business?"

"Not exactly," I say. A flute of perfectly chilled champagne presses into my hand.

"Here." He pilots me away from the chatter of the main room and follows me into a nook. We sit in easy chairs flanking a bay window overlooking the blurry, illuminated grid of the San Fernando Valley. "A moment of privacy." His trademark voice plays language like an instrument, all the vowels aspirated and consonants correct.

He hasn't locked the door or pulled out the handcuffs. So far so good. "I'm not exactly in the business. Most recently, I was a production intern on a low-budget feature." *Unmentionables*, a soft-core thriller set in the lingerie modeling industry, bit the dust when one of the producers snorted the funding. The distribution deal fell out while she was in rehab.

Paul Street steeples his hands below his cleft chin. "Anything else?"

"Before that, a screenplay I wrote was optioned, but nothing came of it." Nothing good, anyway. *The Thing That Came From There* was about an intergalactic virus that permeates Earth's atmosphere and mutates an entire high school into flesh-eaters. That hellish ordeal ruined my friendship with the producer who optioned it and installed the case of writer's block I'm still pounding my forehead against. Still, I think Ashe would be impressed by my professional self-blurb. "Before that, I won a couple prizes in film school for my thesis project."

"Congratulations. I don't keep up on the 'real' biz so much since the infomercials. In fact, I'm debuting a new one tonight. I'm sure *Wonder Abs* will change the world." Self-deprecating. I like that. "Tell me about your thesis."

I explain how *White Man Dancing* intercut family home movies (mine) with animal behavior footage from the fifties I'd discovered in a dumpster while I was doing an internship at Paramount. Dad wasn't impressed by my visual exercise of juxtaposition and composition that re-examined Eisenstein's theories of filmic metaphor; he was deeply hurt, however, by the pair of shrieking blue-assed mandrills that appeared directly after a snippet of him and Mom having a screaming match that began over burnt toast. It wasn't flattering to my parents or the monkeys. Mom was upset I'd hurt Dad's feelings and "the *White Man* thing" became a tense topic for us all. When it received Excellence in Vision and Pioneer in Editing awards, I got what everyone wants: a little bit of buzz. For a split second, it seemed I had a future in film.

Front yard lamplight beams in through the window, spotlighting Paul, legs casually crossed, suit barely wrinkling. "And?"

I shrug. "And nada. After graduation, I worked at El-San to pay down my student loan and got used to the money. I took time off to work on the projects I mentioned, but when Dad got sick and needed more help, there was no time for anything else." Which is partly true. The rest of the truth is I couldn't pull together a follow-up. All the juice I developed in school drained away. I loathed everything I wrote, then stopped writing, then quit applying for work. It was as though I stepped into those blue coveralls and drooled myself into a shit-hued sleep. It wasn't until Ashe and I got together that I began to rededicate myself to my so-called career. And all *that's* got me so far is seven grand in debt.

"You're a good son," Paul Street says, turning to the mirror behind him and smoothing his hair.

My image gawps back at me over his shoulder. *Who, me?*

"Come." He pops up from the floral-patterned chair. "Let's go mingle. It's not a party until you make a connection."

"Or until something breaks," I snort. *Make a connection.* Those were Ashe's exact words just a little over three months ago on the night I consider The End. She had invited me to Musso & Frank to celebrate maxing out my credit card to buy new electronics. She'd tried to reserve Charlie Chaplin's old spot, but table one had already been booked, so we made do at a leather banquette. Ashe looked the part of a fifties *Photoplay* starlet in a silver halter dress. I wore my best Chuck Norris T-shirt that says "I don't step on toes, I step on necks." We both were amused by our costumes—only one of the reasons I thought she was the perfect girl for me—and ordered bone-dry martinis from a waiter with a face like a spit-shined leather boot. What Ashe didn't know was not all my seven grand of debt went toward the camera and computer. I had a black velvet box in my pocket that held the ring we'd seen in the window at the Beverly Loan Company, a popular celebrity pawnshop. She'd ooh'd and aah'd and wondered whom it might have belonged to and why they might have had to sell it. "I could never sell something like that," she claimed. "Not that ring, anyway." While I was waiting for the martini to work its magic so I could work up to popping the question, she was craning her neck to see who'd gotten Chaplin's table. "Look! Over there! No, wait. Don't look yet. Now! No, stop! He's looking. Wait. Oh, God. He saw me." She straightened up, turned her face to her "good side," and waggled her fingers at an unseen someone. "Hello," she mouthed, a much sexier word to mouth than "hi." I turned my head to see Oggie Bright at table one, mouthing his own frog-lipped, tongue-curling "hello" in the direction of my date. Ashe went on to tell me what an up-and-comer Oggie was, as though I weren't painfully aware of my status at the bottom of the ladder. Then I watched my beloved take a big gulp of martini, rearrange her breasts, and stand up. "Let's make a connection, Sander. Come on!" I refused, staying at the table and ordering myself another martini as I watched her congratulate that douchebag, watched his tumescent eyes lean into her cleavage while he pulled her toward him to whisper something in her ear, watched the light and shadow play on her white throat as she threw back her head and laughed deliciously. I never made it to my question and the velvet box never made it out of my pocket. Later on that night while we were fighting, Ashe was furiously explaining that making it in Hollywood, making it anywhere, was not about talent, though that didn't hurt. Not about education, but that certainly helped. It was about connections, which she tried to help me make that night, and which I had stupidly refused. There's no red flag like hearing the woman you love echo your father's advice. Tonight, inside Paul Street's pink villa, I'm not sure whether I'm doing it for Ashe or for Dad, for me or for Paul Street, but with Preston Sturges' name stitched close to my heart, I plan to enter Paul's party and connect.

But this party is not what I expected. This is a grand room of antique armoire, crystal chandelier and marble-topped étagère. A room filled with murmured conversations with the occasional throaty chuckle scored by live performers on flute, viola and harp. Punctuated with flower arrangements that complement the floral design in the ankle-deep carpet. The guests skew older, with leisure suits and artsy-craftsy sweaters sprinkling the fashion landscape. Many faces look eerily familiar, yet I can't identify anyone by name, something that happens a lot growing up in L.A.

"These people are mostly *Wonder Abs* colleagues," Paul explains. "Nobody you'd be interested in." He scans the crowd, then

snaps his fingers. "I know! You should meet Vana LeValle! Wait here."
Exit stage left.

I snatch more champagne from a passing tray. I usually set
up camp in a corner at parties, but the damn living room is *round*, so
I settle for the edge of a curved picture window. Outside, muscular
marble nudes stand sentinel around a lagoon uplit with colored lights.
Even though I'm standing under a glacial blast of A/C, perspiration
soaks the pits of the Sturges. Producers are to Hollywood what
cockroaches are to New York City, and of all the cockroaches in this
bug-infested town, Paul Street is going to introduce me to one I've
already worked with.

I remember a few facts from her "Film Encyclopedia of 1986"
entry. Born Esther Kuhns in Vienna, 1950. Daughter of an Austrian
opera singer and a German aristocrat. A former model, she married
French director Georges LeValle, famous for naming the sixties "Anti
Wave" school of filmmaking and featuring his exotic-looking wife in
his experimental features. After Georges' murder in a crowded café
in Rome in the seventies, Vana moved to Hollywood. She became a
producer of soft-core thrillers. Not exactly an A-list player at the
white-hot core of the film world. I wonder if she'll remember me as
her production intern. No perks, no pay, but invaluable, hands-on
experience was promised.

Unmentionables' production office, a.k.a. Vana's West
Hollywood carriage house, was a maze of cardboard filing boxes that
broke a large room into four smaller cubicles. Unfortunately, the
boxes contained working files, and the walls often came down when
files needed to be accessed. Desks were made of doors balanced
on sawhorses, and held old-school computer monitors, dot-matrix

printers and fax machines. Lights, cables, coffee cups, sugar packets, half-empty pizza boxes and Chinese takeout containers littered all other available surfaces.

I was revising call sheets based on the number of scenes we were behind (eight, at that point, for a total of three weeks) and watching my computer screen crash yet again. I'd already worked thirteen hours that day and mechanically attempted a sip of coffee from the same empty cup I'd been trying to drink from for the past half-hour. I heard Vana's unequivocal clipped accent along with footsteps on the gravel drive outside. My breath smelled like garbage, and I knew Vana always kept a small tin of mints on her desk. I went to her cubicle and found the engraved tin container. Lavender? Who the hell sucked lavender mints? When she burst into the office, she was dressing down the three crew members who still hadn't quit. "Vy I hire such idiot as you tree in first place, I not understand!" Vana's voice scratched the air like a feral parrot's.

My first instinct was to grab the tin, drop to my knees and crawl to the bathroom, which I did. The plan then was to pee loudly to let them know I was here, which would cool down Vana, after which I would emerge with minty breath and an empty bladder and no one would be the wiser. And after I flushed, the tirade did indeed subside. But when I opened the tin, instead of breath lozenges, there was cocaine.

Vana rapped one of her giant rings on the door. "Call sheets finish?"

I clamped the tin shut. "Yes, but the computer keeps crashing whenever I try to print. It's rebooting."

"Ve go now. You fax me at home when print finish. I sign off and you deliver, yes?"

"Sure." It sounded easy, but it meant I had to hand-deliver the call sheets to the three actors who'd be filming tomorrow. Two of them lived together in Laurel Canyon, which was just over the hill from the production office, but the third one lived in Echo Park, which meant I had to drive the beater I then owned deep into gangland at night. With at least an hour of work to do on the sheets, an hour for Vana to review and approve them, and then a good hour and a half of driving, it'd be almost 2 a.m. before I was through. Then I had to be up at six the next morning to pick up the Echo Park actor at seven. Such was my glamorous life.

I heard Vana and the others leave, and went back to my computer. It was still rebooting, amber code filling and refilling the small screen. The tin was still in my hand. As instinctively as I'd dropped to the floor, I wet my finger, dipped it into the powder, and massaged it on my gums. Nice. I tapped a little pyramid onto the desk, then lined it up with my driver's license, Al Pacino's monologue from *Scarface* at the ready. "What you lookin' at? You all a bunch of fuckin' assholes. You know why? You don't have the guts to be what you wanna be. You need people like me. You need people like me so you can point your fuckin' fingers and say, 'That's the bad guy.'"

I got the computer up and running, reduced the number of weeks we were behind from three to two (no small feat), got Vana to approve the new schedule, ran the call sheets to Laurel Canyon and Echo Park, and had time to stop off at Barney's Beanery for a late-night chili dog and round of pool before going home for a few hours of shuteye. I never found out whether Vana missed the coke I "borrowed;" production shut down the next day.

I grab another glass of champagne from a passing tray, wishing I had my VMX with me. The harpist looks like Groucho

Marx, and he gazes theatrically into an arrangement of flowers before scowling and then dropping his hands ever...so...slowly to pluck his huge instrument. *Did I snicker out loud?* A pair of men in matching wheat-colored sweaters tip their heads together and look my way. The one that would make a nice-looking woman leans in my direction. "Are you with Paul Street?"

"Yes. I mean, he invited me." *Shit. I just said something really gay. Stupid gay, not gay gay. I must not think about gay.*

They crinkle up their faces—though no wrinkles appear—and look at each other. Before they can turn back to me, I surprise myself by having the presence of mind to wave to someone I pretend to recognize across the room and make my exit, wondering, really, how bad it would be to spend the remaining trillions of seconds left on my Death Clock shoveling shit from pipes. I slide along the wall and duck down a shadowy hallway, where framed black-and-white photos of male nudes are spotlit from above. Where the hell is the bathroom? Elevator doors whisper open and I stumble inside: all the surfaces are mirrored and I can't tell if the thing's going up or down. When the doors slide open again, I step out into some kind of pasha's bath palace. Gold and purple silk scarves drape from ceiling to floor. Oversized pillows are piled about. Decanters of amber liquids are clustered on a low table. Crushed-velvet shades block out the early evening light, and intensify the incense-heavy air, which I can barely pull into my lungs. I hear running water. Voices murmuring from a half-open door.

The water screeches off and a pipe knocks from inside the wall. Sounds like there might be a loose washer in the faucet, too. Then, a woman's voice: "If bastard not give me film, I vill rrruin him."

The trilled Rs and Franco-Slavic goulash accent are unmistakably Vana LeValle's.

Another voice responds. "V, I can't help you relax if you don't stop talking about work."

I move one step to the left to peer into a candle-lit water closet. My eyes snap open.

Vana leans against a tiled wall, a metallic bronze dress pulled up above her hips. On her knees before Vana: a brunette in jeans and a brown lace bra with a circular tattoo—is it a doughnut?—at the small of her back. Vana sighs and closes her eyes. "Ees zat best you do?" she demands, something she said more than once on the *Unmentionables* set.

A muffled moan from the brunette on the floor, followed by a burst of zealous bouncing. Vana's face furrows with the effort of oncoming ecstasy, her mouth a furious concentrated O. My head says "scram," but my crotch says "don't move a muscle," and Vana is coming, both her eyes open now, watching herself in the mirror, bucking the brunette's face, "I coming, coming, coming, I svear I kill him if he fuck viz me."

I scram as quickly as possible, locating my feet, the fun house elevator, the wall of nude dudes, the round room, the panoramic window, more champagne, and Paul Street.

"Having fun?" he asks, beaming as he scans the room, recognizing, acknowledging, as if parties like this constitute his most intimate milieu. Apparently, they do. He leans in conspiratorially. "It's good to get out and about during the grieving process. I find I do my best creative work after suffering an intense emotional trauma, don't you?"

I squelch an urge to lick the inside of my empty glass. "You'll never guess who I just…"

"Here she is!" Paul calls out across the room as Vana strides toward us, her bronze dress rippling like tiger skin across the body I have just witnessed in the throes of ecstasy.

My fingers sweat around the stem of my flute. I set the glass down before it can slip to the floor.

"You're a vision," Paul says, when she's close enough for him to kiss her personal space.

My inner animal disobeys my command, and sniffs the air around her for a whiff of musky sex and sweat.

"My favorite movie star in ze vorld." Time has been generous to Vana in the way cosmetics and procedures make older women tighten and glow. Her plump lips maul the air adjacent to Paul's earlobe.

"Sander Sanderson, meet Vana…," Paul Street says.

"Vana LeValle? The producer?" It's been almost ten years since I worked for her; there's no reason for her to remember me, but if I learned anything from Ashe it's that people like to be recognized. "I'm honored."

"I am talent manager now. You know Destinée? Used to be beeg? Vell, she about to be beeg again, zanks to me." Vana oozes ballsy bravado; her hand hangs in the air as she scans me. "Ve know each ozzer?"

"Really?" Paul does this arched caterpillar move with one eyebrow that I've only seen before on screen, but it works. "From where?"

Wasn't someone just talking to me about Destinée? I grab another glass of champagne and drink while I formulate my response and, luckily, Vana's brunette friend shows up, waving a padded envelope and running toward our little group. "It's here!" she cries, now wearing a gauzy tunic that's a mere distraction over the lace bra.

"About fuckeeng time," Vana barks, snatching the envelope. "Paul, come. I vant opinion." She strides away through the crowd.

"What's up with her?" Paul asks the brunette, and then introduces us.

"Hey," Faun says, barely acknowledging me before addressing Paul. "Destinée's commercial was due three days ago, but the director's been refusing to deliver the footage, and V's livid." With her huge brown eyes, delicate features and triangular face, she resembles a human deer. "I've been trying to calm her down all night; maybe you can help."

I doubt Paul Street is the type to kneel before Vana the same way Faun did, but the image pops up anyway. "Come," Paul says, his hand settling languidly on my shoulder. All the eyes in the room covet my exalted position as I follow them down the hall. This should feel fantastic, but I feel like I'm walking through water at the bottom of a deep, dark lake.

Dark leather and wood furniture fills Paul's Old-World style office. Bookshelves hold hundreds of videos. Faun turns on the massive television and slips the disc into the DVD player. Vana sits in an ornately scrolled chair behind the dining-room table-size desk, ranting the entire time. "I *know* meestake let talent peek deerector. But he *seezling* right now. Fact he even vant to *smell* my leettle project ees good, yes?"

Numbers count backward on screen; the music starts. The tune has a techno edge, a funky bass riff. Standard girlpop turdfluff. We open on what looks like a motel room interior, with patchwork bedspread and curtains, framed Western movie poster, pine cupboards above a small kitchenette. A fuck-me-I'm-a-little-girl voice sighs over the drumbeats, as on screen a young woman in a T-shirt and jeans falls backward onto the bed, kicking her legs in the air. A man's hands reach in from out of frame and we smash cut to the woman's hips rising up from the bed, then cut back to the man's arms, pulling the jeans off her kicking legs. The lyrics are not words, just groaning, moaning, babbling, intercut by ecstatic shrieks—or are they shrieks of terror? The man's arms pull off the woman's white T-shirt amid a tangle of red curls. We never see her face, or his, and so far we never see anything of the man but his hands and his arms. Beyond a perfunctory prick of professional jealousy, I'm mesmerized by the crisp cuts, the jarring continuity and complexity of form. I'd be hard-pressed to determine if the woman is being forced to submit or if she is participating in pre-sexual roughhousing. The song builds to a driving rhythm now, pure drivel at optimum output. More clothes fly, but limbs move, too. Their movement is in slow motion, but the editing is at top speed. The bodies merge as they thrash and grind. The images make the music sound better, lending the vapid tune an undercurrent of emotion. The song ends on a scream, the screen goes white, and the room is silent.

"Wow! That was fantastic!" I say, forgetting no one has asked my opinion.

Faun looks over with the tiniest shake of her head. *No it wasn't.*

"Zat vas sheet!" Vana yells. She hurls the remote at the wall, where it bounces off the gold frame of a still life with decomposing fruit and a dead rabbit. "I can't send to Vestern Burger! Is not approve script! Budget already gone! Ve behind schedule!"

"Sweetheart." Paul retrieves the remote. "Nothing can be solved until you relax."

Rainbow prisms flicker on the fresco'd walls of the bathhouse, where a large hot tub churns up a bubbling stew. My feelings about hot tubs are Hunter S. Thompsonesque—I fear and loathe them. I disappear onto a lounge chair, hoping no one notices I don't plan to participate in their aquatic adventure.

"So give us the back story," Paul Street says from behind a changing room door.

Ever the European, Vana nonchalantly tosses the bronze dress aside. "Faun write script, Vestern Burger approve, I put up money." She kicks away her sandals, snaps her floss thong, and descends into the tub. "Zen, deerector hold film hostage and now he give me porno!"

"What are you doing putting up money for a commercial?" Paul Street emerges in a black Speedo, looking like the tan, buff youth-serum spokesman he is. He follows Vana into the water, then notices me trying to blend into the cushions. "Coming in? There are extra suits, all sizes."

"No, thanks. I'm fine." I try to check for exits without looking like I'm checking for exits, then decide the least I can do is take off my jacket.

Even Vana's sigh has an accent. "Is only deal Vestern Burger make. Since rehab, Destinée is consider beeg rrrisk. She can select deerector only if I, caring, beeg-heart manager, make cash up front.

Zey reimburse ven I turn in commercial and zey approve." Vana pours a glass of champagne on her head, then throws the glass across the room, where it shatters against the wall. "Zis deerector very expensive. I can't afford lose all ze work, ze prep. Ze MONEY!"

Faun pulls her tunic over her head and steps out of her jeans. Brown lace lingerie hangs onto her stick figure body—punctuated by Thanksgiving Day parade balloons of breast and ass—for dear life. "I hate to say I told you so, but you wouldn't have this problem if you'd let me direct," she says as she follows Vana into the water and slips behind her, massaging her shoulders. I try not to stare as her floats...float.

"Zen don't say," Vana snaps, twisting away from Faun. "Get me champagne."

Faun pouts but obeys and exits the tub, slipping into a robe and heading toward a wet bar and mini-fridge.

Now Paul eases into position behind Vana. "The footage *was* kind of interesting," he says, before rubbing his hands together quickly and putting them over Vana's eyes. "You are so tense. Are you even breathing?"

"Too stress to breeze. Sure, vas interesting! Vas fucking art! I don't hire for fucking art. I hire for fucking script for fucking Vestern Burger."

"They might like it if they see it," I offer. "That footage could sell anything."

Vana pulls Paul's hands from her eyes and lasers me with a withering stare. "No von vill ever see. Ees garbage. Deerector do on purpose. Slap my face. I need deerector vis no ego, no new idea, no flashy tricks. I just need fuckeeng Vestern commercial like I hire him to make."

"*I* could do that," I shrug.

"We need a name," Faun says quickly from across the room. "Or Destinée won't agree."

"Destinée do vatever I say from now on," Vana flings her hands in the air.

"Sander's right," Paul continues. He winks at me and kneads Vana's shoulders. "You need a foot soldier. With no reputation, no celebrity, no agenda. Someone who can just come in and execute the shoot."

"Right zere," Vana sighs. "I vish somevon to execute deerector."

"I could do that, too," Faun says, eager to be all she can be for a shot at the gig.

Paul Street intensifies the massage while humming a deep, chesty hum that reverberates off the domed ceiling, creating a demented, Tibetan monkish spell. "Sander's an up-and-comer."

"Really?" Vana's arched eyebrows arch even higher; the corners of her mouth curve up.

"You need someone completely objective." Paul Street runs his hands through Vana's hair, massages her scalp, runs his elbow down the length of her spine. "You've never met Destinée, have you Sander?" He laughs. "Sorry. That's just bad dialogue, isn't it?"

"And corny." I re-cross my legs, slippery with sweat. "And no, no dates with Destinée here."

Faun shoots me a look and pops the cork off a fresh bottle of Dom. "What about the schedule? D goes on tour in a couple of weeks."

Vana's head lolls back on Paul's thigh. "And how to make sure no more meestakes?"

Paul puts his lips close to her ear. "You trust me, don't you?"

"Von zouzand percent." She doesn't move. "But you're not deerector."

"How many sets have I been on in my life?" Paul asks. "Directors don't need talent. They just need a script, actors and stamina." He winks at me. "I'll produce it if you like. And to show you how much I believe in Sander, I'll cover any monies you lose."

"Really?" Vana lifts her head, opens her eyes and smiles her first, full-fledged smile of the night. "Vould be very nice to fire zat bastard Oggie Bright anyvay. You send demo, Zander, yes? Eef I like, ve make deal."

She wants to fire Oggie Bright and hire me? "Sure. I'll send a demo," I say, feigning a casual voice that I hope is masking explosive mental fireworks of joy.

"Great!" Vana claps her hands. "Faun, let's make a toast. Zander, you going to vork viz me, you must come in."

Faun's pillowy lips curl into a scowl as she pours bubbly into flute glasses and arranges them on a tray.

"Treat yourself, Sander," Paul says. "You've had a rough week."

Normal me wouldn't dream of taking Oggie Bright's gig. Normal me doesn't direct commercials. Normal me doesn't even go to industry parties. Normal me is at home, re-reading Ashe's breakup email, re-writing our love story with a happy—or maybe even more tragic—ending. But normal me doesn't drink glass after glass of expensive champagne. And normal me didn't get here by being normal me. Screw normal me. I take off my shirt and drop trow, the belt buckle clanking as it hits the tile floor. But in my champagne-muddled haste, I've neglected to take off my shoes. I tug the pants down over the shoes, determined to remove them through my pants, which are now inside out, with my feet. This can be done, I'm sure, one foot at a time, with some well-balanced hopping.

"Sander, what are you doing?" Faun says, with obvious disdain. Suddenly, they are all staring at me and my tangle of pants and shoes, which distracts me. Their laughter echoes and amplifies off the arched, tiled walls, as I hop, then topple, into the hot tub, ass first.

Instantly, I feel like normal me.

5

MONDAY MORNING

Shin & Shin's eighteenth-floor Century City law offices have about as much charm as a bathroom stall, but they're impressive nonetheless. The walls are streaky marble, the windows bare of rod or drape. There's a tufted carpet below a granite slab that fulfills the semiotic function of a desk without appearing to actually be one. The overall effect is unfriendly, stark, and expensive. I find it amusing that the future CEO of El-San Pipe & Drain—me—had to take the bus to his first board meeting. A rubbery squeal calls my attention to the window washer in his carriage, hanging on ropes outside the floor-to-ceiling windows with a squeegee and a bucket, and I notice our freakish family portrait reflected in the glass. Me in my outdated funeral clothes (again) slumped on a leather settee between Mom, imperious in a navy outfit and refusing eye contact, and Ellie in her "dressy" track getup, sucking down a swamp-green health drink slung in a net sack across her shoulders. Jerome's working today and couldn't attend, so it's just us three, so unnatural and stiff we could be posing for Mom's annual holiday card.

One of the Shins, I'm not sure which, clears his throat and begins to read Dad's last will and testament. Knowing where this is headed and dreading the destination, I dial down the volume and turn inward. Soothed by the back and forth arc of the window washer's squeegee, I drift to a mental place that's as familiar and soothing to me as a baby being rocked in a cradle: my personal archive of humiliation. In reverse chronological order, I run through the classics.

SUBJECT: adios
FROM: ashe
REPLY-TO: ———@aol.com

Dear San – Sorry to spring it like this, but I think you'll agree: you & I are pretty much over. I need to be with someone whose career goals are more closely aligned with my own, and Oggie's a really sweet guy. I hope you write your screenplay some day and shoot it – It'll be great, seriously. I'd hate to be famous & need a plumber & have you be the one to come clean out my pipes. No hard feelings, okay? Can you move your stuff out by Saturday? I'm in rehearsals all week & won't be in your way. Mwah, A.

Then there was award night at film school. We had piled into the family Oldsmobile after the ceremony. I cradled the cheap statuettes like silver twins, my head swimming with notions of an exciting and challenging future filled with creativity, success and girls turned on by same.

"Let's celebrate," Mom said from the front seat. "Ice cream! Champagne! Both!"

Ellie grabbed a statuette and held it like a microphone. "We're here in the back seat of his parents' car with recent award winner Sander Sanderson. Tell us, Sander, how does it feel?"

"Fan-freaking-tastic, Ellie. Disney and Warners have both called, inviting me to write my own ticket. It's going to be a difficult decision." Not true, of course, but it felt great to say it.

"Sounds like you're on your way to a successful career."

"I am, Ellie. And, since you didn't ask, I thought you'd like to know I'm wearing Levi's tonight, and the T-shirt is from a boutique stall on Venice Beach..."

"Dammit!" Dad hollers, but only we can hear him. He lays on the horn at the line of cars parading behind him that won't let him back out of the parking space. "A couple film school prizes don't mean shit in the real world!"

His outburst got Mom going, and then no one was in the mood to celebrate so we just went home. The statuettes seemed somehow shameful and tainted. I stashed them in the back of my closet behind the sweaters I never needed to wear.

Then there's the high school debacle of running track in front of the cheerleader tryouts, wondering why all the girls were laughing. The cute one from Algebra yelled out, "Hey Sanderson, what are you running from?" I had no idea what she was talking about until I turned to see a streamer of toilet paper trailing from under my shorts. The nickname TP stuck my entire freshman year.

The earliest and most traumatic took place in fifth grade. Red velvet drapes transformed our dingy cafeteria stage into a grand auditorium. Miss Sweetland introduced me and my one-boy play, *When I Am King of the World*. Applause thundered—or so it seemed—as I made my way to the microphone. The handwritten script trembled in my hands, and all I could hear was Ellie, in the front row, whispering "Don't mess up. Don't mess up. Don't…" Mom slapped Ellie's arm, but the spell had been cast. My forehead bled sweat. Words clogged my throat. After an interminable thirty seconds, Miss Sweetland mercifully escorted me off-stage.

Back in the present, in the law office, I try to envision a future that redeems my big, fat loser history: Oggie Bright presents me with a Clio award for Best Commercial of the Year. Western Burger underwrites my new indie film project featuring Paul Street, who makes a resounding career comeback in the surprise hit. I move into a modern studio loft space and am working on my next studio-financed project when the doorbell rings. It's Ashe, with a puppy, apologizing for dumping me. I forgive her, we kiss, the puppy barks like crazy…

Wait. That barking dog is not in my brain movie. It's Ellie, coughing a big whooping croak. Both hands fly to her chest and swamp brew dribbles onto her velour hoodie.

I thump her back, politely at first, then harder, as Ellie continues to choke. Mom pulls a handkerchief from the sleeve of her sweater and dabs her nose. The hankie flits about like a tiny deranged ghost, trailing wisps of Shalimar. *What did I miss?*

The choking has subsided, but now Ellie bawls so hard she gets the hiccups. "No-huh-no, I do-ho-hon't wa-hant it. El-San was sup-po-hosed to go to Sa-hander."

And there it is, as cliché as the nose on my face: I, Sander Sanderson, Bobby Sanderson's first-born son, have not inherited El-San Pipe & Drain. I got the big TV and its BarcaLounger companion. Ellie got the business and Mom's in charge of everything else.

This is my moment of truth. What I've dreaded happening, didn't. I didn't want to be a plumber; I don't have to be one. I'm supposed to feel great now, right? I'm waiting. For satisfaction. For the flood of relief. To feel vindicated, triumphant. Instead, a new truth chills me: I wasn't good enough to be a goddamn plumber. Sure, I always suspected that, but it's fucking lousy to have that read aloud to you in front of your family. Now, there's no fallback. No sorry lot to bitch about. No workaday paternal memory to honor or rue. No uniform to assume. No depths of shit to plumb.

Shell-shocked silence reigns in the black-marble elevator that carries us down to the lobby, until Mom articulates what's on all of our minds. "That was certainly a surprise."

The elevator bumps to the ground floor and we walk through the black marble lobby to wait for the valets. Mom sighs, looks at me, then turns away, as though she's either disgusted or contemplating something far off in the distance.

If she's not talking to me, I'm not talking to her. I extend the cold war by waiting with them at the valet. It's the least I can do. Once they're both safe in their cars, I'll head back to my bus stop.

The sun shines brightly, and a tangy ocean breeze ruffles the palms lining the wide boulevard. The pistachio Land Rover arrives first, but Ellie makes no move toward it. Her temple veins bulge, her hands twitch at her sides. "I can't," she whispers. Her whole body trembles.

"I'm lunching with the Shins," Mom says, and at first I think she's talking to the valet.

"I'll drive her home," I shrug, guiding Ellie into the passenger seat.

"And you might want to swing by the house," Mom continues as she heads toward her Oldsmobile. "Sander's inheritance is already out on the curb. There's a truck on the way."

"You what?" I can't help myself.

"Your father didn't tell me he changed his will, so deal with it!" Mom slaps some bills onto the valet's palm and slides into the driver's seat, which is weird because Dad always drove. She refuses to give up the behemoth even though she can barely see over the wheel, and barrels onto the boulevard, acknowledging neither lane marking nor pedestrian.

I hop up into the pistachio driver's seat. "To the family home, Mrs. El-San?"

"Just fucking drive, moron," Ellie sniffs.

When we arrive at Mom's, the guys from Goodwill have already begun to load her curbside donation into their truck. If this were my neighborhood, the stuff would have been spirited away or at least graffiti'd or damaged long before Goodwill showed up. As it is, the guys are none too pleased to learn their booty has been reduced to a set of bookshelves and an Exercycle, and grumble at my request to unload the TV and the chair. Ellie surprises us all with a convincing argument when she unzips her hoodie. I'm no freak, but I've watched my sister's tits develop from pancakes to muffins, and what she's flashing the boys now are decidedly flashier than her standard set. The guys from Goodwill don't seem to care about the particulars; they grudgingly wedge the television into the back of the Rover and lash the recliner to its roof. When Ellie and I finally head toward my apartment, it's like I'm driving a rumpus room on wheels.

There are no shortcuts from Mom's place to mine, but the fast food joints create an ethnic topography that marks the changing neighborhoods. French cafés and bistros in her neck of the woods give way to Eastern European delis and tabouli shops as we inch through WeHo; cheap burgers and dogs as we head through Hollywood; taco trucks and panaderías from there to my house. On the last leg of the journey, traffic flow on Sunset Boulevard is constipated, so we sit at an intersection. The light changes from red to green. No one moves.

Ellie's success with her cleavage seems to have helped her recover her composure and she's now griping about Dad's will, about Jerome's weekend plans for a Harley ride with his new "friends," about low blood sugar. Without missing a beat—about Mom getting rid of Dad's stuff, about me and Mom having to kiss and make up someday—Ellie opens the cooler console and pulls out a half-gone package of Oreo cookies. "I'm starving," she says. "Are you hungry?"

"Since when do you keep snacks in the car?" The light turns red again. I avail myself of a handful and waggle them at her. "Is this why the twins are gaining weight?"

"Shut up." She glances down at her plunging neckline and blushes before zipping the sweatshirt up to her neck. "Actually, the cookies are part of our earthquake preparedness kit. Jerome and I could survive in the Rover for ten days if we needed to." She puts a stack of the wafers on the console lid and waggles one back at me. "I'm gonna kick your ass, brother."

"Bring it on, sister!" I tilt back my head and insert the Oreo into my mouth, delicately balancing it *en pointe* between upper palate and lower gum, a special talent Ellie had always lorded over me when we were kids, but which I have since mastered. "Huh," is all I can say with the cookie propping my mouth open like this.

She inserts a cookie into her mouth the same way.

We glare at each other. She holds up three fingers. I nod. She does a manual countdown and the contest begins. The goal is to separate the two cookie halves without breaking them and remove the sandwich cream using only your tongue. This nearly impossible feat was achieved only once, by Ellie. She was in the eighth grade and spending a lot of time in front of the mirror. The best part about it is the black and white chaos clearly visible inside the mouth. As kids, we would laugh deliberately and obnoxiously throughout the contest, blackening our teeth and tongues, and showering ourselves with crumbs. This drove Mom nuts. We, on the other hand, are still rendered hysterical.

"God, Sander," she says slowly, after we catch our breaths. "I can't believe I got El-San. Plus, I'm going to be a mother."

I smash another cookie into my mouth with the heel of my hand. "You'll be a *muvvah awright*." I spew crumbs into the air. "Seriously, did Jerome buy those for you? Like, he got a Harley and you got knockers?"

"He did give them to me, in a way." She beams at me, idiotically radiant, nibbling a second Oreo. "I'm pregnant."

"What?" More crumbs fly out. "Since when? How long?"

"I've suspected for awhile, but I found out yesterday for sure. I haven't told Jerome yet." A fleet shadow crosses her face.

"Wow." She's breeding. Daddy's golden girl gilds her halo. Too bad he missed it. "Congratulations to both of us. You're going to be a mother and I've got new furniture."

She's used to my snarkiness; she's in her own world anyway. "You think I'll be a good mom?"

"You'll be a great mom. Your kid will be a genius. I will be a great uncle and world-class director. And we'll all live happily ever after."

She brushes crumbs from my shirt. "If not, you can always work for El-San."

"There's a dream come true."

She flips her hair over her shoulder and looks in the mirror like there's something new to see. "I'm just saying, if everything doesn't work out, there's always a back-up plan." The light turns back to green.

"You don't think I can make it?" I check all the mirrors, too, like I'm actually driving, like the cars are moving, and there's somewhere to go, but stationary we remain.

"That's not what I mean and you know it." She puts her hand on my arm.

I shake it off and look out the window.

"I won't be able to manage a newborn *and* the business. Not the first year, anyway." A whine is creeping into her voice. I know where this is going.

"Forget it." I punch on the radio. Metal. Loud.

She flicks it off, then does that thing with her voice. The thing that made me clean the bathrooms when it was her turn. That made me trade her all my favorite issues of *MAD*. The thing that made me never fink on her, even when I busted her royally for coming home at three in the morning through my bedroom window because Dad locked hers. "You won't have to go out on calls. There's still Fabrizio and maybe Sam, I don't know. Just keep the paperwork going and the money coming in."

"You don't need the money. Sell the place. Who cares?"

"Mom would kill me."

"Nah. Blame it on me. She hates me already."

Ellie looks down at her hands in her lap. "I can't sell it. It's Dad."

"It's a *plumbing company.*" She doesn't say anything. "What about Jerome?"

"He doesn't have time for El-San. Not with his career."

This stings. "His career is more important than helping his wife? His new family?"

Her face goes dark. "At least he has a career." She unscrews the cap on her green drink and I notice its label for the first time: Vitamin Babe-E.

I punch the radio back on. "Maybe I have a career you don't know about."

She's had so much practice yelling at me she doesn't bother turning the radio off. "Really? Do tell!"

How much should I reveal about me possibly taking Oggie's place? Nothing's on paper and I don't want to jinx the deal. "There might be a directing gig. I need to keep my schedule open."

I love that she looks shocked. "For who? What? How long is it supposed to last? *If* it comes through?"

"Couple weeks maybe."

"'Couple weeks maybe' is a hobby, not a career."

Traffic is finally moving, so throttling her is momentarily out of the question. I punch the pedal. Her head snaps back from the forward thrust and we barrel down Sunset towards Echo Park, the late afternoon sun glowing over our shoulders, reflecting off car mirrors, windows and chrome. We screech to a halt behind a banged-up gardener's truck taking its time. I angrily lurch into the right lane. If I had been looking ahead instead of fuming, I would have noticed the light had changed from green to red. I might have said something, or thrown my arm across her chest in warning. But I didn't. I only hear the blare of the minivan's horn as it swerves to avoid smacking us as we careen through the intersection. Ellie flies against her door as I wheel right during a frantic/calm one-Mississippi second that seems to last hours. I squeal into a corner gas station. Ellie opens her door and retches on the asphalt.

"Now we're even on the puke scale," I wisecrack shakily after she settles back into her seat and wipes her mouth with a tissue.

"This is the last fucking time I let you drive my car!" Her chin is shaking and she looks like she's about to cry, so I don't remind her I was only driving because she couldn't. "That was close," she finally whispers.

Too close. "Look," I say, "I'll do whatever you need me to do. But if I get this gig, just give me the time to pretend I'm doing what I want to be doing, okay?"

I hate it when she cries on me like that.

After tacos from the truck at the bottom of the hill and a beer from the back of my fridge, I rearrange things to make room for my inheritance, which transforms my place into a kind of in-home theatre bachelor pad. I sit in the BarcaLounger before turning on the giant screen, looking at but not seeing my stupid reflection. Why didn't Dad give me El-San? My inheritance has been a given for as long as I can remember. When did he change his will? Was it before or after the pink glove incident? Or was it even before then, during the *White Man Dancing* days, when he decided he wouldn't leave shit to a son who thought his parents were a couple of monkeys? I wonder if he thought I loved him. I wonder if I did. And how the hell did Oggie Bright come up with such a kickass piece of filmmaking? It felt great to hate him when I thought he was just the toad who stole Ashe. And after seeing his work, part of me hates him even more. Still, now that I might be getting his job...despising him isn't as much fun. I resent that being taken away from me. And what will I be adding to my résumé, if I even do get the job? A Western Burger commercial. *That's* going to open some doors.

I thoughtfully peruse my movie collection. Grouped by director—Hitchcock, Wilder, Welles, Ray—nothing appeals at the moment. I review my porn classics: *The Devil in Miss Jones, Behind the Green Door, Deep Throat, Debbie Does Dallas.* But I feel the need for plot, too, which is why I select my guiltiest pleasure, Brian De Palma's *Body Double.* I must have watched it ten times after Ashe dumped me, but today I'll see it for the first time from less than six feet in front of my new 42-inch screen. Every time I watch it, I'm hooked right from the start, when B-actor Jake Scully in vampire drag snaps open his glittered eyes while shooting a scene inside a coffin. Of course my phone rings. I pause on poor Jake, paralyzed with claustrophobia, and pick up, expecting it to be Mom laying down an olive branch, offering detente.

"I send you contract on email. Before you sign and fax back, I tell you von zing vonce." It's one thing to talk to Vana LeValle in person; it's another to try to decipher her voice on the phone. I have to concentrate. "I know you vork for me time ago. I know you sneetch my coke. I only hire you because Paul Street my friend and Oggie Bright sheetbastard. Eef you steal anyzing else from me, you never vork in zis town again. Capiche?"

I'm *already* not working in this town again. How could working for Vana be any worse?

6

SUNDAY AFTERNOON

Massive auto malls and cookie-cutter McHousing developments border Interstate 10 as it cleaves through the Inland Empire uber-suburbs in San Bernardino and Riverside Counties. The air is bronze with smog; traffic thick and malicious. Any other day, I'd be snarling and cursing my fellow Interstaters. But today I am smiling, even as a Mexican kid in the passenger seat of a Honda is bare-assing me and giving me the finger while the driver hoots with laughter. For I am cruising through L.A.'s armpitty outskirts behind the wheel of Paul Street's glossy black Lexus. What an upgrade from La Rubble! I backed up a few extra times before I pulled away from my apartment to watch its door mirrors tilt down automatically. I reset the power sunroof every half hour in accordance with the angle of the sun. I read and re-read the electro-luminescent analog gauges *in direct sunlight.* And my VMX3000 gets the star treatment, too, nestled in the leather passenger seat with heat and power lumbar support and seat-mounted side air bags. When I told Paul I planned to visit the location early to wrap my head around the project, he offered to lend me his car "so he wouldn't worry in case my ride couldn't take the heat." Actually, he wanted to come with, but he had to stay in town for a *Wonder Abs* book signing. Given Betty's unstable condition,

I could hardly refuse the wheels. I confess: this lavish favor makes me suspicious. But what choice do I have? When life hands you a Lexus, baby, just fucking drive.

Traffic opens up as I approach the grid of windmills just outside Palm Springs. Their skyscraping blades symbolize the official threshold to the desert, and seem to spin according to whim rather than in accordance with the gusty dry blasts. I bear north on Highway 62, a two-lane straightaway. With no cars in sight, I give the Lexus its head.

90, 95, 100 mph. The twin-cam V-8 powers the sedan like a dream. Destinée's as-yet-unnamed, soon-to-be-released song—the Western Burger commercial's soundtrack—blasts through the Nakamichi system with seven speakers and one-touch six-disc CD changer. After only one viewing, the images from Oggie's footage are already inextricably linked in my mind to the music. The kick of legs on a mattress, arms reaching, pulling, legs spreading, an open mouth, teeth. But I'm not complaining: Vana's loss is my gain.

I roll down the window and cup my hand against the speeding oven of air, air that affects me naught thanks to automatic climate control with dual temperature settings. Tall birch trees border the 62, their coin-shaped leaves flashing silver and green. "Me? Oh, yes. I'm the director," I inform the lighted mirror behind the visor. Forget Destinée's pop crap. I need something inspirational. I open Paul Street's CD binder to browse his collection, and tucked right in the front pocket is a sweet little pinner. How thoughtful! I light up for a taste. Man, the shit is strong. I stub it out after three tokes; I want to chill out, not journey back to the womb. I slip in a random CD. Johnny Mathis warbles *Misty* and that's all right with me.

Emotions are exhausting; as a rule, I try to avoid them, but my stoned, rabbity brain hops relentlessly from one to the next. From elation at finally getting a gig to fear that I'll screw it up. From mild despair (it's only a commercial, for a burger I don't eat to the music of a teen singer I don't listen to) to resignation (sure El, I'll trade my life's dream to make your life easier). Finally, I settle into my customary sinkhole of regret. Had I known Dad was going to go when he did, I'm sure I would have been more civilized, more mature, in what were then his last days.

I try to focus on the road as the Lexus winds upward through hills that look like piles of pebbles. As the asphalt evens out at the summit, a hawk descends to coast alongside the car. I'm alone on the road, so I slow down, swoop the VMX from the passenger seat and frame the big bird in the viewfinder. Its white neck band dazzles in stark relief to the brown feathers covering the rest of its muscular body. We cruise together until the road slopes into Morongo Basin, where the creature catches a thermal and tips away. This spontaneous tandem flight leaves me giddy. I floor the pedal, aiming for the hazy stripes of heat at the horizon—that hovering illusion that's always just out of reach.

The Greasy Spoon coffee shop marks my turnoff onto Buckaroo Trail. For a short block, the trappings of a small town remain: the Motor Inn motel, Dusty's Liquors, Auntie Rose's Little Bo-Teek. But once I pass Coyote Trail, a quieter energy prevails. On either side of the winding two-lane highway, open washes of bright white sand give way to log cabins and stone bungalows tucked into foothills. Next come orange-red rocks, gently rounded and golden at first, quickly becoming jagged crags. Twisted Joshua trees spike the fantastic landscape, which alternates patches of hardy scrub with clumps of tiny yellow flowers. "Magicville" is painted on a bleached wooden door nailed to a post; its doorknob dots the second "i." I experience an unusual need to perform the lamest of all lame activities of my generation: I need to share.

Ellie's machine picks up. "Listen." I toot the horn. "Paul's Street's Lexus. I'm just saying. Just saying. Um. I'm just saying. Shit, El, I haven't been this stoned since..." I crest a small summit and, heading down the other side, brake hard to avoid hitting a dog standing in the middle of my lane. The Lexus responds instantly; the red Doberman shivers and whines. "Ellie? I'll call you back."

A shadow ripples the ground. A hawk—my hawk?—circles above. Transcendently trashed, I am inspired by this scenario, its palette. There's no time to move the Lexus; I don't want to miss the moment or the light. I snatch a Slim Jim from my duffel and my VMX, and step out of the car into dry, baking heat. Wind and blood pound in my ears as I climb onto the Lexus' hood to record a long take of the surreal desert landscape with its bone-white sand, golden boulders, and rusty scrub that ends on the shivering dog's gold, unsure eyes. When I finish, I take a bite from the Slim Jim and wave it at the dog. "Here, boy, girl, whatever you are."

The Doberman whines and circles, flashing generous testicular twins.

"Impressive," I tell him, waving the beef stick, loving the heightened sense of perspective from the hood of the car, my spontaneity, this shimmering moment, Paul's pot. The dog's nostrils twitch, catching the stick's meatish scent on the hot breeze. His tail stump half-wags to one side. "Whatcha doing out here anyway, boy? How'd you end up in the middle of nowhere? I mean, out in *Magicville.*"

The dog runs playfully to the shoulder of the road, then back to the center line, barking and prancing. I break and run halfway to the shoulder; he follows. He runs back to the middle of the road, with me following him. He runs back to the shoulder, then lets out a series of shrill barks, like a warning, then runs further off the road, clambering up the hill.

"What do you want me to do? Huh? Where do you want me to go?" I follow him onto the shoulder, with him backing away as I approach, maintaining a constant distance from me until I'm standing on a mound of rocks. I hold out the Slim Jim again and the dog tentatively pads closer, until he can just reach the treat. His brown lips quiver as he daintily removes the Slim Jim from my palm, then he snaps his alligator jaws once and swallows it, not even bothering to chew. He raises his muzzle into the air to catch some seductive new scent and I follow suit. What *is* that? Smells like...

Burning brakes! A horn blares above their metallic shrieking. From the other side of the summit, a land yacht of a vehicle fishtails down the grade directly toward the Lexus. "No!" I yell so hard my throat hurts as the 1970s-era blue Cadillac Eldorado comes to a full, quaking stop no more than three inches from the Lexus' rear bumper. But that's it. Nothing else happens. Other than the Eldo's ticking, hissing engine, the scene is eerily silent. When I finally focus on the car's occupants, the image is indelible and bizarre.

The driver is a young girl in pigtails; her passenger is an older gentleman in a white cowboy hat and mirrored shades. The couple in the back looks like refugees from the Sixties. The woman has wild, henna-red dreadlocks; her bearded counterpart wears a long, dirty-blond ponytail and a cream, Nehru-collared jacket. "That your car?" the cowboy-hatted man says, hanging his arm out over the door.

"Kind of." This whole mess is my fault for stopping in the middle of the road, but there's no way I'm gonna cop to that, not the way people are with lawsuits and whiplash. But when I jump down from the rock, my foot lands sideways on a crack, my ankle twists, and I topple. I twist my body to cradle the VMX from the impact, and hit the dirt in a patch of gravel. I notice for the first time that the Lexus's license plate spells out SPRSTAR, and silently forgive the bareassed bird-flipper for mooning me on the Interstate. The dog trots over, delighted that I have joined him at ground level. He licks my face and barks twice, then gallops back to the car, where he sniffs around the front tire and lifts his leg to squirt onto its dusty rim.

"You all right?" the passenger drawls, whipping off his shades. "That's quite a gash there, mister." His full-lipped, high-cheeked features lend him a certain Elvis aspect. He opens the huge door from the outside and unfolds his frame from the bench seat. White jeans, white boots and a red, white and blue sash complete his costume.

"I think so," I answer, but when I touch my hand to my nose, it comes back smeared with blood.

The girl gathers her long, pioneer-style dress above her knees, and leaps over the driver-side door, after which there is a metallic crash. "Crap, Grandpop," she says, in a surprisingly deep voice. "My camera! I forgot it was in my lap and now the lens is broken!"

"Let's take care of the wounded first, honey," the old man says to the girl, who clamps her lips together in a tight pout.

"Can I help, Harry?" The back-seat gypsy lady slowly rises to her feet.

"First Aid kit in the glove box," the old man says.

The woman flings a fringed shawl from around her shoulders, then lumbers to the front seat. She is gargantuan with child beneath her red peasant dress. Kit in hand, she slams the door behind her, one hand pressed against her lower back.

Which is exactly when the Cadillac, by some absurd fart of physics, shoots forward, rocking on its shocks and tapping Paul Street's heretofore untouched Lexus. We all watch transfixed as the luxury sedan rolls onto the shoulder and downhill into the sandy wash. The dog leaps away from me, barking and leaping at the car as if he were suddenly reliving old SWAT-team memories.

The long-haired dude in the Caddie's back seat looks over, one hand shading his eyes. "Tell your dog to chill out, man."

"It's not my dog," I answer, then yell at it, "Shut up!"

The dog instantly quiets down and sits on the ground next to me. I am *so* not stoned anymore. My raw nose burns and throbs and the skin around my ankle grows tight. I gingerly test the VMX, and she obediently responds.

"The middle of the road isn't the best place to park. You got people cresting that summit." The old man gestures behind me.

The gypsy lady waddles my way. "Leave him be, Harry. Carson," she says to the kid, "You come here, help me." Close up, the gypsy lady's pale Negroid features are freckle-splashed, her eyes a translucent blue. She carries a cloud of spiced, hippie incense about her and wordlessly hands the antiseptic wipe to the kid, who has stomped in a quiet sulk to her side. "What's your name, friend?" the gypsy asks me.

"Sander," I tell her. The kid squats down and swabs the bridge of my sniffer, her wheat-colored eyebrows scrunched tight with concentration. "And I was parked in the road because I was trying to avoid hitting the dog." No need for them to know about my stoned little video. At this, the dog leans his body weight against me, and steps heavily on my left hand. Now the gypsy hands the kid some strips of white tape, which she applies with a light touch. "Thank you," I say, even though it feels like I suddenly have an Elephant Man-size proboscis.

"You're welcome," the girl says politely, and returns to investigate the ruins of her camera.

The grandfatherly Elvis joins us now, and extends his hand. "Name's Apple. Harry."

Damn; Harry Apple is my contact. "Sander Sanderson."

"Ah," he smiles. "Paul Street said you'd be comin'. You're early, ain't ya?"

I nod. "I wanted to check out the place before everyone gets here. Do some homework."

"My motel's just up the road, behind the Saloon." He nods in the general direction of "yonder." "That there's my granddaughter Carson."

"That was some nice driving, Carson." Might as well suck up to everyone.

Carson cradles her camera and cracks the tiniest of smiles. "Grandpop taught me how to drive the Eldo when I was ten. Just on the back roads, though."

Harry continues. "The happy couple is Starshine and JC. Jerry Cartwright." He gestures to the gypsy woman now handing me a swath of Ace bandage—"for your ankle," she says—and the John Lennon guy in the cream suit, who gives a little wave-salute and taps his wrist. "Now, let's reconnoiter this." Harry mountain goats into the wash to examine the Lexus's bumper. "There isn't a goddamn scratch on this car," he marvels. "Ain't that somethin'?"

I quickly wrap the bandage around my ankle, haul myself up from the dirt, hobble down into the wash, and squat next to him. Harry's right. SPRSTAR is super clean. "Let's hope it runs," I say, trying to sound positive, even though my mind is racing ahead, with visions of getting stuck in the sand, calling for a tow, during which the car is damaged, and when I try to pay for repairs my credit card is rejected, and Paul Street dumps me as quickly as he found me and I end my days in debtor's prison, eating rats and keeping a firm grip on the soap.

Carson jackrabbits over and joins Harry to watch me hunch behind the wheel and put the car in gear. I rev the engine, and the spinning tires spew arcs of white sand behind me. The Lexus lurches forward, then sinks back down on its wheels. *Shit!*

Harry winces, taking off his hat and scratching his head.

"A little slower," Carson calls out.

One more time. Flying sand suggests cartoon clouds of velocity, but I only sink deeper into the wash. I let up on the gas, then give it another tap. The Lexus lurches forward, and I sway wildly as I maneuver it at a long diagonal up the tilting incline. I breathe again. My new amigos cheer and I clasp my hands above my head, Rocky-style.

JC joins us, bowing into the group. "No pressure, anyone, please," he apologizes, making prayer hands at his chest. "But the astrological window is closing. If Star and I don't get married in ten minutes, we'll have to wait two hundred years for such an auspicious planetary alignment."

"You musta done something right, honey," Harry calls over to Starshine. "JC here is just itching to be your ball and chain."

"Baby can't wait much longer either," Starshine laughs.

"Let's do this then!" Harry rubs his palms together and I easily imagine a twinkle flashing off his smile, like in that old toothpaste commercial.

"What about the video?" Carson stops twirling. "That was supposed to be my present."

I'd really like to get settled in and start reviewing my project. But they just taped my nose. And what are the odds a guy with a VMX burning a hole in his pocket would literally run into a group of characters in desperate need of a camera? The Sturgesness of the moment does not escape me. In *The Palm Beach Story*, when Texas sausage mogul the Weenie King catches Claudette Colbert hiding out in the shower of the tony apartment she and Joel McCrea are about to be evicted from, he is so appreciative of the momentary pleasure of ogling a pretty girl that he forks over $700 cash so the poor little rich couple can pay the rent.

The wedding party splits up into teams. JC, Starshine and Harry make their way up one side of a little box canyon. Carson and I hike with our camera equipment to a boulder across the way. While I extend the tripod's legs, Carson's inspects her busted lens. "What kind of camera you got there?" I ask.

"Keystone Capri," she says, holding up the small metal box. "Eight millimeter. Nineteen-fifty-something. It has a hand-crank on one side, A.S.A. chart on the other. The lens is a three-header and rotates, see?" Her nails are chomped to the nubs.

"It's pretty cute." I screw the VMX onto the tripod. "Where'd you get it?"

"My Grandpop," she says, twirling so the ruffles on her strawberry-and-pony-printed dress lift up in waves. "'Cause I'm cra-yay-yazy about movies."

The Doberman runs from bush to bush below, then bolts after a rabbit that suddenly leaps above the brush. "You'll never catch it," Carson calls out to the dog.

Across the way, JC, Starshine and Harry find their places on a bolder. Harry clears his throat. "Camera ready?"

"Almost." I set the viewfinder on their rock, positioning the wedding couple center frame, with Harry between them, tuning a guitar. Behind them, cloud columns rise above the jagged silhouette of the Sawtooth Mountains, creating a dramatic tableau: light and dark, earthy and ethereal, man and woman. "Camera set," I call out.

JC and Starshine turn to each other, holding hands. Harry strums a flamenco arpeggio, then speaks. "*The Owl and the Pussycat went to sea in a beautiful pea-green boat.*"

"Zoom in," Carson whispers.

"Roger that." I tighten focus until their faces fill the frame, the sunlight seeming to create an aurora around them, or maybe it's the beatific, trance-like expressions on their faces. These people are stoned or in love or stoned on love. "Do they always look like that?" I ask Carson.

"Pretty much," she sighs.

"They took some honey, and plenty of money, wrapped up in a five-pound note. The Owl looked up to the stars above and sang to a small guitar." Harry goes into extended strumming now, with a series of intricate picking, before he sings, *"O lovely Pussy! O Pussy, my love, what a beautiful Pussy you are."*

I struggle to contain my laughter as Harry continues, completely serious. "JC, Starshine, you may now recite your vows."

Gazing into JC's eyes, Starshine begins. "You are a child of the universe no less than the trees and the stars." The acoustics in the small box canyon are astonishing. Her speaking voice is clear, as though she were standing right next to us. Harry plucks a light weddingish melody in the background. "You have a right to be here. And whether or not it is clear to you, no doubt the universe is unfolding as it should."

JC picks up. "Therefore, be at peace with God, whatever you conceive Him to be. And whatever your labors and aspirations, in the noisy confusion of life, keep peace with your soul."

Starshine places his hand on her belly. Together, they recite: "With all its sham, drudgery and broken dreams, it is still a beautiful world."

The whole thing is a big Kansas cornfield, but somehow beautiful for its total lack of cynicism and display. And then comes the topper. In a gravelly voice twanged with country, Harry sings, *"You are my sunshine, my only sunshine."*

When I was a kid, my parents sang that song to each other on Saturday mornings, while we all did house chores. None of us knew all the words or bothered to learn them. We just kept singing the four-line chorus over and over. My eyes unexpectedly fill with tears. I hope no one notices what a sap I am.

3

7

STILL SUNDAY AFTERNOON

The Eldorado, now with Harry at the wheel, sways along the twists and turns of Buckaroo Highway. I follow in Paul's Lexus, watching the newlyweds make out vigorously in the back seat, Starshine's dreads flying about like red Medusa snakes. A half-mile up, a sign announces "Welcome to Buckaroo Proper, Est. 1946." In the foothills behind is a log cabin, its front cactus garden dotted with rusty remnants of a tractor, a harvester and a railroad car. Past that, more rocks. And these aren't just any rocks. They're rocks like I've never seen before. They're Stonehenge, pyramids, monoliths. A bit farther, there are glimpses of an illuminated neon sign: a tan boot, the word "Saloon." Finally, the whole thing: a kicking cowboy boot, below the words "Shitkicker Saloon." Figures. I'm cursed by the nursery rhyme Dad quoted when we were kids: "No matter where I roam or stray, crap is never far away."

I follow the Cadillac into a sandy parking area. Weeping willows create a kind of oasis around the Saloon's thick, clay walls, into which moonshine bottles and musketry have been pressed for effect. A red London-style phone box marks the entrance. The dog, which has galloped alongside the Lexus all the way, now runs laps around the two cars, tongue lolling. Carson gets out of the Eldo and directs me to park near the phone box; Harry and the newlyweds wave as they drive slowly toward the back of the establishment.

I step out into the oven of still air.

"They got wedding stuff to do," Carson says, "so I'll check you in and make sure you get something to eat, okay?"

"Great." The Doberman emits a whiny yawn and rolls over in the dirt at my feet. "Any idea who this guy belongs to?" I thump the dog's barrel chest as I explain to Carson how he lured me away from the road just before their car appeared at the top of the hill.

"Never seen him before." Carson says. She lies down on the ground next to him and he licks her face. "He looks like a Jake, doesn't he?"

Weird she should mention the name of *Body Double*'s hero, but, hey, what's not weird about this place. "What's a Jake look like?"

"You know. Jakie. Jake-sterish." Carson jumps up. "Hey, Jake. Are you a Jake?" She runs around the cars in figure eights, the dog gamely trotting at her heels. "Come on, Jake! Inside! Come on, Sander, follow me!" She gallops to the entrance and holds the heavy plank door open.

The inside of the Shitkicker is cool relief from the heat, and rings with wedding chatter and excitement. One wall is covered in rusty license plates and buzzing neon beer signs. Glossy photos of country bands paper the walls behind the corner stage, which also features an archway twined with white roses, a band setup and a hand-lettered banner reading "JC + STAR = HITCHED It's about time!" Mismatched coffee mugs filled with white daisies dot the red-and-white check cloth-covered tables. The jukebox plays classical music. Bizarre, but folksy.

Carson runs across the room and scoots under the bar counter, yelling the entire way. "Mom! Mom! My lens broke so this guy filmed the ceremony instead and it was so CO-OL!" She throws her arms around the woman behind the bar.

The bartender, Carson's mom, covers the receiver of an old-school wall phone with her hand. "I'm on hold here. Stop flea-hopping and speak slowly."

Carson looks back at me, rolls her eyes again and turns back to her mom, standing stock still and speaking in rubbery slow-mo. "Mmmmmyyyyy lllleeeeenssss brrrrroooooke..."

Smart aleck. I like that. Her too-hot-to-be-a mom gives her the "shush" hand, to which Carson shrugs and runs off with the dog.

The mom speaks firmly but quietly. "No, I cannot wait until Tuesday. The party is in an hour. People will need to use the facilities." She listens and paces, unaware she's winding the phone's curly white cord around her jeans and T-shirt in all the right places. "You want to charge WHAT? Are you serious? You're banned from here, okay? Blacklisted. The Shitkicker is out of bounds for you. Thanks for nothing." She repeatedly bangs the receiver onto the phone hook, little bells tinkling with each slam. "Plumbers are evil!" She sees me watching, composes herself, and smiles. "Can I get you something?" she asks, moving toward me, but she can't—the cord holds her hostage. "Shoot! Carson, come here and help me? And how did you break your lens?"

"I can't, I'm busy. Look!" Carson is dancing in front of the jukebox with Jake, who stands on his hind feet with both paws on her shoulders. His head hangs off to the side and his eyes are half-closed.

"Carson Jean, you come when I tell you to come!" She does a mean impression of an annoyed mom, which her daughter ignores completely.

"Here." I lean over the counter and grab the receiver. "Just twirl..."

"I can do it!" she snaps, snatching it away. She spins and twirls, but the cord just gets tangled up tighter. It's actually fun to watch.

"Be nice to Sander," Carson calls over the dog's shoulder. "Grandpop promised him dinner and drinks."

"Don't tell me how to act, young lady." She spins in one direction, the wrong one. "And you tell your Grandpop...Oh never mind." She spins the other way. Wrong again.

I lean over the bar, remove the receiver from her hand and hold it away from her. "Just stand still. Let me do it." I circle the receiver around her.

Carson's mom crosses her arms and taps her foot. "Twelve years old and knows everything, doesn't have to do anything I say. I'm about ready to trade her for a new model, I swear." Her breath smells of Dentyne; her red-brown hair of barbecue smoke. She looks up at me. "Sometimes I just want to run away. Have you ever just wanted to up and leave and start life somewhere else, where no one knows you?"

"Why do you think I'm here?" I say, suddenly the rogue. "Left the wife and ten kids behind. Robbed a bank. Came up here 'cause I heard the beer was cold and the bartender was fine. Hopin' I could maybe find someone to hit the road with me and see the world. You available?" This is certainly not normal me; must be Elephant Man talking.

"More than I was a minute ago." She's finally freed; I hand her the receiver and she returns it to its hook. "What happened to your nose?"

"Sander fell when he jumped off a rock," Carson calls out.

"That would be the correct answer," I nod.

"Happens a lot out here." Carson's mom smooths her hair and smiles. She's got those same big eyes as her daughter, only cat-green, and something about her face is wide open. "What can I get you?"

"Rolling Rock'd great. Big day today?" I indicate the wedding decor.

She sets a bottle in front of me, flips off the cap with her thumb, then does that under-over-handed move and flicks the cap into a corner onto a mountain of other caps—a high-school parking-lot move I have always admired. "The whole town's invited and my ladies' room toilet's on the fritz."

No matter where I roam or stray, crap is never far away. "I'm pretty handy with toilets." *Toilets? My pickup line?* Ellie would piss her pants.

She looks sideways to make sure Carson's out of earshot, then leans over the bar and dips her head in close to mine, fluttering her lashes and affecting a southern accent. "Mah name is Patsy and ah'd loooooove to talk about toilets." Her breasts plump sweetly between her crossed arms.

"I'm Sander." I finish off my beer. "Talk potty to me."

"Well, as of fifteen minutes ago, when we turn on the dishwasher over here," she says, drawing a circle on the cigarette-burned, plank bar, "the contents of the Dispos-All come up out of the toilet over here." She draws another circle a short distance away. "And when you flush over here," she marks the spot with an exclamation point, "vice versa."

"Oh. Bad. Mm. Not pretty. Terrible. Oh. Yeah." Furrowed brow and chin strokes. "Health Department wouldn't want to hear about that."

"Who said anything about the Health Department? Not out here. Not if we fix it first." Another Rolling Rock appears, another bottle cap shoots into the corner.

"From what you just said, ma'am, I don't believe you're talking about toilets." *Ma'am?* I guess a shitkicker on a roof makes everyone under it a redneck.

"I'm not?" Patsy's shoulders hitch up as if her whole body is engaged in the conversation. Not like women you meet in bars back home, always looking over your shoulder or to the side of you to see if someone better is around.

"Nope. You're talking about septic tanks." I say, sucking down another half-bottle. "Do you know where yours is?" My intention was to slip into Buckaroo, check into the motel and hunker down into the script and the schedule – collect my thoughts, make some notes, find my zone. I still have all night tonight, and all tomorrow and tomorrow night before the crew arrives. But right now, there's a cute damsel in distress and her septic tank's calling my name.

Around the side of the Shitkicker Saloon, a slab of beef turns on a spit in a massive barbecue. It smells great, but it intensifies the desert heat that much more. Patsy watches from the shade of an overhang while Carson pretends to film me with her busted Keystone. I smile pretty for the camera, then plant the shovel, press my heel onto it, and carefully remove a clump of daisies from a patch that has taken off like wildfire, a sure sign of a septic below. Already, sweat furrows down my forehead and under my nose bandage, stinging a salty assault on my scraped skin. It drips from my eyebrows into my eyes, furrows down my back, my front, the insides of my legs, the cheeks of my ass. The closest I've ever been to heat like this was at one of those Woodland Hills ranchos. Place was a furnace.

My shovel hits the top of a tank, and I make short work of exposing it, then clear away dirt from two more. I motion for Patsy and Carson to come look. "Not too close," I warn, and point to the lid of the first tank. "See that crud seeping out there?"

Patsy stands back and nods, clamping her nose with her fingers, while Carson affects a manual zoom in.

"What you have here is a waterlogged tank that needs to be pumped out. Until that's done, you're gonna have burritos coming up out of the toilets when you flush or crap floating in your sink when you use the dishwasher."

"Can you fix it?" Patsy asks.

"I don't have the equipment to completely pump out your tank. I'll do what I can to tide you over for the rest of the day. If I were you, I'd apologize to your plumber friend, invite him to the party, then ask him to come back and pump your tanks as soon as he can."

"Damn!" The screen door whacks Patsy's back pockets as she stomps inside.

Carson rolls her eyes. "Mom hates to apologize."

"Want to see what happens when you don't clean out your solids?" At Carson's apprehensive nod, I position my shovel under the lip of the lid, count to three, and open 'er up.

"Gross!" she yells, then leans in and cocks her head to one side. "How's that work?"

There's really no artful way to describe the feces, paper and food waste that accumulates in these systems, or how bacteria transform it to liquids and gases, but I do my best. "Then, when the liquid in the first tank reaches this line," I grab a piece of dead wood from a nearby cactus display and stir up the surface layer, "gravity helps distribute it to the other tanks via this outflow pipe."

"Cool," Carson says. "Then what?"

"It drains off through subsurface pipes and gets absorbed back into the soil. That's why, over here, you get daisies. You see this a lot in Topanga Canyon, out in Malibu." I stir the thickest of the gunk away from the outflow pipe, at which point, punctuated by loud sucking and gurgling noises, it begins to drain. I sit under the shade to let gravity do its job, while Carson pretends to film Jake, who has fallen asleep in the pile of cool dirt next to the tanks. After about twenty minutes, I dispatch Carson to perform a test flush.

Patsy emerges from the kitchen with an update. "Roto-Rooter and the missus are putting on party clothes, the kitchen sink's flowing, and, last I checked, the toilet flushed everything down instead of up."

"Great." I close the lids on the tanks, return the wood to its display and wipe my hands on my now filth-encrusted pants, and notice her as though for the first time. She's changed into a shiny Chinese dress that fastens across the shoulder, down the side, and stops about mid-thigh. The light blue fabric has tiny red birds on it, with suede cowboy boots to match. "Wow. You look super."

"Thanks, plumber." When she hands me another beer, her fingers brush mine and she smiles right into my eyes. "You stink."

I look back at her and—suddenly extremely aware that smoke, shit and B.O. are the major components of my personal funk—give her everything I've got. "Thank *you*."

No way am I driving Paul's Lexus like this. I limp beside the car as Carson drives the roughly one hundred yards from the Saloon to Coreen's Oasis Motel. "So what's the deal with this town anyway?"

"You mean Buckaroo?" Carson asks from behind the wheel. "It was built in 1946 by a bunch of Hollywood people as a Western movie set," she recites by rote, like an official tour guide. "The people who worked in the movies built their houses around it so they could have a place to live right next to where they work. Roy Rogers was one of the most famous ones." She parks the Lexus and pops the trunk so I can grab my duffel.

"So the whole town's a set? Sweet." I wonder why I've never heard of the place and follow her down a short flight of stairs bordered by roses, cacti, wagon wheels and shot-up road signs. "Do you live around here?"

She points to the one-story, barn-red motel. "Me and my mom are around back in Room Ten and Grandpop lives in Room One. John Wayne stayed in Room Eight one time," Carson says as she opens the door to Room Three and drops my duffel on the bed directly inside the door. "Mom said for you come over later and we'll fix you something to eat."

The first thing I do is peel off the Elephant Man bandage from my face. The scrape beneath it is not too bad; I'm glad it was covered while I was cleaning out the septics. I unwind the bandage and test my ankle. Not bad either. The small bathroom has a horseshoe for a toilet paper holder and a branding iron for a towel rack. The shower is an old-model, self-contained, free-standing metal job. I don't expect much, but for a mid-day shower in a desert motel, I'm surprised and impressed by the spray's forceful pressure and consistent temp. They must have a large-capacity water heater. Even the low-flow head doesn't seem to compromise the quality of the spray, compared to most I've installed. They can't have access to water mains out here. I wonder if they have a tank. Maybe their own well? An underground spring? Who'da thunk I'd be parsing plumbing while I'm preparing to direct my commercial, but this modest contraption is producing one of the best showers I've ever had in life.

I wrap a towel around my waist, have a seat in the rocker and put my feet up on the patchwork bedspread to air dry. I open my laptop and review the materials Vana's sent over in a series of emails. Prep schedule, location description, crew bios, script and shot list. Fuck, I'm starving. I'll just grab a quick bite and then come back to work. As I button myself into the Sturges—it is a wedding party, after all—I study the small room. There's a small pine-paneled kitchenette with a cactus cookie jar, a kitschy ceramic panther on the fireplace mantel, and above it a framed movie poster from *High Noon*. A teensy Gary Cooper has his hands at his sides, ready to draw against three large-legged opponents below the tagline "The story of a man who was too proud to run!" Too proud to run? Life in the old Westerns was always so dramatic, so elemental, survival so tough. I sling my camera bag over my shoulder and, when I open the door, nearly stumble over Jake, sitting like a stone lion sentinel next to my doormat. "Howdy Pardner," the mat reads. "Welcome to Your Home Away from Home!"

8

SUNDAY EVENING

The Shitkicker Saloon looks like a scene from *Fellini Satyricon*—if *Fellini Satyricon* had taken place in Buckaroo and featured a wedding party scene where the guests wore costumes ranging from traditional Western wear to neo-Renaissance-era hippie gowns and knickers, from formal gowns and tuxedos to buckskin Indian get-ups. People of all ages pack the venue, plus a handful of dogs. There's a goat decked out in a flower lei. Dancers crowd the dance floor below the small stage where Harry Apple fronts a band—The Homeboys, a flyer on the wall announces—consisting of a drummer, bass player and rhythm guitarist. Judging from their white hair and beards, authentic-looking hippie getups, and the way they plow into the free-form guitar jam, they seem more like The Old Home Boys. When the music quiets, Harry croons velvet as if he were the King himself: *Dark star crashes / pouring light into ashes. / Reason tatters / the forces tear loose from the axis.* I recognize the Grateful Dead song from junior high, when my best friend Nathan and I spent an entire summer listening to it over and over—stoned, of course—in bean bag chairs in Nathan's basement bedroom. We pored over the lyrics for hours, searching for deep meaning in its pothead poetry.

I'm still surveying the incongruous scene when JC himself draws me into the throng. There are too many people to do anything much like dancing, so I just bob my head as JC undulates away from me in his white tails. He dances toward Starshine in the center of the floor, sitting on a chair decorated with flowers. Someone pulls me into a crooked conga line and soon we're circling JC as he freestyles modernist twirls and huarache toe taps, and Star, who waves her arms in Balinese/Hawaiian/Flamenco gestures. The conga line splits and reconfigures into a two-line *Soul Train* formation. I extricate myself just in time to avoid having to dance down the center. Jake skitters to my side. Man, I need to record this.

I head to the back, grab a barstool and pull out my VMX to check it out before I shoot.

"Sander!" Carson's voice bullhorns across the room. "Are you having fun?"

"I sure am," I say, which surprises me. Weddings usually give me hives. And it wasn't long ago I was thinking of one of my own. Ashe's idea of a great wedding would probably be some grand, outdoor Malibu affair with paparazzi hovering in helicopters.

"Omigosh! I'm supposed to fix you a plate. Don't move." Carson gallops into the kitchen, slapping her thighs as she goes.

Patsy appears behind the bar with a tray of empties and catches my eye. "Nice suit, plumber," she says, then bumps—awkwardly, and with an unfeminine *oof!*—into the wall. The tray crashes to the floor, bottles clatter, plastic cups roll.

I jump down from the stool. "Nice move, barkeep."

We crouch awkwardly, our eyes locked in a confused gaze, mouths gaping. She points to a tributary of cream running toward the toe of her blue-suede boots just as I reach for the red plastic cup on its side on the wood-plank floor.

"*So much depends upon a red wheel barrow glazed with rain water beside the white chickens,*" a man's voice intones. The voice is soft and its cadence slow, with a swinging drawl this California boy can only identify as "southern." The source of the drawl has a mullet, a bull neck and beefy shoulders, and wears patchwork denim overalls over a short-sleeve dress shirt. He's sitting in a stripped-down wheelchair with fat, off-road tires, and compulsively strokes a chicken resting—roosting?—on his lap. *Satyricon* redux.

"What?" Patsy's voice is sharp. Her fuse seems to be on the short side.

"The William Carlos Williams poem. It's all right there." The man's features are classically handsome with thick brows and a cleft chin. "See? The red cup is the wheel barrow and the white inside is the chicken and the milk is the rain..."

"I just see spilled milk." Patsy places the cup on her tray.

"It's more than that," he sighs. "So much more." He one-eighties his chair and wheels away. The raccoon tail pinned to his backrest sways.

"Who's the poet?" I ask, collecting an empty from under a nearby table and placing it on her tray.

"Who? Donnie?" Patsy snorts, shaking her head. "He's had a thing for me ever since we made out once behind the Post Office when we were squirts." She grabs a rag from her apron and mops up the milk.

"You were that good?"

She blushes—I like that—and laughs. "We were twelve! In his head, we're still an item."

"How does the chicken fit in?"

"Donnie breeds birds. Prize winners." Patsy sighs. "Thanks for cleaning up, plumber."

"My pleasure, barkeep." We idiotically ignore each other some more.

"I hope this is enough." Carson hands me a plate heaped with barbecue, three mounds of salads (four if you count Jell-O), two kinds of beans and a biscuit the size of my head. Patsy abruptly stands and stalks behind the bar, while Carson starts picking up stray bottles and cups that her mother and I didn't get to yet.

"For starters." I settle at the bar and tear into a rib. "Meat good." And so is the view as Patsy lines up beer mugs, chats with guests, and laughs, looking over at me occasionally to make sure I'm watching. I don't hide the fact that I am, and I'll let her wonder if the smile on my face is from the food or her proximity.

I'm wiping up the last of the sauce with a biscuit when Carson arrives with JC and Starshine in tow. "Can we show the video now? It'll play on the new monitor!" She points to a screen mounted in a corner over the bar. "It's so cool! It's a computer, it's email, it's TV, it's anything you want!"

Starshine pulls Carson toward her, chiding the girl. "Let the man finish eating, honey."

"It's all right." I wipe the barbecue sauce from my hands and retrieve the memory stick, which Carson takes into to a small office nearby. Next thing I know, the musicians have quit playing and Harry's at the microphone inviting everyone to watch. Guests gather at the bar, eyes glued to the screen. But nothing happens.

"Check the plugs," I say. "Try pulling out the stick and putting it in again. Reboot."

Carson calmly tries everything, not getting flustered by the waiting crowd.

"Hey, there *is* something on the screen!" somebody says.

And there is. A very faint impression of the letters X, M and V.

"Ohmigosh. SANDER FORGOT TO TAKE OFF THE LENS CAP!" Carson announces, her built-in bullhorn amplified by everyone in the room falling silent.

"Impossible." I turn on my camera, insert the stick when Carson brings it to me, and press REVIEW, confident the ceremony will replay. Until it doesn't. I remove the memory stick, replace it, and try again. But the stick is as blank as my brain. Where the *fuck* is the goddamn wedding ceremony? "This camera's brand-new. There must be a factory malfunction," I protest lamely. All eyes are on me: the stranger, the interloper, the idiot who can't work his own camera. I have *Deliverance*-style visions of being made to squeal like a pig. Perhaps a good old-fashioned hanging at noon. If they kill me now, they'll have two days before anyone from the production is due to show. I wonder how long it takes buzzards to pick a skeleton dry. There's not that much meat on my bones to begin with...

Carson tugs at my sleeve. "What are we gonna do?" Her eyes well with tears, and her chin starts to wag.

Patsy's hand covers her mouth, but not fast enough to muffle a snort of laughter. Her eyes are mischievous and sparkling. Her shaking belly gives her away and in that very instant, there is a pang of attraction in the bottom of my gut. A pang so loud and clear I wonder if Carson can hear it. The same sort of pang that told me to sit next to Ashe before the start of *Jules et Jim*. Which is how I am inspired to spend the next two hours filming all the guests telling their love stories, one by one. This time, I let Carson set up.

Rainbow-colored streamers dangle from the beams on the overhang above the Shitkicker's small outside dance floor, and white satin bows decorate the spiky arms of the Joshua trees that surround it. Carson and I sit at a picnic table in the soft night air under a sky like an ocean of stars, studying the love stories on my VMX. There's the Native American Indian couple from the same New Mexico tribe who met on a cattle call at Paramount in the forties. A set designer who claims he built the set for *Quo Vadis* in Rome where he met Sophia, the script girl, during production and they've been married for thirty years. A teenage boy mumbling rhyming couplets of the girl he hoped to meet, a kindred spirit who would be his artistic muse and listen to his poems and maybe put them to song. And just because they were there, three little girls on their backs in white dresses hanging over the back end of a pony cart, squealing with laughter as their pigtails trail in dirt. "Which one's your favorite?" I ask.

"All of them," Carson says dreamily. "Hey! What about yours?" She jumps to her feet. "Sander, we forgot to do yours!"

"You don't want to hear my love story, kiddo. Weddings are supposed to be happy."

A Ford Bronco approaches the outside dance floor. The tricked-out truck has five-foot-high tractor tires with fancy metallic flames painted on the sides. Giant speakers and a very large gift fill the truck's bed. The ultimate redneck road machine's driver is my poetry-quoting friend with the chicken. I hit RECORD and slide him into frame. "What's his deal?"

Carson fills me in. "Donnie's real name is Adonis. He had a twin brother, Apollo, but he died."

"Apollo and Adonis?" I zoom in.

"Lonnie and Donnie," Carson says, "Donnie's in love with my mom and everyone knows it, but Mom always says she's never falling in love again so he shouldn't waste his time."

"Fascinating." When the engine turns off, a woman in her eighties disembarks from the elevated cab like she was hopping down from a horse. In a fringed skirt, vest and boots, she looks like she just doh-si-doh'd off the set of *Annie Get Your Gun*. "Who's the lady?"

"Donnie's grandma, Willamette," Carson says. "She owns the bowling alley and the Costumery. Used to be a bareback rider. Did stunts for the movies. She's the only one lived here in Buckaroo longer than Grandpop. Raised Lonnie and Donnie since they were little."

I bet she's got some stories. A hydraulic platform slides out from the chassis below Donnie's door and his driver's seat—his wheelchair—rolls out onto the platform. Willamette folds her fingers between her lips and blows a piercing whistle. When the music dies down and she has the crowd's attention, she calls out, "JC and Star, let's have at ya!" Her voice is girlish, with a bell-like, Jean Arthur lilt over a hick twang.

The newlyweds cut each other hesitant glances, then link arms, and head to the dance floor. Donnie wheels his chair over to his grandmother, who clears her throat before she speaks. "We been waiting for you two ta tie the knot for a long time. 'Bout nine months now." The guests chuckle like an appreciative laugh track. "Things are gonna change when the littl'un comes along. So to celebrate our friendship and help keep the honey in the moon, here's a gift to say good luck and good lovin'!"

The crowd whoops and hollers: "Speech! Speech!"

JC's hands ball up into fists, and Star grabs the tails of his tuxedo coat, holding him back. They whisper to each other behind their mutual hair before JC gently pushes her hand away and steps forward. "Adonis, Willie. We're proud to be your friends and we're overwhelmed by your generosity, but we really can't accept." My VMX captures JC: his mouth is smiling, but his eyes are marked with fear.

Donnie's chicken clucks excitedly, as though it has some inner antenna reading the moment's undercurrent of anxiety, but Willie smiles and opens wide her fringed arms. "Nonsense. Ya'll are family to me and my Donnie-kins."

"Grandma!" Donnie complains. "Don't call me that in public."

"Oh, shush!" Willie waves her hand again. "You can't say no to family." She draws JC and Star into her python's embrace, which the couple stiffly leans into, their hands remaining tightly clasped.

"Well, then," JC says weakly when Willie finally sets them free. "I speak for both of us when I say *namaste*." He directs prayered hands her way, then bows deeply. Star waves Carson over to open their gift.

Carson scampers up into the back of the truck and tears away the paper, leaving the huge ribbon and bow in place, to reveal an elaborately carved, mahogany canopied bed, complete with a purple velvet comforter. "Wow!" she screams, as she jumps on the bed, then looks up into the canopy. "Hey! Mirrors! Is that so you can watch yourself fall asleep?" The crowd laughs, pushing toward the truck to see, while the band picks up where it left off.

I make my way to the bar and order another beer from Patsy, who wordlessly sets it in front of me, not bothering to shoot the cap into the corner. She turns to Willamette, who's wheeling Donnie into place next to me. "The usual? Or would you like some champagne?"

"The usual, Pats," Willie says. "Who's the stranger with the busted beak?" Her face is nut-brown and remarkably unlined. There's a smile on it, too, but her eyes scan me like a cop's.

"Willamette, Donnie, meet Sander. He fell off a rock today," Patsy says, pouring out two shots of Patrón Añejo and a tall glass of lemonade with a cherry on top.

"Poor baby," the dame says before tossing back both shots in quick succession.

"My condolences," Donnie says, making a show of pawing Patsy's hand and kissing it.

Patsy very casually slips her hand away. "Then he filmed everyone's love stories for JC and Star as a gift from Carson."

"That bed was a great gift," I lie, meaning one of the strangest gifts I've ever seen. "You must do good business to be able to afford something like that. What do people do out here anyway?"

Donnie squints. "What do you mean by that?"

I step back. "What do you mean 'what do I mean?'"

He looks confused, I am confused, and Willie steps in to dig us out of our conversational hole. "We do it all up here. We keep the town running as a tourist attraction first and a working film location second. Lots of artists up here. Retired Hollywood people. We're just like any other town except we live in a magic place, right Donnie-kins?" She tousles her grandson's hair.

"Grandma!"

"Sorry!" She waves across the room, where Harry beckons from the dance floor. "This old lady needs to boogie."

The VMX is calling my name. "Can I film your love story, Donnie? I'd hate to leave anyone out." Especially if his story concerns Patsy.

"Everyone knows Patsy is the apple of my eye. Right, Pats?" Donnie deliberately places the cherry between his lips, and pokes it into his mouth with his finger for punctuation.

"And everyone knows Patsy Apple is a free agent," Patsy says lightly, slamming the cork into the tequila bottle with the palm of her hand.

I pick up the VMX. "May I?"

Donnie pats his sprayed-in-place mullet. "How's my hair?"

"Perfect," I tell him, panning slowly from his man-model features to the black-and-white chicken in his arms. "Whenever you're ready. Just ignore the camera and tell the story."

"Until Patsy realizes she's madly in love with me, my heart belongs to my chicken here. Her name is Little. She's a pedigreed vanilla and chocolate Silver Sebright." Adonis puts the chicken's beak to his mouth and gives it a peck of a kiss. "Give Daddy some sugar." The chicken pecks him back, and when he tucks her under his throat and strokes her, she coos at his touch. "When an amorous rooster wants to perform intercourse, he drops his wing to the dirt and does a little song and dance. With any luck, this will excite one of the hens in his harem, who will respond by raising her rump, at which point her suitor will hop on and ride her, clasping his beloved's neck with his wings. Like in 'April is the Saddest Month,' you know?"

"Let me guess. William Carlos Williams?"

He nods, clears his throat and looks off-camera. With one hand held aloft, he recites, "*There they were stuck, dog and bitch halving the compass. Then when with his yip they parted, oh how frolicsome she grew before him—playful, dancing—and how disconsolate he retreated, hang-dog, she following through the shrubbery.*" He sets his hand back in his lap and continues. "There's been similar behavior right here at the Shitkicker on the occasional Saturday night, wouldn't you agree, Pats?"

Outside the frame, Starshine whispers and giggles with Patsy behind the bar.

"I said, 'right Pats?!'" Adonis' soft voice is suddenly menacing.

"Whatever you say, hon!" Starshine hands Patsy a small white paper bag, and Patsy looks over at me.

"Hear that?" Donnie crows to the camera. "She treats me as though we were married. Anyway, the rooster pumps his lucky girlfriend once, and when the deed is done, the two of them puff up their feathers, shivering and quivering. Chicken aftershock." He coughs. "That's it. There's my story. I can re-do it if you like. What do you call it? Another take?"

"No, that was perfect, man," I tell him, even though Bobby Vinton singing *Blue Velvet* is running through my brain above images of insects crawling through the canal of a severed ear, followed by a flash of Isabella Rossellini, pale and nude, wailing on a suburban lawn. Perfectly weird.

A few minutes later, Patsy leans over the counter to Donnie. Her breasts do that same cute thing they did earlier. "Little want to sit in her spot?"

Donnie listens to the bird as she nuzzles his ear. "Little most certainly does want to sit in her spot!" He hands Little to Patsy, who chucks the bird below the beak and tickles its wattle. She climbs onto the back counter, and places the bird between the raggedy ears of a mounted buffalo head.

"Come on, sunshine. Cut the rug with your Grandma." Willamette's back from the dance floor, doing the twist. She grabs Donnie's chair handles and wheels him away.

I check my watch. If I head back to my motel room now, I can still get in a good two or three hours of work. I work better at night anyway; it gives my subconscious fresh fodder to wrestle with instead of the standard "looking for a good place to jerk off" routine.

"Everything's free tonight except liquor from the top two shelves," Patsy says, whipping off her apron and handing it to a partygoer dressed like Ellie May from *The Beverly Hillbillies*. "And no serving kids or animals." She then tucks the white paper bag under her arm, swings herself over the bar and thumps my chest. "Hey plumber, wanna go for a ride?"

"I was just thinking about heading back. I'm pretty tired."

She breaks into a long, slow smile and bumps one hip out to the side. "I've got something might perk you up."

I'm perked up already.

*   *   *

Patsy jams a screwdriver into the ignition and the '79 Chevy Luv's engine growls into action, knocking like rocks in a coffee can. We barrel along a road that is pitch-freaking black, except for a few twinkly house lights that could be either miles away or a few hundred yards away—without the artificial markers of city lights, it's impossible to tell. When we stop to idle at a fork, the little pickup's headlights give a surreal glow to a lopsided Joshua tree with three arms that point to the left, to the left, to the left.

"That's how I know where I'm going," Patsy says, pointing to the tree.

"What a relief." This jouncing off-roading is killing my ass, which is already sore from my earlier tumble off the Lexus' hood.

Patsy pulls a hard, fast right and we lurch into a blind hairpin, nearly tilting into the wash. A minute or two of hard driving later, she parks next to a manzanita bush. "Yellow Flats. Best natural hot springs around." She grabs a blanket from behind the seat, then hops out of the truck. "Come on." I follow her over some boulders and down into a small natural bowl, where she pulls off her boots. She tosses aside the silky blue dress, a stream of bright, moonstruck water falling from her hand. In a camisole and panties, Patsy slips down into the bubbling sulfuric springs. "Yeeeeaaahhh. Now I'm home. Come on in."

"I'm really not a hot-tub person," I tell her. What is it with everyone sitting around in hot water, anyway? It's like festering in a Petri dish.

"You're kidding, right?" Patsy sinks into a nature-made lounge chair, then floats back up to the surface. Her soaked camisole clings to her contours.

"I'll compromise." I kick off my loafers and pull off my socks. My city-boy feet glow white as I tread carefully, favoring my wobbly ankle, over the still-warm rocks.

She shows me her fine back as she locates the paper bag and

two brownies. "One's for you, but not until you come in." She mows her hand across the water's surface, splashing me.

I duck, my weak ankle crabs sideways, and I fall on my ass, soaking my pants to the knees. "Very funny," I say, in response to her laugh, pulling off the jacket and folding it, lining side out, before placing it on a rock.

"Where'd you get that suit, anyway?" she asks. "It looks like something Willamette'd have up in her costumery."

I rip off my shirt, slip down my trousers, and slide into the water as fast as I can. "It was my dad's," I tell her, bobbing around until I slip into a decent recliner, letting the surface seltzer tickle my nose. Dad and I installed a natural rock spa like this for a couple up in Benedict Canyon, but they didn't have the sulfur springs and they didn't have this sky. "He just died." The energy between us instantly changes—what was light and amusing becomes dark and serious. What was I thinking? *Dammit.*

Patsy winces and her shoulders tense up. She closes her eyes, as though holding something in. "I'm sorry."

"No, I'm sorry. I didn't mean to blurt that out."

"That's all right." She floats over, holding the brownie aloft, then climbs onto my lap. With her free hand she lightly daubs water on my forehead, my nose. "These are healing waters. Good for what ails ya. And this won't hurt either." She feeds me a corner of the brownie, then takes a bite for herself.

"Mmm, not bad."

"Told ya," she smiles, feeding me another bite. "Did you really leave the wife and kids behind?"

"Miles and days and years behind." I nuzzle her neck, breathe in the musky scent of her damp skin and hair, instantly aroused.

She wraps her arms around my shoulder and pulls herself closer. "How big of a bank did you rob?"

"Very big. Getting bigger." We both know what I'm talking about now.

She moves her hips and feeds me some more, resting her finger inside my mouth this time. "Can we go really far, far away?"

"All the way up to that moon," I say, around her finger.

She leans back to look up to the full moon hanging like a giant egg in the sky. I lean way in and we float together on the water. Her tongue laps my ear, my face, my mouth, with urgent animal noises at the back of her throat. After a while of delightful mutual mauling, there's only one thing left to do. She leads me to a rock that looks down across the valley under the star-scattered sky and the bright band of the Milky Way. I ache for her hard, and she's grabbing at her jean jacket for a condom and tearing the packet with her mouth, spitting the foil corner off to the side, and I'm putting it on, trying my hardest to be fast and professional, but the damn thing feels like it's inside out. I'm not accustomed to this kind of urgency. Even with Ashe, it was never like this. And then Patsy points over my shoulder into the dark. "Stop! Look!"

A pair of golden eyes flashes on the boulder above us. "Crap!" I freeze, the condom flag flying above my pole. "What is that?"

"Bobcat," she says. It perches on the ledge, moonlight tracing taut muscles, tawny fur gleaming. The cat leans onto its side and hangs one arm over the edge of the rock, its paw casual and great.

"Shit. I can't do this." Patsy rolls away from me, pops up to her feet, and goes to her truck. She comes back with some rough towels and a blanket.

I don't move, still holding the condom in my hand like an idiot. "What just happened?"

She takes the condom, wraps it in a tissue, and hands me a towel. "I think that bobcat is my ex." She looks straight in my eyes when she says this. I guess so I won't think she's crazy.

It doesn't work. We towel dry and dress without speaking, then she spreads a blanket on the rock and pulls me down onto it. "You want to hear my love story?" Patsy asks, breaking the brownie and handing me half. She snuggles her backside into me, both of us facing the sky and the moon. "Last time I saw that bobcat was the night Tex and I made Carson."

I choke a little. "You have an ex named Tex?"

She playfully backhand punches me over her shoulder. "I didn't name him. Anyway, Tex just showed up in Buckaroo one day, hitchhiking out to L.A. from Dallas. A musician. Checked into the motel and started writing songs and singing on the weekends at the Saloon. Began attracting a following, not to mention, attention. As in, mine. We became lovers."

The bobcat stretches and yawns, showing its large yellow teeth and pink curling tongue. I hug Patsy tight as the animal stands, shakes all over and retreats into the darkness. "Just another moment in Buckaroo," Patsy whispers.

We stay like that for a long time. Neither of us moves. My body is relaxed, but my brain hums with sounds and images. The wind moving through the shrubs. The rustling and bustling of ground squirrels, field mice, jack rabbits, coyotes. The bobcat's padding paws. My heart pumping blood. Air filling my lungs. And Patsy hears all the same sounds, her body experiences all the same feelings. Where Ashe and I transmitted information through one measly elbow, Patsy and I communicate through our brains and entire bodies. It's a good sign. Much better than Violet Crumbles and Truffaut.

9

MONDAY MORNING

Not all erections are created equal.

For example, there's the one that happens on lazy mornings when I read the paper. I call it the Eiffel Tower for its metallic nerve ending twinges, and the fact that it often surges right when I get to the World news section. The Stonehenge is an enduring series of semi-soft chubs that has been known to take hours to reach industrial strength. Once I lasted an entire double feature before I finally caved and beat it into submission. The Pope's Hat refers to a really good hard-on that happens at a really bad time. Like a seventh-grade slow dance with Lani Brown. Or dinner at Grandma's house. Old Faithful is the kind that stands through the entire wrinkled issue of *Playboy* from June 1974, and wants to see that centerfold girl in the green baseball cap, kicking that bat and looking at me, again and again and again.

This morning's wood is an exceptional stiffie, sprung from a Technicolor dream. A dream of extrasensory memory. Of driving down from Yellow Flats in the pitch black night, of Patsy killing the engine to watch a jackrabbit rest, its long ears grabbing for sound, looking strange and false in the headlights. Of falling into bed calm yet stimulated, as though cleansed both inside and out. I laze back into the imagescape. Of roaring mineral waters. Patsy in her wet camisole, breasts bobbing in 3-D. Her breath hot and delicious, moaning *Sander, Sander.* Moaning into my ear, *Sander.* Her voice so real. So close.

"Sander?" Shit. It really is Patsy, knocking on my door. "Sander!"

Without getting up, I crack open the door and look straight into two tan, bare knees. One foot slides up the back of the opposite calf. Frayed cutoffs. A tight white T-shirt. "Mornin', plumber," Patsy says. "Your nose is looking better already."

Her flesh-and-blood presence is shocking on the heels of my erotic dream. "Mornin', barkeep. You drop by to tell me the rest of your love story?"

She waves a steaming mug under my nose. "In case the coffeemaker doesn't work." Then she whoops as Jake squirms through her legs and onto my bed. The Doberman puts his paws on my chest and licks my face. A striped necktie dangles from around his neck.

"That dog has the hots for you," she laughs.

"Lucky me." I push the dead weight of dog off my chest, keeping him far from my crotch. He curls up near my feet. "Come on in."

"Not while you're in bed." She looks away, as though someone were watching. Her voice sounds distant. "You come out."

I wash up, pull on some sweats, and head outside to a weathered picnic table, where Patsy waits with coffee and my VMX. Should I say something about last night? When in doubt: drink. "Good coffee," I say, unable to muster anything more original than that.

"You left your camera in my truck," she says. "I found

Carson fooling with it this morning. She said she was going to take the memory sticks up to the Kicker's computer to burn a disc for JC and Star. I hope that's all right. If she broke anything, she'll be grounded until she pays you back."

"Kid knows her way around a camera," I say, opening the case to inspect it. "Should be fine." A pink Dymo Label pasted on the lens cap makes me smile: REMOVE B4 USE. I set the camera on the table, pretending to focus across the desert on the Shitkicker, its outside dance floor and the yellow rosebushes in the foreground, when in fact I'm focusing on Patsy.

"About last night." She stops, then starts again. "I'm not usually so..." Eyeroll. "Horny."

"I thought you were seduced by my charm."

"No, I didn't mean. I mean, I was. It's not that. It's just my birthday's coming up."

"Oh, now that makes sense."

She crosses her eyes. "I'm freaking out." Makes a freaking-out face.

"Happy birthday."

"Not really. I'm turning thirty."

I like a woman who offers up her age, no nonsense. "I know what you mean. Everything's fine at twenty-nine. Everything's crap at thirty." Not that I fixed the crap. I just learned how to ignore it better.

"I don't talk to Harry, my dad. So what you said about your dad last night..."

"Hey, I'm the worst person to give advice, so you shouldn't listen to me," I say.

But she's already not listening to me. "I've never left this town," she continues. "My kid makes me crazy. I have no life. I meet a guy who's interesting and I try to seduce him..."

"And a fine try it was." She shoots me a look. "Just trying to be helpful."

She picks up where she left off. *"But I can't go through with it because a bobcat shows up.* Obviously, I'm freaking out." She wraps her hair around her wrist and ties it in a knot at the nape of her neck. "Are you filming me?"

"Maybe."

"Goddamn it!" she says, but she doesn't get up.

"You're beautiful," I tell her. The light plays on her skin, casting half her face in shadow. Light Patsy and dark Patsy. Only her eyes look thirty. Not around them, but "in" them, in the part that holds the pain. "Don't stop."

She's suddenly bashful. "What shall I say?"

"Tell me more about Tex."

She pulls her hand away from her neck and her hair slips out of its knot. "The sun came up red that morning, and I'll never forget what he said: 'When I left home, I vowed I was going to L.A. to be a big star. And girlfriends get in the way, if you know what I mean. But I always want us to be real good...'" She stops, staring out of the frame, into my eyes, then far away.

"Oh, shit," I say.

"Oh, shit is right," she agrees. "He wore my handprint on his face for two days." Patsy turns toward me and tosses her hair, hamming it up for the lens. "So what brings you out this way, plumber? Testing out the new camera?"

"Actually, I'm getting ready to direct a project. A commercial."

She becomes serious, folds her hands in front of her. "You're a director?"

"Yeah. For a music thing." There *is* music involved.

"Really?" She crosses her legs and plops her chin in her palm.

I'm surprised the way she's playing me. I don't see her as the type who cares much about Hollywood. But it's just enough to make me brazen. "You've heard of that singer Destinée? It's with her. Paul Street's involved in the project, too. *No One Ever Dies?* That's his Lexus. He loaned it to me." Great. I am now an official member of Namedroppers Anonymous. A dog begging for approval. My brain buzzes with self-loathing.

"You? A director?" She jumps up from the bench. "You left the lens cap on!"

"I never said I was good." I try for that self-deprecating thing Paul Street does.

"Why'd you tell me you're a plumber if you're a director?" She grabs my coffee mug and hurls what's left of its contents into the dirt at the bottom of a rosebush. "Goddamn Hollywood people! Always dropping names and pretending to be something they're not! I knew you didn't have a plumber's butt-crack!" She stomps away toward the end of the motel.

"It's a commercial," I call out as she disappears around the corner. "Sixty lousy seconds!"

A moment later, her door slams.

Jake emerges from my room and lays his head and long snout across my thigh, amber eyes gawping up at me.

"What just happened, man?" I rub circles on the top of his bony skull and he sighs. "Yes, I like you, too."

The dog yawns.

"You're right. I am boring. I came here to work, not fool around, right Jake?" I pound the bench with my fist.

Jake sniffs the coffee in the dirt beneath the rose bush, and lifts his leg on it.

Back in Room Three's rocker, I settle in with the script. A Wild West saloon on a Wild West Saturday night is full of partying cowboys slamming shots, shooting pool and hustling poker. Destinée, a bordello-style madam, and a half-dozen hoochie girls lounge bored on horizontal surfaces: piano, pool table, bar, stairwell banister. When the music comes up, the hoochies come alive, slinking toward the cowboys, grabbing them by arms, shoulders and belt loops, inviting them to the dance floor. The cowboys are game at first, but change their minds when platters of Western Burgers and fries appear at the bar. The girls pout, and Madam Destinée is furious that her girls have been scorned. She leaps onto the pool table and rips off her corseted dress, revealing a sequined G-string and pasties. Cowboy hamburger action stops mid-chew, all attention riveted on Destinée. They are enticed back to the dance floor to worship Destinée, while her girls gleefully devour the burgers and toss one over to her.

How did Oggie get the slamming raw footage I saw at Vana's party from this script? And why did he agree to do it in the first place? So what if Paul Street's coming to baby-sit me to make sure the commercial is exactly as it's set forth on these pages—it's my project now. As such, I need to put my personal stamp on it, to make it better than it reads. I decide to go for a walk, do some brainstorming, play with my camera.

Patsy was checking out my butt.

Mane Street, Buckaroo proper, looks the part of a quintessential Western town. That is, it's a vista of movie clichés that takes two minutes to walk past and two seconds to forget. There's a church, a bowling alley, a row of old-time facades: Jail, Bank, Feed Store, Livery, Gunsmith. The charred sign on a burnt-out building reads Buckaroo Fire Department. A covered Conestoga wagon sits outside a U.S. Postal Office. I take little notice of any of it. My destination lies at the end of the road at the Okay Corral, a split-rail fenced ring overgrown with rose vines and chaparral. Inside the Okay is a large scaffolded structure, walled on three sides, painted in thick strokes to resemble the interior of a saloon. My Western Burger set. Why build an exterior set when there's an actual saloon at the other end of the street? God only knows. I walk around it, squat at various points, film it with my VMX. As inspiration goes, my cup runneth nowhere.

Beyond the Okay Corral is Buckaroo Highway, behind which lie yellow-orange pinnacles below a turquoise sky. It's almost ten o'clock but the town is quiet, still.

A marked road beckons and I look both ways before crossing the highway, even though I haven't seen a vehicle or person yet. *Why did the chicken cross the road? Because a car was coming!* Another one of Dad's goofy riddles from my childhood. The street sign names a fork at Roy Rogers Road and Dale Evans Trail. I take Roy Rogers toward the foothills dotted with modern homes, cabins and RVs. Every now and then I follow a dirt road up onto a mesa, where large land parcels are staked off with crooked wooden fences, barbed razor wire and homemade signs. The third road has a chain across it and a sign:

THIS NEIGHBORHOOD DOESNT JUST WATCH –
WE SHOOT! TRESPASSERS MAKE ARE DAY

Clint Eastwood, crudely sketched, stares down the barrel of a .44 Magnum. Real Hatfield/McCoy stuff. The house behind it is a red-plank desert rancho with a boulder chimney. To one side, a stand of willows shades a chicken coop designed like a Little Red Schoolhouse and topped by a rooster weathervane. Just behind that there's a water tower, piles of junked car cadavers and a rusty dumpster that's filled with something that looks like...golf balls? Off behind the willows lies a corral that warehouses neatly stacked rows of car parts. Around its circular cobbled drive I recognize Adonis London's Bronco, plus a dirt bike, a tractor and an RV. This must be Donnie's place. My hackles rise up as I think about his chickens and his William Carlos Williams and his outspoken designs on Patsy.

I keep walking, winding up into the foothills, until the smooth dirt road abruptly ends at a chain-link gate. There's no fence on either side, just the gate across the road and a rusty, bullet-hole-ridden NO TRESPASSING sign next to it. I hear panting behind me and turn; my chest pounds.

Jake, still in last night's formalwear, sits at my feet, begging for a scratch.

I oblige and he sighs blissfully. "Where to now, boy?"

The dog sallies around the gate and looks back, egging me on. Lassie had nothing on this guy. I look both ways to see if anyone's watching, then trespass, following Jake's lead. There's a rugged road for about a hundred yards which abruptly disappears in a pile of steep boulders. I locate a flat rock far above under the shade of a fat cypress, and make it my arbitrary destination. Spiny shrubs scratch at my legs as I switchback diagonally across the rocks, going way out of my way just to progress a few feet, if any, forward. The hill grows steeper; the sun hotter. I remove my T-shirt, damp with sweat, and wrap it around my head. My throat is dry and dust coats the inside of my nose. I should have brought water. Jake pants, but stays within eyeshot, pacing me. When I finally reach the flat rock, the sun is about straight up noon, but there's shade and a puddle of water beneath the tree. I lap from the puddle, then let Jake lick the leftover moisture, after which he lies down for a nap.

The surprisingly lush valley spreads out below, with a great aerial view of Buckaroo. I turn the VMX onto the one-road town and its surrounding squared-off parcels, then hinge over a jagged mountain range laced with snow. Boulders in sizes ranging from grand pianos to teacups lie stacked in precarious sculptures, delicately balanced yet solid and unmoving for who knows how long. I'm amazed this place is so close to L.A. Its raw, desert topography appears to be from another planet; its idealized, Hollywood-built Mane Street from another time. And the acoustics are incredible. I can hear a car radio on the highway below—some Country & Western song I don't know—as though I were sitting in its front seat. I can hear the breeze soughing through the cypress, creating a low harmonic whistle. Small plants with tiny, brightly-colored buds brush against each other. Streams of multicolored pebbles cascade downhill.

I can't imagine what it'd be like to grow up here, or, like Patsy, never leave here. The fantasy of leaving L.A. and moving here has an appeal. How sweet to never again be bombarded by news from the film world: box office excitement, actresses in rehab, million-dollar deals, hot restaurants with tiny expensive food catering to the heightened sensibilities of the moneyed elite. A man could be himself, without his family's—or anyone else's—expectations or projections. I could forget El-San easily enough. Forget my stupid dream of directing. It's not like I'd be giving up anything. I search for a place to situate a little one-room cabin, try to frame the perfect view from a window over my desk, where I'd write whatever I wanted, inspired by the coyotes and stars and visions of Patsy—never mind we're not talking now—floating around the edges. I'd go down to the Saloon for a cold one. Sit at the bar and listen to local histories of family feuds and tragedies. I wonder if Dad ever dreamed about getting away from his daily grind of pipe and mud and shit, from a wife who spent his cash in continual cycles of redecorating, from unending complaints and demands from two kids who never wanted for anything. I wonder if he ever wanted more out of life? If he ever had dreams for himself?

My cell phone vibrates in my pocket. It's Ellie. "Hey!" I keep the VMX moving, engrossed in my little landscape study.

"What the hell kind of message was that?" She sounds upset.

Message? Oh, that. "I don't know. The kind you never expected to get from me?"

There's a beat of silence on her end. "Are you still stoned?" she asks. "What are you doing? Why were you in Paul Street's Lexus? When did you meet Paul Street?"

"I'm not stoned," I laugh. "And I'm prepping to shoot a commercial." Sort of. "What's going on back there?"

"Where to begin?" Ellie asks, before unleashing a torrential update. "Mom's spending our inheritance on new furniture, I puke every morning before I go to work at El-San which, I might add, is disgusting and the files are a mess and I'm having the office completely redone, *and...*"—she sniffles dramatically—"I need to talk to you about something."

Then, from somewhere, a sudden booming. Jake snorts and whines in his sleep. The bass boom fades, then returns loud, with Bob Seger rasping over the sound of a hefty engine. Nights of Hollywood indeed. When all sound cuts out, Jake wiggles alert and sits up, ears pricked, body shivering.

"Shit," I say, setting down the VMX and grabbing Jake's necktie with my free hand. "Jake, shush!"

"Are you listening?" Ellie's annoyed voice buzzes like a bee in the tiny hand piece.

"Call you back," I whisper, and tuck the phone in my pocket. I pet the dog's back in long strokes and he quiets, folding down to his elbows, but still attentive. Could this be the ill-spelling landowners? Have they seen me? Should I make my trespassing presence known? If I apologize, plead ignorance, would they shoot me anyway? Would that make *thar* day?

It's impossible to determine the location of the sound source; the overhanging rock above me blocks my view, but a vehicle door clanks open, followed by a hydraulic hum. "We came as soon as Patsy called," says a languid drawl. Ew. Donnie. "How is she?"

"Everything's as it should be." I recognize JC's calm, philosophical tone.

"There is a bit of business still." Willamette speaks with her Annie Oakley twang.

"I told you, Willie, I'm retired. Gonna be a full-time Dad, a solid member of society." JC is soft-spoken but firm.

"You can't quit on us now, sugar." Willamette again, and I swear chaw hits the dirt after she says it. "We just got our first order from the Angels. We're going big time."

My mind goes straight to Jerome and his fresh tat. Does she mean the Hells Angels?

"A man's only as good as his word," JC says. "I gave my word to my woman."

"And I gave my word to the Angels." The bells in her voice disappear; the twang grows sharp. "Who you think's gonna be more likely to forgive a broken promise?"

"Grandma! Don't be like that." That's Donnie now.

"You're right," Willamette says. "You boys wrangle the bed inside. We'll talk business later." Footsteps track across what sounds like gravel, then disappear.

"Sorry about Grandma," Donnie says.

"It's not your fault, Donnie," JC says. "But Star and I agreed."

"Between Patsy playing hard to get and Grandma and her damn Angels." Donnie chokes up. "I didn't mean to...I'm sorry." He blows his nose, a loud pachyderm honk.

At this, Jake convulses into full attack mode. Fangs exposed, ruff bristling, he hurtles onto the rock above, barking viciously.

"Oh my God!" Donnie yells.

"Down! Sit, good boy!" JC commands, but the insane barking continues.

I set down the VMX and pull myself up and over the overhang to see Jake springing on his hind legs at the Bronco's wheelchair platform while Donnie swats at him with a crowbar. I clap my hands. "Jake, get over here!"

Unbelievably, the dog stops barking, slinks in my direction and sits at my feet.

Shirtless under red overalls, Donnie stares at me, crowbar raised to strike. Something else I don't anticipate is this: Donnie casually pulls a gun from inside the bib of his overalls and points it at me. "Put that devil-dog between your legs and freeze or I'll shoot."

I grab Jake's necktie and slowly pull him between my legs. He growls quietly at the back of his throat; I hope he doesn't suddenly snap his gator jaws at me. *Yesterday the dog saved my life; today he gets me killed.*

JC, in a white linen tunic and flowing skirt, approaches from a flat rock slab. "There's no need for that, Donnie. We're all friends here." His voice is calming, almost hypnotic; his face is a neutral mask.

Donnie's grapefruit bicep bulges as he turns the gun to JC. "Stay out of it, Jayce. This isn't about you." The gun turns back on me. I swear Donnie's trigger finger twitches. "Have you been listening the entire time?"

"Listening? To what?" Cold sweat runs down the beginnings of a lavish white-boy sunburn on my shoulders, back and chest. "I was trying to catch the dog. He was trespassing."

Donnie looks at JC, then back to me. "Where'd you and Patsy disappear to last night?"

Now is when I'd like to become a human helicopter, kicking myself vertical into the air and hanging motionless in space, cameras circling me à la *Crouching Tiger, Hidden Dragon*. My legs would become the weapons of a lethal ballerina and I'd kick the gun from Donnie's hand, and as I fall back to the earth the gun spins in slow motion high into the air, then drops into my hands so I can point Donnie's own gun back at him. Circular, ironic, poetic.

This is not what happens. What does happen next happens so quickly I'm not even sure it's true.

JC is on the rock slab and then he's at the truck, although never do I see him anywhere in between. Softly, almost tenderly, he places one hand below Donnie's chin, thumb to throat.

Donnie slumps like a rag doll in the wheelchair and JC slips the gun from his hand.

Jake immediately relaxes and wriggles free from my grasp, then trots to the Bronco and lifts his leg on a four-foot-tall tire before racing into the brush.

I'm far away in one of those oddly peaceful molasses-like moments where you've just brushed up against your mortality and escaped it by a feather-stroke of luck, timing, circumstance, or, in my case, JC. "What did you do?" In my high, girly voice. "Is he dead?"

"Just resting," JC laughs. "Feel that little spot?" He moves his hand toward my throat and I instantly pull back.

JC laughs again, then puts his hand to his own throat. "Right here. It's called a hurt spot. There's a little dip above the Adam's apple where it's easy to close off the airway. Lack of oxygen causes a short blackout. A couple seconds is all you need."

I rub my hand across the front of my throat. "I was just hiking. I followed the dog," I babble. "I didn't mean to trespass. He could have killed me. You saved my life."

"No worries. Donnie couldn't shoot the side of a barn if it was sitting on his lap," JC assures me. "How about some lemonade? Fresh squeezed." He motions for me to follow him into a doorway cut right into a two-story boulder.

Not a place I really want to enter. Not with boss lady

Willamette inside. And Sleeping Beauty won't sleep forever. "Actually, I'll be on my way. I have work to do..." Which is true: my big pre-production plan has gone nowhere, my brainstorming session has produced zip.

A female voice calls from above. "How about some quiet around here? We're about to have a baby." Patsy's head pokes out from a window opening carved out of the rock. Her gaze grows steely when she sees me, and a wicked grin turns up the corners of her mouth. "Surprise, surprise. Nice hat, plumber. Sorry, I mean *Hollywood*."

Suddenly vulnerable in my shirtlessness, I unwrap my T-shirt from around my head and slip it back on. Before I can summon a snarky response, JC interrupts. "How is she?" He shades his eyes to look up at Patsy.

"Almost three centimeters. Could be hours, could be minutes. You bringing that bed up soon?"

JC hesitates. "Looks like we'll be having our baby on the old futon."

"Don't be foolish, JC." Donnie Van Winkle's awake and yawning, stretching. "This bed is for you and Star, no strings. We'll talk to Grandma and work it out. We always do." Donnie looks sheepishly at me. "I didn't mean to scare you. Everyone knows I'm a god-awful shot. I've got cynophobia." Off my confused look, he explains. "Irrational fear of dogs."

Patsy's voice ricochets against the rock wall. "It's cute you boys are making nice, but maybe you can bring that bed up before Starshine's vagina explodes?" She smiles at me sweetly. "Make yourself useful, Hollywood."

I check to see how Donnie reacts, but his expression doesn't change—he's either forgotten the last thing he wanted to know before JC gave him the TKO or he's behaving like a gentleman in front of the woman he loves. All I know is that if Patsy and I don't get naked again and finish what we started last night, I'm going to regret it for the rest of my life.

Moving that bed is no easy thing. JC and I dismantle it in the back of the truck and pile its various parts onto Donnie's lap. Donnie then wheels over to the porch, unloads, and returns to the Bronco for more. We work this way quickly, so as to get out of the heat, and it's a relief when we undertake the second half of delivery inside JC and Starshine's boulder home. Part cathedral, part bunker, and remarkably cool, the interior great room has one sheer rock wall that ends in a high ceiling with an opening that invites outdoor light. I note other architectural details as I lug the various frame, headboard and canopy parts from the porch, through the great room, down an arched corridor tucked under the stairs and into a detached wooden structure. Stacked rocks abut a wall lined with dark wood shelves, laden with a collection of books and bongs. A fireplace is cobbled from shiny white rocks veined with silver mica. Hooked rugs and low chairs and tables dot the space. Willamette, wearing an embroidered shirt with jeans and riding boots, squeezes lemons in a compact kitchen area. Stairs lead up to a second level loft. It's somehow rustic and luxurious. I wonder if they have indoor plumbing.

Finally, we're down to the mattress. Donnie rolls ahead, calling out directions as JC manages the front end and I bring up the rear. "A bed for my lady," JC says, as we flop the bulky load onto the fully-assembled frame in the center of the circular room.

"Groovy," Star says from where she lies soaking in a large copper tub. Its nickel lining reflects her flushed skin and her eyes close while Patsy holds a damp cloth to her forehead. A shaft of sunlight spotlights the tub under a window that frames crooked pines and majestic boulders. It's an arresting image; one that makes me smile.

Willamette hands mason jars of lemonade to the guys. "Good thing you showed up." She winks at me, crinkling one thin, drawn-on, fifties-style arched brow. "Thought I was gonna have to help the boys bring the durn thing in mahself."

I refrain from asking how they would have delivered the bed had I not shown up. I just thank her for the cool drink and observe as she pats Donnie's shoulder on her way to a rocking chair, then pulls a pile of knitting into her lap.

Surgical-looking instruments lie on a cloth set on a burled redwood table. A macramé hammock holds a pile of velvet cushions. Scented candles flicker. JC gulps down his lemonade, then spreads sheets and comforters on the bed.

I look up at the domed ceiling while swallowing the best lemonade I've ever had. "I like this space. Is it a—What's that word? Sounds like yogurt?"

"You're thinking of a yurt," Donnie says around ice cubes. "This is a geodesic dome." He maneuvers his chair between Patsy and me.

Starshine puffs out a long, hard exhale. "The circle of a dome is in harmony with the universe. The ceiling is triangles. Sacred equations of a sacred structure."

"It smells good, too." I must have sunstroke to be going on

like this…or is it because Patsy's here, and Donnie. And a pregnant woman in a bathtub. Total weirdness makes me chatty. "Like a temple."

"Krishna lives in the scent of Patchouli," Star says. "It's in my hair." She shakes her dreadlocks, which trail in the bathwater like henna'd kelp.

"It purifies the mind," JC adds, setting up a tripod in front of the tub.

"And the air." Patsy dips the cloth in a bowl of iced water. "You ever smell childbirth?"

"Finished!" Willamette ties off a bit of yarn with her teeth and holds up her handiwork: a pink blanket with the words "Buckaroo Angels" in blue on the borders and white wings in the center. "Just in time."

She can't mean Hells Angels, can she? Donnie looks sharply at his grandmother, who hums tunelessly while she tucks away her needles and yarn.

JC tightens the knee joints of the tripod legs, then unscrews the camera mount. "You brought Carson's camera, didn't you Pats?"

Patsy's shoulders sag. "I forgot to tell you. The camera store was closed this morning. There's still no lens." Then she gives me that look, just like the one right before Donnie recited chicken poetry over us. "You've always got your camera handy, don't you, Hollywood?"

This isn't about getting in Patsy's pants, I think to myself as I monkey down over the rocky ledge with just a few scrapes. *This is survival. If I shoot this for them, they'll have no reason to shoot me.* I swap out the memory sticks from my VMX and pull myself back up over the ledge. Donnie has followed me outside and does little wheelies with his chair in the dirt next to the Bronco. "Patsy tells me you're shooting a commercial out here."

"Yup." I wonder what else he's heard.

"Patsy hates Hollywood. Me, I don't mind it. Puts cash in the pocket." Donnie's soft drawl makes the hair on the back of my neck stand up. I try to keep cool as I head toward the cave, his eyes boring holes into my back. "How long are you planning to stay?"

I turn back to answer him. "Only as long as I have to."

He's really a handsome man when he smiles.

When I return to the dome, its atmosphere is charged, different. Willamette stands at a window, head bowed, praying. Patsy and JC have changed into saffron-colored, kimono-style robes and flank the tub, murmur comforting sounds while Star moans, "I can't, I can't, I'm too tired," between little animal cries.

"Hurry, Sander." JC wraps his arms around Star from behind and nuzzles her neck. "She's waiting for you."

My hands shake as I screw the VMX onto the tripod mount and I'm a little dizzy as I set the frame, but once I remove the cap and get behind the lens, I'm okay. Star squats like a Sumo, nude and voluptuous, flush with excitement and fear, dreadlocks a burning bush around her head. Patsy spoons broth between Star's parched lips. Compositionally, it's a Rembrandt, but instead of vignetting to darkness around the edges of the image, there's a pervasive light. "Ready when you are."

JC dips a tiny spoon into a purple velvet pouch, fills it with a dark powder, then holds it under Star's nose. "Now!"

Star inhales deeply, then violently sneezes. The water at her feet swirls with pink blooms. A mucky bundle rushes smoothly from between her legs, followed by what looks like a plastic bag filled with raw beef liver smothered in raspberry jam.

"It's a girl!" Patsy turns to the camera with both thumbs up.

As I return the gesture, the image in the frame multiplies, becoming a kaleidoscope of blood and flesh, shit and child. Suddenly, everything goes black.

10

MONDAY AFTERNOON

Donnie London hunches over the steering wheel of his Bronco, hands at ten and two, keeping well below the speed limit. His pet poultry, Little, sits on my lap, her head cocked, one flat, black eye assessing her temporary roost.

"I appreciate you giving me a ride," I say. Little stands up when I speak and sits again when I stop. "Why does she do that?" I ask, causing the chicken to stand and sit again.

"She's analyzing your vibrations," Donnie says, carefully checking his mirrors even though we've been the only vehicle on the road since we've turned onto it from JC's trail. "She knows if you're telling the truth or lying."

"You mean like Santa?" Stand, sit.

He laughs. "She's my polygraph."

A jackrabbit bounds in front of us, then stops, paralyzed in the middle of the road. "Holy Moses!" Donnie yells, braking hard to avoid hitting it. The truck bounces on its tractor tires, my head slams the roof of the cab, and Little becomes a crazed ball of fluttering wings. I instinctively hold my camera bag in place with my feet to keep it from jostling around.

"Sorry about that," Donnie says. The jackrabbit saunters to the shoulder before arcing into a stand of Joshuas. "You okay?"

Sure, if you don't count having your gun pointed at my head, fainting during Star's delivery, having severe hots for a girl who won't talk to me because I'm not a plumber (even though I am), and somehow managing to avoid all the work I've been planning to do for the shoot which I'm only pretending is going to change my life when really, what is it going to change? I rub my whiplashed, sunburned neck. "I'll be better when I'm back in civilization," I tell him, snorting when I realize I'm referring to the Shitkicker Saloon. Little's too flustered to do her stand-up/sit-down routine.

"Give me a minute here." The Bronco veers off the main road into a wash of white sand, where, after a few feet, we're suddenly in the crotch of a ravine. Donnie kills the engine and takes a deep breath.

"Why are we stopping?" Looks like a place where a dead body could go unfound for a long time. Little stands again, and doesn't sit down.

Donnie points up to a boulder, where a statue of a torso is mounted on a pedestal. "I always visit on Mondays. Do me a favor?" He pulls a bouquet of plastic-wrapped supermarket flowers from behind his chair and hands them to me. "Go switch out the dead ones?"

"Who's up there?"

"My brother." Donnie's voice goes quiet. "Died when we were in high school after a bunch of Marines snuck us beers at the Kicker all night. Lonnie lost control of our truck when a coyote ran across the road in front of us. We rolled and rolled and landed right here, where we are now."

"Wow. I'm sorry." I touch the bird on the head with my finger; she clucks and sits.

"Lonnie walked away from the mess, but my back cracked in half. He was so tore up, he shot himself in the stomach with a shotgun." Donnie hands me a plastic jug of water and I let him take the chicken from my lap. "I think she likes you," he says.

APOLLO LONDON "Fly, Freebird, Fly" is engraved on the pedestal. The statue looks exactly like Donnie—same classic features, strong jaw, mullet haircut—except for a pair of angel wings that sprout from the back shoulders of his jean jacket. I think about Dad as I dump the old flowers from the coffee can, fill it with water and put in the new ones. I know Donnie's depth of guilt, to feel responsible for yet survive a family member's death. And it sucks.

When I climb back in the truck, Donnie is blowing his nose. "May I show you something? In a man-to-man fashion?" He pats the bib pocket of his overalls.

"As long as it's not your gun."

He chuckles, raising his right hand. "I promise not to shoot you. I just get crazy when I'm stressed. I wave my gun around and never hit a thing. Ask anyone. Ask the Angels."

"The Angels?" I play dumb; as far as he knows, I know nothing about the Hells Angels and their deal with Willie.

"The Buckaroo Angels. Grandma's church group." His hand shakes as he places a small blue velvet box on the console between us. "Go ahead. Open it."

Inside the box is a gold band with a heart-shaped diamond encrusted with smaller red stones. "Aw, you shouldn't have. We just met."

The chicken squawks and flaps from her perch on the dashboard.

Donnie's mouth corners are upturned and smiling, but his eyes are unreadable black stones. "I don't know much about what women want, but you're from the city—you might. Patsy's turning the big three-oh on Wednesday. You think she'll like it?"

"This is a wedding ring," I inform him. In case he wasn't aware.

He nods and straightens his overall straps. "She needs to get hitched before she gets too old. Now you know why I'm stressed."

I'm not sure what he wants me to say. "Looks expensive."

"You flatlanders always think because we live back here we don't know how to make money. I make plenty of money. With car parts and golf balls." His voice cracks on the word "balls" like he's going to start crying again. He closes his eyes for a second, and when he opens them again, there is a fire in them I haven't seen before. *"I have eaten the plums that were in the icebox and which you were probably saving for breakfast. Forgive me, they were delicious, so sweet and so cold. W.C.W."*

"Of course." *How the hell does he make money with golf balls?* I close the box and hand it back to Donnie. "It's a beautiful ring and Patsy's a great girl."

Donnie tucks away the box and the chicken jumps back onto my lap. "You have fun at the wedding last night?"

I wish Donnie would start up the engine. "It was great." The chicken stands and sits.

"You didn't stay very long." Donnie looks straight ahead, one hand resting at the top of the steering wheel.

Is he testing me? What does he know about Patsy and me at Yellow Flats? There's only one way for me to answer. I stare the chicken down, daring her to give me away, and place my finger on the top of her head in case she tries to stand up. "Yeah, I turned in early. Got a lot of work to do for this shoot." The chicken doesn't move.

"In case you were wondering, my pecker works." Donnie's face doesn't change as he revs the engine. "And it's huge." He reverses the Bronco all the way back to Buckaroo Highway and we drive the rest of the way in silence.

In the dim coolness of the Shitkicker Saloon, Paul Street, his back to the front door, leans forward on the wood plank bar. Paul looks the part of wealthy ease in a white linen shirt and pants with a salmon-colored sweater tied around his shoulders. Okay, *gay* wealthy ease. On the other side, Harry Apple leans backward, both elbows on the counter. Carson sits cross-legged on the counter itself, remote control in hand. No one hears me enter and I stand quietly, watching the love story footage from the wedding party on the monitor mounted up on the wall.

On the screen, Harry, in his mayoral sash and white cowboy suit, straddles a chair front to back, and speaks directly to the camera. "First time I ever kissed Coreen—may she R-I-P—we were out behind the bowling alley after the Roadrunners, my team, scored a tournament trophy." Harry's a born actor, turning it on for the camera big-time. "My lips were shaking, I swear, and I steered her toward 'em like I was learning how to drive. I'da missed Coreen's mouth completely if it wasn't she was smilin'. Coyotes started hollerin' right when our lips smacked together. Every time we kissed since then, coyotes like to be callin' out our sweetheart song."

"Wow, Grandpop," Carson says dreamily. "Every time you kissed."

"Pause," Paul Street commands.

Carson snaps the remote and the image stops on an extreme close-up of Harry, one of my favorite shots from that segment. His eyes shine with tears. A silver curl droops down over his forehead. His blistery hands float in the air, as though Coreen's face were right there.

"Damn, I'm a good-looking man," Harry laughs, running his hand through his hair. He wears a brown T-shirt with the Shitkicker's boot logo on the front.

"Not only that, but this is great composition," Paul says. "You can see some of the photos on the wall behind the stage for ambience, but right there, see how the light from that table creates a warm spot just over his shoulder? It's like there's a little spirit there, looking down."

"Thanks for the critique," I crack.

Carson spins on her butt, keeping her legs crossed. "I was showing the love stories to Grandpop then Paul Street came and says you and me have a good eye and make a spec-tac-u-lar team." Rhinestones on her T-shirt spell out FUTURE DIRECTOR.

"One good eye between us," I say. "Not bad."

"Really, Sandy. That footage was nicely executed. How are you bearing up? You ready to get to work?" He claps me on the back.

"Careful." His handprint sears into my sunburn and I sink onto a barstool, ravenous, shaky. Being called Sandy isn't the worse thing that's happened to me today. "I'm barbecued and starving, but I'm ready." For better or worse, I decide to keep this morning's escapade to myself and just get on with the business of the commercial.

"You probably know all this if you read the trades or the tabloids, but here's the official story." Paul Street hands a CD to Carson, who slips it into the player.

"I'll go rustle up some grub," Harry says. "Carson, go find that sunburn cream." He disappears into the kitchen as Carson bounds away, slapping her thigh like she's riding a pony.

Paul Street clicks the remote; glossy red lips appear on the monitor. "Ten years ago, Destinée's post-Mickey Mouse Club mouth launched a billion-dollar TV, film and record franchise." The camera pans downward from Destinée's kisser, matching the descending violins note for note. Faint blue neck veins lead to glitter-powdered cleavage bursting over a red patent leather corset. Alabaster arms end at leather-thong laced fingertips, resting in the V of her crotch. Down fishnet stockings ripped at the knees. Freeze on red-tipped toes. Above the over-produced smorgasbord of every musical trick that might have been hip for a minute, Destinée's trademark singsong voice whines, "In my mouth, we are oooonnnnneeee." Paul Street harmonizes with a respectable baritone.

The onscreen horror continues to a disco beat. Destinée is shackled to a bed, lip-synching in an 18th Century boudoir, surrounded by tapestries, costumed courtesans and a unicorn. Cut away to a castle in the center of a hedgerow labyrinth. Silver clouds smear across a dying sun. A moist, mushroomy field becomes an undulating tongue beneath a wagging uvula chandelier. Zoom out to include stalactites and stalagmites of teeth at the top and bottom of the frame, then zoom out more as Destinée's big lips close, forming a glossy labial sofa. On the last note, Destinée's original pout becomes a dazzling smile, and she giggles girlishly.

"It's garbage," I blurt.

"Maybe so, but that garbage was in solid rotation for eight months, pushed Destinée's single triple-platinum and launched her film career," Paul reports.

"Art vs. the bottom line," I mutter.

Carson returns with some bacon and eggs. "Hope you're hungry, Sander. And here." She slaps a tube on the bar. "Put this on. You won't even peel."

I mumble appreciation and dive into the plate.

Paul squirts schmear from the tube. "Shirt off, Sandy. Spit-spot." He rubs his hands together. "Her film debut was the fourth remake of *A Star is Born*."

"Which was a capital-D dog," I say. I hesitate, then pull my T-shirt over my head and return to my plate, wincing as he rubs the cool goo on my shoulders. "Didn't she have a nervous breakdown after that?"

"If by 'nervous breakdown,'"—he makes gooey air quotes— "you mean a lackluster tour marked by spotty attendance and self-medication to promote an album that no one bought and the critics deemed, quote, a complete lack of creative and musical insight, unquote, then yes."

"I don't remember the album," I say.

"No one does. It was a stinker. The record company dumped her and she started a hate website about them. Enter Vana LeValle. Her motto: every scandal is an opportunity."

Of course. Vana's stock really rose when it was rumored her

own husband Georges was murdered by Vana's lover; she made a handful of deals after that. "Ah. An optimist."

"You might say that." Paul smiles. "Vana convinces Destinée she's the one to get her on the comeback trail, the Western Burger deal is conceived, hotshot Oggie Bright is hired to direct the commercial, the Buckaroo location is set. All goes according to plan until..."

Carson, who's been quiet till now, finishes Paul's sentence. "Oggie hated the script so much he decided he would do something better and filmed himself and an extra doing the nasty in the motel! In Sander's room." She rolls her eyes. "Gross. Her name was Powder or Ember or something like that."

"How do you know all this?" Paul asks Carson, then his hands grip my shoulders. "How does she know?"

"I don't know." My stomach does a somersault. "Was her name Ashe?"

"That's it!" Carson says. "And I read about it on Destinée's website, that's how I know."

I set down my fork and push my plate away. *Ashe* was in the motel footage?

"Destinée has a website? Why would she write that on her website?" Paul unties and reties the sweater around his neck. "Anyway, now we're caught up. I spoke to Vana this morning. This is the last week Destinée can shoot before her Japan tour. If it doesn't happen now, it won't happen. Period. The deadline to wrap this commercial is in three days."

A new surge of sweat. "Three days? Why didn't you tell me?"

"I left you that message yesterday. Apparently, someone

doesn't check his cell phone much." Paul swats at the back of my head.

Shit! I talked to Ellie this morning and never even looked. I check my phone now, but the battery is officially dead. Three days! The words "I quit" are starting to sound pretty good.

Harry comes out from the kitchen. "Is it the exact same shoot as last time?"

Paul karate-chops my spine. "Exact same shoot. Piece of cake. Sander just needs to get in, do the deed, and get out. Vana emailed you everything, right?"

"Yup." A flurry of emails waits unopened in my inbox. If it weren't for stopping for Jake in the road, going to the wedding, getting shanghaied to Yellow Flats by Patsy, hiking into the hills, filming the baby, and stopping by Donnie's grave, I'd have read them all by now. Instead of grabbing the brass ring, I've just been running around in circles.

"You're gonna love shooting up here." Harry leans forward with both elbows on the bar. "Buckaroo's got everything Hollywood's got, only better landscape, cleaner air and bigger sky. Crew chows at the Saloon and shacks up at the motel. We got RV hook-ups for the trailers."

"Breakfast at seven tomorrow?" Paul asks.

"Roger that," Harry confirms. "And Willamette does costumes out of the Soundstage. Buckaroo's gonna make your job easy."

The big front door slams open and Patsy bursts in. "It's official and it's a girl." She smiles, eyebrows high, at Paul Street giving me a massage. "JC and Star said to say thanks again, Hollywood."

"No problem. That's good, Paul." I jerk away, quickly pulling on my T-shirt. I can't look Donnie's beloved in the eye for fear she'll suddenly know what I know—that Donnie's going to propose to her in two days.

Paul Street wipes his hands on a napkin before offering one

to Patsy. "Paul Street, ma'am." He delivers the line like the humble, handsome cowpoke he's played a million times. He's a real pro.

Patsy's no slouch either; she slices him like flank steak with a glance and a fake but dazzling smile. "How do."

Harry purses his lips and stares down into his coffee.

Seeing Patsy and Harry in such close proximity, the unspoken words between them become obvious. There's no greeting. No eye contact. No direct conversation. Father and daughter share the same angled cheekbones; both are flush with the efforts of ignoring each other.

"Carson, honey, you want to see the new baby girl before the town meeting?" Patsy asks brightly.

"Yay!" Carson cheers. "Can Sander come?"

"No," Patsy and I say in unison. We do occasionally agree.

"Some other time," I add.

"Okay. Bye Grandpop, bye Paul Street." Carson hugs Harry around the neck, blows movie-star kisses to me and Paul, then hops over the counter and gallops out the door.

"You should come to our meeting, Hollywood," Patsy says, looking sideways at me.

"I have a lot of work to do." Like opening all those documents and reading them.

"Your work is what's on the agenda." She waggles her fingers and sways out the door.

"Ouch," Paul Street says. "There goes a case of sharpus stickus behindus."

"Actually, you *should* go to the meeting." Harry's eyes change from gray to blue as he stares at the stark desert-scape outside. "And that stick is a terminal case."

The three of us brood quietly until Paul breaks the silence. "How's your mother, Sander?"

He doesn't need to know we haven't spoken since she kicked me and my inheritance to the curb. I wonder if Ellie told Mom I'm here. If Mom would be excited for me. Or would she just want me to hurry home to help Ellie as she flounders at El-San? "I think I'll try giving her a call."

"Good idea. And I'll check in, if you don't mind, Harry." Paul Street slides a cardboard box my way. "You might find this interesting when you have a free moment. It's not pertinent to the shoot, so not to worry."

The old red phone box has been baking in the sun all day, and when I step into it and pull the door closed, I am instantly drenched in sweat. Or is it just because I'm calling home?

My hand is wet around the cumbersome plastic receiver. Not talking to Mom is stupid. I dial her number. As her line rings, a wave of exhaustion overcomes me. There's an emotional wrenching somewhere, too, near my lungs. Whatever anyone says about Donnie being a lousy shot, I could have died today, and if I did, who would miss me?

"Hello?" Mom says. Her voice sounds cracked and tired, as though she's been crying.

For some reason I'm not proud of, I hang up.

11

MONDAY FIVE O'CLOCK

There's something about this high desert shower that leaves me feeling purified and optimistic. For example, here I am, starkers in Room Three, the very room where Oggie made a sex film with Ashe, and *I don't care!* If anything, it underscores the fact that she wasn't The One. And I'm *glad* about it. Maybe it's the water pressure. Maybe it's the minerals in the water. Or maybe I've finally adjusted to the altitude, which Carson says is 3,800 feet. Then again, maybe it's the image of Patsy from yesterday morning before I went and told her I was a director. I just downloaded it from my VMX and made it my screensaver. In the contrasty portrait, one side of her face is in shadow, the other vignettes into a coronal sunburst. Strands of hair float across her forehead, and her eyes somehow look into my soul. God, I sound lame.

This is me, naked in the mirror, which unfortunately works the same way here as mirrors work on the flatlands. I look exactly like myself except for the jagged Z scab on the bridge of my nose. But my life seems as distant, as different, from my own as it's ever been, and that makes me smile. I swipe my comb through my hair the opposite way from my usual direction, left to right, leaving me slightly off balance. Some tufts of hair stand up straight, balking at the unfamiliar direction; others kink in previously unknown cowlicks. My synapses have to snap harder to recognize myself. I could be anyone I want.

* * *

A dividing wall down the middle of the Buckaroo Bowl separates the old-time bowling alley on the right from the café on the left. On the alley side, six lanes run below Western movie posters from the forties. Seating for the players is fashioned from barrels and wagon wheels. On the entire far left wall of the café side is a sepia cartoon mural. A cowgirl resembling Rosalind Russell with gold hoop earrings and a heart-shaped bottom pours coffee into the tin cup of a cowpoke whose flap ears and red nose bring to mind Clark Gable. A shiny zinc counter runs the length of the mural, with scattered tables and a wall of red leather booths opposite. A neon-lit Rockola jukebox holds court over a small dance floor, now lined with rows of folding chairs for the town meeting.

I settle into a booth by the door to watch the café fill up. Some working cowboys trail the aromas of horse and sweat, gabbing with a clutch of artists wearing brightly-colored ponchos. The Roto-Rooter guy who wore the Indian headdress enters with a wild-haired child, his or her fat cheeks smeared with food. Still shirtless in red overalls, Donnie's in his wheelchair at a booth toward the back. Little observes the proceedings from Donnie's lap and a clot of teenage girls gather in the booth around them. No sign of Patsy. I wonder what's so important about this meeting she had to invite me. Harry leans at the counter, where a laminated flyer reads "Reserve a bite of heaven right now! Buckaroo Angels Annual Brownie Sale – See our booth at Hogs for Dogs October 13." Donnie's grandma Willamette, her dramatic face makeup emphasizing arched brows and red lips, leans behind the counter, her eyes glued to a large, fancy boob tube near the ceiling showing *Walker, Texas Ranger*. An oddball group in an oddball town.

"It's about time, ain't it Willie?" Harry asks at the last commercial break.

Willie picks up a school bell and clangs it loudly. "Town meetin' in two minutes," she trills. "Sooner we get it done, sooner Happy Hour begins."

I don't know whether I'm emboldened by the new part in my hair or just inspired by having the VMX at hand, but I suddenly have a creative urge. I suppose a vague movie idea is swirling around the back of my brain, but if I try to pinpoint it too soon, I know I'll lose it. I thread my way over to Harry. "Is it all right if I tape this?"

Walker, Texas Ranger's theme music swells and the end credits roll. "No skin off my nose," Harry shrugs. "What do you think, Willie? If Sander films."

The SRO room quiets as Willie snaps off the TV and takes her place next to Harry. "Whatcha gonna do with the footage?" she asks lightly. She cuts her eyes at Donnie, who quickly turns his head. He's been watching us. She turns back to me with suspicious eyes and a big smile—a disconcerting combination that makes me wonder if she and JC have managed to work out their "unfinished business."

I ignore the flashing yellow hazard lights. "Nothing," I shrug. "I just want to get the feel of my camera. If it's any good, I'll give it to you. Maybe you could use it for something."

Willamette snorts, organizing a row of ketchup bottles that don't need organizing. "What would we ever use it for?"

"You never know," Harry slaps his hand on the counter. "Make an announcement first."

"All right then." Willie scans the room, waving and blowing kisses. But when she flips open a steno notepad, she's all business. "Town meetin' will come to order. Before we start, I should mention this meeting is being taped. Anyone have a problem with that?"

Harry pats my shoulder. "Sander, wave so everyone knows who you are."

I oblige.

"We gonna be in the movies?" someone asks. "I gotta call my agent."

"I'm just trying to figure out how to work this thing," I say. "No plans for it." Yet.

"Don't forget to take off the lens cap," someone calls out.

I join in the general laughter. "It'll be just for my own personal use. Like a scrapbook."

A couple of men hold dusty jean jackets over their faces and slip out the back.

"Anyone else shy?" Harry asks, taking stock. "Okay, Sander, I guess that's a thumbs up."

I wave a thanks and head back to my seat as Harry clears his throat and begins. "First order of business is the speed limit on Mane Street."

Paul Street slips quietly into the booth next to me. "I miss anything?"

"No," I mouth, but his presence instantly annoys me. I wish he was sitting somewhere else. I feel out the scene through the lens, searching out faces and expressions among the crowd.

Harry continues. "The committee selected a design. Lulu, you have something to show us?" One of the poncho-wearing artists joins Harry at the bar and unrolls a poster that reads "5 – The Only Speed in Town."

"It'd be better if you set up over by the jukebox," Paul Street whispers. "You'll have a nice wide angle and you won't have that tennis-match back and forthing."

I look down my nose at him.

He shrugs. "I like your new hairstyle." He tips his ever-present Evian to his lips.

The big double doors creak open and Patsy enters. I swivel in her direction, inescapably drawn. But I have to twist all the way back to catch Donnie's reaction to her grand entrance. I pan to the opposite end of the booths as casually as possible, as though I'm taking my time, filming everyone in the room. Damn! Paul was right...if I were over in the corner, I would have caught the whole thing in wide-angle with a great depth of field composition. Too late for that now, but I do manage to film two sublime segments: 1) Donnie waving to Patsy and motioning for her to sit next to him, and 2) Patsy ignoring him and bee-lining to the back wall. Though her mom looks neither right nor left, Carson sees me and waves, breaking the fourth wall right off the bat.

While Harry and Lulu discuss the properties of oil and acrylic on wood in extreme weather, I relocate over by the Rockola. Paul exaggeratedly tiptoes behind me, simultaneously deflecting and attracting attention. When Lulu rolls up the poster and returns to her seat, Willie rings the bell again. "Next order of business: Hogs for Dogs."

Harry smiles at this. "I think everyone pretty much knows Buckaroo is launching the Angels' annual event this weekend.

There'll be a couple hundred bikers here starting Friday, with the usual booths, contests and fun. All proceeds will be donated to orphan dogs." As though on cue, there's a series of loud barks outside. Someone pushes the big door open to see what's causing the commotion, and Jake streaks in, greeting each table and booth like a regular politician. "Looks like our poster boy's come to thump his tub," Harry says.

"Buckaroo Angels will be selling brownies, as usual." Willie waves a flyer above her head. "Reserve your batch now."

"Mmm, love the Angels' brownies," Harry continues, their patter well-oiled and comfortable. "We'll kick off with a pancake breakfast at the Shitkicker on Friday morning, followed by a brand-new Dust Drama performed by our very own Gunslingers at high noon. Final Gunslingers rehearsal is..." He turns to Willamette for confirmation.

"Wednesday afternoon. Don't be tardy, or we'll shoot ya." With her trademark wink.

Harry nods to Willie and she rings the bell again. "That's all I got. Anyone else? Going once, going twice..."

Donnie's hand shoots up from the back of the room and Willamette grants him the floor. "Yes, Donnie-kins?"

"Grandma, not in public," Donnie complains to the crowd's good-natured laughter. "Today's Little's birthday, so please stop by for a piece of cake. It's homemade." He gestures to a large metal pan.

"I'll bet it's finger-lickin' good!" a voice from the crowd calls out.

"Not funny, Carl," Donnie says.

Willie rings her bell again. "Donnie, we all know you love that bird like it was your own child. That said, are we about done? Going once, going twice..."

"I've got something to say, Willie." Patsy steps forward, turns toward my camera, and pulls up her faded sweatshirt. The sunlight streaming in from the front window bathes her in a natural golden glow as she pulls the sweatshirt past her chin and shakes out her hair. The sun catches her highlights and blows out her skin. She could be in a Head & Shoulders shampoo commercial. A wolf whistle from somewhere indicates I'm not the only one appreciating the view. Until I focus on the slogan printed across the front of her T-shirt: HELL NO TO HOLLYWOOD! "I'd like to read from this list of incidents since last month's meeting," she says, still playing to the camera, and, by extension, to me.

Harry throws his hands into the air. "Not again."

Patsy reads from a fistful of papers. "Public drunkenness and vomiting."

She tosses the page into the air as a guy in the audience stands and removes his plaid flannel shirt, revealing an identical "HELL NO TO HOLLYWOOD!" T-shirt, this one with "Citizens for a Better Buckaroo" across the back.

"A Jeep tipped into the wash," Patsy reads, throwing a second page into the air, as another citizen stands and removes a jean jacket, revealing another black T-shirt.

"Two Joshua trees knocked down." More page throwing, more shirts removed, now accompanied by booing from the black-shirted citizens. "A broken window at the Saloon; y'all saw the new sheet-glass we just installed—it cost fifteen hundred dollars."

"Theatrical flair, n'est-ce pas?" Paul Street intones at my shoulder. "Nice rack, too."

Patsy continues, ardent and eloquent. "Bright lights and

noise during night shoots on two consecutive weekday nights. And, my personal favorite: They burned down our *fire station*." The entire sheaf of papers flies into the air and nearly everyone in the place jumps to their feet to join in with the booing.

"Not on purpose!" Harry waves his arms.

Willie has to clang the bell four or five times before relative calm is restored.

Patsy's voice is quiet now. "All I'm saying, Willie, is let Hollywood burn itself down. We love our home."

Carson slinks onto the seat next to me and claps her hands over her eyes. "I hate her, I hate her, I hate her, I hate her," she whispers.

"Don't worry kiddo." Paul Street rubs Carson's shoulders. "It'll be fine."

"She'll ruin everything, wait and see," Carson moans softly.

I'm with Carson. The thought of Patsy as the anti-Hollywood ringleader makes my gut ache. Not only because she strikes me as a worthy opponent, but because I want to impress her, which I apparently did as a plumber but now don't as a director. Though she didn't seem to mind when my camera was available to film her friends' childbirth.

"Harry, you have ninety seconds to respond." Willie rings her bell.

The room vibrates with anticipation. With a touch of the evangelical, Harry raises his hands and addresses the room. "Buckaroo was built by Hollywood for Hollywood. Don't tell me when the crews come to the Shitkicker, profits don't peak and tips don't triple. Last time a car commercial shot here, small businesses in the basin showed a minimum 25% increase in sales of goods and services. A working relationship with the filmmaking industry is in the Buckaroo town charter. It's part of our Constitution."

"The charter needs to be updated, Willie!" Patsy flings her arms wide. She obviously inherited Harry's knack for public speaking.

Harry twirls away from Patsy. "Willie, charter revisions can only be initiated by a town official."

But Patsy is on fire. "I have been registering complaints at these meetings for six months and no one ever listens. We need ground rules, a simple permit system, to protect Buckaroo. We're tired of playing games. From now on, the Citizens for a Better Buckaroo will interfere with all future Hollywood productions until our demands are met."

"Shit!" I say out loud.

"I told you," Carson says under her breath.

Willie rings her bell. "Who said that?"

All eyes turn to me and Paul Street, the formerly invisible outsiders.

"Stand up, speak," Paul Street pats my arm.

"May I, we, be recognized here?" My body temperature rises and I turn twelve shades of red as my new, bold self disappears and my old self returns. I set the VMX aside, stand and stutter, "Please, if that's legal for a non-resident...?"

"Speak your piece, honey. Some of us are getting old," Willie says.

Paul covers his mouth with his hand.

My throat is dry, my lips chapped. Paul hands me his bottle of water, but I just look at it, alien in my hand.

Paul Street steps up to the plate, his infomercial voice deep and lubricated, poise unshakeable, shoulders square. "My name is Paul Street. I'm the executive producer on this project and I think what my director Sander's trying to say is he's just a simple filmmaker." Paul is channeling Jimmy Stewart's homespun, apple-pie approach as Jefferson Smith in *Mr. Smith Goes to Washington.* "A creator of stories, a dreamer of dreams."

Dreamer of dreams?

But Paul's on a roll. "And to be able to shoot here, in this special place, we're both moved by its beauty and touched by the heritage of cinema that's so obvious in every plank of this town. And didn't he film all your love stories at the wedding?" The crowd murmurs assent while Paul takes his water bottle from my hand and sips at it, turning attention back on idiot boy me, *dreamer of dreams.* I just wave like the Queen of England, sweating burrito-sized bullets and letting Paul Street do all the lifting. I guiltily wonder if anyone thinks we're a couple.

Paul flings his pink sweater from his shoulders to the back of a nearby chair and strides to the center of the room, a move he's probably done thousands of times on his infomercials. "Sander's not concerned with taking sides in local politics. He just wants to do his job for the next three days. I personally promise that Sander will leave everything just the way he found it and when he's through, he'll remove every trace, every nail, every sequin, of our little production from your town before he's gone. You won't even know we've been here. In fact," he glows with inspiration, "I'd like to invite everyone to the rehearsal tomorrow morning, to watch a fine director at work and to make sure we don't break any safety or nature or any other kind of rules. Thank you." Paul returns to his seat and sits, gesturing for me to do the same.

"That's downright neighborly." Harry steps in, resuming control of his meeting. "I hope y'all accept the invite."

"Our group certainly will," Patsy says, "and we still want to discuss charter revisions."

Paul Street whispers to me. "This place is something, isn't it?"

I decide to postpone my complaint for the "dreamer of dreams" tag. "A big red box of animal crackers," I whisper back, but I'm only half-listening.

"Charter revisions can only be initiated by a town official," Harry says. "And that's me. And it's not on today's agenda. Case closed."

"Thanks for stepping up back there," I tell Paul. "My mouth wouldn't work."

"Dear Sandy," Paul Street shakes my shoulder. "The talents, skills, even vocabulary, previously at your disposal may not be available to you right now. You're grieving and healing, and that takes time."

Grieving? Healing? How can he tell?

"Big day tomorrow." Paul empties his Evian, re-ties his sweater over his shoulders and prepares to leave. "I'm going back to the motel to rest. Shall we meet in an hour? Work through dinner? Or do you prefer to prepare alone?"

I should rest too. Review schedules, the shot list. The weight of this project suddenly hits me like bricks. If I screw this up, I have to start my life from scratch. I'm under-prepared, terrified and distracted by Buckaroo. My thoughts are interrupted by a yell from Patsy from the middle of the room. "It's time for a change!" *Shoot! What'd I miss?*

Willie rings her bell again. "I'm warning you, Pats."

"I think alone is better for me," I tell Paul. "I'll head back in a bit." And I'm engrossed in the town meeting again before Paul Street is out the door.

Harry seems to be half-enjoying the debate—at least he's engaged with his daughter, even if it is an argument through a third party. "Elections aren't until next year."

"Why don't you run for mayor, Patsy? I'll vote for you," one of her black-shirted citizens calls into the fray.

"And be just like him? No way!" Patsy's breathing hard, her cheeks flushed, shoulders heaving. "What we need right now is for our mayor to be impeached!" She spins on her heel and retreats to her spot against the big double doors. A collective wince passes through the crowd. Harry's face becomes an emotionless mask and it makes my stomach ache to see it. Dad and I didn't communicate well either, but most of our confrontations happened at home with Mom playing monkey in the middle.

Willie clangs the bell three times. "Order in my meeting! Firstly, you two need to give it a rest. Secondly, you need to follow specific rules before you start throwing big words like impeachment around."

Patsy shrinks a bit under Willie's glare, but then pulls it together and glares back. "We have to preserve our heritage before we have nothing left to preserve. And I'm appalled that our current mayor doesn't find it necessary to do so."

The room erupts in wild chatter until Willie clangs the bell again. "Order! Order! This meeting is adjourned."

Patsy spins on her heel to make a grand exit. "Carson Jean! Where are you?"

Carson, who's been curled up in a fetal ball of twelve-year-old humiliation, explodes from her chair, dashes to her mother and punches her in the arm before hurtling out the door. Patsy's face clouds and she stomps after her, calling her daughter's name a few more times for good measure.

Harry resumes his role. "To be continued," he says softly, almost to himself. Then to the room at large, "Let Happy Hour begin!" The crowd mumbles and chatters as Harry straps on his guitar, strums a few chords, and sings:

> I know a place, called Buckaroo,
> It'll bring you up, anytime you're blue.
> Yes I know a place, let me tell you how to get there.

Happy Hour at Buckaroo Bowl turns into quite the scene. The counter is packed and the buzz about the town meeting increases the decibel level exponentially, so I take myself on a tour of the alley side. Along the dividing wall is a row of old sepia prints: Roy Rogers throwing the first ball down the alley in 1947, with Dale smiling behind him. Cowboys on horseback lined up at the bar at the Red Dog Saloon. *Cisco Kid* stars Duncan Renaldo and Leo Carillo on ponies in front of a stand of Joshua trees. A still from the set of the *Judge Roy Bean* series. Unit photography of a day's television work, with the boom mike hanging above the set, black cables snaked about the dusty street. Next come the brash Technicolor images of the motion picture lobby cards: *Tumblin' Tumbleweeds, Hostile Country, Overland to Deadwood*. And then some publicity stills of musicians performing at what looks like the Shitkicker Saloon. The first one's a doozy. "The Apple Corps. Family Singers on Stage at Harry's Saloon," with the caption: "Harry, Coreen and Little Patsy sing their hearts out for y'all." A much-younger Harry, his pompadour black as vinyl, strums a guitar and sings with his foot on an upside-down bucket. The pretty woman with the bouffant hairdo, dimples and the rhinestoned denim shirt next to Harry must be his wife Coreen. That makes the kid perched on the bucket in cuffed-up jeans with her hands around her mouth like a megaphone none other than Little Patsy. "Wow," I say to myself.

"You like my ma, don't you?" Carson's voice comes from behind a barrel.

"Of course I do. She's a likable person." I slump down on the bench next to her. "Are you all right?"

Carson shrugs, jamming her hands in her pockets and pointing one scuffed, cowboy-booted toe into each corner of a square of linoleum, then another. "I don't hate her all the time. Just when she's like that." She points her toes on the corners of the square again, before telling me her mom's birthday is in two days. "I want to get her a present, but I don't know what. What do you think she'd like?"

"You know her better than I do. What do you think?"

"I think she'd like to leave here and never come back," Carson says, uncannily echoing her mother's flirting words. "I could buy her a ticket somewhere. I've been saving for a tripod."

That kills me. "Why don't you make something? Like what you made for JC and Star?"

She looks at me like I'm retarded. "Hell-ooo? My lens is broken."

"I have an idea. If you'll be my assistant on Destinée's commercial, then I'll let you use my camera until I can replace your lens."

"All right!" She raises both fists into the air, runs down a lane all the way to the pins and then back, breathless. "What'll I film?"

There's a question I could spend the rest of my life trying to answer. "Whatever you think is amazing."

She answers without hesitation. "I want to make a documentary on everyone who lives here, so Buckaroo history will live forever."

"Like an archive? That's a great idea. Maybe you can make the first documentary and dedicate it to her."

Carson beams; her wheels are already turning. "Thanks, Sander. Now I just have to figure out where to start."

"How about here." I point to the photo of the Apple Corps. Family Singers.

"That's my mom and her mom and pop, my Grandpop. They sang at the Saloon every Saturday night and Sunday afternoon until Mama was ten years old. People came from all over to hear them, mostly 'cause of Mama. Everyone said she was born to sing. She used to sing to me when I was little, but not anymore."

The hater of Hollywood used to be in show business? "Why not?"

Carson looks at me sideways, gauging my story-worthiness. "Mama says the Saloon wasn't doing so good so Grandpop sent her and Grandmom to go make a record in Nashville to make some money. Neither of 'em wanted to go, but Grandpop packed them up, said they had to or they were gonna lose the Saloon. Grandmom's car never made it to the Interstate. Got hit by a trucker who fell asleep at the wheel. Insurance money saved the Saloon. I love my Grandpop anyway."

Shit, that's deep. Patsy and Harry, two survivors, each with their own bucket of guilt. A group of girls bursts into laughter near the big back doors. Donnie, in the center of the bunch, waves. "Carson! Sander! Come watch the champ." He balances two bowls of birthday cake on his thighs. "Last two pieces have your names on 'em." Carson bounds over to join them but I stop near the Apple Corps. photo, where I press my finger to my lips then lightly touch the image of the little girl Patsy used to be.

Carson and I eat cake and watch Little repeatedly trounce her contenders at tic-tac-toe, to more laughter and applause. When Carson sits down to challenge Little to a game, Donnie leans in to me and whispers, "I've never seen Patsy like she was today. She's a real pistol, isn't she? I'm gonna have my hands full, right?"

I'd prefer *my* hands were full of Patsy. "Good luck with that, man." I bend down to address his chicken, who's just beat Carson in four moves. "Happy birthday, Little. I bet you were a cute little egg, weren't ya?"

Little clucks excitedly. I wonder if she recognizes me as I head outside toward Coreen's Desert Oasis Motel, the sky behind me a perfect cliché of vibrant sherbet colors and pillowy clouds.

*   *   *

Luckily for me, all the usual pre-production decisions—script, location, cast and crew, wardrobe—are already made. How difficult can this job be? Paul even gave me Oggie's original shot list. I compare it to the script, making notes and visualizing the flow of images, the pacing, when to go to Steadi, the juxtaposition of A and

B cameras—impressive for just a little old commercial. Tomorrow, there'll be reconnaissance with the A.D., mini-meetings with art, props, wardrobe and makeup, then a sit-down with the D.P. so we can talk through my vision. What the hell *is* my vision? An hour in front of the computer becomes two and two shots from a half-full bottle of Jack Daniel's I found in a top cabinet of Room Three's kitchenette become three before my brain starts to feel like Western Burger meatmush. The facts in my head need to simmer. I study my Patsy screensaver like an idiot, remembering her wet skin under the moon at Yellow Flats, our inspired makeout session, that surreal ride home. Paul Street's radio next door plays classical music; he sings along in occasional baritone bursts. Why didn't Dad support me the way Paul does? Did he think I had no talent at all? When one more whiskey shot has me checking my Death Clock and naming my penis (which inexplicably comes up as Elvis four times in a row!), I decide to take the VMX out for a stroll.

The nearly-full moon hangs low, a copper frying pan in a blanket of stars. Next door to the Saloon, a log cabin's front yard features a rusty bathtub planter holding a flowering cactus and a pair of upside-down cowboy boots. Just up from the bowling alley, a barn-like structure has SOUNDSTAGE across the top in old-West lettering with a small sign below: The Costumery. Across from that is the faded steeple of the Church of All Creatures Great and Small. Crooked letters on a small sign advertise yesterday's sermon: "It's Never A Cold Day in Hell." Next door to the church, a white clapboard bungalow with pink curtains at the windows and a dilapidated porch sofa. I peer into the cobwebbed windows of the Bank, Livery, Feed Store—all pure façade behind which is more dust and scratchy desert scrub. I end up at the "Okay Corral" and join Harry at the edge of the stage inside the three walls of Destinée's set. "Isn't the real O.K. Corral in Tombstone, Arizona?"

Harry nods and raises one hand, clutching his ever-present cup of joe, then sings softly, *"Camptown ladies sing this song, doo-dah, doo-dah."* I try to picture him as the black-hearted father who sent his wife and daughter away to make money to save their saloon, only to have his wife die in a car accident and his daughter never forgive him. Harry must live in a heartache world.

Harry sings another verse, and then keeps whistling the tune over and over. Soon, other sounds punctuate his whistling. They sound like bird calls, a coo-cooing which I instantly associate with the doves that nervously flitted in our backyard fountain growing up, and a clattering, possibly a woodpecker. Harry holds his hand out, motioning for me to keep still. Soon there is dun-colored movement near the rose vines that climb up the fence. A pair of birds approach, bushy crests bobbing, strong black tails jutting out from lighter-colored bottoms. They look up at Harry, waiting.

Harry takes a plastic baggie from his pocket, then tosses something to the ground. The two birds pounce on it, lustily scrapping over what I now see is a nugget of barbecued chicken. Bits of meat fly into the air, and the birds' bills clatter against each other in the hubbub. The larger one finally triumphs, and runs with the prize clutched in its bill to the base of the rosebush. The smaller one looks up at Harry and blinks expectantly, coo-cooing. Still whistling, Harry drops another piece of meat to the ground. The bird snatches it and follows its mate to safety.

"What are those?" I ask.

"Roadrunners," Harry says, taking another gulp from his mug. "They breed for life. Members of the cuckoo family."

"Aren't we all."

Harry smiles. "I went and got 'em hooked on barbecue. They come out whenever I sing. Aside from that, they're dumb as horseshoes."

We quietly watch the birds' fussy tics beneath the rosebush. At the opposite end of Mane Street, the Shitkicker's neon sign glows yellow and brown. "This couple's been around the corral for a few months now," Harry says. "There's another pair at the motel. Good thing, too. They keep the tarantula and scorpion population in check."

"Tarantulas and scorpions!"

"Oh, my!" he smiles. "Carson didn't tell you? Make sure to check the bed before you get in it every night. And shake out your shoes in the morning before you put 'em on."

"Will do." Just what I need—killer insects.

"You look different. Did you do something?" Harry asks.

I pat my hair.

The moon has risen above us now and dimmed to a golden hue. Coyote yips and yaps pierce the silence. Joshua trees twist and bend in mute postures of joy and pain. Purple and lavender foothills loom in the distance. Harry nudges my shoulder. "This ain't Los Angeles, is it Dorothy?"

"Harry," I say, "I don't know what this place is."

I watch the Shitkicker logo on the back of his T-shirt as he shuffles down the dusty road. When he disappears inside Room One, I click on my VMX and replay the footage from the meeting. Maybe it's the fatigue, maybe it's the whiskey, but I think it's good. I pause on an image of Patsy, caught looking into the lens. I wonder what I'd do in her situation. If I'd forgive myself for being alive, forgive Harry for sending his family away. Does losing a parent change as you get older? Is me losing Dad more or less of a loss than Patsy losing her Mom? How does child grief compare to sibling grief? Do you grieve more for someone you've known longer or for someone you haven't had time to truly enjoy? What is the true measure of loss anyway? How loudly one grieves? Or how well those left behind go on living? On the VMX's small screen, emotion lurks deep in Patsy's eyes; her cheekbones are like knives. I try to envision her power on a big screen; shivers run up my spine.

I must have been six or seven the first time I ever went to the movies. Mom and Ellie had gone off in the station wagon for some all-day adolescent girl party, and Dad was stuck with me. He wouldn't say where we were going, but he pointed me toward his work van, which I thought was fantastic. Amid the thick smells of dirt and grease and the sharp clanking of tools, he drove us to the Cinerama Theatre in Hollywood, which was one of the country's only round theatres and a big deal at the time. A concrete geodesic dome that looked like the top half of a golf ball, the Cinerama used three 35-mm projectors and a curved screen to show the widescreen movies that were popular then. The seats were plush red velvet—fit for royalty.

No matter that it was made in 1940, *The Thief of Bagdad* blew my little ass away. The saturated Technicolor, the flying horse, the gigantic genie, the all-seeing eye, the magic carpet, the boy Abu— *"I am Abu the thief, son of Abu the thief, grandson of Abu the thief, most unfortunate of ten sons with a hunger that yearns day and night"*—who turns into a dog, "master of a thousand fleas." For days after, I was an Arabian prince and magic carpets could fly. The one I drew was deep blue, and curled up in front like a snow sled. In my flying carpet daydreams, I swooped into backyards and circled around trees. I have Dad to thank for that. Now if only I could muster the emotion I absorbed from that movie and write something as colorful and enchanted, as strange and wise, as magical and terrifying. *I am Sander the plumber, son of Bobby the plumber, most unfortunate only son with a hunger that yearns day and night.*

When I wobble back to the motel alone, all the lights on Mane Street are out. Around me are stacks of boulders, medieval mountains beyond them, and a wildly starry canopy above. The moon is a hair smaller than last night's full disc, the Milky Way a faint white stripe. Stars arc and fall like fireworks. This moment requires punctuation. I find a Joshua tree around the back of the Bowl, and throw my head back for a long, dreamy piss. Suddenly, a squawking bird flies out at me from the base of the tree. Wings beat the air, feathers fly, and a pointy yellow beak pecks at my shins. Stunned, I step backwards, right onto the weak ankle that I crabbed on the highway. I'm flat on my ass again and the Satan chicken or rooster or whatever the hell it is dances away, dragging its wing in circles, clucking and cackling. There are feathers in my nose, stickers in my hand, and pee on my pant leg. My foot throbs, and I laugh so hard my eyes fill with tears.

12

TUESDAY MORNING

A chicken the size of Godzilla, the color of piss—like Big Bird on steroids—stomps down Mane Street. Feathers fly as it demolishes the Buckaroo Bowl, scattering horses and townsfolk alike, when I am awakened by a pounding on the door. My muscles ache, my scabbed-over nose itches and my sunburned skin is stretched tight as sausage casing. I pull on my sweats and step outside in my bare feet to a vision of Paul Street, in tangerine running shorts, executing Royal Canadian Air Force-caliber jumping jacks. "Let's go for a run, Sandy," he calls out, his breath even. "It's gorgeous out here."

"Jack LaLanne?" I yawn. "I thought you were dead."

"Not J.L.!" Paul Street laughs, launching into vigorous windmill toe-touches. "You remember in '75, when he towed that boat the length of the Golden Gate Bridge?"

"Not really." The outside air is fresh; the sky a post-dawn pink.

"The man was sixty-one years old, shackled, did the entire swim underwater and towed a thousand-pound boat." Paul is on his back now, ferociously crunching his abs. "I was on that boat. And guess what he said when he finished that swim."

"'Somebody throw me a towel?'" I've never been any good without coffee.

"I'll never forget it. J.L. leans over to me and he says, 'I could have done it faster, but my boner was creating drag.'" He cracks up without missing a crunch.

"I don't get it."

Paul wipes tears from his eyes. "You'd have to have seen him in the hot tub at the party the night before." He falls into another round of laughter, resumes crunching, and hops to his feet after a hundred. "Come on. A short run. You'll feel better." He's on leg lifts now.

"Run bad," I grunt. "Coffee good." I'll need it after last night's whiskey and the crew due to arrive in two hours.

"It's made up in my room. Go grab some." Paul shadowboxes a rose bush, then points himself toward Mane Street. "Today's the first day of the rest of your life, tiger. Make it count." He consults his sports watch, then takes off running.

I set up at the picnic table, connect the coffee to a vein, and open my laptop for a final read-through, hoping a visionary word or phrase will leap out at me. Patsy appears from around the side of the motel and walks across the desert toward the Saloon, her shoulders squarely set against the world. Jake prances across the desert to greet her. She stoops to scratch the dog's head midway, then waves as a YYY Desert Rooter van pulls up to next to the Saloon's oversized barbecue pit. For one ridiculous moment, I think: that could be me, coming to clean her pipes and save her day. That's one thing about being a plumber: the lady of the house—and it's usually a lady—is always glad to see you. I've been greeted with coffee, a martini, even a set of golf clubs, and sent home with cookies or flowers. Once an invitation to dinner, but I think the woman was planning a kitchen re-do and hoping for a cheap estimate. The sky has now become pale turquoise. It's about time to go inside to shower when a Navigator turns off Buckaroo Highway and pulls in at the berm above the motel, with Jake running and barking beside it.

Jake turns his attention to a hole in the ground while a woman descends from the truck, tapping into a BlackBerry. I recognize the signifiers of ambition and determination: clipboard and walkie-talkie at the ready, bleached-white T-shirt sans sweat stains or wrinkles, khaki cargo pants and rugged work boots, fashionably-faded denim shirt and ponytail tied back in a leather strip. It's me, a dozen years ago, on Vana's production of *Unmentionables.* "Hey!" My voice cracks. "Off to a rolling start, hey?" Hey? What is "hey?" *What am I, British? Righty-ho!*

The flat of her hand bids me wait while she spins, turning her back to me and continuing to tap into the BlackBerry. Jake joins us, greeting her with a friendly nose-poke to the crotch. She swats his snout away without missing a beat and that's when I see it. Peeking over the low-slung waistband, peering from its owner's crack: Faun's circular snake tattoo. Faun finishes her correspondence, slips her device into a pocket marked "BB" on her shoulder pack and finally looks up at me, extending her hand. "Hi Sander. Remember me?"

"Of course. Faun." The image of her going down on Vana at Paul's party is seared into the archives. "What are you doing here?"

She bats her eyelashes. "I'm on the crew list. F. Scott. I'm your A.D. *And* your P.A." Smiling a cervine smile at what I'm sure is my blank look, she says, "When Vana said most of the funds were gone, she meant it. Basically, I'm the right hand that does everything but shake your dick."

Bambi just became Godzilla. "Faun Scott," I say, grasping her right hand firmly and trying not to let myself visualize a dick at the end of my arm. "I can't wait to get started."

"Me too." She bares perfectly-spaced and polished canines in a facsimile of a smile. "There's something you should know." She waits for a moment off my look. "I hate you."

"Sorry?" *Have a crumpet?*

"Hate you, hate you, thoroughly despise you. Vana promised me I would direct her next project," she says. "Then suddenly, 'New Boy' shows up at the party with Paul Street and gets the gig. Anyhow, no hard feelings. That's how things happen in Hollywood. With any luck, I'll get the next one. By the way, you look like shit." She pulls out a cellophane baggie and shakes out a handful of pills. "Vitamins?"

My stomach flip-flops. "No thanks. I'm watching my weight."

She wolfs them down and follows me into my room, chugging orange juice from a sleek, Germanic thermos, growing healthier and more alert by the second. "Crew's on the road about fifteen minutes behind me." She sets up her notebook computer on the small table. "I know we're working from a pre-set sched, but I have a few ideas that might save some money, maybe some time. I know we're tight on both."

Fucking hot dog.

A small voice pipes up from behind Faun. "I brought coffee."

"No interruptions! We're working." Faun barks over her shoulder.

"Hey, that's my assistant you're talking to." I wave Carson over.

Her red wagon has a milk crate and basket piled on it, filled with thermoses and bottles and baked goods. "Coffee, tea, juices. Croissants, power bars, trail mix, fruit. I can make smoothies too. Destinée's is banana-strawberry with a wheatgrass back. I stocked up. And the trucks are here. I showed everyone where to park and where the bathrooms are and where to get coffee and stuff."

Lethal fumes rise from a cup of French roast. "Carson, you're the best."

"That's what they all say," she sighs, hooking her thumbs in the pockets of her jeans, then tying the front tails of her denim shirt into a knot. "But my forte is directing. Breakfast is in fifteen minutes at the Saloon. You'll want to eat your largest meal now, before it gets too hot. And drink lots of water so you don't get dehydrated. Also," she turns to Faun. "Someone needs to come up to the Saloon to talk about lunch and dinner chow with Grandpop."

Faun looks to me for corroboration, her pillowy lips a-pout.

"Sounds good," I tell Carson. "Faun can handle that."

Carson U-turns her wagon with swift precision, and I mention to Faun to be forewarned; everyone in town is invited to watch today's rehearsal.

"What?" She yells. "We can't have a bunch of people watching. It'll be too distracting."

"I'll explain later. I'll meet you up there. Go! Scoot!" I wave them both away.

Faun scowls. She's not happy but she holds back, not wanting to appear inflexible or, worse, a threat to my leadership—yet. As she follows Carson across the desert, I hear Carson ask her how many shoots she's done and with whom. Sweet.

Finally. A moment alone in the bathroom. I'm checking out the patches on my back and chest that are starting to peel and waiting for the water to heat up for another glorious shower when someone knocks at my door. I bet myself a hundred bucks it's Paul Street, and

I win. I know this because the window is ajar, and has been since I arrived—it's painted into position. I can see his tangerine running outfit through its spacious opening. "I'm just getting in the shower," I call out, wrapping a towel around my waist in case he can see back in.

"Wow. Running up here is fantastic. Jackrabbits all over the place." Paul peers through the crack. He's drenched with sweat; a small white towel is draped over his head. "A director's first impression is important, so I thought I'd go into town for breakfast. You need anything?"

I sense he would like me to say, *No, don't go. Stay.* And the scared-shitless part of me would like him to be there, to back me up if I get another case of mouth paralysis like I did at yesterday's town meeting. "No, I'm set. Thanks," I tell him.

"I'll be back to watch the shoot. Break a nail," he says. Is that a tear in his eye?

I give myself a little pep thought in the shower. This is no time for thick tongues or weak ankles or hesitation. It's all I've got and may be all I'll ever get. I check my shoes for scorpions and tarantulas, then rifle through my duffel bag. My fashion statement should say powerful but nerdy. Fascist but fun. Because I'm not superstitious (or maybe because I am), I pull on my Chuck Norris T-shirt, the same one I had on at Musso & Frank when I didn't give Ashe her ring. "I don't step on toes, I step on necks," my chest proclaims, and I'm ready to bluff my way through whatever fresh bowls of steaming shit the day might serve.

Two white equipment vans, a smattering of SUVs, and Donnie's Bronco are parked in the Saloon's parking lot. Signs are posted on all the Bronco's windows and doors: "Save Buckaroo – Change the Charter!" Inside the Saloon, Patsy's refreshing the egg platter on the buffet table. She's wearing her "Hell No to Hollywood!" T-shirt—I appreciate the medium, if not the message—and her tawny hair drapes both sides of her face. It's not easy for me to catch Patsy's eye and make it look casual, but I give it a shot.

"What?" Patsy asks, eyes flashing. I hadn't noticed the flecks of sage in them before.

"What?" Yeah, I'm a genius.

She shakes her hair away from her face, and I'm surprised at my all-over craving. "What is your desire, oh, dreamer of dreams?" she says.

"There are so many ways I could answer that question, but right now I'll settle for eggs." I wave a plate at her.

She snorts—I can't tell if she's amused or annoyed—then turns and pushes through the swinging door into the kitchen. I watch her above the counter, talking to JC, whose long, hay-blond hair is encased in a hairnet and tucked up under a tall white chef's hat. *What's he doing here?* He smiles over Patsy's head at me and waves.

"Congratulations," I call back to him, and make a note to myself to ask him what was in the pouch Starshine snorted that made their baby slip out like a fish. Ellie might like to get in on it. He nods, smiling solemnly.

When I sit down at the table, Faun complains. "I told that woman to cover up her T-shirt, but she just ignored me. What's up with that?"

I tuck into breakfast while I explain about the town meeting and how the Citizens for a Better Buckaroo threatened to protest our shoot. "It was Paul's idea to invite them. And it's a good one."

Faun sighs and I listen half to her as she briefs me on the six-person crew and six dancers and half to the talk among the tables that surround us. *I heard she had a nervous breakdown because she was a lesbian and couldn't decide whether to come out or wait to be outted. I heard she was a sex addict and tried to pick up the youngest guy on the set and was pissed when he wasn't interested. I heard she wouldn't talk to anyone but the director. I heard she couldn't get one of the shots and everyone had to stay for fifty-seven takes. I heard she was in seclusion and wouldn't talk to anyone. I heard a crew shot one of her videos so coked-out there was an orgy afterwards and a tape of it made the rounds and no one on the tape has ever worked again.*

I let them talk themselves out. Watch them group and re-group, until cluster by cluster, the hot food and the quaint surroundings and the desert landscape quiets them. I stand and raise my hand in greeting, my own version of benevolent dictator. "Thanks for coming out on short notice, everyone. We all know we're the second string team here."

There are grumbles from the tables. Faun coughs in my direction, muttering, "No, we don't." I look at her. She shakes her head *no!*

Suddenly, the front door bursts open and Adonis London wheels into the Saloon. He's wearing his PJs and a plaid flannel robe with matching slippers, and his normally sprayed-on mullet hair sticks out in spikes. He either just woke up or had a heck of a night.

"Sorry Donnie, but the Saloon's closed to the public right now," I call over to him.

"I'm not here to make trouble," he says, "but somebody urinated on my chicken, and I need to find out who." He holds Little in the air. She is decidedly yellow.

"Somebody *peed* on your chicken?" Patsy asks, incredulous.

"That's disgusting."

The crew members look wide-eyed at each other, holding in laughter, eyebrows raised.

"Little had too much birthday last night. She wandered away and when I finally found her, she was yellow and smelled like urine. People are sick. Sick! I've never seen anything like this." Donnie slams his ham-sized fists on his armrests; Little clucks loudly.

"Calm down, Donnie," Patsy says.

"I am calm!" he yells, then says quietly. "I just want to tape up a sign."

"You can tape up your sign," Patsy says, "But then you have to go."

I can't let this continue and risk Donnie's trigger finger again. I take a breath and stand up. "Donnie, everybody." The Saloon falls silent. I clear my throat. "It was me. I relieved myself on your chicken."

"I knew it!" Donnie yells, ignoring the crew's muffled laughter.

Patsy interrupts. "Shut up and let the man speak."

Donnie cringes like a misbehaving puppy.

I take a big gulp of water. "It was an accident. I had a few drinks. It was dark and I found a Joshua tree near the Bowl. She flew at me like a bat out of hell. Knocked me down."

"Little knocked you down?" Donnie smiles.

"On my ass," I confirm. "Donnie, that chicken of yours is no chicken. She's a fighter, a brave warrior...ess."

"Yeah, this one always had spunk." He looks down at Little on his lap, then back to me. "Thank you, Sander. I appreciate your honesty."

"You're welcome." Then I'm inspired. "Hey Donnie, how about some WCW?"

"Really? Sure!" He pets his bird as he considers his words. *"As the cat climbed over the top of the jamcloset, first the right forefoot carefully, then the hind, stepped down into the pit of the empty flowerpot."* Donnie salutes his fist into the air, cries "William Carlos Williams!" then wheelies his chair toward the exit and leaves. The room is silent after they leave, until a loud chicken squawk reports from the parking lot. Everyone laughs, except Faun, who shrinks in her chair, which amuses me.

"All right everyone, back to business." I remember Paul's performance at the town meeting and try to become a spokesman for myself, try to connect with each of the faces turned my way. Chuck Norris is damp in the pits. "Firstly, we are indeed the second string. Get over it. We're here to do something the first crew couldn't. Secondly, I did, in fact, pee on a chicken and it did, in fact, knock me into a cactus. There's a needle in my butt to prove it. Big deal."

"I'm holdin' it until this shoot's over!" someone shouts.

I raise both hands for quiet. "It'll be two long days of hard, sweaty, dusty work, but we're in a really special place out here in Buckaroo." My peripheral/carnal vision catches Patsy's perked-up ears. "Strange, beautiful, hot. This town was built as a Hollywood set, but it's not just that. It's home to some really nice folks, all of whom have been invited to watch us rehearse today." Groans from the crew. "Which is an excellent opportunity for everyone to demonstrate what you do best. Faun will review the shot list, and then we'll head over to the set. We have one day to work out the kinks and one day to get it perfect."

A crowd of townspeople surrounds the Okay Corral, with some cowboys on horseback, a handful of pickups parked ass-in toward the rail with folks sitting in the beds, and the Citizens for a Better Buckaroo sitting on folding chairs in the shade of a canvas tarp stretched across four poles, clipboards on their knees, Patsy at the fore. Harry Apple holds court with his cronies. A brown, beat-up Chevy van is parked nearby, with Star and the baby settled in an easy chair in the back, while JC plays proud papa to visitors and well-wishers. Paul Street watches from a golf cart, his ice chest stocked with Evian. The white production vans are parked off to one side; the crew eviscerates them of equipment. In a flourish of last-minute inspiration, I decide on my visionary catchphrase: "flashmeat." We film the burger like a beautiful body; we film the dancers like delicious meat. It's the best I got for this mishmash of a project.

Carson accompanies Faun and me as we make the rounds with the crew. In fact, it was her idea to film us with my VMX as a sort of "making-of." We thought it would be an interesting piece for the archives, but agreed it wasn't the ideal birthday gift for Patsy. Each member of the crew gets a short but intensive dose of close-up face time, with an encapsulation of the overall vision we're trying to achieve. Faun's specialty is creating the instant hook-up, using pet names and a physical gesture to seal the deal. For instance, she calls the sound guy Mr. Do-You-Hear-What-I-Hear and strokes his massive boom-built bicep, while I deliver the directive. He watches her ass twitch on her way to the dancers, where she exhibits intricate choreography of her own involving flipping pony-tails, swatting the girls' fannies, and tweaking the boys' pecs, and conferring pet names to their best attributes. She gives the hair and makeup stylists advice regarding same, and manages to get them to both lift their shirts to compare abs, which she playfully smacks. We inspect the prop burgers and discuss the all-important burger toss at the climax of the piece. There's a lot of laughter and joking, hugging and, oddly, gratitude and affection. I've never seen a crew in a better mood than the people working here today. Perhaps it's because Carson's filming them; everyone has a good-natured crack about my peeing on Donnie's chicken, yet everyone also seems open to the "flashmeat" experience and excited to work on this project that now has this eccentric sheen.

The more I watch Faun manage the nuts and bolts, the more I appreciate her military-minded troubleshooting skills and diplomacy. She asks the right questions; I give simple answers. We find our places in a way that becomes about the work. Let the lighting techs go with their guts on scrims and light. Talk through the lenses and dolly moves with the D.P. Discover how heat affects tools, how light bounces off linen, how the sand shifts under tracks, how sweaty hands hold equipment. How sweat springs up from no movement at all, but comes from quiet breathing and sitting and looking, listening and playing with light and sound and perspective. Once the first round is done, Carson hands me the VMX so I can film my portion of it. I film the crew playing with light, choreographing intricate camera ballets, hammering a scaffold skeleton. Exploring the options the strange set has to offer, its vibrant thick paint surreal in the fierce sunlight. As we radar in on the latitude and longitude of position and angle, an industrious thoughtful silence supplants the previous informative chatter. One-word questions are answered with nods. Details are finessed.

Finally, we're ready. While Carson and Faun take a last-minute bathroom break, I head for Craft Services to check out a snack. When I get there, Donnie's shaking hands with the Crafty. "Hey Donnie, you enjoying yourself?" I grab a handful of trail mix and flip through the herbal teas. The guy behind the table sobers instantly and busies himself with measuring coffee beans into a grinder.

Donnie smiles. "Just great, Sander. How you doing?"

I realize I'm throwing trail mix into my mouth and speed-chewing like a freaking chipmunk. "A little nervous. But in a good way."

"If you ever need to chill out..." Donnie coolly unhooks and flips down the bib of his black denim overalls, showcasing an organized display of joints, plastic-bagged buds and glittery pink pills in smaller plastic bags. He points out his wares with quick precision. "Singles, artisan buds and Dove, a highly-recommended local product you've got to try to believe. Excellent for the creative spirit. Most of your crew's on it already," he grins.

"You're kidding!" I say, just as the Crafty hits his grinder, its ear-splitting whirr making conversation impossible. Car parts and golf balls, my ass. No wonder the crew is in such a good mood. Do I call Donnie out for dealing on my set and possibly trigger another bout of gun-waving? Or do I play it cool? The grinder stops. "No thanks, man. I need to be able to concentrate. We're ready to start in about five minutes. Would you mind joining the observers? Craft Services are really only for cast and crew."

"Sure thing, Sander." He wheels his chair around. "Break a leg. Isn't that what they say?"

"That's what they say," I tell him. If his legs weren't already pretty busted, I'd like to break one of his.

"Quiet on the set!" Faun calls, holding the slate clapper in front of the camera.

Willamette runs over from the bowling alley, an old-time megaphone in one hand. She thrusts it at me. "For luck," she trills. "All the directors use this when they shoot in Buckaroo. Nice T-shirt," she says, winking at Chuck on my chest.

I grab the worn wooden handle of the cone-shaped device, feeling slightly ridiculous yet somehow humbled, perhaps honored, by tradition. I raise one arm and hold the megaphone to my mouth. "Action!" I love saying that. My thumbnail tucks against my lip as I squat on my haunches. Alert, relaxed, watching. Dancing girls dancing in leggings and camisoles. Cowboys fake-brawling in short-shorts. Paul Street gesturing to Carson, who's pretending to film with her funny old Keystone camera that's no doubt still minus its lens. Faun signaling, measuring, counting. The precise interplay of camera, operator, hand signal, light, shadow.

I remind myself it's not even a movie. It's a commercial. For a burger I don't eat and a pop star I disdain. With a concept that's not mine. With Paul as my own personal babysitter to guarantee success, plus an A.D. who is banging, if that's the proper term, the producer. But all eyes ultimately look to me for answers. I say "action" and I say "cut" and nobody, right now, can take that away from me.

From the first of the shots to the very last, we start out rough and improve shot by shot. Throughout our rehearsal there is one image that propels me: Patsy, spooning out scrambled eggs.

Her freckled bicep, her grip on the aluminum spoon, the way her tongue tapped against her teeth as she spoke. *What is your desire, oh, dreamer of dreams?* She watches from the edge of her seat, guardian of every grain of sand, making sure no harm falls upon her beloved Buckaroo.

Even if the crew are all high as kites, by the end of the run, we operate as a unit, all parts oiled and integrated, moving in the same direction to create the same vision. "Cut!" I say into the megaphone, and look over at Faun.

This commercial may not be my idea, and it's certainly worlds away from art, but of one thing I'm certain: with all its high-voltage, tricky camera angles and Vegas dance moves, our "flashmeat" shoot is true to the script. But I understand now what Oggie rejected about it. Meat, even lowly burger meat, should be gritty, real. If you're hungry for a burger, you want to smell blood and smoke, not greasepaint and cologne. "Not bad," I venture, so as not to jinx the works.

"Not bad?" Faun throws her arms around me without restraint. "That was fantastic!"

The crew slaps fives and chests and spikes empty water bottles, bouncing them high into the air. Those sideline observers who have hung with us this long actually join in and *cheer.* Paul Street is at my side in a single bound. "That was terrific," he says, looking weepy around the eyes, swear to God. Patsy looks mildly entertained.

"We should wrap now." Carson's at my elbow, her face smudged with glitter courtesy of the makeup department.

"Wrap? We just got started."

"The air tastes funny." She squinches up her face. Jake pads over, whining, eyes searching the crowd, nose in the air. "Like a bad wind's coming."

"There's plenty of time for another run-through," Faun says. "Should be easy, seeing as how the first one went so well." She throws her head back to glug water, signaling it's my call.

"Wind doesn't seem that bad," I nod. "Two run-throughs are scheduled. Two we'll do."

Faun looks at me and shrugs her shoulders. "Let's do it then. Same as the first."

Wrong. I call the group in for a huddle and announce this time we'll do it differently, with a new catchphrase this time: "authentic." Faun throws up her hands—a symbolic washing of—but she takes my notes, smiling and nodding more than once as I explain how I want the dance steps less precise, the camera moves longer, the attitude less Vegas, more fun. When I finish, she calls for quiet and claps the clapper.

My next word is as sweet as a second kiss. "Action!" Totally in the zone, I raise the VMX to catch the dance. The framing is instinctive now, transitions smoother this time, hesitations erased, anticipations eased, the dancers more joyful, the natural light soft.

Until a single gust of wind—supernatural in speed, immeasurable in force, arbitrary as to victim—picks up and slams across the corral, toppling anything that's not nailed down. Which is just about everything.

Scrims sail, cranes crash, lights pop and darken, extra bits of costume rise up into the air like rhinestone cowboy ghosts. The sky darkens and a boom fills our ears, stopping the wind as if by some godly toggle. Everyone's hair falls back to their heads, mouths open in disbelief, and a brilliant artery of lightning strikes down from the daylight sky to anoint the set with flame.

I am too stunned to say "cut."

But my VMX doesn't miss a thing. It catches the drivers, wakened from their catnaps, running unevenly from their trucks with fire extinguishers over the lousy terrain pocked with holes, knees buckling as they drop their canisters, pick them up and run again. Captures the flames growing swiftly in the absence of opponent and response, hungrily devouring the painted saloon interior as a main course, with the roses and chaparral twined around the fence of the Okay Corral for dessert, exploding in a single, massive ball of fire. Records the screams and actions of the observers, particularly Patsy, stunned by this act of Nature suddenly joining and validating their cause. Finds Paul Street pulling Carson into his golf cart and driving away to safety. Sneaks up on Faun, pulling cords and cables away from the blaze as fast as she can. It's not until raindrops spatter that it dawns on me I should be helping instead of filming. But there's not much to do anymore. Water pours down from a sky that a moment ago held not even the faintest wisp of cloud. Billowing sheets of bullet-like rain, with the sun still laughing at us from behind the San Gorgonios. Sand turns to mud. The set resembles an over-sized campfire, doused mid-blaze, in the center of a group of wet, muddy onlookers, silent and stunned.

Harry grabs the megaphone from my chair, and calmly announces, "Emergency meeting at the bowling alley! Five minutes!" He looks at me, shaking his head as he tromps through the mud to the Buckaroo Bowl.

"Cut," I whisper, and turn off the camera.

13

TUESDAY AFTERNOON

Whipped cream farts from an aerosol can punctuate the soft twang of steel guitar, as Willamette finishes off two mugs of cocoa and sets them on the counter for Carson to hand out. Here in the café side of the Buckaroo Bowl, Paul Street and I are the only outsiders among most everyone who witnessed the firestorm, plus a few regulars and canyon-dwellers waiting out the rain. Gathered in the bowling alley side of the Bowl, my crew stands with their backs to each other, creating individual personal spaces to murmur into cell phones. Calling their friends. Alerting the press. Who knows. Shivering in her sweatshirt, Faun huddles with the hoi polloi. I should be with them too—rallying, consoling—but I need to sit through this meeting first.

They don't need to know I'm completely demoralized, the paralyzed fourth grader, the high-school senior trailing TP from his shorts. From my post next to the back window near the jukebox, I can see down the muddy length of Mane to the remains of the Okay Corral and Destinée's Western Burger saloon set: a pile of charred, soggy bones. Miraculously, the freestanding structure kept its blaze, explosive as it was, to itself. Gray sheets of rain pound what few embers might remain amid the corral's old-wood posts and the set's painted walls. I'm amazed at how quickly it all happened. How people came together, how the rain came to our rescue, how my project disappeared in billowing clouds of black smoke.

Harry doles out blankets and towels. "No sense tryin' to swim through the flash floods that're sure to come next," I hear him say. A nerve-wracking gust of wind buffets the building. The long sheet-glass windows buckle and moan; the dark ceiling beams grimace.

"Where's his crazy daughter and her vigilantes?" Paul Street whispers in my direction. "They're the ones who worry me."

Patsy and the Citizens for a Better Buckaroo are conspicuously absent. "Probably tying knots in the old hanging rope," I say, suddenly feeling as though I'm being watched. I am.

Donnie's squeezed up to his regular booth, cooing to Little and patting her with napkins, his drug-dealing eyes glaring at me. No wonder all the girls gathered around him at the town meeting yesterday; girls always know where to get drugs. I wonder if Carson knows what he does. Or if everyone here already knows and doesn't care. If I should say something to someone official, and maybe mention his penchant for gunplay.

Willamette finally clangs her bell and Harry takes his place in the center of the café. "We're all sad about losing our favorite, most famous landmark. It's a real shame..."

"I know what we need to do," Paul says, snapping his fingers and slapping my thigh. "Let me handle this."

But right then, the doors bang open. The Citizens for a Better Buckaroo silently file into the bowling alley. Patsy's wet hair is a flattened skullcap. Dirt smudges her forehead and cheeks. She looks sadly defiant as she leads the procession into position across the back wall.

"Wait," I tell Paul, anxious to see how the Apple family drama plays out.

Carson runs to Harry and leans into him, burying her face in his damp denim shirt. He smoothes her hair and asks if she'd be kind enough to share some cocoa with their friends who just arrived.

Carson shakes her head no, refusing to look in her mother's direction.

Patsy's shoulders sag at this, but she says, "We're fine."

Harry clears his throat. "As I was saying, it's a real shame..."

As a group, Patsy and the Citizens raise placards above their heads that read IMPEACH HARRY.

Paul shifts in his seat and whispers, "This is becoming a TV movie." He shakes his wrist and looks at his watch. "We need to move this along."

I stand up from my seat. "It wasn't Harry's fault. It was mine." The words come out barky and dry. I can feel Patsy radiating dismay in my direction and do the same right back; I can't let her blame Harry for this mess.

"Not like that!" Paul Street pulls me back down to my chair. "What's wrong with you?"

Harry smiles at me sadly. "Nice of you to say, Sander, but you're out of line. We need to follow protocol here. As I was saying..."

Now Patsy and the Citizens take up a soft chant. "Im-PEACH! Im-PEACH! Im-PEACH!"

Harry finally shouts over them, "Message received!" They quit abruptly and Harry calmly continues. "Willie, will you please add the requested item to next meeting's agenda?"

"Item noted," Willie says, but she shoots daggers at Patsy and under her breath mutters something about respect and parents and kids.

"Thank you," Patsy says. *What a snot!*

Harry takes charge again. "First things first. Is anyone hurt?" There are murmurs from the crowd, but nothing specific. "Sander, all your people doing okay?"

"Fine, fine," I say, peering across the way into the lanes, where the crew mills together, talking softly. "Just wet and cold and wondering if there'll be another day of work." And humiliated for being part of my shoot, I add silently.

"Filming should have been prohibited in the first place," Donnie says, pumping one fist; Little loudly beeps *ba-KAWK!* at the sound of her master's voice.

Paul pulls at my sleeve and nods toward the bowling alley. "Huddle. Now."

"We need to hear this," I whisper, glued to my seat. Paul looks surprised, then stalks away to join the crew.

Patsy rolls her eyes, something I can see but Donnie can't. "Filming isn't the problem." She slicks back wet bangs from her forehead. "It's not having permits and standards. If we required permits, we'd have insurance against catastrophes like these."

"Really?" Harry's head snaps in her direction. "I'd like to see the permit that could stave off a desert storm. Lightning is an act of God." He flings an arm to the sky.

"Actually, it's caused by charge separation, although there are two major schools of thought as to why that might occur," Donnie offers. He turns to Patsy for some props, but another *ba-KAWK* interrupts. It's not his chicken this time; it's his cell.

Someone probably needs a party pack, calling in their pot order like Chinese takeout.

"Don't get smart with me," Harry yells after Donnie, who's already snapped open his phone and is rolling toward the restrooms with it clapped to his ear.

"Don't you holler at my Donnie-kins!" Willamette trills at Harry, the Indian beads around her neck rattling.

"Dammit, Willie, he was out of order," Harry protests. "Even if we change the charter, no one here can change the weather."

"We can change the mayor," someone calls from the crowd, and the chant starts up again.

"Im-PEACH! Im-PEACH! Im-PEACH!"

Harry's supporters begin their own chant of "Har-RY! Har-RY!"

Someone lobs a balled-up napkin. A handful of marshmallows gets tossed back. Mustard and sugar packets follow, with opposing sides pelting each other with condiments, leftover food, whatever's handy. When Carson squirts a stream of ketchup at Patsy, the skirmish officially escalates to war.

In the midst of the ruckus, I might be the only person who sees Donnie speed-roll from the back vestibule across the bowling alley to JC's booth. The only one who witnesses the whispering, and JC's calm, negative response. The only one who sees Donnie draw his gun and lay it across his lap in front of Little, and deliver a few choice words to JC before hurtling out the doors and down the access ramp. Back inside, JC confers with Starshine for a moment, then calmly tucks the baby into her basket, helps Star to her feet, and guides them outside and down the stairs toward their old brown van. The Bronco's hydraulic lift is just shifting Donnie behind the wheel when I see our crew descending the front stairs of the bowling alley and scattering in various directions.

Paul walks toward me slowly, his hands in his pockets. "The entire crew quit." His face is flushed. "You satisfied now?"

"You're kidding?" Outside, Donnie spins the Bronco in a wild U-turn before tearing away down Mane Street. "Ratbastards! Can they do that?" I ask.

"Sure," Paul shrugs. "There's another gig. Better pay. Longer shoot."

I watch the clump of them disperse, climbing into their vans and SUVs. "What about their contracts? The equipment?"

Paul smiles ruefully. "Not for this gig. This one was under the radar. We hired them specifically because they come with their own toys. If they take the toys, we have nothing."

"Shit!" My head is starting to ache and there's ringing in my ears. This isn't my fault, too, is it? Something tells me it is. "This is a disaster."

"Don't worry." Paul Street puts his arm around my shoulders. "I have a plan."

I toss his arm away. "Never mind!" My face burns red-hot. "I quit!"

Paul's neck stiffens and he steps back. "Excuse me?"

But my train is already bulleting down the track. "What's the point? I'm the director, I suck and I quit! THIS SHOOT IS CANCELLED!" My voice echoes in sudden silence; the War of Condiments is over as quickly as it began.

"No!" Carson cries, her hair matted with mustard.

"Sander, how can you quit something you never really started?" Paul Street calmly finishes his cocoa, swipes a napkin across his mouth, and makes a quiet but effective exit.

The place is a mess. Ketchup, mustard, relish and marshmallows splatter the Buckaroons like a Jackson Pollack painting, but no one seems to notice. They're all looking at me. There's a collective gawk as amused "ooh, lover's quarrel" glances ricochet around the room, then Patsy and her Citizens erupt in cheers.

From the porch outside, I watch my failed babysitter return to the motel. I've let him down. I've let everyone down. I've let me down. The big doors open again and Patsy exits, carrying Carson in her arms like a baby. The kid kicks her coltish legs and bawls, small fists thumping her mother's back. I know exactly how Carson feels.

The wind tosses bits of char around Mane Street like black snow. The last of the SUVs, with Jake in pursuit, turns onto Buckaroo Highway. Jake gallops back to me, head down, a rusty blur. He shoves his snout into my hand, then sets his chin on my thigh looking up into my face as though I had all the answers. "Not me, bud." I scratch his ears and he chuffs in reply. I dig for my cell phone to call Ellie, but, of course, its battery is dead.

"Charges? I'll accept, I suppose." Ellie's voice has a serrated edge. "Sander, what the hell?"

The Shitkicker's phone box is much cooler than the last time I was in here. Through the red-framed glass panes, the roiling thunderheads glide away from Buckaroo and hover above the mesa below. I haven't figured out what to tell my sister. But it's okay; she's not ready to listen. "You cut me off yesterday, I leave a million messages on your cell, and you never call back! I need to talk to you. Come home. I'm going out of my mind."

"I'm talking to you now, I *am* coming home and you *are* out of your mind. Whatever's wrong, can't Jerome take care of it?" I'm exhausted, but my body hums strangely, as though I can feel blood surging through my veins.

"No, he can't. Or he won't. Or I don't want him to. I don't know." The buzz on the line makes her voice sound like a little girl's, chopping her words in half.

"What language are you speaking? And what could possibly be wrong that Nurse Perfect can't fix?" My lungs move like an accordion in my chest and my heart pumps rhythm. I can scarcely catch my breath. Is this a panic attack?

"Never mind," she finally says. "I'll figure it out."

"Okaaay." The sky crackles brightly; the green, gold and orange rocks and flora gleam as though scoured. "So, how's Mom?"

"Oh. My. God." Ellie seems relieved not to talk about herself—a personal first. "Mom. Kidnapped. Dad."

"What. Are you. Talking about."

"On Friday, after the cremation, she went to the cemetery to make sure they were using the right urn. As they were going to seal it in the drawer, she grabbed it, ran to the car, and took off." Ellie lets loose a snort; I crack up, too.

"She can keep it at home, can't she? Lots of people do that. It's not so strange."

"Normal people don't buy the drawer then not use it. Normal people don't keep the urn in the bedroom and talk to it."

"She talks to it? About what?"

"God only knows. Probably about redecorating."

"Wow." The thrum in my head prevents me from riffing back.

But Ellie doesn't need my help to continue the conversation. "I haven't gained any weight yet, thank God. I'm so busy getting El-San in order, there's no time to eat."

"And how's that going?" She's hating it, I'm sure, and it's comforting to know I'll be needed somewhere, even though it's the last place on earth I want to be needed.

"Great! I created a filing system and upgraded the computer and accounting software. It practically runs itself. I make calls from home in the morning and check in on the guys in the afternoon."

Of course my sister would be even better at being me than I am. Was. Whatever. "You still need me there, don't you?" File *that* under "Words I Thought I Would Never Say."

"Of course, but probably just part-time. You can still work on your screenplay. Isn't that great? How's the shoot going?"

I study the ground, where my tennis shoes and pant cuffs are splattered with yellow mud and my name on the cardboard box from Paul Street has almost completely faded away. "Come pick me up and I'll tell you."

"What'd you do, crash Paul Street's Lexus?"

"I'll tell you on the way home. It's a long story."

Ellie sighs. "I can't make it until tomorrow; Mommy Yoga is tonight. Lots of potential clients. I'm thinking of expanding into diaper service, what do you think? Where are you again?"

My ears ring as I explain how to get here, wondering how I got here myself.

14

TUESDAY AFTERNOON

The storm has left the sands in the wash alongside Buckaroo Highway damp and hard-packed and they're easy to walk on, unlike when they're dry. Easy to walk away from the latest installment in my hall of shame, away from guns and exploding vaginas. Maybe this fiasco is a sign. Are there still canneries in Alaska? Is there still a Foreign Legion to join? Do hobos still ride the rails? Does anyone still say hobo? I wish I had some of Donnie's dope now.

The landscape seems oddly familiar—a shark fin-shaped boulder, distant jagged mountains. I'm clearly headed in the direction from whence I arrived two days ago, yet am completely turned around; the highway's twists and turns could have me facing west again. I clamber up an almost-trail over a few mounds of rocks and I recognize JC and Starshine's wedding location. Looking out on one improbable rock pile after another—spectacular sculptures that fly in the face of gravity, physics and engineering—I see why they wanted to be married right there; the boulders above are shaped like two perfect hearts. That means the scene of my rendezvous with Jake and the Eldo that first day must be nearby, too. Searching for the main road, I return the way I came over the hills, which now all look identical. I'm back at the wash, but not where I left off. I must be further down the road because when I emerge, there's a sign on the opposite side of the road: Magicville, with a small arrow pointing to a trace of a trail.

I follow the tributary of bone-white sands as best I can, wondering how exactly a flash flood works out here. The curves are nearly always blind ones, winding through mounded hillocks of sand and dirt that seem to be just a foot taller than me. I run up the side of one to get a clear view, but the next hillock is just that much taller. A familiar guitar riff floats up. Where would music be coming from? I pound up and down a couple more hills. Robert Plant sings the first line to "Stairway to Heaven." I laugh out loud. Why not? The song floats in pieces, until the path lets out onto a sweeping plateau. A tan Chevy van is parked in the middle of it, doors open, music blasting. On a rock nearby: a man, a guitar, an amp. JC, naked but for beat-up Birkenstocks, jams with Jimmy Page. The song builds, then ends quietly. "Yeah," JC laughs to himself. "*I'm not no rock, I got to roll,*" he shouts, fumbling the lyrics, then laughs and laughs. His laughter turns into a wolfish howl, then abruptly stops as he looks directly at me. "Salutations." He waves me over. As I scale the rock, he slips the guitar over his head and pulls on a white caftan.

"I didn't mean to interrupt," I say. "I had no idea where I was going. I just heard the music."

"I used to want to be a rock star. I come here every now and then to kick it out." He settles into a cross-legged position and pats the spot next to him. "You see Elvis?" He points across the way to a pile of boulders.

Hard as I try, I don't see the King of Rock 'n' Roll in the mish-mash.

"Don't look harder. Look softer." JC closes his eyes. "Remember when you were a kid making stories in clouds? See his guitar? His hair? The hip made by that shadow?"

I close my eyes halfway and unfocus. Sure enough, a guitar appears, a protruding hip, a lush mound of hair carved by wind, grit and time. Directly below the rock of Elvis, tall trees stand in a crooked circle on the high plateau. Their arms stretch out, like regal dancers, apocalyptic apostles. They look simultaneously serious and absurd, natural and artificial, calm and chaotic. "Those trees are freaky," I say. In the center, a tall column of rocks, balanced perfectly, create an obelisk.

"Joshua trees only grow in certain parts of the world," JC says, pulling a baggie and rolling paper from the kangaroo pocket of his dress. "Here and in the Holy Land. And slowly." He sprinkles bud along a cigarette paper and with a graceful slip of the fingers of one hand rolls a perfect doobie without even looking at it. "Because of their height, these could be the oldest Joshua trees on the planet. That's why it's called the Mother Circle." He tokes deeply, easily burning up half the cigarette, and passes it to me.

"Why does the sign say Magicville then?" I close my eyes and inhale.

JC finally exhales. "Magicville. Mother Circle. Different words; same meaning. It's the place of creativity. Songs are written, prayers are shouted, love is made."

The word "jabberwocky" comes to mind as I hold the swirl of smoke in my lungs, savoring a layered bouquet of vanilla, rosemary, and something I can't pinpoint.

"Cognac," JC says. "My proprietary blend."

I exhale in a juvenile burst, followed by a coughing fit. *That man just answered my thought.*

"I tend to do that," he smiles. "People up here have gotten used to it."

Now I'm afraid to think anything for fear he'll be able to read it. Did he hear me think "jabberwocky?" I think about Mom and the jerking off thing, and then wonder if he knows that I'm thinking that, too. "Have people gotten used to you being able to put them down by touching them under the jaw? How did you do that, anyway?"

"Easy," he says. "Same way you just saw Elvis, by opening your mind. Enter the cosmic classroom and whatever you see, let it be real."

I don't know what the hell he's talking about, but I shut my eyes.

JC and I are squeezed into kid-size desks. John Lennon sits Indian-style on the teacher's desk, singing Lucy Sky's namesake song. The Walrus does a modern, interpretive dance in front of the chalkboard. JC nods, like he understands. I run to the Walrus and beat him on the chest. "Talk to me! Tell me what to do!"

Back in the Mother Circle, JC says, "Good try, but not quite," his eyes still closed. "All you ever hear is third-eye this and third-eye that. Everyone going around with their foreheads all scrunched up trying to visualize. Once you realize the third eye is in your heart, you can actually see a whole lot better. Try it with your eyes open this time."

I look around. Golden boulders in the near distance stand out in stark relief against the surrounding mountains. The sky shimmers electric blue. The air crackles with the arguments of mockingbirds and rabbits twitching their ears in the brush.

"There. That's better." JC claps me on the shoulder.

"I didn't do anything!" I tell him.

"That's the first step," he says.

Enough of this. "I saw Donnie show you his gun at the bowling alley. Are you in trouble?"

JC tokes again, passing the joint back to me and holding the smoke in a long time before he speaks. "Donnie's really not a bad guy. I mean, come on! He's president of the William Carlos Williams fan club. He just acts like a thug around Willamette to keep her off his back."

"He showed me the ring he's going to give Patsy for her birthday. He's going to propose."

"Poor dude. He's been carrying around that ring since high school," JC sighs. "Says he's gonna ask her every year, but he never does."

"So he's sensitive and he loves poetry," I snort. "A sensitive, poetry-loving thug is still a thug."

"Everyone needs to excel at something," JC smiles. "Me, I was slick with chemistry. Coupla cats taught me righteous basics back in the day. Bathtub acid, synthetic mescaline. I partied with a lot of musicians. But then, then..." He smiles wryly, touching a finger to his lips, as though bidding himself to be discreet. "I got tired of people abusing the medicine and fucking themselves up." He pulls a small quarter-baggie of pink capsules from his kangaroo pocket. "So I developed this. It's my baby."

"Hey, Donnie was selling that to the crew this morning."

JC takes my hand and pours a small pink-capsule waterfall into my palm. "A completely organic blend of THC, lysergic acid amides from morning glory seeds, mescaline from pedigreed peyote and some other good stuff."

"No, really, I don't..." I protest lamely as I inhale the tasty smoke again.

"It's my last batch." JC closes my hand around the little pink pyramid and locks his hand around mine. "They'll be collectibles." His deep-set eyes blaze like a modern-day Charlie Manson's, hypnotizing me into joining his pink pill-popping cult. He laughs. "I'm a Dad now. Upstanding citizen of the U. S. of A. You saw me at the Saloon this morning. I'm the Shitkicker's new Executive Chef." He laughs and starts howling again.

When a coyote responds from the other side of the Circle, I can't help myself, and join in. I doubt I sound much like a coyote, but the sound of our voices evolving and devolving into an otherworldly animal scream is oddly comforting, somehow beautiful. I am good and trashed again and I love it.

"What's this stuff called?" I open my hand.

"Dove," he says, "It's ninety-nine percent pure. See my signature?" A small, cursive "JC" is scrolled onto the side of each sparkling pill. "The glitter is a recent development. Ground mica. Ravers dig it." JC continues, a convinced salesman hyping his product. "You can drop it with a nice California Merlot, or break it open to smoke it, sniff it, cook with it. However you ingest it, the result is the same: serene euphoria, expansive thoughts, creative expression and a pillow-soft descent. No aftertaste, flashbacks, or hangover. Guaranteed."

Sounds familiar. "Was it in your wedding brownies?"

"That it was, my friend," he smiles.

"Thanks." I tuck the capsules into my pocket. The air is exceptionally still, yet charged with an energy that seems to emanate from the trees. Like I'm inside a giant, natural cathedral, a feeling I haven't had since Dad took us to Grand Canyon back in the seventies. I remember looking out at the view from Bright Angel Point. A layer of blue haze hung above striking orange and red stone towers. "The right rocks and light can make any place into a church," Dad said quietly. I haven't thought of that moment in years. Back then, I thought it was a weird thing to say. I remember rolling my eyes and kicking a stone over the edge to see how long it took to hit bottom. But now I understand what he meant. Some places have something about them that remind you how measly you are in the scheme of things, not in a way that makes you feel helpless, but in a way that makes you feel like you're part of the plan and connected to everything else, no matter how inconsequential you might feel. My eyes tear up at the thought of Dad having that feeling. Somehow, I conspired to see him as my own personal pain in the ass, instead of another piece of the cosmic pie, same as me, with doubts and fears and grandiose dreams. Something loosens around the center of my chest.

And then I have this vision: *Dawn gently illuminates the Mother Circle. The camera tenderly pans the ring of the trees, zooming out slowly to heighten the incongruity of their twisted limbs creating a perfect circle. We ascend the obelisk, its crannies granting purchase for tiny, brightly colored desert blooms and nests for birds or animals. Atop the stony pedestal is Destinée, nude and singing, with no pretense of costumes or makeup or storylines of medieval knights, labyrinths, cowboys or saloons. Just her, natural and vulnerable, in stark contrast to the spiny trees and rocky surfaces. Her natural red curls move slightly on the breeze. Her eyes are closed. The camera is so close and its movement so slow that it's impossible to tell what part of her body is being filmed; she becomes soft knolls and valleys of flesh juxtaposed against a dramatic background. The light lapses so that time is understood, clouds pass under the sun, shadows darken the body and the land, as though Destinée herself were crossing the sky.*

"Nice," JC nods, eyes slitted in appreciation. "You oughta make it happen."

Okay. He's a mind reader. Get used to it. "Too late. I quit. The shoot is cancelled. I'm outta here tomorrow. It's not what I was hired for. And how does it sell a burger, anyway? Unless it just showed the burger after her clip and said something like 'the natural choice.'" Oh, man. That could work. For the sake of normal conversation, I recount to JC the major plot point of what happened after he left the bowling alley.

JC's hair whips his face as he shakes his head. "I adore Patsy, but she and her Citizens are terrorists, man. You can't quit because of them."

"I'm not," I argue. "I quit because I suck."

"That vision you just had didn't suck."

I know that too.

"Check it out." JC points to a shelf-like outcropping not six feet away.

The rattlesnake's tawny stripes blend in with the rock as it sprawls in the afternoon sun. "Rattlesnakes carry hemotoxic venom which basically annihilates tissue and organs. Then your blood stops clotting," JC says calmly, rhythmically waving his hand until the snake's head rears up. Its body curls into a loose "S" and it slithers toward us, hollow tail beads clattering.

"What are you doing?" I pull my legs into a crouch, ready to leap. Snakes scare the shit out of me.

"Rattlers aren't aggressive by nature, but if you disturb a nest or a hunt, they'll strike." JC pulls his hair away from his face. "Their bite is always potentially fatal and the younger they are, the more potent the venom, the more apt they are to deliver a fatal dose."

"Come on!" I grab JC's arm, but he calmly shakes me off.

It's like he's in a trance now. "The snake's nature is to protect itself, its food, its young. Does that mean we never go where rattlesnakes might live?"

"Yes!" I crab-crawl away, backwards, down, anywhere that's away from the snake, which is now about three feet from JC's face.

"No." JC's voice is soothing, mesmerizing. "We must always go toward what we fear. We must kiss the enemy and offer our cheek to let him kiss us back as best he can." In one swift strike, the snake extends its body, as though flying through the air. It's in and out in one precise movement, then disappears quickly under the rock. The sound of trickling sand is the only evidence of its presence. That, and the two bite marks in the center of JC's right cheek.

Floating in the middle of my forehead is me and Dad in that hillside garden, on either side of that shitty pipe. "Fuck! What do I do? Where do we go?"

JC sprawls across the rock and hangs his head backwards off the ledge. "Keep my head below my heart and suck the bite as hard as you can. You want to draw blood to the area to help drain the toxin. Most important: don't swallow!"

I press my mouth to the wound on his cheek. I am present in a relaxed, floaty way, as though directing myself in the scene from above. Part of me relies on instinct to coordinate the sucking and spitting. Another part of me wonders if JC did this on purpose. But why? A tiny part of me hopes Dad is watching, and proud.

JC's van is not the turd I thought it would be. Its off-road tires grab the ground as the back road shifts from hard pack to soft sand. I drive slowly to keep JC from swaying in the passenger seat. "Give me a landmark," he groans, head between his knees.

"Pile of rocks that looks like a bag of French fries," I say. The metallic taste of blood—JC's blood—tingles in my mouth. My breath smells like a butcher shop.

"Bear left. Give me another one."

The van careens to the left around the bag of fries, up and over a smooth hill, then through a narrow canyon. We're heading straight into the sun now. "Stand of pine on the right growing out of a boulder that looks like the prow of a Spanish galleon."

"Stay straight." JC turns his face up to me. "How do I look?"

"Jesus Christ!" I nearly veer off the trail. His right cheek has doubled in size; blood weeps from the puncture wound. Sweat beads sprout on his brow.

"Try to maintain, Sander," he says. "Am I yellow?"

"Light green. How do you feel?"

"In about fifteen minutes I go into shock, so step on it, my friend. Just follow the road."

The Chevy lurches forward and its rear fishtails a bit, but I'm getting the hang of driving on sand. You need to go fast, so the vehicle floats. I'm amazed at my calm demeanor in the face of jeopardy, amazed that I'm able to focus and drive, given that I'm stoned off my ass.

"It's because my shit is clean, that's why," JC murmurs. "We should be here now."

And we are. The back road has delivered us to the Oasis Motel, right to the door of Room Ten. Patsy's room. "Now what?" I kill the engine. JC's slumped against the glove compartment. "Help! Help!" I run around to the passenger side, pull JC from the seat and position myself under him, fireman-style.

"Shush!" Patsy calls out in a loud whisper from the cracked door. "The baby's sleeping!"

I drag JC from the car to her threshold, where classical music leaks from the space above the crack in the door. "Rattlesnake!" I whisper.

"Shit!" She steps outside the door and closes it behind her. She's wrapped in white towels—one around her body, another turbaned around her hair—but this is no time to enjoy the view. "Come on." She leans into JC's other shoulder and together we drag him around the motel—the long way, to avoid going past Harry's windows—and deposit him on his back on my bed. "Make him comfortable," she says from under the sink, where she pulls out a green metal box.

The piano music from Patsy's room seeps through the walls, scoring the scene of me stuffing pillows under JC's knees and head, then tucking a knitted, field-of-daisies comforter under his chin. If his head didn't look like it was about to explode, he'd look peaceful.

Patsy calmly digs through the box. "Hold him," she says. I clamp down on JC's biceps while Patsy swabs antiseptic on his face.

The melody marches on, accelerating, as notes fill the air with swirls and flourishes. She tosses aside the cotton and brandishes a gleaming safety razor. "Don't faint on me, Hollywood."

"Just do it!"

With the ease of a French chef, Patsy lances the swollen snakebite. Black blood and acid-green pus geyser upward, straight into my chest. She daubs the wound with hydrogen peroxide, then swiftly plunges a hypodermic needle into his cheek. JC's body convulses, then visibly releases into what appears to be a restful sleep.

The music quiets again as Patsy listens to his chest, his heart, takes his pulse. "He'll be fine." She grabs my hand, presses it to her heart, and bows her head.

I try to memorize her gingery freckles, the soft rise of her chest as she breathes, lips moving in silent prayer or poetry. There is a quality about her I could watch forever. She is part animal, part human, part angel—unlike any other person yet somehow more like everyone than anyone I've met. The moment is natural and intimate, as though we are an established couple, long accustomed to saving people's lives. I suddenly want to apologize for everything rotten I've ever done. "I'm sorry about the Corral," is the best I can muster.

"I know," she sort-of smiles. "Me, too. I thought about what you said, about your dad. I don't really want to impeach Harry. But sometimes, it's just hard to quit being me." She releases my hand to collect and dispose of the bloodied gauze easily, efficiently—the same way she makes drinks behind the bar in the Saloon. The way she pumps the cactus-shaped soap container exactly three times before scouring her hands is adorable.

"You can change if you want," I offer, with a sudden flash of Paul Street-like wisdom.

"So they say." She eyes the toxic goo slathered over my front. "You can change your shirt too."

I take a quick shower and put on a clean shirt and pants, and when I come out of the bathroom, Patsy has moved the rocker to the edge of the bed and is massaging JC's feet on her lap. "Best not to move him for a while. Give his system a chance to stabilize. Can he stay here until...when are you leaving?"

"Tomorrow," I say. "One night on the floor won't be so bad."

She points to an upper cabinet. "There's a bottle of Jack up there. I could use some."

I take it down and find two shot glasses. "I know. I discovered it last night. Did you put that there?"

"No, but I grew up here. I know all the secrets." I pour us each a finger and she raises her glass to me. "You saved JC's life," she says quietly. "Not bad, Sander."

"Thanks, Patsy." I raise my glass. It's the first time we've addressed each other by name. Not that I'm keeping track.

We knock back our shots and are quiet a moment, looking off to opposite sides of the room, JC, Gary Cooper on the poster, anywhere. Patsy breaks the silence. "Oh my god." She points at my open laptop's screensaver. She cocks her head and stares at herself, her light and darkness, the sun's halo, that straight-on gaze. "I've thought a lot about that bobcat. I think it came to say I should live my life, and not be stuck in the past."

"That's funny," I say, enjoying looking at her looking at herself. "I thought it came to watch us having sex and was disappointed that we didn't finish."

She looks at me and laughs, revealing two silver fillings on the right side and one on the left. She moves JC's feet back to the bed and gets up from the rocker. "Show you something?"

As I step outside to follow Patsy down the corridor, Jake streaks in and jumps on the bed, settling in next to JC, who I swear has a smile on his face.

Room Ten has a modern Palm Springs sensibility. White walls, white carpeting and white linen curtains with orange Formica countertops and kitchen chairs for contrast. Starshine sits cross-legged on the orange-and-white-flowered sofa, smiling and cooing into a basket made of twigs. Her henna-red hair is wrapped into a tall bun, Nefertiti-style. "Where'd you run off to, Pats?" She looks up at me. "Hi, Sander." She looks to us for explanation, eyebrows up.

I start in on the story of JC and the snake. "I went out to the rocks and found..."

"...Sander needed fresh towels," Patsy interrupts. She chews her lip; the sign of a bad liar.

"Really." Starshine smiles at Patsy's towel-based getup.

"Shut up," Patsy says, disappearing down a short hallway.

I don't know why Patsy doesn't want Starshine to know about her own husband, but I back off. There must be a good, female reason. "How's the papoose?" I ask, to be polite, peering into the basket. "Wow. You just sneezed her out. What was in that powder anyway?"

"I have no idea. You'll have to ask JC," Star laughs. "Here, Lucy Sky has been waiting to meet you." Starshine lifts the tie-dye flannel-wrapped bundle and prepares to transfer it into my arms.

"No thanks. Babies aren't really my thing."

Starshine laughs. "Don't be silly. Everyone loves babies. Sit down."

There's a molded-plastic rocking chair behind me, so I back into it and let Starshine deliver her daughter to my lap. The infant's limbs jerk and curl, and her watery blue eyes stare up at me. "Can she see me? Aren't babies blind when they're born?"

"You're thinking of kittens. Go ahead, pick her up. Just support her head."

Lucy's tiny body thrums against my heart, her sweet-sour breath a gentle breeze. Maybe it's the fact that her father is in my room, moments from death; maybe it's the fact that I burned down a historical monument; maybe it's just that my sister has got one of these cooking in her own inner oven—I have no idea—but, with an unexpected pang, my eyes well with tears. I see Dad in this creature and wish he were here. To meet these characters. To hang out with his friend Paul Street. To watch my almost-perfect shoot. To console me when it went to shit. He might have liked Buckaroo. Might have set up a cabin on a little piece of land as a weekend getaway from weekdays of reaming pipe. Which is ridiculous, because I'm just wishing that's what he would do. Lucy squeals, a tiny, toy-like moan. "What does she want?" I ask.

Starshine loosens her wrap to expose part of her breast. "Here, I'll take her now."

My hands shake as I pass Lucy back to Starshine, the warmth in my arms and chest cooling from her absence. Lucy's face creases like a balled-up washcloth as she suckles at Starshine. The intimacy of the moment is overwhelming. I wipe my eyes with the back of my sleeve, fully realizing I'm missing a Dad who didn't even exist. "Kids are so needy. Such a huge responsibility."

"Ow." Starshine grimaces as the infant spastically pats her breast. "They're just like everyone else, learning to make the most of what they've got, finding love where they can and figuring out how to be happy. They need us less than we think."

Patsy rejoins us, hair half-dry and tousled. She leans against a kitchen counter, her T-shirt absent political comment for a change. "I usually make a light supper after work on Tuesday nights. Nothing fancy. Would you like to join us?"

We make a date for ten o'clock, and as I float back to my room and pass Room Two, there's a loud exclamation of "Shit!" from the other side of the small bathroom window.

"Paul?" I rap on the window. "Are you all right?"

A second later his door opens. What is it with towels as a fashion statement around here? "Goddamn hot water practically scalded me." He looks up and outside. "Oh, it's you." He re-ties his towel skirt around his waist, crosses his arms and looks off into the distance.

I hate that I suck at apologies, and I owe him a big one. "Let me look at it."

"Don't go to any trouble." He flips his hand at me.

I step past him and go straight to the small closet behind the shower. "Scalding water is a simple fix." I adjust the pressure balancing valve, then turn on his shower and run my hand under the hot water. "Try it now."

He watches me thoughtfully. "Bobby had the same instincts. Always knew right where to go, exactly what to do."

"Regular chip off the block," I say. "It never hurts to have a skill people need."

"You're like him in so many ways you don't even realize."

I give it a shot. "I'm sorry I blew up at you. This opportunity wouldn't have been mine to blow if it weren't for you. I had no right to be such a dick."

"You just hit the anger stage of your grief, that's all. And I was a handy target." He makes actorly faces in a mirror, then pulls on perfectly-faded jeans. He uses the towel-skirt to rough-dry his hair, then concentrates on combing, the nuances of which require focus and finesse to create his windswept, natural look. I find myself studying his jaw line, looking for the scar from his youth, when the pony ran into the clothesline and nearly decapitated its rider. There's no sign of a scar; he must have had a great doctor. Paul catches me staring. "What?"

"Nothing."

He gives his trademark hair one final spritz. "Did you get a chance to open that box yet?"

Shit. When was the last time I saw that thing? "Not yet."

He bends down to pull on silk socks and fancy cowboy boots, and seems different when he sits back up. Pulled together.

I want to tell Paul Street about JC playing *Stairway to Heaven* naked. About getting stoned and having my mind read, and the snake biting JC, and Patsy being part angel and inviting me to dinner. I want to tell him about how I let Dad down, let him die.

"Sander?" Faun calls out, banging on Room Three's door. "Sander! Where are you?"

I step outside Paul's room. "Right here. What's going on?"

A small posse of locals is with her: Harry, Willamette. Carson pretending to film us with her Keystone. "This is an intervention," Harry says.

"A what? For who? You trying to save me?"

"Not you, jerk, the commercial." Faun rolls her Bambi eyes. "While you were off doing whatever, we've been making a plan."

Fucking Mickey Rooney she is. Fucking Judy Garland. Come on kids, let's save the show! "Oh, have you? And what plan is that?"

Faun hands me a paper bag. "Can you walk, eat and listen at the same time?"

Paul Street watches us silently, arms folded across his chest.

"I'll give it my best shot," I say.

15

TUESDAY EVENING

The bowling alley frank inside the paper bag is as satisfying as any Dodger dog I've ever had. As we walk the stretch of desert from the Oasis to the Kicker, I chew while Faun talks. "This project isn't just about you. It's a big opportunity for me, too. When the crew quit, I made them sign waivers saying they couldn't tell anyone about the fire until Saturday. So Vana won't find out. Just in case there's a way we could still make it happen."

I wish I'd thought of that. "Why didn't you tell me?"

Faun's arms fly out in frustration. "I couldn't find you! I left a bunch of messages on your phone but you never called!"

"My phone died." While I was moping and getting high, my P.A./A.D. was already on the rebound, charting an alternate course. I feel sheepish and threatened at the same time. "Anyway, a bunch of waivers aren't going to keep Vana from hearing about this. You know how the grapevine works. She probably already has a new director booked."

"Nope," Paul Street says, trailing behind us, as he clicks off his cell. "That was Vana. Everything's still set. She'll be here tomorrow at seven a.m."

Am I the only one not delusional here? "They took all their

gear with them, remember? And what about the dancers?"

Willamette steps forward. "Costumery has everything you'll need. Lights, reflectors, tracks. They're old, but they work."

A solution right under my nose. How extra embarrassing. The vintage equipment might even give the project the authentic feel I was shooting for. Could be cool.

"The Gunslingers can dance like nobody's business," Harry adds. "And you've pretty much learned how to use your new camera now, haven't you?"

"Ha ha." It sounds too plausible; they must be overlooking something. "I don't know."

"Come on, Sander," Carson says from behind her little Keystone camera. "It'll be great."

"What are you doing? Is that even working?" I point to her camera.

"Paul Street took me to pick up my lens today." She pans over to Paul, who waves.

I experience something which might be pre-emptive heartburn, but which also might be a tiny stab of jealousy that it was Paul who picked up the lens and not me.

"He let me drive the Avanti, too," she whispers. "Man, that baby flies! But only on the back roads. Never outside Buckaroo." She cranks the handle. "Now I can be just like you!"

I decline to point out the futility of her goal. "Why are we even talking about this when we have nowhere to film?" I mash a handful of fries into my mouth as I already start to picture something daring and fresh that still satisfies the original Western Burger concept.

We're already at the entrance to the Saloon. Harry opens the heavy plank door and points me down a narrow hallway just off the entrance.

"This doesn't go anywhere," I say, looking up the staircase that dead-ends into the ceiling. The small room looks exactly like the Western Burger set that just burned down. Same rustic bar, round tables and chairs, barrel kegs along the wall, everything.

"Actually," says Harry, "there's a little trap door that goes up into the attic. Patsy keeps the good whiskey up there."

"Never was supposed to go anywhere," adds Willamette, then covering Carson's ears, whispers, "One of them original producers got it into his head he needed a staircase with a banister for his hoochie girls to grind on. I mean for his dancing girls to audition on." She lets go of Carson and tousles her hair. "He was too cheap to build a second floor, so he decided stairs would do the trick."

JC's rendition of Led Zeppelin oozes through my overcooked brain. "And they're the same stairs as the ones on Destinée's set?"

"Her set was built to look exactly like this room, actually," Harry explains.

Faun starts in. "First, we make amends with the Citizens by rebuilding the Corral."

Willamette waves a baton of rolled-up paper. "I dug up the blueprints. Folks that originally built it were on a tight budget, being as it was all their own dough. Shouldn't cost much to clean up the mess, get a bunch of lumber, and follow these here plans."

"And we're paying for this how?"

"Obviously, I didn't pay the crew for work they didn't do," Faun says. "The rest of their salary is still in the budget."

Okay, so I hadn't thought of that. "Yeah, but who's going to build it?"

Harry thumps his chest with his thumb. "My Homeboys."

This takes a moment to sink in. "Your band?"

"Sure. Carl knows his way around a table saw almost as good as his bass. Ed and Buzz used to work at Paramount building sets before they retired and moved out here for good. In fact, I think they built the sets for *Star Trek*; you'll have to ask 'em. They've certainly done bigger jobs than rebuilding the Okay. Should be a piece of cake."

"So why didn't Oggie Bright just film here the first time?"

"Patsy," Harry and Willamette say together.

"Wouldn't let 'im," Harry chuckles.

"No way!" says Carson.

"Not till hell froze over," Willamette adds.

"You're darn right I wouldn't," says a voice. "What's everyone doing?" Patsy stands at the threshold, head cocked to one side, hands on her hips.

"Nothing," murmurs Willamette, handing off the blueprints to Harry as she scurries across the room. "I got to get back to the Bowl."

Faun moves to take the blueprints from Harry, but he gently steps aside, gesturing for her to follow Willamette outside the door. Faun looks at me for corroboration. I can tell Harry's got something on his mind, something big, but the way his eyebrows and mouth are working, it seems he's not sure where he's going or how he's going to get there. I motion for Faun to follow Willamette and she shrugs, but does as I ask.

Harry makes the first move. "Patsy, we'd like to shoot the commercial here."

"Smile, Mom," Carson says, cranking the Keystone's handle and focusing on Patsy.

"Carson Jean, don't you film me!" She points a warning finger at her daughter, then turns to me. "I thought the shoot was canceled."

Carson ignores her mother and pans in my direction.

"It was," I say, sputtering like I'm lying even though I'm telling the truth. "This was all Faun's and Harry's idea."

"And mine!" Carson calls out.

Then something clicks and I'm on board. "And it's not a bad one. We fulfill our contracts and shoot here, you make some money, we all go back to L.A. the next day and you never think about us again."

"Last time we made a deal, you burned down the Okay!" Patsy says matter-of-factly.

"*Lightning* burned down the Corral, not me." I take the blueprints from Harry and unroll them on a table. "And we can build a new one. Just like the old one."

"Then what kind of disaster falls upon the town? Locusts? The plague?"

"Dammit!" Carson screams, her face turning red. "Sander's being nice! Why do you have to be like that?"

"Watch your mouth, young lady." Patsy crosses her arms. "Be like what? What am I?"

Carson narrows her eyes. "You're a B..."

"Don't you dare," Patsy whispers.

"I..." Carson continues, glancing sideways at Harry and me. "T..."

"Carson Jean," Harry interrupts. "If you finish spelling that word, you're grounded!"

But Carson ignores her grandfather too. "B. I. T. C. H! Bitch, bitch, *bitch!*" she screams, then sprints toward the door.

Patsy lunges to the right to block her daughter's escape.

Carson wheels in my direction and throws her arms around my waist, sobbing into my T-shirt. All I can think to do is rub little circles on her back like I've always done for Ellie. Patsy looks at me with a sad, little-kid expression on her puss—something I haven't seen before—as though she were asking me a question. Whatever it is, the answer can only be yes; I nod my head. The room crackles with tension as Patsy slowly fills a glass with water behind the bar. She drinks it, rinses the glass, then puts it back on the shelf, upside down. Very deliberately, she walks across the room and puts her hand on Harry's shoulder. "So. Pop. How would this work?"

It's nice to see Harry smile for a change, even if he's crying at the same time.

*   *   *

The Shitkicker Saloon is hopping. I want the Okay Corral rebuilt before Vana arrives tomorrow, so Harry's Homeboys, Carl, Buzz and Ed, have set up a mini-headquarters in the pool room, making calls to friends for lumber and materials. Willamette has offered to loan us some old Studio Pro lights stored away back in the old soundstage so they can work through the night. Willamette, Faun and I are at a table in the center of the main room, auditioning the last of the available Gunslingers to fill the roles of our saloon dancers and drunken cowboys. The Gunslingers are a loose-knit group of men, women and kids who entertain Buckaroo's Sunday tourist trade by dressing up in Western garb and having themselves an old-time shoot-'em-up on Mane Street. As far as auditions go, anyone's eligible, as long as they bring their own costumes and can memorize a few lines and some dance steps for the hootenanny afterwards. Harry, Patsy and Carson have set up a buffet-style table of eats for everyone to serve themselves so the three of them can enjoy their Apple family reunion dinner without interruption. Father and daughter sit at a back table below a large, amateurish portrait of Harry in his twenties astride a spotted pony, while Carson films them talking together, recording the reunion. Seeing them animated, joking, catching up after fourteen years of feudal silence is fantastic. I am satisfied, calm. Or maybe that's just what happens when Roy Rogers sings *Happy Trails*, as he is from the jukebox right now. Whatever it is, I feel good, even though we still need one more cowdude to complete the cast.

"What about that long drink of man?" Faun points over to a cowboy at the bar. "There ought to be at least one guy a girl wouldn't mind hitting the sack with."

"Go for it."

Faun stands up and arches her back, displaying her silhouette to its fullest advantage. "Hey you. Come here." She crooks her finger at the cowboy, who looks over each shoulder before pointing to himself. Me? "Yes, you."

He moves his toothpick from one side of his mouth to the other and strolls lazily to our table. His archetypal Marlboro Man looks—sharp cheekbones, sun-squint eyes, lean bod in a tight T and jeans—are tempered only by dingy yellow teeth. Perfect.

"You want to be in a commercial?"

"Mebbe," he considers the proposal. "Do I get to work with you?"

"Mebbe," she says back. "Can you dance?"

"Ballroom, cha-cha, tango and rumba. Some disco. Vegas style."

Faun pinches my leg and I pinch hers back. She smiles and asks the cowboy his name.

"Spit."

"Spit what?"

He moves the toothpick back to its original corner. "Cowboy Spit."

"Can you be here at eight tomorrow morning, Cowboy Spit?" she asks.

Spit leans down on the table with both arms and smiles his yellow smile at Faun. "I can be wherever you want me to be."

"Eight is fine." She shifts in her chair and twirls a lock of hair around in her fingers.

Spit tips his hat and winks before turning away from our table to head toward the bar.

"Sweet Jesus in heaven, that cowboy is a dish," she says, watching him strut to *Happy Trails'* pokey beat.

"I thought you liked girls."

"I love girls," she says. "But every now and again, a cowboy is a fine, fine thing." We crack up and look around the Saloon, alive with business and plans and music. Faun taps at the keyboard of her laptop. "Take a look at the new schedule."

"Sure." I hunker toward the screen. The schedule looks fine—

it's exactly the same as our original one, only shot indoors instead of out, which makes it a helluva a lot more stable; and with one camera, my VMX (instead of many), shot by me (instead of a D.P.), which eliminates the stability factor right there. I can't stop peeking out the sides of my eyes at Patsy; she's a hot, white bulb to my mothy gaze. Carson walks through the room, filming the crowd, then stops at the jukebox and waves to her mom, who waves back, mouthing, "Go on." Carson drops in a quarter, punches a few buttons, and suddenly the music changes from Roy Rogers to an R & B oldie. *"Rescue me / take me in your arms. / Rescue me / I want your tender charms."* Good old Fontella Bass. As if we all drank the same Kool-Aid, everyone in the place migrates to the dance floor. Willamette two-steps with Paul Street. Spit sweeps Faun to her feet and twirls her in a series of professional spins that make her yelp with delight. Harry leads Patsy from their table. The Gunslingers, still in costume, practice their routine in two lines. Everyone is smiling at everyone else, for no other reason than it's Tuesday night, we're kind of hard at work and we're kind of having fun. I haven't felt this giddy since I was stoned up at the hot springs with Patsy.

Carson sits at my table and turns the lens on me. "I'm filming my mama's birthday present. You think she'll like it?"

"She'll love it because she loves you."

"I know," she sighs. "Say something for the video."

But before I can begin, Patsy grabs my arm. "You know how to swing?"

Swing dancing was Dad's passion, before it was replaced with television, and when we were kids, swing dancing meant it was Sunday afternoon. (No boring church for us!) Dad would mix up a couple of cocktails, with Shirley Temples for Ellie and me. Mom would haul out the record player and the suitcase of old 45s. And then we would just go crazy. Dad would throw Mom in the air. Ellie would throw me on the floor. Dance until we were exhausted, laughing most of the time. I never swing danced in high school or college—it would have been the opposite of cool. But I do remember Dad's whispered advice: "Watch for good dancers, Sander. They can make a man happy." To Carson I say, "Film this."

To Patsy I say, "East Coast or West?"

She smiles broadly at me. "West is best."

I grab Patsy's waist and spin her. She whoops loudly, twirling three times, landing face to mine. Her Dentyne breath and the barbecue smoke in her hair are intoxicating. We swing easily together. She glides away, I reel her back in. She's a good dancer and I'm a happy man. I'm the kid in the wood-paneled variety room, bare feet in orange shag, Mom and Dad laughing, Fontella singing it like it is.

After a few more stretches of dancing and mini-meetings with folks to figure out tomorrow's shoot, I notice it's ten after midnight. "That's my curfew," I tell Faun. "There's nothing left of me. You knocking off soon?"

"Go on ahead," she says, from Spit's lap, with her arms entwined around his neck and his nose nestled in the vee of her T-shirt.

I cut across the dance floor to the big back doors and step outside to head toward the motel.

"You turning in already?" a voice calls from the shadows. It's Patsy.

"Big day tomorrow," I say. "I mean today. Hey, happy birthday. I guess it's official."

"I guess so," she says. "The beginning of the end."

"Maybe the end of the beginning." We both look up to the waxing gibbous moon, and a star shoots across the night's spectacular cathedral dome.

"Wow, did you see that?" she says.

"Yeah. That'll have to be my birthday present to you, because I didn't have a chance to leave a note for the wife and kids. Or rob that bank. I'm a little behind schedule."

"I know what you can give me," she says quietly. "If you want."

I know what I want to give her, but I know better than to say. "What?"

"You want to go for a ride?"

"Again? I'm not sure."

"You don't even have to get out of the truck. I just need someone with me," she says. "Please?"

The radio suddenly blasts as Patsy's Luv rounds a curve on Buckaroo Highway toward the valley. Gilbert O'Sullivan sings that sappy song from the seventies. It always slayed me as a kid, not just because the lyrics spoke of suicide and death so casually, but because I couldn't get it out of my head the afternoon Nate and I decided to run through the girls' locker room while the girls were changing from their uniforms into street clothes. It was a thrilling extravaganza of tops off, bottoms up, smells of powder and musk, and the ever-present Herbal Essence shampoo. Every night when I went to bed, I kept the radio on low, just waiting for the song to come on between 9:40 and ten o'clock, and drifted off to sleep with my hands between my legs, a smile on my face, and visions of bras and panties dancing across the ceiling.

"God this song kills me," Patsy says, and snaps it off. We're just past Coyote Trail at the intersection of the main road. All the landmarks are present and accounted for: The Greasy Spoon coffee shop, Auntie Rose's Little Bo-Teek, Dusty's Liquors, the Motor Inn. Patsy turns right, down Highway 62 in the direction of Morongo Basin and Palm Springs.

About a half-mile before the Interstate, at Desert Hot Springs, the wind buffets the little pickup. Patsy pulls to the shoulder at the on-ramp to the 10 East. "This is it."

"What?" The columns of windmills stand like an alien army, powerful and silent.

"The furthest away I've ever been from Buckaroo."

"Oh." The wind howls and gusts at the intersection of the grass-covered slopes from Morongo and the jagged peaks of the San Gorgonios, where snow dots the uppermost reaches. A rusty tin shack leans between the two cloverleaf on- and off-ramps. Bits of shredded plastic blow sideways and tangle in the cyclone fence parallel to the road.

"I don't have a solid memory of this, but when I was little, the Saloon wasn't doing well and my parents were arguing about money a lot." Patsy's voice is small and raspy. "Uncle Ray-Ray and Mama and I were going to Nashville, where Mama was going to cut a record. But the car flipped on the highway, right here. Uncle Ray-Ray and Mama died. I was asleep in the back seat and thrown clear. I was bruised and scraped and stuff, but not broken." She looks into her lap. "Well, not broken so you could see."

That lovely outer shell has finally cracked. I step out of the truck. "Chinese fire drill." Patsy climbs over to the passenger side while I circle round and take the driver's seat. She jams the screwdriver into the ignition, and I accelerate onto the on-ramp. I just drive, keeping my eyes on the road; Patsy looks out the window. I pull off about thirty miles down at the Wheel Inn, a diner with a 50-foot-tall dinosaur in the parking lot that's lit up green at night. It's air-conditioned inside. The coffee is hot, the apple pie warm. We don't speak a word the entire time. When we return to the motel, we go our separate ways.

In my room, the bed is made; JC and Jake are gone. Two shot glasses and the bottle of JD on the counter and the bloodied debris in the trash are the only evidence this was a scene from *E.R.* just a while ago.

16

WEDNESDAY PRE-DAWN

I have twisted and tangled in this bed for hours, my brain buzzing with lists of everything that could go wrong today shot with jolts of adrenaline from orbiting around planet Patsy. Finally, I dress and sit on the bench outside to count shooting stars. Some of them are green and move across the sky in formation; I chalk that up to my tired eyes and sleep-deprived brain. Finally, sunrise—a bloody, Heinz ketchup smear.

I'm on my third cup of coffee when a taxicab-yellow HumVee with tinted windows turns off the Buckaroo Highway at the Saloon and rolls toward the elevated embankment in front of the Oasis, with Jake trotting alongside it. The huge machine lurches into Park, and as the driver door opens, there is a mighty rumbling deep in my gut suggesting a confluence of fear and French roast: my producer knows nothing of our change of plans.

Vana LeValle hops down from the high seat in a khaki safari costume complete with multipocketed jacket, cargo pants and a panama hat trimmed in leopard with a matching neck scarf. "Ve ready?" She rubs her jeweled hands together.

"Ready and waiting!" I chirp. A minor improvement over *Righty-ho.* "There are a few things we need to talk about first." Urgent intestinal cramps send shooting signals to my ass.

"Vat ve need talk about?" Jake sits on his haunches at Vana's feet, one paw lifted for a shake. "How sveet," she gushes, shaking his paw, then squatting down to throw her arms around him. "Who he is? Yours?"

"That's Jake. And he's nobody's, really." I try not to gag as Vana kisses Jake on the mouth and lets him lick her lips, but I'll take any time he can buy me. "There have been some minor changes."

Her face dewy with dog slobber, Vana appears nonplussed. She thumps Jake's chest and laughs when one of his hind legs goes into a ticklish frenzy. "I zink I falling in love, Zander. Vat changes?"

"Listen, I need to... I just, can you give me five minutes?" There's no time to wait for a response. My insides are churning as I run to Room Three, but my feet are not fast enough.

There's a voice from the HumVee. "Saaanderrr? Hiii!" The back door bounces open and Destinée leaps from the truck. She is stick-thin with a clot of gingery red curls hanging to her waist. A plaid flannel robe flies behind her like a superhero cape as she barrels down the hill in Eskimo-style suede and fur boots. "I'm sooo haaappy to meet youuu," she cries, and throws herself at me with such force that I involuntarily let loose a tremendous warning fart which I hope my donkey bray of laughter will camouflage.

"Destinée! Hello to you too!" I disentangle myself from her enthusiasm and head toward the door. "Just give me five..." As soon as I'm inside, my pants are undone and dropped. I'm on the throne and ready to produce what I can already tell is going to be one of the all-time greats, a personal best, when something stops me cold.

"Darlings. How was the drive?" Paul has joined Vana and Destinée outside my painted-open bathroom window. He sounds rested and sincere. I know this because I can hear them—and see snippets of their bodies—as clearly as if I were outside with them.

"Hiii Paaauuul. I can't waaait to work with Sander. I loooved his demo reel. It was greaaat." That girl is way too excited. I don't trust her or her super-elongated vowels.

"Ve don't vant great." Now it's Vana. "Ve vant vestern. Zander say new plans. Vat new plans?"

Jake mumbles as though he's telling her all about it, and ends his aria with a whine.

"I should probably let Sander tell you," Paul says. "Where is he?"

Right here, I want to say, but I'm too busy restraining what a moment ago I was gung-ho to release. Who knows what sounds effect might accompany sewage of this magnitude? What flatulence, splashing, plopping will echo through this tiled room? What aromatic aftermath might waft their way? But the pain of holding it in is unbearable, and goes against my personal code of conduct anyway. I try to let it emerge slowly, try to manage the splash, and keep the special effects to a minimum.

"Zander inside. I zink he had to make shit. He had zat look."

The jig is up. I let it rip and can't hold back a snorting laugh, knowing full well as the mongoose exits that it is, indeed, a perfect drop. Texture is firm but not hard. Odor is rich, instantly filling the room. I take a quick peek. A Loch Ness beauty curls in the bowl. I scrub up, flush, and wave an entire book of lit matches around to diffuse the stench. If I know anything about people, I'm confident everyone will be too polite to say anything once I join them outside.

"Nice one, Sander." Paul slaps my shoulder. "You been saving up?"

Faun emerges from Room Four, on the other side of my room, pulling a T-shirt over her head. "Sorry, people. I overslept. Good morning."

"Perfect timing," I say, heading away from my bathroom window and motioning for everyone to follow.

Faun joins us, tucking her shirt into her pants, looking unsurely at Vana, who offers her cheek for a European double-kiss. While Faun obliges, Cowboy Spit, looking rumpled and freshly-sexed, emerges from Faun's room, stretches and lights a cigarette.

"Mornin' everyone," he drawls, winking as he cowboy-strolls towards the Saloon.

Vana's nostrils flare. "Wampire?" she asks, pointing to the pink love bite on Faun's neck.

Faun turns bright red.

Paul looks at me.

I clap my hands once. "Let's take a ride." At least everyone's forgotten about my shit.

Vana navigates her HumVee up Mane Street, with me in the front seat, Paul and Destinée in back, and Jake trotting apace at ten o'clock. Harry Apple is at the intersection of Jackrabbit Lane, digging a hole. His new speed limit sign lies on the ground nearby. He waves as we slow down to five miles per.

"People in small towns are sooo friendly," Destinée chirps, waving back. "I remember hiiim."

But Vana doesn't notice. She's staring at the end of the street where Harry's Homeboy Carl perches atop a ladder next to the freshly-built corral, nailing up a sign across the main posts: "Vana LeValle's New Okay Corral."

"No vay!" One hand flies to her mouth, as though she might burst into tears.

"Yes way," I say, before launching into the story of the firestorm and the rest. By the time I get to my brilliant idea of adding Vana's name to the sign, both Destinée and her manager are singing my praises and saying how thrilled they are to be working with me. We have a little tête-à-tête about our modified approach to the existing script, which everyone loves, and I promise to stop by Destinée's room to walk with her over to the set. As we head down Buckaroo Highway toward the Saloon, Paul flashes a thumbs-up. This is going to be a breeze.

*   *   *

There's so much going on in the Shitkicker's small side room, it doesn't occur to me to be tired. Harry's other Homeboys, Ed and Buzz, have set the lights to create a certain dangerous, late-afternoon atmosphere that's more a perception than a measurement, something that comes from spending lots of leisure time in bars and knowing how the light looks when things turn to trouble. The Gunslingers in their homegrown costumes people the set with an authenticity that the previous dancers—God love their muscular, sculpted bodies— never even approximated. Take away the lights and the equipment, and the set could easily be an extension of the actual Saloon. A place where anything could happen, from marriage to murder.

"Everybody take five. Destinée's due on the set in fifteen."

Faun slaps my ass as I pass by. "Looks super, doesn't it?"

"Super fucking super. You're awfully fresh this morning."

She pats the red bandanna tied around her neck. "Don't know what's got into me." She winks and turns to look at Spit leaning against the bar, who touches the brim of his creased, greasy hat when she looks his way.

"Whatever it was, Vana didn't look too happy about it."

"I'll take care of her," Faun laughs.

"I'm sure you will." I head toward Room Eight. Poor Destinée. It must be hard to go from having a personal trailer and entourage to checking into a tiny motel bedroom in a backwater town. But what enthusiasm! She's obviously a pro. My palms sweat as I rap on the door.

It cracks open. "Vat?" At the sound of Vana's voice, Jake mumbles from his napping place in a patch of shade below the eaves.

"It's me. Time to walk over to the set."

The door closes. Vana's voice, a half-octave higher, floats through the wood. Jake raises his head. The door cracks open again and I can hear some kind of rustling inside, as though someone were thumping on the bathroom door. Vana sticks her head out now. "Destinée prefer valk over alone. She be zere in fifteen. Guarantee." The desert sun catches the wrinkles around Vana's eyes and the corners of her mouth. She slams the door so hard a blast of swamp-cooler chilled air huffs out at me.

This is bullshit. Back at the Saloon, one half-hour, then another, passes as we wait for our diva to appear. Ed, Buzz and Carl amble among the lights, confirming last-minute adjustments of position and intensity while I run through the camera shots again and again, like a martial artist making my moves, eyes closed, totally in control. I see the whole piece in a way I didn't yesterday, when I was just executing a pre-set list of shots for someone else's vision. This is going to be so fucking good; I'm determined not to let something like Destinée being a little late bung it all up. Carson and Faun work the room, keeping everyone's spirits high while the Gunslingers practice moves for Sunday's show.

I decide to take a walk around the building to work off some nervous energy and come across JC manning the Craft table in the Saloon's main room. He wears a trucker cap down low over his eyes and dark shades. The only sign of yesterday's brush with death is a small Band-aid across his right cheek. "You never tasted egg salad until you've had it fresh from Donnie's hens," he says, behind a mountain of hard-boiled eggs.

I try not to imagine egg salad squirting from the rear ends of hens. "How are you?"

"I'm great, thanks to you and Pats. I think with the new kid and all, maybe I just needed a snooze," he says, looking over his shoulder as though he expects someone to jump out at him from the shadows. "Sleep is nature's workshop, you know." He rolls an egg on a cutting board and palms off the entire shell with one hand. "You and Patsy work well together."

The thought springs to mind that JC plotted his snakebite as a matchmaking ploy. Or maybe it was so I wouldn't feel like such a failure about my paralysis during the fire. Perhaps it was to eliminate misplaced guilt about Dad's death. *Am I reading JC's thoughts?* "Where'd you go off to last night?"

"I'm a desert creature. Nighttime is my day." JC pops the egg into a slicer one way, than the other, resulting in perfectly diced cubes that he tosses into a large bowl. "You did good yesterday, Sander. I'm proud of you."

"I haven't seen Patsy today." I try to sound casual. "To wish her happy birthday."

"She and Star and Lucy went out to Patsy's teepee for a little tea and Tarot. It's a birthday tradition. They'll be down later, don't worry."

"I wasn't worried."

Cowboy Spit and a couple of Gunslingers come out of the small room. JC watches them from the corner of his eye, and waits until they go into the men's room before he speaks. "You know much about that cowboy? That tall one?"

"Who, Marlboro Man? Not much. Faun spotted him leaning against the bar when we were auditioning so we hired him."

"He's not a Gunslinger, that's for sure. Feels funny to me."

"I take it you don't mean funny ha-ha."

"Funny like FBI." Outside, Donnie's Bronco pulls into the parking lot, dust whirling in his wake. JC leaps from his chair and crouches behind it. "Whatever you do, don't tell Donnie you've seen me!" He monkey-runs down low to the kitchen. Seconds later, the screen door slams. Paranoia, suspicion. His is a brain on drugs, all right. I take JC's seat behind the table and start chopping eggs.

Donnie rolls in, all dandied up in yellow overalls, a light blue dress shirt, blue and yellow striped tie, white oxford shoes. With a huge smile on his face, he wheels a three-sixty to show off his outfit. "Today's the big day. Got to look nice for Patsy's birthday. So? What's the verdict?"

He looks like a cross between a pimp and an Easter egg. "Can I be honest?"

"I hope so."

"You won't shoot me?"

He bugs his eyes at me. "I promise."

"What you need is a total makeover."

"What?" Donnie's face clouds up.

"You heard me. Get out of those overalls and get a haircut."

He looks down into his lap. "*Each time it rings, I think it is for me, but it is not for me nor for anyone. It merely rings and we serve it bitterly together, they and I.*"

"And you gotta quit with the William Carlos Williams. It's weird and the chicks don't dig it. I'm sorry but I had to say it. We okay?"

Donnie sighs. "We're okay."

I look around. "Where's Little?"

"I thought Patsy might be here. Had to leave her in the truck." He leans in to whisper. "She used to like Patsy. But ever since I decided I was gonna pop the big one, Little's been acting all strange and peckish. Married life is gonna be a big transition for her. She's been the only girl in my life, but once I'm married, she'll be...the other woman."

No comment. "You know, I was curious about something. How do you figure a chicken's birthday anyway? I mean, is it the day the egg is laid," I hold up one of Donnie's glistening, hard-boiled poultry products. "Or the day the chick is hatched?" I bite off the ovoid top.

"Hatched." Donnie's brows furrow; his expression grows dark. "Patsy around?"

"I haven't seen her. Took the day off for her birthday I think, although she's supposed to work dinner for the crew tonight."

"Hmm." Donnie flicks an imaginary speck off his lapel. "Grandma tells me you convinced Patsy to shoot here in the Saloon. That's big news."

"Yeah, she's talking to Harry, too." Good Lord, I'm gossiping like a local! "Things are changing."

"This is just the beginning, my friend." Donnie reaches over and slaps my shoulder. Too casually, too hard. "You seen JC?"

"Nope." Thank God Donnie left his high-maintenance lie-detector chicken in the truck.

Cowboy Spit and his cronies come out of the men's room now. He doesn't look like FBI to me. In fact, I might be imagining it, but I swear Donnie nods at him.

"You see JC, you let me know, all right?" Donnie makes this pronouncement too loud, as though more for Cowboy Spit's benefit than mine.

"Roger that," I say, making a note to myself not to do anything of the kind.

Two hours later, Vana and her protégée arrive at the set. "Ve ready," Vana announces, leading Destinée, still in her ratty flannel robe and with most of her face hidden by her hair, to her chair.

I'm furious. We worked all night to be ready for her and now she's wasted everyone's morning. *What would Paul Street do?* I pull my chair to hers for a knee-to-knee conference. "Can I get you anything? Do you have any questions about what we're doing today?"

Destinée cuts a look over at Vana, then looks up at me, her professional happy face buttoned back on. "No. I'm ready. Let's dooo this." She tosses her robe aside, revealing her costume: a flashy corset above diaphanous strips of skirt, fishnet stockings and lace-up ankle boots. Willamette approaches with hair feathers and bobby pins, while her helper Lulu dips in for last-minute applications of brushed-on lip color, a whoosh of hair spray, an oversized puff of body glitter. In a few moments, the technicians, such as they are, the Gunslingers and Destinée find their marks. At last, almost three hours late, Faun hands me the megaphone. "Action!"

The music begins. The six male Gunslingers slam shots, shoot pool and play poker as though they've been doing it all night and will continue once the shoot is over. Their female counterparts brazenly drape themselves across the furniture, their everyday aspects and unstudied positions more authentic and subversively suggestive than the original dancers' clichéd, Hollywood-tinged concepts of allure. And I'm right where I need to be, with Faun behind me, hands on my waist, whispering short instructions in my ear as I frame and move with the dancers, taking it wide first, taking it all in. After the first sixteen bars, the music changes and the ladies begin to dance. Their group history as Gunslingers allows for a sense of play and mutual camaraderie, whereas the original dancers tended to fight for space, everyone pushing stage front and outdoing the others with explicit, masturbatory moves. As the women pull the men away from the table and the men demur, comic undertones become apparent. The war of the sexes, played out on the dance floor on a Saturday night.

On cue, Destinée moves center stage and up onto a table. Her slick moves, bright makeup and sparkly corset look out of place, unnatural, among the muted tones of the Gunslingers' costumes. Which is fine. She is not of them. She is above the common folk; she is artificial, the icon, the archetype. Until I realize something is wrong. Destinée's lip-synching is spot on, but her body moves to its own rhythm. This, in turn, throws off the Gunslingers, who until now have all been in synch with the beat and each other. We can maybe, somehow, fix it in editing. I just want to go through this once to see how the whole piece plays out. We'll get coverage, close-ups and such, later.

Suddenly, Destinée stops. "Cut!" she cries.

The other dancers look at her, then at me. Everyone knows only the director can call the cut. I repeat the call and pretend to fiddle with my VMX as I walk over to Destinée. "Everything all right?"

"Sorry." She nods her head briskly, betrayed by a nervous eye tic.

"Can you hear the music all right? Is there an echo?"

She shrugs and her chin quivers. I remember Harry's words: *it's your talent that'll screw you.* "Just forget everything else. Listen to the music and have fun."

"I *aaam,*" she says, then marches back to her mark. "Let's go. I'm ready!"

Faun claps the clapper. "Action!" I call again, motioning for the music.

At first, Destinée gamely powers through the moves, but it's as though she can't coordinate her movements to the tempo. Finally, she stops and just looks at me until I call, "Cut." I set my camera down on a chair.

"I told Vana I couldn't do it but she wouldn't believe me," Destinée says, her voice empty of emotion. She rubs her eyes, dragging glittery streaks down both sides of her face.

Jake keeps his eyes on Vana as she approaches from the sidelines. She takes Destinée's hand, pets her hair. "Baby, relax.

You'll mess makeup," Vana whispers. "Remember vat ve talk about?"

That's when Destinée loses it. "Of course I remember. All I do is remember." She throws herself to the ground and screams, a huge, redheaded insect in the throes of being burned by a lit match. (I was eight and only did it once, I swear.) "Last time I was here the same thing happened, I couldn't do it. And Oggie got mad and screwed that girl and we broke up. And everyone acts like nothing happened and everyone says I should be fine. But I'm not." She looks at Vana, then at the rest of us, who look like we're playing a game of freeze tag. "Can't you see my heart is broken?"

"Darling, you are fine," Vana pulls her up by one arm. "Now get up!"

"No, I'm not!" Destinée mule-kicks Vana with both feet, landing a wallop on her thigh.

"You crazy beech!" Vana shrieks, and, teetering off-balance, catches herself by grabbing Destinée's hair. The flame-colored tresses come off in her hands. Vana screams, dangling the hairpiece as though it were a dead animal.

Billiard ball-headed Destinée pounds the floor with her hands and feet, screaming, "I'm the one that does all the work and pours out my heart and all I get is treated like crap!"

What would Paul Street do? Thus far, he's standing across the room, shell-shocked, shaking his head and looking at me. I point at him and then Vana. As he tends to her, I head over toward Destinée's chair and tell everyone to take an hour for lunch.

There are groans and sighs all around from Harry's Homeboys and the Gunslingers. "Carson, go tell Harry I need to borrow the Eldo and bring me his keys."

"Yessir," she salutes me and dashes out of the room.

I lay the plaid-flannel robe across Destinée, whose crying has faded to a whimpering whine. Paul drops her wig in my lap as he leads Vana out the back door toward the motel.

Welcome to the glamorous world of commercials.

17

WEDNESDAY AFTERNOON

I'm in that second stage of exhaustion after a sleepless night, where my mind and body are operating on different planes. I steer Harry's Eldorado along the back road from the Oasis, following yesterday's landmarks in reverse—stand of pine growing out of a boulder like the prow of a Spanish galleon, narrow canyon, smooth hill, bag of French fries—and park the Cadillac in the shade of Elvis' stony arms and guitar. As soon as I turn off the engine, the particular sound of this place takes over. That contained call of wind moving through brush. Silence that grows more dense and complex the longer you listen to it, and the longer you listen to it, the simpler your thoughts become. Nature's own meditation tape.

"Why did you bring me here?" Destinée asks. Her crooked wig makes her look like a kid playing dress-up.

There isn't a course in film school that tells you what to do when your pop star has a broken-hearted meltdown. I explain about the Mother Circle and the Joshuas, and the calming effect they had on me when I was upset yesterday. "They might be able to help you, too."

She looks around, eyes darting from rocks to sky and back. "It is kind of preeetty in a spaaacey way." She drops her face into her hands and bawls. The wig falls onto her lap.

I dig around on the back seat floor. "You've got a spectacular head." I hand her a dusty box of tissues. "Architecturally, I mean. It's balanced."

She honks into a square.

I place my hand on her head. "So soft, too. Did you cut it yourself?"

"Yeaaah. Bad night," she snorts, launching a snot bubble from her nostril. "Sorry."

"It's really kind of striking." I flip down the visor so she can check herself out in the mirror.

She studies both profiles, then smiles for the first time, sincere and shy. "I don't mean to be difficult. I'm just an aaartist. Things need to be a certain waaay before I can perform. My body is my instrument. So if something isn't riiight, I can't find the beat. And after what happened last time? And the stress I'm under? I'm a nervous wreck." She sighs. "Do you have any gum? Or Xanax? I could really use a Xanax."

Feeling like Dr. Feelgood, I fish around in my pockets for the baggie of Dove JC gave me yesterday.

Destinée's eyes brighten. "What are those?"

I shake two pink capsules onto my open palm. "Local sunshine." We take one each and swallow, washing them down with warmish water from my canteen. The effect is almost instantaneous and very, very good.

Nature is on its best behavior as we stroll around the Mother Circle. The air is electric with light and the rocks shine gold beneath its buzzing blanket. Birds call out perfect hymns; rabbits arc furry rainbows. The trees themselves sway and sing under the soft caress of the thermal current. "Toootally," Destinée murmurs, taking my hand and swinging it as we stroll. "Oggie Bright is an aaasshole."

It's getting easier to tolerate her vowels. Maybe it's the Dove.

"A briiilliant asshole," she continues. "My therapist says I'm attracted to them. Like that's my paaattern. We were great while we laaasted, but we just didn't operate on the same plane of consciousness."

Of course you didn't.

"I'm not like sooome people who always have to be invooolved with their director," she continues, tears forgotten now that she's on topic. "Like that new cunt he's working with since I dumped him."

I thought Oggie dumped her, but no matter. Here's my cue. "That cunt he's with now?"

She nods, narrowing her eyes. "Ashe Standish," she hisses.

"Ashe used to be my girl. She dumped me to be with him."

"No waaay!" Destinée throws her arms around me. My ass instinctively clenches.

"It's all right. I found someone better."

"That is sooo cool!" Destinée cries, and hugs me again.

"I knooow!" We both crack up, comrades in Oggie Bright's waste-dump, wastoids in Dove's blissed-out euphoria, laughing until our stomachs ache, then convulsing into fresh gales. "You know? I had the most amazing vision of you yesterday." I tell her about the naked dance, the play of light and shadow, the resonance of the landscape, the eternity in the serene rocks and comforting dirt and trees that create their own visual ballet.

"Wow. That would be a great music video for my song." She touches her head. "I think I'm getting sunburned."

"Wait here. I'll go grab your hair." As I jog the short distance to the Eldo, I feel loose. Life is good. The project's fucked. So what. We're alive.

"I love Dove!" Destinée yells from the rock, and when I turn around to wave, she is dancing. Which is interesting, because tucked in the back seat next to the canteen is my VMX.

She laughs when I plop the wig on her head, and she continues to sway, drinking greedily from the canteen, water spilling down her throat, wetting her flannel robe. "That feels good," she says. "But this feels better!" She pulls off the robe, then the corset. "You should film me now, Sander. Film your vision. Let my fans see what I'm really like."

She doesn't have to ask twice. I set the VMX and frame my subject. "Naked except for my wig," Destinée purrs. "That'll show Oggie. Let the whole world see what he threw away. He'll be sorry. I just had my whole system purified, so I know I look great." She smiles and, for the first time, her lip size seems right. "Just keep that thing on me, baby. I'll give you footage that people will be longing about for a talk time." She giggles and laughs. "You know what I mean. And Sander," she stops for a second. "Call me D?" The rest of her clothes follow swiftly and she starts to move, dancing to the sound of the wind.

Without thinking, I move the camera around her. With this footage, I can easily recreate my original vision. Lay in the day-to-night sky work with some low-tech software. The point isn't for it to be perfect anyway. This is Destinée *au naturelle*. And then, the kind of magic that only happens when God finally tires of throwing rocks at the side of your barn.

A cloud of white butterflies appears from behind the rocks. D coos and dances with them as they flutter and swarm around her.

She's naked in their snowstorm: innocent and sexy, natural and clean. Her skin radiates health and there's laughter in her eyes. She could sell used cars or makeup or even a lame-ass Western Burger. She performs at her own personal sea level, a level that experiences life more deeply, loves more fully, renders intimacy more exclusively and invitingly and more meaningfully, in the most spectacular of all spotlights: the sun.

The Cadillac glides away from the Mother Circle over bumps and waves on the sandy wash. "It's like we're traveling on another planet," D whispers. We agree to shoot the commercial exactly as Vana wants it—offbeat or on—partly because I can't bear Faun and the Gunslingers pulling an all-nighter for naught, partly (mostly) because it's in my contract. I promise to make a dupe of the Mother Circle footage so D can show it to Vana to see if she agrees that those few trillion pixels of a few thousand butterflies cascading over her naked body would make the perfect video for D's single. D said it like this: "Even if you're the worst cinematographer in the world— because, no offense? I don't know you from Adam?—this has to be great, because we just witnessed a fucking miiiracle."

I roll down the window of Harry's old Caddie and smile. "Our bodies are such amazing machines. I mean, my brain thinks, 'Some air would be nice.' Then without even verbalizing it, my arm moves the crank that rolls down the window, and then before I know it, there's a breeze on my face."

D nods. "And see those jagged mountains over there? Don't they remind you of that statue of those soldiers planting that flag in that Japanese island?"

Apparently, thanks to Dove, D and I are both still at one with the universe. We ride the rest of the way in blissful silence; D with her wig in her lap and her almost bald, lightly pink head leaning out the window, me wondering how to drop massive amounts of Dove into the world's water supply. As we approach Buckaroo proper from the back of the Oasis Motel, a gunshot blast pierces the silence and echoes off the distant rocks. Another blast, then another. I jam on the gas pedal and swerve around the side of the motel and up Mane Street.

A man in black lies in the dust in front of the Bowl between two men pointing guns at each other in a face-off. Now what? Is Donnie going gun crazy again? D grabs my arm.

The men yell at each other, angry-sounding words I can't make out because of Buckaroo's odd acoustics. There's another shot, and one of the men staggers backwards, trips and falls over the body already lying on the ground, then goes into a series of convulsive seizures, his body jerking like a spastic rag doll.

I have no idea what I'm going to do when I get there, but I throw the car into park, leap from the driver's seat and run toward the men. I can do CPR. I know I can. I fall to my knees next to the body and recognize Cowboy Spit. "Okay," I say, as calmly as possible, rolling the tall man onto his back. "Help is here. Can you see me?" I remember something about clearing the throat before applying the mouth seal, and hope to Christ this guy's not got a mouthful of vomit. There is vague shouting, but I'm focused on saving a life here.

Suddenly, Cowboy Spit goes limp in my arms. "Come on, buddy," I tell him. "Not yet."

I put both hands on his face and lower my mouth to his.

Cowboy Spit starts to laugh and sits up, shaking his head.

"Jesus Christ, are all you Hollywood people gay or what?"

Harry's standing next to us now. "It's just a rehearsal for the Dust Drama," he laughs, an oversize sheriff's star gleaming down at me from his white lapel. "That there's about the best endorsement we ever had." Now a crowd laughs, and for one weird, hopeful moment, I entertain the possibility that this is a Dove-induced fantasy, and I am really somewhere else. In the relatively safe refuge of Room Three, perhaps, taking a fantastic shower. Or asleep and dreaming a deep, hyper-real dream. The two erstwhile corpses, including Cowboy Spit, are already fully resurrected, lighting each other's cigarettes and dusting off their costumes. The Gunslingers critique each other's performances. Carson, palming the steering wheel like a pro, drives Harry's Eldorado, with Destinée in it, from the middle of the street where I left it to the horse rail at the side of the Bowl. I am still on my knees, sitting on my heels, in the middle of Mane Street, when Patsy appears and squats down to look into my eyes. "You all right there, cowboy? You look like you've seen a ghost."

But she's confusing and confounding me too, with her muslin peasant blouse, pioneer skirt and workmanlike frontier boots. "I'm perfect," I say, letting her help me to my feet and brush dust off my jeans. "Have you converted? Are you a Gunslinger now?"

She nods and wryly smiles. "That Harry sells one helluva bottle of snake oil."

More laughter rings from the bowling alley porch, where Gunslingers and other small groups have gathered at picnic tables. Destinée, Paul Street, Faun and Vana LeValle, with the now-ubiquitous Jake. A few tables over from them, Ellie and Mom. *Ellie and Mom?*

"Shit." I place my hand on the small of Patsy's back and take a deep breath. "Come."

We climb the stairs to the bowling alley and wend our way through the crowd to a picnic table in the corner. "You made it." I stick my head between my mother and sister and give them each a kiss on the cheek. "Welcome to Buckaroo."

They swivel in tandem and look me up and down with identical wide-eyed stares. Ellie pulls it together first. "Sander? What happened?"

"It's his hair. He parted it on the other side." Mom brushes my hair the opposite way, the way it used to be, but it falls back into its new place.

"And his beard." Ellie laughs. "It's all red."

"I'm disguised as a local," I say, making What's-Mom-doing-here? eyes at Ellie.

"Yokel," Ellie says, under her breath, just for me. "She insisted. I need to talk to you. Alone. It's important."

But I wave her off for the moment. "I'd like to introduce you both to Patsy," I say, pulling her into our threesome. "Patsy, my mom Madge, my sister Ellie."

"Pleased to meet you," Patsy says.

Ellie grunts a response, so I pinch her. "Nice to meet you too," she says, on auto-polite.

I squat down to whisper in Mom's ear. "I meant to call a thousand times."

Mom's brow furrows, her blue-gray eyes focus across the porch. Her mouth opens, then closes, then opens and closes again. She points a coral-polished finger at a table half the porch away. "Is that Paul Street?" Her voice quavers.

"It is," I tell her. "You want to meet him?"

"I want to meet him," Ellie says. "Sander drove his Lexus here." Tattletale!

"I've met him," Mom says. "Why were you driving his Lexus?"

"You have?" Ellie asks, her voice rising dramatically.

Patsy backs away to give us some privacy, but I hold her hand to keep her near. I start with meeting Paul at Dad's memorial and bring them all up to speed. I squeeze Patsy's hand when I explain how I got this gig, so she understands I'm mostly a plumber.

"That's fantastic," Mom says, but she won't look me in the eyes and her smile indicates otherwise.

But I'm too caught up in my story to ask what's wrong, because as far as I'm concerned, it *is* fantastic. Bizarre fantastic, anyway. "Well, it would be. Except during yesterday's rehearsal I burned down the Okay Corral..."

"Omigod!" Silent during the good-news portion of my tale, Ellie responds loudly to the bad-news portion.

"*Lightning* burned it down," Patsy interrupts.

"But it's right there," Mom points at the end of the road.

As I'm trying to explain the rest, Paul Street rushes to our table and gathers up Mom into a full-body embrace. "Madge? Is it really you? How are you holding up? What are you doing here?"

Mom is shaken, which only Ellie and I would know because of the way she tucks her hair behind her ears, then flips it in front of her ears, then tucks it behind again.

I try to keep things moving. "Paul invited me to his premiere party for *Wonder Abs*."

"Don't buy them," Paul says. "They're a crock."

Mom's still staring at me and not answering Paul. Patsy nudges me, but I've already shot my conversational wad.

Paul tries again. "Did you come up to watch our shoot tomorrow?"

"We came to take Sander home," my sister sticks out her hand. "I'm his sister Ellie."

"Sander can't leave." Now Paul turns to me. "We're shooting first thing in the morning."

"We are?" That's news to me.

"We need to talk," Paul nods.

Patsy steps in. "There are two vacant rooms at the motel, ladies. You can come to the Saloon for dinner tonight, too. There's going to be a big celebration for the New Okay Corral."

Mom looks nervous and weak. "Yes, I would like to rest. But first, Sander, why don't you take me for a walk? Ellie, I'll meet you at the room." She picks up a tote bag from the seat next to her. "Shall we?"

"I need to talk to Sander, too," Ellie pouts.

But my priority right now is Mom. I set up a meeting with Paul at the Bowl in fifteen minutes and ask Patsy to walk Ellie to the motel.

"Madge?" Paul tries yet again. "Will I see you later?"

Mom smiles blankly and looks out onto Mane Street as though she's already sightseeing.

I shrug my shoulders at Paul, who looks away, and follow Mom and Patsy down the stairs.

"My, this place is lovely. Isn't it just lovely?" Mom views the hokey Mane Street facades, distant boulders, huge sky.

"Before we go anywhere, Mom, Ellie, Patsy." The three of them turn to me with questions on their faces. I make eye contact with them all as best I can. "I deeply, deeply apologize for missing Dad's memorial. And for being a jerk..."

Mom stops me with her hand.

But I must speak my piece. "And for making Dad go back out on..."

"I said it's over. Stop. You didn't make him do anything. Nobody can make anybody do anything." Her eyes are soft and serious. "We forgive you."

"You do?" I've prepared for theatrics: gravel scraping, hair pulling, crow eating.

She pulls a jar from her tote bag and tucks it under her arm. "Your father convinced me it was more important that the three of us get along as best we could rather than stay angry with each other. I mean, I could kick the bucket any day now, you know?" She gazes lovingly at the jar that says BOBBY SANDERSON "My Darling." Dad's *urn*?

"Sander must take after his father," Patsy says, putting her hand on the urn. "He sort of did the same thing with me and Harry. My dad."

"No way!" Gotta love my sister.

But Mom ignores Ellie; her eyes mist as she addresses the urn. "You were right, Bobby. It's much easier than I thought it would be." She raises the urn to her lips and kisses his name. "Love you still. Always will."

"I'm glad. Really glad." I give her a bear hug like I never have as an adult. It feels great. Not forced or fake. Just real. Which allows me to venture into new territory. "Maybe you didn't mean to be, but you were a little rude to Paul Street back there."

"Oh! The nerve of that man!" She shoves Dad's urn in the tote bag and is all prickles again. "I can't believe he met with you in secret and then didn't show up at the house."

"It wasn't like that," I start to explain, but Mom puts her fingers to my lips.

"I don't want to talk about that man, all right? I just want to walk up the street with my son. Is that too much to ask?"

It's weird, but it's not too much at all. I feel like a local as I point out Buckaroo landmarks. Give her the inside scoop on filming JC and Starshine's wedding without the cap on. About filming Starshine birthing Lucy. About celebrating a chicken's birthday only to be attacked by it while peeing on it later. About burning down the Okay and building the new one. About JC inviting the rattlesnake to bite his cheek. About Destinée having a meltdown. About Patsy. She smiles and nods but doesn't say much. Once we've gone up and down both sides of the street, I walk her to the Oasis before backtracking to the bowling alley to meet up with Paul, where he, Faun and Vana have taken over a booth.

"What's going on?" I ask, as I slide in next to Faun. "You're all smiling. It makes me nervous." And suspicious.

"Zanks to Faun, everyzing figure out," Vana says, viciously texting into her Palm Pilot.

"The Gunslingers will return tomorrow morning," Faun taps the keyboard and swivels the laptop screen toward me to show off her latest schedule. "There's still time for a complete run-through before D leaves for Palm Springs."

"Look!" D shakes her red curls. "Willamette gave me some wig tape."

"It's actually a little crooked."

"It's okay. We just make it part of the look." Faun looks pleased with herself. "People will talk about it. That's what we want. Buzz."

"Ve love buzz," Vana says, not looking up.

"Buzz is great." I vaguely remember enjoying those few moments I thought I had it.

Someone calls out my name. At the booth across the way, Adonis London has evidently heeded my makeover advice. Gone is the mullet; his hair has been streaked blond and cut in layers that fast-forward him from the early eighties into the mid-nineties. He wears a light blue wide-collared shirt that laces at the V-neck and an updated pair of jeans, ironed and creased as is his style. "Well?" He spreads his arms wide. "She can't say no to this. Am I right?"

"I think you're onto something," I tell him, thinking the whole time about how I don't want to be here when it happens. "Good luck. You look great. Gotta run."

"Go! Go!" He waves me away. "Thanks for your help. Next time you see me, I'll be proposing to my ball and chain." He crosses his fingers on both hands, the lunk.

"Everyone! Everyone!" Harry stands on the zinc-topped counter. "In case y'all didn't know, today's a special day here in Buckaroo."

"It's my mom's birthday! She's thirty today!" Carson yells from the booth in the front, where she's sitting with Patsy and Lucy and Star.

"Great! Thanks," Patsy laughs, as Willamette rolls out a huge sheet cake on a trolley and the entire bowling alley bursts into song. Patsy blows out all thirty candles and cuts the first slice, while Willie,

Harry and Carson deliver cake to everyone. I look over to Donnie's regular booth, but my madeover friend is nowhere to be seen.

Carson puts her index fingers at the sides of her mouth and whistles. "This is a birthday present I made for my mom!" The lights dim and a white screen slides down from a slot in the ceiling and covers the mural behind the bar. Opposite the screen, a film projector is set up in the wall dividing the café from the bowling lanes. Someone pulls heavy blackout curtains across the long windows. Dailies must have been shown here back in the day.

Images from last night flash on the screen. Harry and Patsy talking, their hands clasped on the table. The Gunslingers practicing their moves, line-dance style. Harry and Patsy dancing. Patsy and me dancing. (Faun elbows me in the ribs at this.) Faun and Cowboy Spit making out in a corner. (I elbow her back, and Vana gives her a sharp jab.) When the images end, the lights come up. The room explodes with applause. And then a surprise. "Now here's Sander's part!" Carson cries.

The room quiets as the next film begins. A circle of tall, twisted Joshuas, each one unique, commanding, alive with light. Then, dark against the sun: Destinée's nude silhouette.

You never know when you're squinting into a quarter-inch viewfinder what the image will look like when it's projected large, but our moves are instinctive, in sync. She's deconstructed in swooping bits and pieces, then reconstructed with a slow, tender pan. I barely recognize most of the footage. It's as if it were created by someone else, and I were just the conduit. The nudity is not necessarily seductive, though her movements seduce. Not overtly sexy, though sensuality is apparent. But innocent. Playful. The camera captures

Destinée enjoying her moment, slowly, the sunlight intermittently blinding and harsh, becoming soft and golden. And then, the butterflies, like winged snow. A cheap trick, right? Like throwing in a puppy when the lovers reunite. It's gorgeous, but I could be wrong. I could simply be in love with it, the way I've loved all the drafts of my total crap screenplays before coming to my senses and deleting them.

The screen cuts to white, all is silent. Acid churns my stomach. My throat is dry. My leathery lips prepare the standard litany: it wasn't my fault, it was an accident, I was depressed. I am momentarily blinded when the lights come back on, but it might be because everyone is looking and clapping and smiling at me.

18

WEDNESDAY NIGHT

The VMX is starting to feel like part of my face, and I like it.

The Shitkicker is full to the rafters in honor of the New Okay Corral. The tenor of the celebration befits the historic occasion. The Citizens for a Better Buckaroo are hard at a game involving tequila shots and ringing horseshoes around the pool table legs—each player's take on the rules seems to differ—while the Gunslingers shoot pool around girls dancing on the table. One spot over, Vana taps her toes, texting into her Palm Pilot with one hand while the other scratches the top of Jake's head. Carson teaches Faun to two-step to a psychedelic jam courtesy of the Homeboys. Ellie has joined Patsy behind the bar and is mixing drinks into jelly jars for Cowboy Spit and Donnie, who's still decked out in his madeover duds. The two men smile and clink their jars to seal the deal on something. The hairs on the back of my neck stand up, as though JC's paranoia has somehow become mine. But who am I to judge anyone else's weirdness? I'm at a table in the corner with my parents, one of whose cremated body is in an urn with a bandanna tied around its neck; the other one—the living one—watches me film the scene.

"Your father and I are very proud of you, Sander." I film Mom straightening Dad's bandanna. "No matter how this little project turns out."

When Mom and "Dad" forgave me for missing Dad's memorial, I vowed I was done with the part of my life where I blamed my parents for not being perfect. But once an old habit dies, it simply resurrects. "You and Dad never believed I had any talent, did you?"

Mom kisses Dad and arches an eyebrow at me. "What are you talking about?"

"You know. Not wanting me to go to film school. It was because you didn't think I had any potential. You still don't, and your last statement proves it."

"Not really." Paul Street twirls a chair so its back faces our table, and straddles it. "Sander, I've noticed something. You seem to suffer from a tragic flaw in emphasis."

"My tragic flaw? *Emphasis?*" I look to Mom for corroboration, and to see how she reacts to Paul Street joining us after her blatant snub earlier this afternoon.

She takes a deep breath, closes her eyes, and clasps her hands around Dad's urn, as though waiting to "feel" his answer. She opens her eyes and makes a pronouncement as though it were a line in a script. "Paul knows people, San. He's been in therapy for twenty years."

"Twenty-five," Paul corrects her. "What I mean is, your mother just said she and your father would be proud of you no matter how your project turns out. You chose to hear only the negative. 'No matter how your project turns out.' But you're ignoring the most important part of the statement, which is: 'your father and I are proud of you.'"

"You should have come to the house," Mom says quietly, and only because it makes no sense to me do I realize she's addressing Paul.

Paul smiles sadly. "I was there in spirit. I didn't want to take anyone by surprise."

"*Wonder Abs* took me by surprise!" Mom says, with a crack of passion in her voice. "You're so much better than that!"

"I am what I am," Paul says softly.

"I know," Mom says. She wraps her hand around his.

My brain cannot grok this scene. "How do you two know each other again?"

"We go way back," Mom whispers, as the Homeboys take five and the jukebox kicks in.

Ellie plops into a chair nearby. "Bartending is hard work. My back is wrecked." She slings a nylon mesh sack on a strap around her shoulders to the front and unscrews the top of her power drink. "San, can we talk now?"

"Sure," I say, unable to look away as Mom and Paul wrap their free hands around their already-clasped hands and gaze at each other. "Check out the floor show," I whisper to Ellie, as they hum along with Patsy Cline on "Crazy."

Ellie clamps both hands on either side of my head and forces me to look at her. "I'm. Leaving. Jerome."

"What? Why? Since when?"

"He should have told me he wanted a motorcycle, he should have asked me to help pick out his tattoo, and he's going away this weekend. Without me. Is that how a man in love treats the mother of his child?" She has the self-righteous delivery down pat, and slams back her green drink as though it were whiskey.

"Where's he going?"

"Road trip, he said." She shrugs and slugs more green stuff.

"He invited me, but I told him forget it. Anyway, I had to pick you up."

Christ on a stick. I never thought I'd be advocating for Jerome. "Maybe he's nervous about being a daddy."

"Maybe I haven't told him I'm pregnant yet. Maybe he isn't ready to have a kid. Maybe he's having an affair." Ellie has a twitchy gleam in her eye the likes of which I haven't seen since she was in high school.

I say this slowly, so it sounds like I'm just being practical. "Maybe you're filled with hormones and you need to talk to him."

She actually takes it the way I meant it. "Maybe that's true," she sighs, "but maybe he's never around."

"Go. Call him. Now." I point Ellie toward the phone booth outside and watch to make sure she gets there.

Mom and Paul stop singing at the second chorus to let Patsy Cline go solo. "Bobby adored that song," Paul Street says, ripping napkins from a metal dispenser and dabbing his eyes.

"We practically fell in love to it," Mom adds, her eyes dreamy. "Gosh, I remember the day she died. Bobby and I were having hot dogs, remember San? At Tail o' the Pup."

"Sure." We'd gone there tons of times as kids. Ellie and I loved the old hot dog stand shaped like a giant wiener. We'd run screaming around the parking lot, high on Pepsi while Mom and Dad ate quietly. Dad would kiss Mom on the cheek and pet her hair for a few minutes before backing the station wagon out of its space. I watch my sister in the Shitkicker's red phone box. Her back is to me, one hand cupped over her ear.

"We heard the news on the radio right there." Mom curls Dad's urn in the crook of her elbow. "Your father put his head on the table and wept and I remember thinking, there's a sensitive man. I could live the rest of my life with a man like that."

"I never realized you were that much in love," I say.

"We were crazy about each other, don't be an idiot," Mom snaps. "Where's your sister off to now?" Outside, Ellie passes the Saloon's long window, crossing the sandy parking lot toward the motel. I consider following, but the jukebox suddenly cuts out.

"Is this thing on?" Donnie's deep voice cuts across the chatter in the main room. He taps the mic. "Can y'all hear me?"

A piercing feedback squeal has everyone wincing and clapping their hands to their ears.

"Loud and clear," someone calls out from the audience. "Where's your chicken?"

"You look pretty, man!" someone else cries. "Who does your hair?"

"Sorry," Donnie says into the mic as the Homeboys lift his chair up onto the stage. "I'd like to take this opportunity to wish happy birthday to someone today. Patsy, come on up here!"

"She's working," someone calls out.

I crane my neck to watch Willamette fetch the reluctant birthday girl from behind the bar, both of them hamming it up for the crowd with Willie grimacing while she yanks and Patsy waving her hands and shouting, "No more birthdays!"

"Hey, Sander?" D pokes me on the shoulder with one hand, the other hooked on Vana's arm. "Check me out." Her shaved head has been painted sky blue and decorated with glittery stars. She beams. "You like?"

"Great," I say, as Patsy steps up onto the stage, where Donnie waits with open arms. She leans down for a hug and Donnie pulls her in and kisses her full on the lips, to the crowd's whooping delight.

Patsy pretends to be shocked and playfully smacks his cheek. "Donnie, don't be fresh!"

"Zander, you are artist after all. You see vat he make?" Vana hands Mom her Palm Pilot, where D's butterfly video plays, and throws her arms around me. "I can vatch million time and alvays be heppy."

Part of me is aware that Mom is smiling as she watches my video; the other part of me is magnetized to what's happening on the stage.

Donnie takes a deep breath. "There's been a rumor going around for about twenty years now that I have a crush on Patsy Apple." The audience whistles and stomps, and he laughs a bit. "I'm here to say, tonight, in front of God and everyone, that rumor is true."

"Sander," Mom says. "This is amazing." Her eyes are soft and I know she means it. Praise from my family is not something I'm used to, but the glory of the moment is dimmed by Donnie laying his heart on the line for Patsy.

Vana rubs the top of Paul Street's head with her knuckles. "Zat Paul Street ees not fool."

"Who said I was a fool?" Paul asks.

"Nobody," Vana laughs. "Ve talk very soon. About you." She points to me.

"Patsy," Donnie grabs Patsy's hand, "you're a very special woman. And on your special day, I have a very special wish."

Patsy crinkles her nose and smiles, then looks out to the crowd and asks, "What could that be?"

Which is why she doesn't see Donnie pull the ring box from

beneath his thigh on the seat of his chair. "Patsy, if you would accept this and be my wife, then my wish would come true." Simply and honestly stated. I'm impressed.

Patsy appears stunned. At first, she barely shakes her head no, then more wildly. Finally, she jumps off the stage, threads her way through the crowd, and disappears in the direction of the ladies' room.

The hushed crowd awaits Donnie's response.

Donnie fidgets in his chair, putting on a brave front. "It's all right. You don't have to answer me now." He's starting to get a little wild around the eyes. I've seen that look before.

Harry takes the stage, gently places one hand on Donnie's shoulder, and takes the microphone away with the other. "Gosh, Donnie, that was real sweet. I know what it's like when Patsy won't talk to ya." He winks at the crowd and signals for the Homeboys to help Donnie down from the stage. "I wish you a lot of luck with that."

I push back from the table. "I need a drink."

But the dynamic of the Saloon is shifting. The hard partiers at the back are crowding up front to the dance floor, and I might as well be standing in place for all the progress I'm making to the bar. Everyone seems to be rushing the stage. I can just pick out Carson, front and center with her Keystone. Faun stands on a chair and Cowboy Spit lifts her up to perch on a rafter, where she holds out her BlackBerry to focus on the microphone in the spotlight. Even Paul and Vana have joined the crush up front. The lights dim and a spotlight circles Harry. "To celebrate the New Okay Corral, here to sing for the first time at the Shitkicker Saloon is...Destinée!"

I finally squeeze my way through and am relieved my regular barstool is unoccupied. I can see above everyone's heads from here. D bounds onto the stage and the crowd goes wild. With her simple white t-shirt and jeans, her star-spangled scalp and million-watt smile are actually striking. "To say thanks to all the incredible people of Buckaroo, I'd like to debut my new single. We only got to practice it once today, so be nice everyone, okay?" She turns to the band. "One, two." The Homeboys don't have a keyboard, so there's no techno edge to this version, just that mildly funky bass line under a guitar and pedal steel. D talk-sings it this time, to the beat, thank you very much. And without the Vegas business, she's actually watchable. *Where the hell is Patsy?*

I make my way through the swinging doors into the vestibule outside the restrooms. The door of the Saloon's tiny office is ajar. Light shines off a bit of chrome wheel on the chair where Donnie weeps. The blue-velvet ring box is open on the desk.

It's very peculiar to feel bad for a guy who could whip out his gun at any second.

Patsy motions for me to disappear when she sees me, but too late. "This is all your fault!" Donnie bellows.

"Mine? Why?"

Donnie reaches for his bib pocket, but he's not used to his new outfit; his overalls are not there. As he fumbles with his jacket, I dart in, putting my hand at his throat, trying to do JC's move, the one where Donnie falls instantly asleep and wakes up fresh as a daisy. But Donnie slaps my hands away. "What are you trying to do, strangle me?"

"No, I..."

Patsy cuts me off. "Don't you fucking dare," she says softly, aiming a small pistol point-blank at Donnie. "Not at Sander. And never in my bar."

"Patsy! What the hell?" Donnie looks up at her, stupefied, and raises his arms. "You know I wouldn't..."

Which gives me just enough time to stick my hand in Donnie's jacket pocket. I have my hand wrapped around his gun, but then his hand—bigger than mine by half—wraps around mine. "Give it," I grunt.

"Let go," he grunts back.

"Drop it, both of you," Patsy says, pointing her gun back and forth at both of us. Maybe Carson can disobey her, but we know better. We put up our hands and Donnie's gun clatters to the floor. "Sander, pick it up," she commands.

"Not me! I'm a city boy. I don't play with guns."

Patsy has the steely eyes of Gary Cooper in Room Three's movie poster. "Pick it up!"

"Sheez." I dangle the butt of Donnie's gun between two fingers.

"Hold it right! Point it at him!" She motions at me with her gun.

"Shit!" I point Donnie's gun at him. "I'm sorry, Donnie. I won't hurt you. I don't even know how to work this thing."

"It's easy," Donnie says. "See that little hook? That's the trigger. First you cock that..."

"Shut up. Both of you. God, you're like two twelve-year-olds. Sander, give me that."

She grabs the gun from my hands before I can say a word.

"Now put those on him." She points to a pair of handcuffs hanging on the wall above her desk.

"Sorry about this too, guy." I clip a bracelet around one

wrist, then pull both arms behind him, while Donnie weeps quietly, chin to his chest.

Patsy puts her gun away, picks up the blue-velvet ring box, and tucks it in Donnie's jacket pocket. "I'm real flattered you asked, but you know I can't say yes." She kisses his cheek.

And that's when Donnie really starts to blubber. "You know I wouldn't hurt you, Patsy. It's all right you don't want to marry me. I never thought you would. But Willie'll kill me if I screw up this deal. I gotta find JC or she's gonna sic the FBI on him." The tiny hairs on the back of his neck are freshly cut and bristly, shiny with hair dye and mousse.

I position my hand above the nape of his neck and make my mind a blank. Donnie doesn't notice, just keeps blabbing full-speed. I move my hand around to the side of his jaw and search for his Adam's apple. "Hey!" he yells at me, but I shift up about a half-inch above the hard, knotty lump, slip my fingers into the trench just under his jaw, and press firmly against his windpipe. The crying stops and Donnie's head slumps forward.

"What did you do?" Patsy asks.

"JC's move! I fucking did it!" I kiss her, then grab her hands, draw her into a basket whip turn and spin her back out again. "Quick! We only have a few minutes. Bring the truck around."

*   *   *

The Luv's headlights illuminate the Joshuas that line Buckaroo Highway, then both sides of Roy Rogers Road and Dale Evans Trail, where the trees become sinister, haunted. We turn into a circular driveway and I recognize Donnie's ranch house from my hike that very first morning. We drag Donnie down from the truck bed and into his chair, then up the ramp toward the back kitchen door. The chair's front wheels catch on the lip of the ramp, and no matter how we push, the contraption won't go forward. I grab Donnie under the shoulders and nod at Patsy, who runs to the front of the chair and picks up his feet. On the count of three, we lift him from the chair and carry him into his kitchen, where an empty bottle of cooking sherry lies on its side on the table. We carry Donnie through his living room, where a dozen chickens roost on cushions, chairs, tabletops and lampshades. The air is dense with the aroma of chicken shit. A British production of Shakespeare is on the big screen television.

"Public television," Patsy comments.

The chickens cluck softly at her voice.

"Smart birds," I say.

Patsy and I snort in unison and I will myself not to lose it as we carry Donnie down the hall towards his bedroom. She unlocks his handcuffs, then we pull off his boots and jeans and tuck him into bed. I turn out the overhead light and wait in the shadows while Patsy lingers at Donnie's bedside, brushing his newly streaked hair from his forehead. "How long till he wakes up?" she asks.

"He's awake," I tell her.

Donnie yawns and smiles when he sees Patsy at his bedside. "You change your mind?"

"No." Patsy's face shines under the glow from a chicken-shaped lamp on the nightstand. "But I'm glad you finally got it over with. The anticipation was killing me."

"Killing *you*?" Donnie burrows into his pillow, looking like a teenage boy in the half-light, relief and pain raw in his features. *"It is a willow when summer is over, a willow by the river from which no leaf has fallen nor bitten by the sun turned orange or crimson."*

Patsy lays her hand on his cheek. "I like your makeover, Donnie. I bet the right girl will too." She turns out the light and closes the door.

I stop in the living room to turn off the television. The telephone's old-school receiver lies next to the base, its disconnect signal beeping frantically. As I hang up the phone, I notice a small notepad, with the words Spit and FBI scratched on it, and some numbers. I reach for it, wondering if I'm reading it wrong or if I'm making up evidence to fit the mystery. But then Patsy comes up behind me and takes my hand. "Harry is babysitting Carson tonight," she says, and I forget about everything else.

The moon is a sliver more than half full. Once my eyes adjust, it's easy to walk in the desert. I follow Patsy up a twisting staircase of stones between two provocatively balanced boulders, where we proceed in total darkness. I shiver in the chilled air as I try not to think about the tarantulas and scorpions that might be wandering around under here. When we come out the other side, the moon hangs high above the Milky Way's glittering belt. Scattered yard lights dot the mesa below. Beyond that, the Shitkicker's small yellow-gold neon boot kicks. And kicks. And kicks. "See the orange light?" Patsy points across a canyon to a blurry glow. "That's JC and Star's satellite dish."

Of course. And he probably uses it to track satellites, too. "I'd never want to leave if I lived there."

"I guess," Patsy sighs. "Me, I wouldn't mind getting out of Dodge a little more often."

I hold my breath as we creep along sheer rock walls, listen hard for rattlesnakes as we clamber down another jumbled pile, then finally relax when we emerge in a sheltered box canyon. Patsy leads me through a stand of willows, past a small pond and toward a clearing with a cone-shaped structure. "A teepee?" I ask, as Patsy fishes a key from her jeans and opens the full-size door complete with a stained-glass window of a full moon in a dark blue sky.

"My teepee. One of the reasons I stay," she says. "Close your eyes."

I blindly follow her in, happy to obey until she instructs otherwise. "Of course, a teepee," I blather on as she rustles around. "You live in a Western town, and you identify with the Indians, with nature, the native, the primitive. Another manifestation of your rebellion."

"Yes, Doctor Freud," she sighs, and I hear the snap of a lit match, then some kind of smoky incense. "Sage," she answers, without me asking. Fabric rustles, burning wood crackles, and weak, tangerine light flickers against my closed eyelids. "Okay. Now."

We're in a small, circular room tall enough for us both to stand in the middle, with a futon under the sloped ceiling on one side. There's a pot-bellied stove on the other side, and two large cushions on either side of a low table.

Without a word, I pull Patsy into me for a kiss that makes me feel like I've spent my entire life crawling through a desert, and only now have I dared to dip into an oasis, and actually discovered cool, clear water. I want her to feel the same way too. Our hands wander, hers through my hair, mine on her breasts, hers around my shoulders, mine down her waist. I extract the little silver pistol from the back of her jeans and dangle it by its pearl handle as far away from us as possible.

"Bartender's best friend," she smiles, taking it from my hand and placing it on the low table next to some Tarot cards and a china teapot. "It's more for show than anything else."

Reflections of flame dance in the gun's silver barrel. "You showed me all right," I say. "You're just like Donnie."

"Not really," she laughs, unbuckling my belt. "I know how to use mine."

We fall to our knees on the futon, and down.

Making love with Patsy. Making love with Patsy. Making love with Patsy.

Making love with Patsy is as easy and right as dancing was the night before. She likes it upside down then right side up, just like I do. We laugh a lot in the middle. We come hard and quiet and fall asleep quickly, with no need for dumb conversation. It's close to three a.m. by the time we head back to the motel to catch a few hours of sleep before crew call at six.

*   *   *

I don't remember leaving the light on when I left Room Three, but the dim glow from my window indicates otherwise. The air outside my door has a balmy, tropical texture and a familiar skunky scent. I unlock the door and push it open, but the chain is latched. Some Eastern music plays, chanting and a sitar. Through the three-inch opening, I can just make out a gowned figure, cooking at the small kitchenette. "Who's in there?"

JC's eye fills the crack. "Dude! Quiet!" He unlatches the chain and pulls me inside.

Bowls, measuring spoons, scales and jars clutter the small counter, tiny eating table, my bed. "What the hell are you doing?" I ask.

JC takes a tremendous hit from a small wood-carved bong, hands it to me, and rushes back to the kitchenette, where pots boil on the range. He is clearly in an otherworld zone, murmuring above a steaming kettle, hands raised in prayer at his forehead.

"You can't stay here," I tell him.

JC nods and ignores me, pouring pink liquid from a pitcher into a blender and wrapping a towel around it to muffle the grinding whine of Puree. He slowly exhales the smoke, tapping his foot to the music and shutting off the appliance just as the singer begins to wail.

I pop open the top of one of six small Tupperware containers stacked on my bed. There's enough Dove in one little tub to put all the residents of Buckaroo in a very good mood for a long, long while. I grab his arm. "Listen to me. You have to get out of here."

JC pours the mixture from the blender into a flat plastic tray, pops it in the microwave and sets the dial to High, then turns to me, a weird, beatific smile on his face. "Now I understand why it freaks people out when I know what they're going to say. And yes, it is paramount that I get out, but first I need to ask you something very important." The whites of his eyes are shot through with pink, but his speech is clear and deliberate.

"No, I will not make a munchie run."

"Man, this is serious." He clamps his hand on my shoulder and puts on a Cheshire cat smile. "Will you do me the honor of being Lucy's godfather?"

"What? No! Who do you think I am?"

"Who do I think you are?" he repeats. The Cheshire Cat smile grows, and I imagine him vaporizing into thin air, leaving me with the pots and pans and drugs and his fucked-up smile.

He's annoying me now. "You're the fucking mind reader. You tell me." I set his bong aside and start to gather the paraphernalia he's strewn around the room.

JC folds his legs Indian-style on the bed and watches me fill the cardboard box he must have used to cart everything in. He calmly takes up his bong, packing the bowl with more dope as he speaks. "Even mind reading's not the purest form of communication."

"Fuck your goddamn guru-speak!" I grasp his shoulders. "This is serious!"

JC smiles and gently removes my hands. "People's minds are messy. Chaotic," he continues, taking off his beret and letting his skinny braid swing down like a vine. "But I'm off topic. Will you be Lucy's godfather? Please."

The microwave dings. I yank out the tray of what is now pink, crystallized powder and place it on top of the crap in the box. "I'm not godfather material."

"Sure you are," JC laughs. "You're the guy who does his best not to disappoint other people. You're kind to animals. You saved me from a rattlesnake bite. You take risks for what you believe in. You get excited by beauty. Patsy's taken you into her heart. Lucy told me she picked you out special. And Carson thinks you're neat."

"She does?" Screw Paul Street and my tragic flaw of emphasis. I like JC's version of me better.

JC puts his hand on my shoulder. "You know what the purest

form of communication is, Sander?" He thumps his chest, then mine. "Your heart. I like the way you use yours. You're beautiful, man. Swear to God."

How do you say no to that? I take the bong and the matches from him, take a big hit, then stash them in the box and sit next to JC on the bed. Cognac-infused smoke swirls into my brachial tubes, and I suddenly remember what was scribbled on that note pad next to Donnie's phone. "I think you were right about that Cowboy Spit being FBI."

JC turns serious. "Look. I'm not gonna shit you. I made some less-than-excellent dope in Florida. Kid OD'd on it and his idiot friends traded my name to reduce their charges. I hit the road and ended up here, where I met Donnie and Willie, who had a little operation going."

My jaw drops. "I thought Willie was an actress."

"She was," JC says. "Retired with a load of cash, too. Just fell for the wrong guy, who got her to invest in a moneymaking project that fizzled away, then—mysteriously—so did he."

"She killed him!?"

"No one knows for sure." JC shrugs. "You know how the rumor mill works around here. Anyway, I offered to make her some product so she could sell it and recoup her loss. That woman negotiates like nobody's business. She bought the bowling alley with her first deal. Willie sets up the deals and Donnie makes the deliveries. They give—gave—me a nice cut so I could buy some land, build my bunker up in the hills."

"How long have you lived here?"

"Ten years. Got one more year before Florida's statute of limitations runs out. But then along came this deal with the Angels."

"The Buckaroo Angels?"

"Not Willie's church group," JC says. "The *Hells* Angels. Willie wants to grow her backwater empire and play with the big boys. Ever since I knew I was gonna be a father, I told Willie 'no more.' I'm gonna be a law-abiding citizen rearing his daughter in a free society where people get along. In a weird way, we do that here in Buckaroo."

"A very weird way," I say, considering everything I've seen. JC's bloodshot eyes are full of worry for his wife and child, and I feel it too, as though somehow Star and Lucy are in my blood. What's the worst thing that can happen if I become Lucy's godfather? I finish shooting tomorrow morning and head home for L.A. Twenty-one years down the line, Lucy will look me up, and I'll buy her a beer and we'll talk about how I filmed her Mom and Dad's wedding, and how I fainted when she was born, and how lucky she was to grow up in Buckaroo.

19

THURSDAY MORNING

Eerie silence wakes me. Honest to God, there is no sound.

No wind moves through the birch leaves, no coyotes yip, no roadrunners coo or clack their bills. The motel walls and floorboards don't creak and, now that he's dumped me for his new mistress, Jake isn't muttering in his sleep at the foot of my bed. I try to quiet my brain, to make it as silent as Buckaroo is right now, but thoughts keep cropping up. Is Cowboy Spit really FBI? What's JC going to do if he is? Is Patsy awake? What will Donnie think when he stands in front of the mirror this morning and sees a man without a mullet who no longer has being rejected by Patsy to look forward to? Paul Street's questions from the day of Dad's funeral percolate in my brain: "Who are you, Sander? What turns you on? What wakes you up in the morning and makes you glad you're alive?" I have to admit: lying here the few moments before my day starts, skin bare against the sheets, anticipating the opportunity to finally shoot the commercial does. I'm showered and out the door in minutes.

At 5 a.m., the Saloon is already bustling. Cowboy Spit or FBI Agent Spit or whoever the hell Spit is sits at a table with Faun, checking in Gunslingers, both of them grinning like they've had another night of rambunctious fooling around. Harry's Homeboys huddle, checking lights and wires. Paul Street is at a table with Mom, chowing down bacon and eggs. I head over and give Mom a kiss, steal a strip of bacon. "You're all up early. Did you sleep well? Have fun at the party last night?"

"Sleep?" Mom grins girlishly and looks at Paul.

"We never went to bed," Paul laughs throatily.

"I haven't partied like that since 1978," Mom says. She pats Dad's urn reassuringly. Evidently, he partied all night too.

"Where were you?" Paul Street asks me innocently.

"Conspicuously absent." Mom poses with her hand to her chin. "As was Ellie. I never saw her again after she went back to the room."

The pair of them smirk at me, but I don't bite. "I've got to check in with Faun. We ought to be shooting soon." I hear them chuckling as I walk away, but my hands grow warm with the memory of Patsy's skin. My ears ring with the catch of breath in the back of her throat. I can handle anything anyone tosses my way.

"Have you seen Destinée?" Faun calls to me. Up close, she looks hung over and tired, which makes me feel strong and more alert.

"Not me." I pull a chair over to her table.

"Vana just went to check on her. I thought you might have run into them. Everybody else is about ready to go. If we keep to the schedule, we'll be able to wrap before lunch."

"Excellent." We've rehearsed this sucker so many times we should be able to sleepwalk through it. Once we wrap it the way Vana wants it, maybe she'll let me shoot it again. I'm thinking I'll try it Scorsese-style, maneuvering the VMX through a crazy-long

Goodfellas take, then drenching it in faded saturated color as though it were from original film stock, ratcheting Destinée's Western Burger commercial to a new level of authenticity and art. Oggie Bright can kiss my ass.

"Zander!" Vana strides into the Saloon, carrying the outside air in with her and pacing in figure eights like a hungry tigress. "Von meenute I turn my back and eet all go sheet. This vat happen ven I make deal vis Paul Street." Even Jake seems nervous, hanging back and tracking her with his liquid eyes.

Not even Vana can dim my good mood. "What happened?"

"Vat happen ees you fuck up. You don't vatch D and now she gone." Vana's head moves spastically, her shoulders contort with each subsequent phrase. "Goddammit, Zander, you better find."

As far as my contract is concerned, I'm the babysitt*ee* not the babysitt*er*, but something else is bothering me. "Hang on." I push past Vana to the barbecue area outside, where JC stands with deep purple rings rimming his eyes, beard unkempt, hair in a limp yellow tangle. I push him around the corner to my old friends, the septic tanks. "What are you doing here? That FBI cowboy is inside."

"I have a message for you," he says. The whites of his eyes burn red.

"I'm working." I jab my thumb toward Vana's accented operatic cursing.

"It's from your father." JC's dead serious; his hands knead the air.

I start to remind JC he's never met my father, then realize humoring him may get this over with sooner. "I'm listening."

JC tells me this as if in a trance. "I was in a canoe with

John Lennon and the Walrus, you know, hanging out, hitting the bong, digging the light on the water. And when I pass the bong to the Walrus, he has to take off his head to hit it because he's not really the Walrus, it's just a costume, right? The Walrus is your dad, Sander. And he said, 'When you put one finger in the water, the whole lake responds, just like the Universe, man.' That's so far out and beautiful."

Bullshit makes me impatient. "You dreamed you and John Lennon were in a rowboat doing bong hits with the Walrus, who is my dad?"

"I didn't *dream* it. I astral-projected. I was *with* them." JC seethes with exasperation at my inability to grasp the physics of his supercosmic event.

"My dad doesn't smoke pot." What am I saying? Dad's dead! John Lennon's dead! JC is a fugitive killer on the lam and I'm here talking to him when I'm supposed to be filming and my star is missing and one of my backup dancers is an FBI agent! What the fuck?

Vana shrieks again.

"Thanks for the message, but I gotta go. Take care of yourself, all right?"

JC places his palm on my heart. "Your pop's a cool cat. He's trying to help. Check this out."

I am unable to move, and suddenly I get this vision.

In the middle of a foggy lake, John Lennon, JC and Dad sit in a canoe. Dad wears a shaggy fur walrus suit; the walrus head sits on his lap. "You were in that really popular group, right John?" Dad hits on the bong and passes it to JC.

John smiles. "You can ask Jesus how effing popular we were."

Dad turns around the walrus head to look into its empty eye holes.
"Tell me, honestly, what do you think of modern music?"

"Modern? You mean like her?" John points at the surface of the lake,
where a watery image of D appears, singing, surrounded by arms grabbing
and pulling at her.

Great. According to JC, D is floating in a lake. I'll just drop
whatever he's tripping on, go project myself out wherever projectors
project themselves, bring D back to Vana, and live happily ever after.

JC looks at me sadly. "You'll never find anything with that
attitude, man."

"Sorry," I say. "I'm listening."

"You're listening with your ears," he says, knocking on my
forehead. "Try listening with your soul."

How do I do that? Cup my hands around my soul's ears?

"Destinée's singing somewhere out there, man, surrounded
by little arms waving around in the air." JC closes his eyes as though
he can see her. Then he cracks up. "John said she's pure shite as an
artist, but she's got a good heart." JC hugs me just as Patsy's truck
comes tearing around the side of the Oasis from Room Ten toward
the Saloon. *Now what?*

The screen door to the Saloon's kitchen bangs loudly.
"Zander!" Vana screeches, her arms windmilling crazily. "Vere you
are?"

"Sander!" Patsy leaps from her truck. "Carson didn't come
home last night!"

Suddenly JC's message makes sense.

*   *   *

The Mother Circle's Joshua trees are purple in the early shadows below the vista point on Elvis' forehead, where Patsy and I stand with binoculars, searching for our missing persons. A sudden jostling in some scrub turns out to be gray squirrels chasing each other's ratty tails. Patsy chews on the inside of her cheek, inspiring a dimple in the opposite one. I wish I could say something to make everything better. "Has Carson ever not come home before?"

"My kid is not a runaway," Patsy snaps, then stamps her foot. "If only I hadn't taken you out to the teepee, this never would have happened. Dammit!"

"Hey!" I put my arm around her. "We'll find Carson. I promise."

Patsy softens. "She was a great kid until she hit twelve. Then she turned into a monster. You've seen her."

"Yes I have, and she's a lot like her mom."

Patsy shoots me a look.

"Smart, independent, passionate."

"That's what worries me most." Patsy's voice is soft. "When I was ten, right before Mama died, I was pissed at her for something—I don't even remember what—so I hitchhiked out of town. Wasn't even wearing shoes. Willamette picked me up and brought me home. Mama took me straight to Yellow Flats; remember the hot springs we went to that first night?"

Of course, I nod. Her camisole, the bobcat, that Dove brownie.

"We had a heart-to-heart in the waters and went home best friends. It was our last time together before she died. But we didn't know that then." Patsy swipes the back of her hand across her nose.

"Wish I had a heart-to-heart with my dad before he croaked."
I pan the landscape again, looking past the Mother Circle to the back
road I traveled with JC just two days ago. Past the rocks that look like
a bag of fries, the pines that look like the prow of a galleon, to a pile
of boulders I never noticed before. "What's that?" I point to a phallic
boulder that leans at a 45-degree angle and points to a flat-topped
mesa.

Patsy scans the horizon. "Right there? Some people call
it the Cockpit because there are supposedly lots of UFO sightings
around there, but other people call it the Rowboat."

"The Rowboat?" This is too weird.

"Yeah. There's an old, dried-up rowboat been out there
forever. Ever since I was little. We'd go out and play..."

"Tell me later! Come on!"

Patsy's Luv bounces down the trail from Elvis' forehead,
through the Mother Circle, past the French fries and the Spanish
galleon, where we find Harry's Eldorado parked at the Rowboat's
entrance. Carson stands on the open convertible's back seat,
stretching grandly and yawning wide, happy to see us. "Mom, you'll
never guess what happened..."

But Patsy has already jumped in the Cadillac and wrapped
her arms around Carson. "Probably not. And you'll never guess how
long you're grounded."

Carson continues. "Mom, you're not listening. Aliens took D.
I saw it."

I grab Carson's arm. "You were with D?"

Carson hops up and down. "She flew right up into the green
lights. It must have been a flying saucer."

"Flying saucer?!" Patsy shakes her daughter. "Were you drinking with this Destinée? Because you're underage and if you were, you're both in huge trouble..."

Carson pulls away. "Mom, I'm her number one fan! We weren't drinking. She wanted to see the desert stars."

Patsy grows stern. "Carson Jean Apple, this behavior is not acceptable."

"I didn't do anything." Carson looks to me for reinforcement, but I look away. She's not dragging me into this one.

Patsy lays into her. "Young lady, you do NOT disappear with Destinée or anyone else without telling me where you're going. You do NOT stay out all night. You were supposed to spend the night at Grandpop's. Do you care how worried he is about you?"

"Don't get mad at Grandpop! He took me home like he was supposed to," Carson pleads. "It's not his fault."

"You're right about that. The only person in trouble is you."

Carson stomps her foot on the back seat in frustration. "I just wanted to show Destinée our stars. After she disappeared, I couldn't just leave, so I waited in the car and then fell asleep..."

Patsy silences her with a look. "And you do NOT make up stories about flying saucers." She grabs Carson's arm, deposits the now-bawling kid into her truck, then slides in after her and drives away, leaving a plume of dust hanging in the air behind them.

"Thanks for helping me find my daughter, Sander," I yell after her as I jump behind the wheel of the forgotten Eldo and steer the hulking machine back toward the motel. "Oh, you're welcome, Patsy."

The air outside Room One is rich with the aroma of baked goods. Harry opens the door, his usually tame pompadour gone wildly Einstein. "We found her," I say.

"Patsy told me." He fills a mug with coffee and hands it to me along with a warm muffin. "Banana nut. I always bake when I get the jeebees. Damn kid was asleep when I checked on her. If anything happened, I'd never forgive myself and neither would Patsy."

"Carson said aliens came and took Destinée away in a flying saucer." I rip off the muffin top and stuff it into my mouth.

"She saw it?" Harry's eyes widen.

The muffin's decapitated body follows. "That's what she said. Kids and their stories, right?"

Harry gazes out the window, his eyes suddenly a strange milky blue.

"Don't tell me you believe in aliens? Harry, have you been probed?"

He abruptly fetches a bottle of 3 Amigos from under the sink. "People say you're crazy when you talk about that stuff," he says, splashing tequila into each of our mugs.

The mug is still too hot to handle. "Wonder why."

He ignores me. "Patsy was a trooper when her mama, Coreen, died. Took it like a champ. Me, I drank myself silly for six days. Hell-bent to wreck everything around me, too. Punched a horse in the face and broke my hand. I wish that dastard Ray-Ray never set foot in my Saloon."

"Uncle Ray-Ray? Patsy mentioned his name."

Harry looks stunned. "Uncle my ass. I'll bet she didn't mention Ray-Ray was messing around with her mom who he promised to take to Nashville to cut a demo."

I shake my head.

"I figured if I let Coreen go, she'd miss Patsy so much she'd come home and we'd sort it out. I didn't figure on her packing Patsy's bag, too. Didn't figure on anyone dying. But then, who does?" He looks into his Mexican coffee and sighs before dumping it into the sink and pouring himself a fresh cup of virgin joe.

"Jesus, Harry." The tequila gives the coffee just the bite I need. In fact, I could use a little more. I hold out my mug and Harry obliges with a second pour.

"Of course, I felt responsible. Practically throwing my wife at Ray-Ray so she could follow her dream." The harsh light through the window bleaches Harry's skin to white marble.

"So you were drunk when you saw the alien. That's understandable."

"Sober as a preacher." Harry settles into his story. "On the sixth day of my binge, Patsy and her little friends went to the bowling alley after school. I was sitting on the steps, stinkin' drunk in broad daylight, and overheard one of 'em say to her, 'Your pa's drunk.' Plain as day, Patsy answers, 'No he's not. My pa's dead.' Looks right at me when she says it, too." He sips from his mug.

"Ouch."

Harry sighs. "Those words sunk in. I grabbed a rucksack and went out in the rocks. Some people call it the Cockpit and some people call it..."

"The Rowboat?!"

Harry nods. "It was cold as a witch's tit, with stars enough to make you believe in God. I laid my head against a rock, when five green lights come straight down at me. Light came out of the bottom, like from a giant flashlight. I was calm, not freaked out at all. And then she came down, like an angel. And even though she didn't look like my Coreen—she had a little body and big head, slanty eyes—I knew that's who she was. She said 'come on, Harry. Let's go fly the friendly skies.' And I said 'no, I gotta stay home and take care of Patsy.' And the alien said, 'right answer, Harry. You finally got it right.' And she kissed me on the mouth. Best kiss of my life." Harry closes his eyes, lips trembling as though Coreen were kissing them right now. "I went home to tell Patsy I was done drinking, but it was too late. She already decided I was dead and gone."

Outside, the desert vista is a layer cake of orange dust, purple mesa, cobalt sky. All I can think of is that crappy Little League game in junior high. A beautiful pop fly dropped plunk into my right-field mitt and then, as though it had changed its mind, hopped right back out. The Beverly Beavers lost the pennant. My teammates berated me mercilessly. I held back tears all the way to the station wagon, where Dad tried to give me a hug. I roughly elbowed my way out of his embrace, which actually felt worse than dropping the ball. Dad seemed sad as we drove home, and I always thought it was because he was embarrassed by me. Now I realize he knew he was losing me because he had not been able to console me. *Walruses, aliens, John, oh crap.*

Harry offers me another muffin and freshens up my coffee from the new pot.

"I gotta head back out and find Destinée so we can finish the shoot today." I rip off the muffin top, shove it in my mouth and raise the steaming mug to my lips.

"Too late." Harry gives a rueful half-smile. "Vana sent the Gunslingers away and told the Homeboys to strike the set."

"She what?" The planet's hottest coffee spills down my front, soaking my t-shirt and the crotch of my chinos. "Ow! Jesus! Fuck!" With muffin crumbs cascading from my mouth, I do a spastic dance out Harry's door, drop the mug into a flowerbed, tear off the wet shirt and dash into my room, dropping my pants and kicking them off, but of course, they get wrapped around my shoes, and I take a tumble onto the small table, causing my laptop and VMX to crash to the tile floor. "Fuck! Fuck! Fuck!" The laptop splits into two pieces; its screen is shattered. The camera's power light won't turn on. My brain feels the same: split in two, shattered, no power, no light. No commercial. No future. No life. Wearing only my wet briefs and with my pants still tangled around one foot, I carry the broken equipment outside and hurl them one at a time across the desert. The laptop halves land in the sand with satisfying bursts of dust. My stupid VMX hits the roof of Vana's HumVee as it veers around the corner from the back side of the motel, Faun's Navigator close behind. The HumVee swerves; the Navigator follows suit. Vana and Faun look over at me, in my shorts with my pants tangled around my ankles. I can hear their laughter through the closed windows as they head toward me.

I start to yell before they even shift into Park. "I can't believe you shut us down! After everything! We were almost there!"

Faun's window slides down. "Aren't you Mr. Déjà Vu!" She eyes me head to toe.

Yeah, I'm going out the same way I came in. "How could you let her shut it down?"

"The director disappeared. We thought maybe you quit again." Her bulbous lips grin.

"I was looking for Destinée! You knew that!"

Vana sticks her head out the window. "Better not dent HumVee!"

I run over, pants trailing in the dust. "Why did you shut us down?" I ask again. I hear a dog bark, and notice Jake in the passenger seat. "Where are you taking Jake?"

"I going to make Jake honest dog." She pulls his ears and I swear the fucker smiles. "Go ask Faun vy I shut down."

Faun can't wait to deliver the news, and jumps out of the Navigator to accost me outside Vana's car window.

"We're shut down because we already have what we need." She's all business now, despite a fresh hickey peeking over her neck bandanna. "Remember that first rehearsal before the corral burned down? That perfect one? We're using that, superimposing the dancers against the background of the set burning down. Then we'll use the video I took on my BlackBerry of D at the party last night—remember how good she was?—dancing in front of the wind and the fire."

Vana grabs her protégée's cheeks and plants a kiss on her lips. "Smart girl!"

"You can't use cell phone video on television!" Foamy spit flecks shoot from my lips.

"Sure you can," Faun laughs. "It'll look all rough and distressed. The kids like that. Then, out of the fire, a giant burger and the words: 'The Big Charbroil.' The Western Burger people already signed off on it. They love it."

Vana glares at me. "Paul vaiting at bowling alley. If D not back by midnight, he file Missing Person. And if D miss Vite House concert, I going to sue. You." Vana points a wicked witch fingernail at me, then one-eighties the HumVee toward the highway.

"Jake was always an honest dog!" I yell after her.

Faun smiles as she switches her ass back to her truck and hops in. "Sorry it didn't work out, Sander. It was fun, though. Hope we get to work together again some time." And then, as though she didn't just ruin my career with a single blow, she navigates her Navigator away from Buckaroo.

The craggy rocks shine lavender and crimson.

Crows circle and call.

Joshuas welcome with crooked arms.

Perfect puffy clouds slide overhead.

My camera and computer in pieces, reduced to desert debris.

Shit.

If Destinée left with Carson, she must be somewhere around the Rowboat. But how to get there? On the berm above the cactus garden, Paul's Lexus is coated with dust. No. I can't go dragging my tail to Paul, not again.

Around the back side of the motel, both Mom's and Ellie's rooms have placards hung on their doorknobs: "Do not disturb! This means Y'ALL!"

I bang on Ellie's door.

"What?" She yells groggily from the other side.

"I need to talk," I say, fully expecting her to tell me to fuck off.

"Fuck off."

"Fuck off yourself."

She cracks the door a bit.

I should know better. First we have to talk about her. "What happened when you talked to Jerome?"

She swings the door open. "Nothing." She crosses her arms over her chest and a to-do list shows on the page of her folded-back

DayRunner in her tiny chicken scratch that only I, as her sibling, can decipher: lawyer, papers, child support, credit cards. "He wasn't there. I'm definitely leaving him. How much do you think I can get for unborn child support?"

Part of me wants to rub her back, the other part of me wants to slap her. "You need to *talk* to him. Did you call again?" Is it genetic with us, not wanting to talk? Is this our idiot destiny?

She shakes her head. "When are we leaving this place?"

"Mom's been up partying all night, she's still asleep."

Ellie groans. "Go wake her up."

"Not yet." Finally, it's my turn. "I need to borrow the Land Rover."

She slits her eyes at me in a familiar sisterly fashion. "Why?"

"What's it to ya?"

She stares me down with a look that convinces me she is going to be a fine parent.

I give up. "*Please.*"

"The last time you drove it you nearly killed us both," she snipes, flipping her hair over one shoulder.

To which I react accordingly. "Well you wouldn't be in it with me this time so I'd have no reason to want to kill myself!"

"Sander, you're so frickin' immature." Ellie slams the door on me.

I'm starting to wish an alien *would* drop from the sky and abduct me, just to get the hell out of this mess. The more things suck, the more things suck.

20

THURSDAY EVENING

Ellie and her divorce drama piss me off. My broken stuff pisses me off. D's disappearing act pisses me off. This fucking project pisses me off. I pull Patsy's bottle of Jack Daniels from the top cabinet and pour myself a shot. Room Three's patchwork quilt comforter pisses me off. Gary Cooper on the kitschy *High Noon* movie poster pisses off.

If I hadn't busted my laptop, right about now I'd be surfing the Internet. In my current sadistic mode, I imagine the Death Clock apologizing, indicating I have already been dead for six months. I imagine new names for my penis: Woody the Tiniest Big Pink Cock. Mr. Nobody. I'd lose fifteen games of Solitaire in a row. I'd drag out the old screenplay and play the "what if?" game. What if a guy is a big fat loser and his dad dies but he doesn't leave his kid his plumber's business like he always said he was going to and the guy misses his father's memorial where he meets an interesting guy who seems to want to help him and out of that meeting the guy… I'd write a one-paragraph version of my dumb life story like it's someone else's, a speedy, third person scrawl, hitting the big beats. At first it all sounds clever and cool, but the closer I get to the guy screwing up his gig and not knowing what to do, the more I can only picture darkness at the end of his tunnel. What I need is the Preston Sturges ending, the one where a long lost twin appears and the story turns on a ninety-degree dime. Maybe if I get some sleep I'll be able to figure out an ending that doesn't include running away to someplace like Cleveland.

As I crawl into bed, I notice the box from Paul Street on my pillow. I don't remember hauling it over from the phone box myself, but here it is. Inside are loose sheets of rough, fibrous drawing paper, with scene after scene of crayon-scrawled wars and soldiers, mountains and rivers, horses and guns. Towns with churches and trees and family scenes inside houses. Blood and gore, dragons and kings. The images are detailed and the scenes themselves considerately composed. And they're all signed by none other than me. I remember spending entire afternoons drawing these pages, making up stories as I went along. Giving one soldier a nose like a pie and another one a deformed leg.

Beneath those, an aged manila envelope with "Bobby, Madge & Paul – Rosarito Beach" in faded blue ink. Inside is a black and white photo of the three of them reclining in a hammock under the shade of a straw palapa. In the background, palm trees lean sideways in the wind on a sandy beach. They are young and laughing, each one raising a bottle of rum into the air. Mom lies in the middle, her hair loose and softly curling around her shoulders, wearing a white one-piece swimsuit that ties around her neck. Her legs are across Dad's thighs; her back rests on Paul's chest. Dad and Paul, both shirtless and in plaid Bermudas, each have a free arm around Mom. Paul is looking at Dad, Dad at Mom, Mom at the camera, though her free hand is on Paul's thigh. On the backside of the photo is the year before I was born. I stare hard at the picture, willing it to magically impart some understanding as to who these people were.

At the bottom of the box is a large white envelope, a brad-bound manuscript inside. On thin, watermarked onionskin, the fat courier type splashes ink on the S's, a small shadow under the capital H. The cover sheet says "MORE THAN YOU KNOW – An Original Screenplay by Bobby Sanderson & Madge Reilly & Paul Sternberg." I thumb through the script. 150 pages—long by today's standards. I deliberately place it on the bed next to me as though it were a malignant rodent. My parents? Screenwriters? If it's no good, then I'll have inherited Dad's untalented literary genes. If it's good, then why am I just learning about it now? I finally succumb to nearly comatose sleep in which I am conscious, in my dream, of not dreaming.

Taps on the window wake me. It's Carson, holding my broken laptop and dusty, cracked VMX in her arms. "I found your stuff in the street! What happened?" She has a horrified look on her face. Dust streaks her face.

"I don't need it anymore," I say through the glass. "Aren't you grounded?"

"Open the door!" She stomps her foot. *Wonder who she picked that up from?*

I swing the door wide open. "What?!" I'm really not in the mood.

She drops my camera and computer at my feet. "I know where D is!"

"Who cares?"

Carson stomps her other foot. "I do! And so do you! Don't you? You cared about me when I was missing. How can you not care about her?"

Because I don't need her anymore? That's a crappy answer. What if she's mixed up with Willamette and Donnie or is stranded and lost out in the desert somewhere? Finding D isn't really my responsibility—I didn't sign up for that—but as long as Paul's waiting until midnight, I have a few more hours to try to redeem myself, if not in his eyes, at least in my own. I must have slept for some time. The sky behind Carson is pink and orange now, casting a surreal glow on the streamlined fins of Harry's convertible.

Carson bounces excitedly behind the steering wheel as we roll up Mane Street at four and a half miles per hour. "I just checked out Destinée's website, where she keeps her diary. It's not supposed to be public, but I figured out her password."

"Carson!"

"It was easy! Any fan could guess it. I could, anyway."

"So what's there?"

"It's not just that she's heartbroken, like she said. Last time she was here, she had a dream she was abducted by aliens. Her and Oggie..."

"*She* and Oggie." I can't help myself.

"Whatever. They drove out to the desert to look at the stars and she thought he was going to ask her to be in his next movie but he broke up with her instead. They got in a fight and she refused to get back in his car, so he left her out there."

"What a jerk!"

"Totally." We pass the Buckaroo Bowl and stop at the Soundstage, the cavernous wood building that houses Willamette's Costumery. Carson parks in the alley between the two buildings and looks over both shoulders as she turns the combination lock. *Great.*

We're breaking and entering on the drug empress's property.

The raft-sized sliding door screeches on its castors as we tug it open. Inside, the vast warehouse is quiet and cool, the last rays of sun beaming spotlights through the skylights. Doves coo in the rafters and small animals—probably mice—scratch themselves into hiding. One entire wall is hung with saddles and tack. A stagecoach is parked off to one side, next to a battered truck and a dusty, taxidermied horse. "Is that...?"

"Trigger's brother. His stand-in," Carson says.

"This is amazing." Rack after rack of metal shelves hold all manner of old-school cameras, lights, cables, reflectors, costumes, cowboy boots, hats—any kind of paraphernalia you would need to film, star in and edit a Western movie from the forties is right here. "Look at this." I wrap my hands around an old 16mm Bolex camera wrapped in alligator skin. "This is the real deal. You could set up a studio in this place."

"Totally," Carson nods. "But Willie says there's no cash in the movies, and the bowling alley takes up all her time." The back wall is lined with shelves holding hatbox after hatbox. Carson points to a top shelf. "Can you reach that one?"

I stand on the bottom shelf to pull down a ladies-style hatbox covered in blue velvet with a silver star pattern on it. Carson dusts off the lid with a rag before she removes it, then lifts out the headpiece inside. It's got ear flaps and a chin strap like an old-time aviator cap and is made of plasticky garbage-bag material. "What the hell is that?" I ask.

"Here, there's one for you too." Carson hands me a plastic helmet, then straps hers onto her head. "They're for protection."

"From what?" I put the musty-smelling thing on my head and make a dork face. "Fashion?"

"No," she replies with dead-serious, pre-teen gravity. "Aliens."

*   *   *

The heft of Carson's Keystone in my hands is somehow comforting.

She squats on her haunches at the lower left corner of the frame, illuminated by our small bonfire, the Rowboat's prow jutting behind her. The sky overwhelms the composition—a real "human versus the universe" image. "Okay, that's great. Now, Miss Apple, please explain for the camera why we're here."

In the flickering flame light, Carson examines the hot dogs on her stick with the purse-lipped authority of a Michelin chef. The alien helmet actually makes her look like an alien, only with traces of Patsy in her cheekbones and Harry in her eyes. "We're waiting for the aliens to return Destinée," she says, in all seriousness. "And since you're not wearing protection, I'm waiting to see if they take you."

"You realize this is going into the archives," I say. "Someday your grandchildren will watch it and say, 'Grandma was a teenage nutjob.'"

"Why would I ever have kids?" She holds the wieners in the flames until they catch fire, then looks straight into the camera. "I don't want to ruin anybody's life." That twangs me. When the blackened dogs burst, Carson bites off the end of one and chews thoughtfully, mouth open, while tucking the others into buns.

"Destinée's diary said she fell asleep in a place that looked like a rowboat. Like that." Carson points with the roasting stick to the flat rock. "She wrote about five green lights. If they brought her back here once, they'll totally bring her back here again."

"Right, totally. And you saw these five lights?" I saw five lights myself just the other morning, and Harry mentioned seeing the same thing. Five lights do not a spaceship make.

"I saw fiiiiive greeeeeen liiiiiights," Carson enunciates, as though I'm intellectually challenged. "D left the Eldo to pee and when she pulled down her pants and squatted, the five lights crashed together into one big green light. When the light went away, D was gone." Now Carson pokes marshmallows onto a stick, balances it on rocks over the fire, and sets out graham crackers and chocolate bars. "You don't trust me because I'm a kid. But she's up there, I know it," she says, tilting back to gaze into the sky. "Sander! Look! I told you!"

I pan up to film the five green lights in the half-mooned sky above us. They move at a consistent pace—neither slow nor quick. Connect the green dots and they'd form a house, the kind kids draw in kindergarten, a box with a triangle on top. "So what. Green lights. They're military jets doing exercises. Or some golf pro flying to Vegas from Palm Springs. Disco space junk." I try to sound like the hardened skeptic I know I am in my soul, but still. It's weird.

A high-pitched cry quavers in the distance, sounding like a frightened child. "What's that?" A hot wind kicks up and passes across the small plain, across my face, on my arms, and then nothing. Everything was as it was before. Shivers race up my spine and I turn off the camera. For a moment, I feel disconnected, like I'm floating outside my body. I flash on the morning after Dad died, when I was convinced he was standing next to my bed, and I swear his hand touched my pillow, and I felt, more than heard, his cold breath whisper, "It's okay." I swear I heard it again in the wind. *Maybe I should have worn that helmet.*

"That's a boy coyote calling for his girlfriends and telling the other boy coyotes to stay away," Carson says. "Shoot! The lights are gone! Where'd they go, Sander?"

"I don't know," I say, scanning the sky. Yup, they're gone. "But look who's back."

Destinée stands alone in the Rowboat, stretching as though she's been asleep. When she sees us, she waves. "Hey! Boy, am I glad to see you guys!"

"I knew it! They brought her back!" Carson leaves her marshmallows in the fire to run and throw her arms around Destinée. "Did you see the inside of the spaceship? Were there aliens? How tall were they? Taller than me? Did they walk like this?" She thrusts out her arms and goosesteps. "Take me to your leader."

"What are you talking about, you crazy girl? I fell asleep. There weren't any aliens." Destinée laughs nervously.

Carson bites her lips and looks at me. "Did you have any dreams?" Carson asks hopefully. I hope she realizes that if she says anything more specific, Destinée might figure out her online diary's been hacked.

"Nope," Destinée says, a bit too casually. "No dreams." She vigorously rubs her embellished scalp, now sporting a five o'clock shadow. "Damn, my head itches. And what is that on *your* head?"

"Nothing," Carson says dejectedly, pulling off the helmet, then turning and running back to the bonfire. "My 'smores!"

"Omiiigod!" D checks her wrist for a nonexistent watch. "The shoot! I'm sooo late!"

I hook my arm into hers as we head toward Carson. "More like *too* late. Vana shut it down." I explain to D about Faun's idea to revamp the Western Burger commercial.

"It doesn't hurt to be sleeping with Vana, either," D says. "I'm really sorry I let you down. I just got bummed and passed out," she says sheepishly. "You know, I actually did have a dream, but I didn't want Carson to hear it. I don't remember a spaceship, but there were lots of little creatures, lots of little arms. They told me they picked me because I was special. I was supposed to lead them, to teach them about love. But that's all I remember. Then I woke up. Weird, huh?" She brightens. "But who cares about a stupid old commercial anyway? Your video with the butterflies is going to play behind me, on stage, at the Whiiite House! It'll be so cooool." She kisses my cheek and runs ahead of me to the crackling flames. "I'm starving! Do I smell hot dogs?"

I listen to them chatter as we chow down on dogs, and when we're done with those, I film into the beautiful, chocolate-marshmallow-laced mess of their open mouths as they gobble 'smores. Never mind the similarities between D's dream and my vision, all the little people with the little arms. Or how my footage at D's concert Saturday could change my life. I'm still freaked about that wind and hearing Dad's voice. As though he was watching me, and maybe, finally, a little bit proud.

This time, I drive. In the back seat, Carson and D hang their heads out the side windows to let the warm night rush against their faces. The Caddie's high beams create a hyper-real glow around the twisting roads in the night, while off in the distance, the Shitkicker's neon boot kicks shit over and over. When we arrive in Buckaroo proper and turn onto Mane Street, I head toward the motel. "To the Bowl," Carson commands. "Service for D is door to door."

"Won't your mom be mad?"

"Don't worry," Carson says. "I know how to handle her."

Paul Street runs out as I pull up in front of the Buckaroo Bowl. "Thank God! Destinée, are you all right? Where were you?"

D's cool as a hungover cucumber. "I'm so sorry, it's all my fault. I made Carson here take me out to look at the stars, then had a little too much to drink."

When Carson hops out of the car, Paul Street picks her up and spins her around.

"I don't know how we missed her when we found Carson this morning. I guess I'll go find Mom and Ellie." My work here is done. No reason to hang out and cry in my lake of spilled milk. I'd rather head back to L.A. than drag out goodbyes.

Carson shrieks happily as Paul swings her onto his shoulders. "Oh, Harry took them into town for dinner and then they stopped by here before they all went back to the motel. Said to tell you they kept their rooms an extra night."

Patsy arrives, breathing heavily from her sprint up from the motel. "I came as soon as I saw the Eldo." She groans when Paul Street delivers Carson into her arms, and covers the kid's face with kisses.

Carson hugs Patsy tight. "Mom, I'm sorry I disobeyed. If you have to ground me longer, I'll accept my punishment." That kid is so smooth; I'm in awe. "But we found D. Isn't that cool?" She extricates herself from the hug. "Can we get some nachos?"

"There weren't any aliens?" Patsy asks.

"Nope." Carson and I exchange looks. "Can I, *May* I please have some nachos?"

"Nachos for everyone," Paul shouts, speed-dialing Vana to relay the good news.

We all troop inside the Bowl, where one of Paul Street's infomercials plays on the ceiling TV. Willamette sets us up in a big corner booth. I slide along the banquette across from Patsy, who warms one hand around her white diner mug while the other one smoothes Carson's hair from her face. Carson and D compare how many nachos they can stuff into their mouths at one time. I am just happy to be here, next to them, momentarily mesmerized by the infomercial's cheesy soundtrack and the lush mansion grounds where Paul strolls in a cream linen suit, extolling the virtues of Star Hair Care.

The real Paul Street bangs open the doors with a flourish. "Vana's on her way. The White House is on!" he announces, hopping onto a stool and twirling around on the seat. Carson and D screech in delight, but I can't tell whether it's over this news or the second basket of nachos Willie sets before them. I study Paul as he watches his onscreen self interview a vaguely familiar starlet about volume and shine. The same passion blazes in his eyes right now as in that picture from Rosarito Beach over thirty years ago.

I join him at the counter. "I opened the box," I say, focusing on the infomercial. "Tell me about that photo."

"Beach bum took it." He watches himself on screen as well. "Goodness, we were crocked. Get a little rum into her and your mother was quite the sexorita. And your father? He could dance all night, talk about anything. Movies, history, psychology, art. The man had focus, you know, and incredible insight."

He's talking about someone I never met. "I'd forgotten all about those drawings."

"I thought you might like them back." Paul smiles. "Your dad gave them to me. He thought you had more talent in your little finger than he had in his whole body. He was so proud of them, proud of you."

Funny, that's how I felt when I heard that strange wind. I guess I'll choose to believe it.

Paul claps his hand on my shoulder and finally redirects his attention to me. "Did you read the screenplay?"

"Not yet." I don't want to mention I'm scared of what I'll read—whether I'll hate it or love it, whether it'll have anything to do with me—and it dawns on me that my parents might have felt the same way about anything I might decide to create.

"I think you'll find it intriguing," Paul says. "Here's the best part." He points to the screen.

I sit through the hard sell from volume to gloss, but I'm really thinking about my parents. How I've been afraid to know them too intimately and assumed they've been afraid to know me. There's no telling whether my fear was a result of their fear, or theirs developed as a result of mine. My own personal parent/child chicken/egg dilemma.

End credits are rolling just as the whup-whup-whup of chopper blades beats the air. Outside the Buckaroo Bowl, it's a little *Apocalypse Now* as we traipse under the churning blades, dust devils curling up around us.

D bends down and kisses Carson's forehead, then whispers in her ear.

Carson's grin looks as though it could slice off the top of her head.

D turns to me. "And you." She pulls my arms around her. "Make sure to watch on Saturday. I prooomise you, the butterfly video will be on!" She presses her huge lips to my cheek and I'm engulfed by fake red curls, with their bouquet of desert and campfire smoke. "I have been on sooo many sets over the years," she says, "after awhile they all blur together. But I will never forget one miiinute of the time I spent in Buckaroo. It's totally magic. Sander, you should write it up and send me a script! Seriously!"

"Maybe I will." Like in a million years. "I'll try to catch the show." I wouldn't miss it for the world.

She whispers in my ear, "Any chance you can get more of that Dove?" Her cell phone blasts snippets of a cheering crowd, one after the other, louder and louder. As she digs for her phone, I check to see whether any of those little pink capsules are still in my pocket from yesterday. "Hello? Omigod! Oggie?" she says, as I slip some into her hand. "Hang on," she says to the phone, then blows me a kiss. "I'll call you." She blows one Patsy's way, too. "Bye, honey. Y'all make a real cute couple." Into the phone she says, "I don't even know why I'm taking your call, you creep."

Dust swirls around us as the chopper lands in the middle of Mane Street. The door swings open and Vana jumps down, racing through the cloud to embrace Paul Street. "Zat son of yours not loser after all," she yells above the roar, as she rubs her ringed knuckles on top of my head, twisting my hair with a noogie.

Like the movie star hero he is, Paul Street lifts Vana up into the chopper, then D, then swings himself up into the cabin on one muscular arm. The doors close behind them and the copter takes off like a giant dragonfly into the night. I hug Patsy and Carson, and we all wave like nutheads, out there in the wind on our high-desert top of the world.

That son of whose? A noogie?

21

FRIDAY MORNING

The air is bracing; the stacks of orange boulders surrounding Buckaroo are no longer surprising with their visual drama, but comforting and friendly. Like Dad's church of rocks and light, they seem to create a sacred place, safe for secrets. I've been out at the picnic table in front of Room Three since sunrise, alternately watching the sky brighten and reading *More Than You Know*. Here's the synopsis:

Two high-school sweethearts dream of making it in the movies. Robinson, the writer, stays up nights scribbling script after script, while steady girl Marlene waitresses at Schwab's between acting classes, hoping to be discovered. In a unique twist, Robinson is discovered by an older, gay actor, Pavel, who mentors the boy and befriends his girl. Pavel dotes on the couple, and introduces them to his underground, glamorous world. Through Pavel's connections, Marlene lands a role as a screaming murder victim in a sci-fi B movie called *The Beastess*, and Robinson meets the dean of a local film school, who suggests if he were to apply for a scholarship, he might receive special consideration. Pavel invites the couple to his beach house in Mexico to celebrate, and a boozy, maryjane-laced night ends in the three friends sharing a sweaty, confusing bed. Marlene becomes pregnant shortly thereafter, unsure which of the two men is the father. Robinson trades his scholarship for a socket wrench and proposes, while Pavel, now linked to a high-wattage lesbian starlet as her beard, agrees to step out of the picture.

My first reaction is that the universe has somehow turned inside out. My world not what I thought it was. Dad not my Dad, Mom not Mom, me not me. Questions twitter through my head like psychotic birds. Mom was in a B movie? Dad wanted to go to film school? Did he resent me for being the reason he didn't go? Was he jealous I went? Was Paul in love with Dad? *A three-way?* I try to imagine myself a father-to-be at twenty, with a scholarship and connections, and begin to see him as someone else: a complicated stranger.

Harry's roadrunner couple appears amid the roses, and begins to fuss. The sun creeps ever higher. Rose petals slowly unfurl. A trio of crows alight on the birch tree and caw. Everything is different, though nothing changed.

At eight on the dot, a caravan of Harley-Davidsons thunders into town. Arriving in twos, they glint under the sun. Their rippling engines shred the air, and Mane Street's yellow dust rises to the eaves of its faded facades. Leathered and helmeted men, women, children and pets ride vintage, new, classic, authentic and well-detailed hogs. A terrific scene to get on film, but for the moment, I'm tired of filming. Anyway, I'm sure Mom and Ellie want to get back to L.A. ASAP. Mom probably has some painters coming or is getting carpet delivered. Ellie no doubt has a date with a lawyer, a Baby Pilates convention and the final tweaks on a new El-San business plan. I guess I'm going back to an old chair and a big screen TV in my dingy apartment to watch

D sing at the White House with my video behind her. If the phone doesn't ring after that—and I know better than to count on that it will—I'm back to El-San coveralls and service calls.

Harry ambles down the breezeway in his Indian blanket bathrobe with two familiar mugs; Mom follows with tea in heavy crockery. I hide the screenplay on my lap, below the table.

"Isn't this thrilling?" Mom yells to be heard above the ripping boom of the engines and joins me at the table. "I'm so excited."

"About what?" I ask, trying to picture Mom as a screaming teenager in *The Beastess*, trying harder *not* to picture her in a three-way with Dad and Paul. Harry hands me coffee.

"About the Dust Drama," Mom shouts. "Harry invited your sister and me to be Gunslingers. Bang bang." She shoots me with her finger and blows imaginary smoke from its tip.

Thrilling. The Harley fleet parks in neat lines down the length of Mane, while riders disembark, hugging and yelling and backslapping their way to the Saloon. When the commotion dies down, Mom says, "I'd best get your sister. We have a fitting at ten."

"Hogs for Dogs booked up the motel in advance. Most of 'em been on the road since dawn. They'll be checkin' in soon," Harry's hand slides onto Mom's arm; she doesn't seem to mind. "Y'all can leave your bags in my room till after the show. You know your lines?"

"My, what a strong, handsome sheriff!" It's been thirty-seven years since Mom's last role, but her voice is trained, flirtatious and clear. I notice Dad's urn hasn't joined us for coffee.

Ellie appears at the motel breezeway, still in her sleep sweats, her hair bent and unruly. She scrunches her nose at the sight of all the Harleys. "God, I hate those things."

"How 'bout you? You been practicing?" Harry asks Ellie.

"Now that's what I call sexy!" she says, in a voice flat with sleep and disinterest. She pulls her cell phone from her pocket and fusses with it.

"Could use a little punch, not a bad start." Harry's hand rests on my shoulder. "Sander, would you mind filming the Drama today? Carson's all in a tizzy about this archives hoo-ha."

"Can't," I tell him. "I busted my VMX."

"Actually, I was hoping you'd use this." Harry pulls a parcel from his voluminous pocket. "It's for you."

The 16-mm Bolex Paillard with alligator finish and dual lens. Carson must have whispered something in his ear. "Wow. This is fantastic."

Harry puts his arm around my shoulders. "I'm gonna miss ya, kid."

I pummel down cresting emotion in my chest, and it's not just from the sharp perfume of Harry's Brylcream. "Me too," I say, my voice cracking.

Harry tousles my hair like I'm twelve or something. "Now get on up to the Saloon and get you some grub before them bikers eat it all. Patsy's been prepping since near 5 a.m." Indian bathrobe flapping, Harry ambles off to greet the line of bikers forming at Room One to check in.

"Such a nice man," Mom says, playing with her pearls.

"Do you hear that?" Ellie asks, walking toward us with her phone pressed to her ear, looking around. "That phone? You know Jerome's ring tone, that Beethoven thing?"

We all stop, our ears perking to catch the digital *Ode to Joy*. It's here all right.

"Jerome? Can you hear me? What?" Ellie looks perplexed and closes the phone.

"Why'd you hang up?" I ask her.

"He told me to." She looks at me, then her phone, then back at me, as though she's forgotten who and what we are. "I haven't a clue."

"Honey, you need coffee." Mom takes control. "Let's go to breakfast."

"Oh. My. God." Ellie breaks into a run across the desert toward the Saloon.

"What on earth?" Mom asks, and we stop in our tracks as Ellie approaches a group of bikers, and begins to slug one of them, whaling on him with both hands. "Sander, do something. Your sister's gone mad."

"Nothing I can do about marital bliss," I say, as Jerome Green-Sanderson grabs Ellie's arm and walks her away from the group. They're in a nose-to-nose standoff now. Their voices are shrouded by the crowd, but two sets of neck veins bulge tautly. I feel bad for Nurse Perfect, who's about to experience the wrath of Ellie. But what's this? They embrace. Jerome covers my sister's eyes with his palm, leads her to a vintage Harley and holds her hand as she steps into a sidecar. More embracing, laughter, kissing. If only everyone's problems were as simple as El's. She's all smiles as Jerome drives them at a low roar to join me and Mom at the table.

"Look what Jerome got me for our anniversary!" my sister exclaims, jumping out of the sidecar. "Isn't my husband a prince?" She jumps up into his arms and kisses his face. "Ow, those whiskers. Sander, check out his tattoo." She waves her hands under the orange and black band around Jerome's bicep. "Isn't it awesome?"

"My princess," Jerome laughs. *Barf city.* He swings Ellie up out of the sidecar and pretends to stagger before gently setting her on the ground. "Oof. Did you finally put on some weight? I've been trying to get her to gain some," he explains to me and Mom.

"Maybe she's having twins," I mutter.

"We'd have to be pregnant first," Jerome laughs. "And that's not in our plans for a long time."

"Sander!" Ellie hisses at me, then looks sideways at Jerome, crinkling her brow.

"Ellie?" Tough biker boy Jerome's nostrils flare. He's either terrified or about to sneeze. "Is there something you're not telling me?" My vote is for terrified.

"Ellie?" Mom's voice trills as her brain's redecorating cogs whirr into grandmother gear.

Ellie looks at me. I point to her husband. "We're pregnant," she says, invoking the annoying royal pregnancy. "And I didn't tell you because, well, I wasn't sure we were ready. We didn't exactly plan this. And then you bought the Harley, then Dad..."

"It was mojito night, wasn't it?" Jerome says, smoothing her hair.

Ellie laughs and nods, then starts bawling into Jerome's leather vest and when she blows her nose into his signature Harley-Davidson bandanna, he doesn't even wince. They really are fucking perfect together.

"Congratulations," I tell them. "All you need is a baby seat for the sidecar and you're set. Now can we go to breakfast?" I stand up and the forgotten screenplay slides to the ground.

"Hey, what's this? You finally finish your opus?" Ellie grabs the script, shakes off the dust and reads the front page aloud. "'An Original Screenplay by Bobby Sanderson & Madge Reilly & Paul Sternberg.'" Her brow furrows and she suddenly looks very young and confused, like when she ate liver for the first time and then learned what it was.

"Goodness." Mom takes the script from Ellie and puts on her pearly, cat-eye bifocals. A crooked half-smile crosses her face as she thumbs through it. "Did Paul give this to you?"

I slip the photo from its envelope. "And this, too."

"Oh, dear," Mom says. "Look at us. Look how cute we all were."

Ellie snatches the photo from Mom. "Oh my God!"

Jerome regards the photograph over her shoulder with interest.

Mom looks at me. "It's not my story," I say, throwing up both hands.

"Mommy," Ellie whines. I love that she reverts to this, as though suddenly she's six. Jerome strokes her arm, making shushing noises. *Fucking nurturer.* "Tell us." Ellie again.

"Sander, you tell her. Please." Mom sighs and folds her glasses with careful precision, the way she always has. She holds out the script to me.

"Tell me what?" Ellie shrieks. She hates being in the dark about what's going on, which makes this moment extra sweet.

I thumb to page thirty-two and read aloud, "Interior, Cave, Night. Darla, a beautiful blonde bobbysoxer in a revealing lace slip, is backed into a corner, her eyes rolling in terror. The Beastess approaches and..." I point to Mom. "Your line."

"No." She shakes her head so hard her pageboy untucks from behind her ears.

"Who's Darla?" Ellie asks.

"Line, please," I repeat.

"Absolutely not." In that voice, the one that instantly shut down childhood arguments, whining, pestering and occasional begging.

But we're not children anymore. I turn my director voice on her. "You're Marlene..."

"Who's Marlene?" Ellie whines.

"...Never mind. You're young, with your whole life ahead of you. A promising career, a boyfriend who loves you, and this monster, this Beastess, has come from nowhere and trapped you, and the two of you are alone and she's going to snatch you away from your dreams and your future."

Mom clears her throat, stretches her lips around her gums a few times and lets out a scream that breaks off almost as soon as it begins. "I'm a little rusty," she says, half smiling. She closes her eyes, puts both hands on the table, and stands. After taking a moment to compose herself, Mom throws back her shoulders, then delivers a bloodcurdling scream.

"Way to go, Mom!" I pump my fist in the air.

In the sharp silence that follows, Jerome breaks into applause.

My sister's jaw hangs open in a perfect cliché of confusion.

Harry rushes out from Room One. "Everything all right out there?"

"We're fine," I tell him.

"Thank you," Mom says with a British accent, bowing formally from the waist.

I thumb to page ninety-two and read some more. "Interior, Bedroom, Pavel's Mexico Beach Shack." I wave the photo for emphasis. "A tequila bottle on the table. Bathing suits and shorts on the floor. The sound of the waves and a soft, sexy mariachi ballad enters the open window, the curtains move lightly in the ocean breeze. A shadowy silhouette of Marlene, dancing around the room. Robinson and Pavel watch from the bed, entranced. They share a hand-rolled cigarette, a sheet loosely covering their hips." The scene is chastely written. Still, your parents having a pot-smoking three-way with a gay gentleman ten years their senior is pretty much a bombshell any way it's written.

Ellie finally closes her mouth, then speaks. "Is this true?"

Mom sighs. "There is a possibility your brother might be Paul Street's child."

I can't tell if Ellie is horrified or jealous. Jerome looks bewildered.

"There seems to be some evidence pointing in that direction," I say diplomatically.

Ellie persists, absentmindedly rubbing her bump of a belly. "So you don't know who Sander's real father is?"

Mom flips her hair out from behind her ears, then re-tucks it precisely the same way it was. "Not exactly. But when your father found out I was pregnant, he asked me to marry him. It never mattered to either of us who the biological father was. What mattered was Bobby loved me, I loved him and we wanted a family together."

Shit, that's heavy. I can't imagine just turning legal and stepping to the plate like that. "Wow, Mom. How did you deal?"

"It doesn't seem so earth-shattering now. But at first, things were difficult. Even when you were young, Sander. I just wasn't..." She stops herself. "Remember the avocado appliances? The flocked wallpaper? Those years were hard. But some days, when I just let it be, it was easy."

"Didn't you wonder if Dad was gay?" Ellie's a regular Baba Wawa.

Mom cocks her head and laughs. "Your father and I enjoyed experimenting. I like to think our friendship with Paul brought your father and me closer."

"That's intense." Ellie still seems unnerved, if not slightly more impressed. "Don't you want to know who your real dad is, San?"

If she'd asked me this question last year or even last week, my answer might have been different. But today, my answer is this: "I already do."

*   *   *

We wend our way through a sea of Harleys to the Saloon. I send Mom and Ellie indoors to get a table, then step into the red phone box and dial Paul Street's number.

"Good morning!" The familiar voice booms, full of life.

"Good morning to you." I don't know how to say it so I just do. "I read your script."

"And?" Paul Street's voice is softer now.

"My first instinct was for a musical, but now I'm thinking low-budge. Keep it simple. Rough around the edges. Retro vérité."

"Interesting," he chuckles. "I always thought at the most TV movie, but you might have something there."

The sun warms my face. The rocks across the way are steadfast in their beauty. "I have a question about the end."

"Damn writers never can get the endings right," Paul laughs. "Shoot."

"Vana called me your son last night. Did you tell her that?"

"In a way," he says mysteriously.

"What way?"

"I don't want you to get upset."

"Why would I get upset?"

"Well." Paul takes a deep breath. "I told her you were my secret love child whose adoptive father just died and that I wanted to be a part of your life..."

"You told family secrets to Vana that my mother never even told me?"

"...and getting you this gig would be a good way for me to feel complete as a father. It's possible. And it's a good story."

I imagine the young Paul Sternberg telling tales as a boy, bluffing and charming his way into the life he was creating. "Why?"

"There was always something special about your dad. But there was this girl he was crazy about. We were best friends. We were kids." Paul's voice catches here and he takes a moment. "Your dad would come by for lunch every six months or so. Fill me in, check the pipes. The last time was just about a month before he died. I think he knew he was going to go. That's when he changed his will so Ellie got the business. To give you a push."

Telephone buzz fills a quiet moment. "I feel terrible about

the commercial," I tell him. *I really suck*, I almost say, but then I figure, why reiterate what he already knows?

"Vana will get what she needs. Her kind always does. Getting to know you was my very greatest pleasure." He sounds sincere.

I hope I do too. "Mine, too."

"If you ever have any questions, I'm here."

"Actually, there is one more thing." I ask him about that story on *Celebrity Profiles*, the one about him riding on a pony into a clothesline, cutting open his throat ear to ear, and how his life changed afterward.

"That was a good one, wasn't it?" He chuckles. "I have your Dad to thank for that one."

"You mean that wasn't true?"

"Nope. Any more questions?"

Actually, yes. "Where did Dad get that suit?"

"The Sturges? Natty, isn't it? I had it made for him when I got my first big paycheck. A thousand bucks was a lot then. He picked out the fabric. For a straight guy, he had a pretty good eye. Funny, my initials are the same as his favorite director's. He was planning to wear it to his premiere. Maybe you'll wear it to yours."

"You mean, the Sturges is really a Street?"

Paul chuckles. "That was part of the joke. Bobby really was a fan of Preston Sturges."

"And you really are a superstar," I say.

"Of course I am, kid. Be seein' ya."

I hang up the phone and head outside into the sun, immediately surrounded by a wave of heat, a swarm of leather and shiny chrome.

I pop in the back door of the kitchen like a regular. JC works the oversized griddle two-fisted, country music blasting, flipping hotcakes at sushi-chef speed.

"Good morning, friend." I clap him on the back.

"Wha?" JC screams and jumps, then turns to me with eyes grave as death. "Shit, man, you startled me. I was meditating."

"Oh yeah?" I make my hands in a little prayer in front of my chest. "How was it?"

"Dude, it was fucked up." JC clamps onto my shoulder. "I saw my family's future and I wasn't in it."

A mountain of bacon waits on a heating plate. "Maybe you were here, making pancakes." I laugh and grab myself a slice.

"Seriously, bro. I just want to thank you for being there for Lucy..."—he hesitates.

"Sure, don't worry. I'm the godfather now." And I'm almost out of here, I'm thinking. On my way home, the Western Burger chapter of this year of my life coming to a thankful close. "Hey, before I go, what was in that pouch that made Starshine sneeze and the baby pop out?"

JC points his spatulas at two industrial-sized spice jars on the shelf above his head.

"Cayenne and black pepper? That's it?"

"Yup," he nods. "Grind them up good with a mortar and pestle."

"Amazing." I grab more bacon and wander to the service window to survey the main room. The tables are full, churning with shouts and laughter. Kids and dogs race through narrow aisles. The jukebox plays something country. Mom, Ellie and Jerome are at a table in the middle of the room, bonding over baby news and tucking into pancakes, an empty chair saved for me. Carson flits from station to station, refilling orange juice and coffee. Patsy's on the phone behind the bar, its long, curly cord wrapped around her, just like the day I arrived in Buckaroo. I slip across the room to stand behind her.

She hangs up the phone and leans in, her forehead against the receiver. I tap her on the shoulder and she yelps. "Shit! Sander! Don't do that!"

"I'm sorry," I laugh. "I just saw you there, like the first time..." Crap, I sound corny. "I'll be leaving after the Dust Drama."

"Yeah?" She won't make eye contact and starts to wind herself out of the cord, tangling it up more, yet again.

I'm not sure what I want to say. *I'm going home now, it was nice sleeping with you? Maybe I can call you some time and we'll talk about how you wind yourself up in the phone cord?* "Let me." I grab the cord. But instead of maintaining a stranger's distance, like I did the first day, I wrap my arms around her, drawing her close. Maybe now words will come.

But she slaps at me and pulls away. "Quit it."

"What's wrong?"

"That was Willamette. You know that stranger cowboy Spit came into town a couple days ago?"

The hair on the back of my neck springs up and my arm flesh goes goosey. "He's new?"

"Yeah, first time anyone ever saw him was when he showed up for your auditions. He'd been staying in his van, up behind some rocks off the road." She goes still. "Willamette was out walking early this morning. Came across the van and found him dead."

Shivers creep up my spine now. "Dead? How dead?"

Patsy looks at me quizzically. "Completely dead."

"I mean dead how? Gunshot? Poison? Strangled? Rattlesnake? Scorpion? Coyotes?"

"Idiot. Coyotes don't kill people." She slugs me. "She didn't say how, just that there were tire tracks coming down the back trail from JC's place. She's calling the cops now. Keep it on the down low, okay?"

All I can think of is JC on the lam from the FBI. How he had a weird feeling about Spit, and now this. I have a feeling Patsy's thinking the same thing. Especially when she finally looks me in the eye, and asks if I know how to make pancakes.

22

FRIDAY – HIGH NOON MINUS FIFTEEN

When I hang my apron on the hook and step outside, the mercury in the thermometer next to the screen door of the Shitkicker's kitchen is at ninety-seven. As I suspected he might, JC split after a short chat with Patsy, leaving me to commandeer flapjacks for the remainder of the morning. After two hours of standing and flipping, my thighs throb, my shoulders ache, the aroma of pancakes and griddle grease wafts up from my scruffy beard every now and again, and I am still in a strange state of stun. No matter how you look at it, a dead body is never good news. While Willie is not to be trusted, I hate to think JC had something to do with it, and part of me—a big part—is really worried.

Mane Street, normally desolate during peak heat, is mobbed. The wooden sidewalks are lined with booths selling everything from studded leather pet fashions to gems and crystals to bouquets of sage and feathers. Local artists display their wares, exhibiting patchwork and lace potholders and aprons, brightly-painted tractor parts and dead wood sculptures. Folks crowd around the Buckaroo Angels' booth to buy Star's famous brownies and Willamette's lemonade.

Outside the Costumery, I slide hangers down a rack, browsing through fringed buckskin jackets, embroidered cowboy shirts with mother of pearl buttons, and woolly sheepskin chaps. And then there's the pile of cowboy boots. Black kangaroo tooled with filigree, seventies patchwork, red ostrich with cream leather insets, brown crocodile with a vista of the Grand Canyon painted on the shaft. And shoved behind them all, a pair of square-toed pony boots. I kick off my sneakers and pull the soft brown suede onto my feet. They're hardly worn and fit as though custom made. I step in front of a full-length mirror set up next to the rack and jump when Willamette slides into the reflection behind me and catches my deer-in-the-headlights gaze.

"Those are the original kickers. Model for the Saloon's neon sign. Went up in the fifties," she announces, her head cocked in professional appraisal. "They look grand on you," she grins.

I trust her opinion no more than I trust that grin. "I never wore cowboy boots before." I test them out, heels clicking against the slats.

She bends down to thumb off some dust with a bit of spit, and when she stands up, her eyes sear mine. "I heard you and Patsy helped bring my Donnie-kins home the other night."

I remember JC's words: *Willie wants to grow her backwater empire and play with the big boys.* I try to keep cool. "He was in a bad way. We didn't want anyone to get hurt."

"That's right kindly," she says, her eyes squinty and unreadable.

A blasting engine approaches and a meticulously restored vintage chopper parks at the nearby hitching post. Its rider, encased in black leather from epaulet shoulders to steel-toe boots, must be sweating like an omelet in grease. He removes his silver bowl-shaped helmet and shakes out his bushy dark hair. "Here to git mah pitcher taken," he mumbles through salt and pepper mutton chops. When he looks my way, I can see my reflection in his Bono-style fly-eye sunglasses.

"Hang on," Willie says to me, then puts on her folksy voice. "Sure now, come on 'n' have yer pitcher taken with Daisy the smilin' buffalo."

She leads the biker inside the Soundstage, past an umbrellaed and lit area dressed with bales of hay and a large, well-groomed buffalo wearing a daisy tucked behind her ear. Willie helps the biker select a costume from a rack of clothes, sets him up in a makeshift dressing room, and heads back my way with a rifle in her hand.

"Nice," I whistle, feigning admiration. "What is she?"

"Winchester '46 original hammerless." Proud, like she just gave birth to it. "Twenty-four inch tapered barrel. Original walnut stock." She buffs the wood with a rag, and holds the rifle to her shoulder, sighting it at various points along Mane. "You hear 'bout Cowboy Spit?" she asks in a low voice. "Scared the life out of me when I came across him this morning. You know the poor man was retiring after forty years serving our country in the FBI? Needed to move to the desert for health reasons. No sooner does he come out to look at a piece of land Donnie and I are selling than he keels over from asthma. Poor bastard." Like a demented pioneer cheerleader, Willie twirls the rifle like a baton, slips it into a rawhide scabbard at her hip, and lets fly a stream of amber spittle to the base of the hitching post.

I wonder how much of Willie's story is true. Even though the news is no longer pertinent to my life now that I'm leaving Buckaroo,

I'd feel better knowing JC can stay and that his vision of being apart from his family was just a paranoid hallucination. I step onto the street and kick at the dust; I'm starting to like the way I feel in these boots: tall. I imagine myself going out on service calls for El-San and arriving at the door in these boots. *Howdy, ma'am. Fix yer outhouse?* "Where'd you get the buffalo?"

"Daisy belongs to Carl." Carson leans against the door frame, holding a large, old-fashioned camera. "Grandpop's bass player. Keeps her out on his property for photo ops." I watch from the street as she screws the wooden box onto the antique tripod and adjusts the brass lens. "We better hurry, Willie. Dust Drama starts at noon."

"Don't worry, sweetie, you won't be late," Willie says, now the reassuring matriarch.

Carson ducks under the brown drop cloth attached to the camera and the biker emerges from the dressing room bare-chested and bare-footed in a pair of familiar overalls. Willie greets him with a hearty "Yee-ha!" then hands him the rifle and poses him with one foot on a hay bale next to Daisy the Smiling Buffalo.

"All right, mister," she says, positioning herself behind Carson and holding a horseshoe up in the air. "Keep your eye on the horseshoe 'n' say 'cheese.'" The hillbilly/biker obeys, Carson's handheld flash explodes, and Willie moves in to guide her customer back to his dressing room.

I wonder what's in store for all of us now—Harry, Patsy, Carson, JC, Star, Lucy. We've become so close during such a short time. While L.A. is only two and a half hours away, I have the sense that once I leave I'll never come back, as though Buckaroo were over the rainbow.

Willie leans the Winchester against the wall and sits behind a makeshift counter created by a plank on two sawhorses. She pulls out a decorative paper frame and a sheet of photo paper. "How much longer you stickin' around?" she asks casually.

Very casually. So very, very casually that I'm quickly reminded she's an actress, acting a part. Reminded of the way she shot back tequila at the wedding. The way she talked to JC when she and Donnie were delivering that bed. A tough broad, she is. Maybe *she* killed Cowboy Spit. Who knows? What does it matter? "Soon as the Dust Drama's over."

"Well, get yourself some brownies and lemonade before you go. Tell the girls at the Buckaroo Angels booth I said to fix you up on the house." She looks me up and down. "And take those boots. You're the only person they've ever fit since the guy they was made for."

"Who was that?" My cowboy feet twitch in anticipation.

"Gary Cooper." She smiles. "Lord, The Coop was a man."

These boots were made for Gary Cooper? I only half believe her, but I surprise us both by reaching across the counter and giving her a big hug. She squeaks at first, but when I hang in there for a beat, she relaxes and returns the embrace, thumping me on the back until there's a cough behind us.

The biker guy is safe in his leathers again. "Kin ah pay now?"

"We'll miss ya, kid. Now get." Willie faces her customer. "Your prints'll be ready in five minutes. That'll be nine-ninety-nine, all framed and everything." She makes her vintage cash register ring, then bangs the drawer with the side of her fist until it opens.

The biker looks at me and I quickly look away, but manage with the corner of my eye to see him pass Willie a fat paper envelope.

Way too fat for nine-ninety-nine. And Willie's all smiles as she thanks him and stuffs the bag into her drawer, not even mentioning it or bothering to count out change. She shakes the biker's hand. "Don't miss my grandson Donnie's booth," she points across from the Soundstage. "His chickens lay the best eggs around."

Directly across Mane, Donnie holds court to a gaggle of teenage girls in a booth set up in the front yard of Buckaroo's little church, whose sign lettering has been changed to "All Angels Welcome." It's not hard to imagine what he's dealing over there. Donnie waves at Willie, then points to a poster mounted on his table, advertising "The Ladies of London – Fresh-Laid Eggs." I can smell chicken shit from here.

There's a bird's-eye view from the top of the temporary bleachers set up in front of Vana LeValle's New Okay Corral. I search for suspicious characters who look like they might have just killed someone, characters trying to blend in with the crowd, but everyone's so uniformly unusual here that everyone seems to fit in. Over by the Bank, I spot Jerome with some biker cronies who, judging from their laughter and guffaws, enjoy watching clown-costumed bikers perform wondrous feats of cycling and drinking amid locals dressed as rhinestone cowboys, dirt-crusted miners and way-out Westerners. It sounds ridiculous, but I suddenly realize: I love this place. I'm going to miss it. I'm fiddling with my new Bolex when I see Carson, in a long pioneer dress and hiking boots, climb the bleachers and sit at the opposite end of my bench.

"Hey, kiddo." I pat the bench beside me. "Come sit over here." She glances at me and shakes her head. Man, she twangs my heartstrings. I hate the prospect of having to do the whole goodbye thing with a kid who thinks I'm neat. "What's the matter?" She ignores me, proceeding to remove her Keystone from its case and set up shots for the Dust Drama below. "Are we both filming this thing?" I ask.

"Coverage," Carson turns to me and glares. "Anyway, what do you care? You're going back to L.A." She bites each word with her teeth, her lips and tongue stained purple from something grape.

"Yeah, but I'll be back." *I will? I guess so.* "Look." I show her lens the cap before stashing it in my pocket.

She almost smiles. "Sure you will. Just like you were going to say goodbye."

Busted by a tyke. Yikes. I familiarize myself with the camera's considerable weight, filming people in the crowd to establish local color. The bleachers shimmy as Starshine enters frame. She carries Lucy, swaddled in a bundle, in her arms and has a beat-up duffel bag slung over one shoulder. "Star, ahoy!" I wave, and film her climbing the bleachers in her tie-dye dress, her face flush from exertion and heat.

When she reaches me, she throws her arms around my neck, nearly knocking me over. "Lucy, you remember your godfather, don't you?" Her voice sounds fragile, raspy, like she's about to break into a laugh or a cry.

"Where's JC?" I ask quietly, hoping I'm not out of line by asking.

Loudspeakers suddenly blast old-time piano player music, which causes Lucy to spastically wave and kick, and turns Starshine's half-laughter into serious sobs. "I'm sorry. I'm such an idiot. This post-partum thing is kicking my ass. Watch Lucy while I go clean up, okay?"

"No, I'm filming," I say. "I can't."

But she ignores me, pressing Lucy into my arms and dropping the duffel at my feet. "I'm sorry. Thank you." She kisses Lucy, then me, and runs down the bench to give Carson—who hardens herself into a stick—a big hug. She's sobbing loudly now as she flatfoots down the bleachers in her Birkenstocks and vanishes into the swirling crowd.

With a complex maneuver that involves all the underdeveloped muscles in my abdomen, back and glutes, I gently place the Bolex on the bench beside me without dropping the kid, who grunts like a piglet. The player piano music becomes spaghetti-Western theme music and Lucy begins a high-pitched guttural whine.

Carson watches disgusted as I attempt to quiet Lucy with little success. "It's starting!"

I weigh my promise to Harry to film and my fondness for Carson against the squirming, needy creature in my arms. "You film it."

"The whole thing?" she gasps. "I can't!"

"Sure you can." Pressing the now-wailing baby to my chest and making hushy noises into her ear, I instruct Carson to sit next to me. She reluctantly obliges, dragging her feet and plopping down an arm's length away. "Now hold frame on Harry."

"My hands are shaking," she says, her fingertips turning red from clenching.

"Relax your grip. And stay with him as he moves. Don't worry about keeping him in the center of the frame. It's okay if he wanders offsides every now and then."

The Master of Ceremonies, all in white, strides to the middle of Mane Street. "My name's Harry and I'm sheriff of this here Western town," he drawls.

"Now pan over easy to my mom."

Carson moves jerkily, holding her breath.

"Breathe," I say, reaching across the distance to gently squeeze her elbow.

The camera wobbles while Carson draws a deep breath, but she relaxes on the exhale, dropping her shoulders and spotting her target. Mom, in a patchwork skirt and a muslin peasant blouse, struts out from the Bank with a sign that says "HOORAY! CHEERS!"

"My, what a strong, handsome sheriff!" she declares as she circles Harry. The bikers go wild.

Lucy's wailing has softened to a whimpering bleat. "Don't worry," I whisper, jiggling the baby. "Everything's gonna be all right." I'm surprised when this ploy works and Lucy quiets.

"I'm going back to Grandpop," Carson says, capturing Harry while he delivers a short speech about hounds, Harleys and the high desert.

I scan the crowd for Starshine and JC, with no luck.

What I do see at the far end of town just beyond the Saloon is worse: JC's Chevy van turning off Mane Street and heading away down Buckaroo Highway. I know in that instant JC is fulfilling the prophecy of his vision. He's not in his family's future. Rather than wind up dead or in jail or locked in a master/slave relationship building the Londons' empire, he's left his family behind. With me. *Jesus Christ.* My stomach turns to mud and my brain switches to high-alert, but somehow I remain calm. I remember the moment in *High Noon* when Grace Kelly goes against her Quaker beliefs and shoots a gunman to save her husband Gary Cooper. "You take the baby for a bit and give me the camera now. Hold her with both hands."

"Like I'm going to hold her with one," Carson says as we make the swap. I wait until she has Lucy securely in both arms before I film the tail end of the Chevy as it chugs down the highway and out of sight behind a stack of yellow boulders.

I don't know exactly what I'm looking for, so I pick up the Dust Drama again as Harry sweeps his arms wide. "Ladies and gentleman, I bring you Belle, the saloon gal with a heart of gold." The Bolex follows Patsy as she sashays into the street in Destinée's original bordello getup, the spangled corset, bustled skirt and lace-up prairie boots.

This time, Ellie carries the "HOORAY! CHEERS!" sign, wearing a similar bordello costume. "Now that's what I call sexy!" she says.

The crowd goes wild again, and I quit filming for a second to join in, whooping and hollering for my girls who are camping it up in front of Donnie's Chicken booth. I want them both in frame, and zoom in close to get my shot. That's when I see that right fucking behind them is Donnie, handing a duffel bag to that biker who just handed Willie a fat wad of cash. *A duffel bag just like the one Starshine left at my feet.* I wonder if Donnie is making his "drop" or whatever they call it. I make sure to record them shaking hands, then pan across the street to the Costumery at the Soundstage, right into Willamette's shining black eyes.

Shit! I pan back to the Dust Drama in the middle of Mane, where Mom points across the street, one hand over her mouth. She's pointing at Willie, with her Winchester hammerless...

...aimed right at me.

Shades of *The Beastess*, Mom lets rip a piercing shriek that sends the crowds' hands to their ears.

Willie squeezes the trigger.

There's a cracking metallic pop.

The rifle releases a gray puff of smoke.

I throw my body across Carson and the baby, then dive to the footboard, holding my camera high in the air in case it catches anything that might be of importance, a fleeting glimpse of evidence, a Zapruder's particle of truth. The bullet's impact on the Bolex throws my arm back with a snap, just one of a multitude of details of which I'm excruciatingly aware.

Carson beneath me, laughing, "Sander, are you crazy?"

Lucy swaddled tightly against Carson's chest.

The crowd gone silent.

Donnie yelling, "I've been hit."

The confused cackling of chickens.

EPILOGUE

SATURDAY

This is me, naked, in JC and Starshine's canopied waterbed, looking up into its mirrored panels with their kaleidoscopic facets that reflect to infinity. Patsy percolates softly next to me, her image adjacent to mine in each and every reflective facet. Lucy sleeps nearby in a basket lined with rabbit skins and soft flannel. I get up quietly to stand at a large window that opens onto a vista of rocks and sky above Buckaroo proper. The final scenes of yesterday's shootout have been looping through my brain all night. The way Harry took control of the crowd of bikers, starting up a sing-along and herding them down to the Saloon. Those two undercover cops arresting Willie and that biker. Nurse Jerome tying a tourniquet around Donnie's arm before the paramedics arrived and took Donnie away. All part of my narrative now, my comedy-romance-sci-fi-western-action-thriller, my own personal version of Dad's *More Than You Know*. I have plenty of time to decide what to do with it.

There's a commotion outside, a rustling in the bushes and chattering of squirrels from the gravel drive below. It's Carson, in my Chuck Norris T-shirt, lying on the ground next to a familiar red Doberman. "Sander!" she hollers. "He came back!"

Jake looks my way too, and when he sees me, he scrambles

up to a formal "sit" and lifts a front paw. "Come on, Jake!" Carson jumps up and pony-slaps her thigh. "Let's go inside."

A moment later, there is heavy clumping up the wooden stairs before Jake hurtles onto the bed and barks once in greeting. "Silencio," I say, and he obeys.

Patsy stirs, then yawns and stretches her arm across the dog, who closes his eyes in response. "You don't think this is a mistake, do you?"

I take her hand. "Some dogs are meant for L.A., but this one belongs in the desert."

"You know what I mean," she says. "Do you think JC and Star will come back?"

"I know." I kiss the inside of her hand. "I don't know."

*   *   *

From where I stand in front of the barbecue, I can see through the front door.

Patsy, Lucy, Carson and Jake lounge in front of the television in the rock-walled living room. Harry sings to himself as he stirs chili in the little kitchen, and baby names buzz as Mom and Ellie squeeze lemons for lemonade at a nearby table.

Outside, just beyond the front porch, next to Jerome's now-dusty Harley, Jerome and I, in the longstanding tradition of males primeval, stare into the coals of a grill, comparing philosophies of barbecue. Smoked vs. clean. Gas vs. coal. Mesquite vs. hickory. For baby names, Zach vs. Jennifer. And, of course, the million-dollar question. "So. Jerome. A Harley? What were you thinking?"

He shrugs. "It was a gift from a client. You know, my patients are terminal cases. My job is to help them live out their days according to their wishes. Last guy's wish was to do this Hogs for Dogs thing. He bought me the bike to go with him."

"You're shitting me. Is he here in Buckaroo?"

"He died the day before the ride." Jerome runs his hands through his thick black hair, which I see now is thinning way up high along both sides. "I couldn't tell Ellie about it. Part of the confidentiality agreement. Still can't. But I trust you. You want to take her for a spin? The ride out was *awesome*, man."

"Sure, I guess." I dig a fork into the coals. Bits of white ash flit into the air, and small embers swirl like fireflies. The sky is intensely blue at the top, ghosting down to a pale sparkle along the mountains' jagged rocky ridge. Ellie inserts herself between us, hands us each a mason jar of lemonade, and hooks her arms through our elbows, joining in our grill gazing. "What are you two yakking about?"

"We figured out the baby's name," I say. "Lucifer or Chiclet."

She smiles and leans into me. "Today's a beautiful day."

I know what she means. "Dad'll like it here, don't you think, El?"

"*My* Dad would," Ellie bumps me with her hip. "No one knows who the hell yours is."

I bump her back. "The good news is, there's a fifty-fifty chance we're only fifty-percent related."

"At least *he* wasn't having an affair," Ellie bumps her hip into Jerome. "That's so cliché."

One thing you can say about Ellie, and, I guess, when I think on it, about me: we're silver-lining sorts.

"Chowtime," Harry calls from the front door. "Get your chili while it's hot!"

It's funny having my whole family here in Buckaroo. Not funny ha-ha; funny odd. Like Family Friday in elementary school, when your parents and siblings descend upon your world, your classroom, and judge it. When they see that your noodle sculpture of the Parthenon is not as well-crafted as the others. I dreaded that day as a kid, but today, I'd say one noodle Parthenon is as good as anyone else's.

"It's on!" Carson clicks the remote and "Rockin' the Rose Garden: A Live Event" scrolls up over a wind-swept American flag. Thank you, JC's satellite dish. If all goes as planned, my Mother Circle video with D in the nude in a swarm of butterflies is going to be broadcast and my life will be changed forever. I can't tell if I'm nervous. Perhaps that means I'm not. Or am.

From across the great room, Patsy says, "There's nothing to be nervous about."

"Thanks." That's when I decide mind reading comes from compassion and isn't so creepy after all.

Carson whoops. "There she is! It's D! This is so cool!"

D takes the Rose Garden stage in a long blonde wig and a skintight tube dress patterned with stars and stripes, looking every bit the superstar she'll someday be again. The music starts with its techno edge, its funky bass riff—old hat for those of us who've been tortured by it the last few days. The professional lip-synch begins, standard girlpop turdfluff, yet catchy still. D might get a hit out of this song after all. Stranger things have happened.

But on the large screen behind her, instead of the circle of tall, twisted Joshuas, followed by Destinée's nude silhouette, we open on the interior of a familiar motel room—Room Three, to be exact. And as D's fuck-me-I'm-a-little-girl voice sighs over the drumbeats, on the screen, a young woman falls backward onto the bed, kicking her legs in the air. A man's hands reach in from out of frame and we smash cut to the woman's hips rising up from the bed, then cut back to the man's arms, pulling the pants off her kicking legs. *Oggie's fucking video.*

"What the hell is this?" Patsy asks, quickly passing off Lucy to Ellie and clapping her hands over Carson's eyes.

"Mom," Carson protests. "I'm not a baby. You don't have to protect me. I've already seen it."

"You have?" I ask. "Where?"

Carson pulls Patsy's hands away from her eyes, but holds them in her own while she speaks. "It's only been on the Internet like for three weeks already."

"Let's watch something else." Harry leans in front of the screen to change the channel.

"Wait," I tell him. "Something's going on."

Someone must have pulled the plug, because the video screen behind D pixillates, then goes blank. When D finally notices, she stops singing, though her music—and vocals—continues. She pulls the mic from her head in protest, spikes it to the floor and leaves the stage, followed by her musicians. The music continues for a few bars, then finally stops. That should get some publicity, for sure. Then, cut to commercial. A Western Burger commercial to be precise. Just as Faun suggested, D's Shitkicker performance is superimposed against the original dancers moving in syncopated rhythm against a background of flames as the original Okay Corral burns. A crazy montage to be sure, but I have to admit it works on a creative level. She sure threw that together fast. Those few minutes of television truly were life-changing for me, only not the way I expected. Harry's already switching the channel.

"In surprising local news," the anchorwoman says, "Buckaroo's annual Hogs for Dogs celebration was interrupted with a flash of violence when a vintage rifle misfired into a crowd, causing one bystander to be taken to Morongo Valley Emergency. In an unrelated incident, a member of the Hells Angel motorcycle club, claiming to have been swindled by a local drug dealer, was taken into custody. A duffel bag recovered at the scene was seized as evidence, only to be found to contain infant clothes, Pampers and baby formula. An investigation is pending."

Harry clicks off the television and the room falls silent.

"Excuse me," I say, and run up the stairs to the sleeping loft. Holding my breath, I unzip Starshine's duffel a few teeth at a time, as though something inside were going to leap out. I open the mouth of the bag and push aside a tie-dye flannel blanket.

Tupperware. Filled with Dove.

One of the best things about JC's house is the variety of comfort stations that don't require conventional plumbing. Just off the geodesic dome, there's the "library," a small water closet with floor-to-ceiling walls of shelves stacked with books. The "outhouse" is a freestanding covered structure with its own septic tank and a front door with a window that frames a remarkable view of the mesa and boulders to the west. My favorite is what Carson calls the "porta-toity," a bucket with an attached toilet seat that you can carry out into the wilderness and set down wherever you like. Right now, I set up for the long view, that view of Buckaroo proper I had on the first day I hiked up into these hills with Jake, and found myself on that rock listening to Donnie and Willie and JC.

My commercial may have been shut down and my video didn't make it on television, but I've lived and seen more life here in Buckaroo than in all my years in Los Angeles. Where else can I watch a stone-colored lizard bask in the sun, throat inflating, protruding eyeballs giving me a serious head to toe? A jackrabbit hops into a small clearing, then gnaws at a spot beneath its haunch, one huge tawny foot straight up in the air. If I were to check my Death Clock right now, I'd have to click the happy mode. I don't know how many more years that will add to my life, but I hope many.

When I rejoin the party, Mom says, "I'm sorry it wasn't your video up there."

"*Or* his commercial," Ellie reminds us.

"I'm not," I say, and I'm really not lying as I flop down on the couch. "Oggie's video is the only reason I got to come to Buckaroo."

Carson drapes a white sheet across the TV screen, while Patsy sits next to me on the couch, slipping her hand into mine. I've already nicknamed the ridge outside the window "Profile of a Sleeping Indian," and as Carson pulls the curtains in front of it, my cell phone, which I actually remembered to charge last night in the middle of post-Dust Drama chaos, buzzes in my pocket.

It's Paul Street. "Sander my boy, did you watch?"

"We were all riveted."

"Don't be discouraged. This is actually great news. Vana reconsidered Oggie's video and thought your initial assessment was right on. Wants to save your butterfly footage for D's single and talk to you about producing a few more projects for her. Can I put her on?"

"Tell Vana I'm busy and I'll have to call her back." I turn off my phone as Carson clicks the reel of film onto the old-time projector.

"Why are we watching something we just lived through two hours ago?" Ellie asks.

"Because it's good," I tell her. "Because it's good." I close my eyes as the images flicker. This is what I see:

HOLLYWOOD BUCKAROO

A Screenplay

by

Sander Sanderson

EXT. — CACTUS GARDEN IN FRONT OF JC AND STARSHINE'S PLACE — SUNSET

HARRY plays guitar softly while PATSY sings "You Are My Sunshine" and CARSON holds her hand.

JEROME and ELLIE stand next to the vintage Harley. Ellie holds LUCY, who sleeps like the baby she is.

MADGE's face glows bright against the violet and amber streaks in the sky. She kisses BOBBY'S URN and hands it to SANDER.

Sander kisses the urn, then removes the lid and flings Bobby's ashes out onto the rocks.

                    SANDER
              I love you, Dad.

A hawk SCREAMS from above; a kit of coyotes
YIP and HOWL. A jackrabbit leaps through the
garden, JAKE on its heels.

                              FADE TO WHITE:

Acknowledgments

Heartfelt thanks to everyone who was around when miracles and bullshit happened daily: Pappy and Harriet Allen; LesLee "Bird" Anderson; Jane Carpenter; John Huff, Ernie and Carole Kester; Carl, Bonnie and Steighsea LaGassa; the Losin' Brothers; Jack McCabe; Dolores Silver; Clive Turner; Victoria Williams; Abbie; Aunt B; Brock; Buzz; Caroline; Cheryl and Kevin; Frederika and Anders; Garth; both Garys; Jake; Jim; Ken and Lori; Kristina; a bunch of Marks; Mary; Naildick; Owl; Patricia; all the Peters, Victoria; Wind; Zipperman, and so many others whose names are writ large in the dust of my brain.

Very special thanks to two fiendishly talented people who transformed my life and my heart: Yaro Prikopsky and Ingrid Willis.

Much gratitude to the friendly readers who assisted the book's development over the years: Hal Ackerman, Seamus Boshell, Cathy Colman, Christine Ecklund, Jane Langley, Lauri Maerov, Rick Mashburn, Meredith Muncy, Wendy Murray, Mary Otis, Leslie Schwartz, Lulu Hali Zucker.

All the love in the stars to my husband Carl Peel.

A Note About
Hollywood Buckaroo

The fictional locale of Buckaroo is based on the larger-than-life town of Pioneertown, California. Perched in the high desert about 35 miles north of Palm Springs, Pioneertown was developed in the forties by a consortium of Hollywood investors, including Roy Rogers, Dick Curtis, Bud Abbott, Louella Parsons, and Russell Hayden, and Western music legends Sons of the Pioneers. It's served as a permanent location for scores of films and continues to be an attraction and getaway for western aficionados, musicians, artists, equestrians, motorcycle enthusiasts, rock climbers and just plain folks. Long live Pappy & Harriet's Pioneertown Palace!

Tracy DeBrincat is the author of the prize-winning short story collection *Moon Is Cotton & She Laugh All Night* (Subito Press/University of Colorado, Boulder). San Francisco is her hometown, but she lives in Los Angeles, where she is a freelance creative advertising consultant and authors the blog *Bigfoot Lives!* www.tracydebrincat.com